BRIGHT STAR

"A TENSE, EXCITING LOOK AT ONE OF THE WORLD'S TROUBLE SPOTS."
—*Tom Clancy*

★★★★★★★★★★★★★★★★

ANCIENT ENMITIES, MODERN WAR . . .

Lieutenant Colonel Scott Dixon: Haunted by his experience as a tank commander in the Iran war, Congressional Medal of Honor–winner Dixon refused promotion—and scuttled his military career. But Operation Bright Star brought him back to the Middle East—and plunged him again into battle . . .

Colonel Nafissi: The second most powerful man in Libya, the short, compact air-force colonel had his own ambitions for Islamic glory. He devised a brutal plan for triggering war between Egypt and Libya—and for bringing the Soviets into the storm . . .

Major Gregory Naboatov: The Soviet advisor to the Ethiopian army was a fighter who had seen too much death and carnage. When he became an aide to a powerful Soviet general, he was drawn relentlessly into the making of a disastrous war . . .

★★★★★★★★★★★★★★★★

(more . . .)

"Coyle writes . . . of slug-it-out army and guerrilla engagements . . . a complex story that moves over a complex playing field. . . . *BRIGHT STAR* is an intense book, well-written and a sure favorite for those who like authentic war stories from an author whose active duty with the U.S. Army reflects his knowledge."

—*Chattanooga Times*

★★★★★★★★★★★★★★★★

Jan Fields: The beautiful network-news correspondent got the story of her life when she witnessed the attempted assassination of the American and Egyptian presidents. She also got war, with all its terror—and a soldier who was the wrong man to fall in love with . . .

Representative Ed Lewis: The American congressman from Tennessee was a hero in the war against the Soviets in the Persian Gulf. But now he had a reckless plan—the immediate withdrawal of all air and ground troops from the conflict . . .

★★★★★★★★★★★★★★★★

"ONE OF COYLE'S STRONG POINTS IS HIS EXCELLENT CHARACTER PORTRAYALS. . . . A GRIPPING MILITARY DRAMA . . . THAT WILL DELIGHT MANY READERS."

—*Richmond Times-Dispatch*

Books by Harold Coyle

Bright Star*
Sword Point*
Team Yankee

*Published by POCKET BOOKS

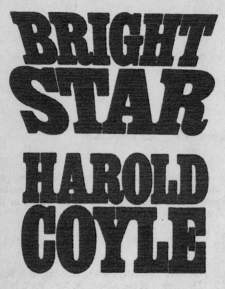

BRIGHT STAR

HAROLD COYLE

POCKET BOOKS

New York   London   Toronto   Sydney   Tokyo   Singapore

This book is a work of fiction. Names, characters, places and incidents are either the product of the author's imagination or are used fictitiously. Any resemblance to actual events or locales or persons, living or dead, is entirely coincidental.

POCKET BOOKS, a division of Simon & Schuster
1230 Avenue of the Americas, New York, NY 10020

ISBN: 0-671-68543-0

First Pocket Books printing March 1991

10 9 8 7 6 5 4 3 2 1

POCKET and colophon are registered trademarks of
Simon & Schuster.

Printed in the U.S.A.

To Leslie

Tell my sister not to weep for me, and sob with droop-
 ing head,
When the troops come marching home again, with
 gold and gallant tread,
But look upon them proudly, with a calm and stead-
 fast eye,
For her brother was a soldier, too, and not afraid to
 die.

—Caroline Elizabeth Norton (1808–77)
Soldier of the Rhine

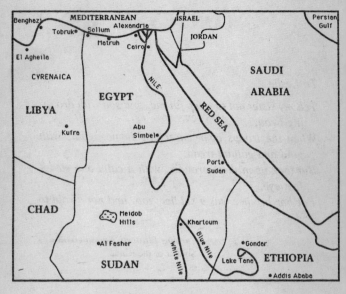

NORTHEASTERN AFRICA

CONTENTS

FOREWORD

Only study of the past can give us a sense of reality, and show us how the soldier will fight in the future.

—ARDANT DU PICQ

This book is neither a textbook nor an attempt to predict the future. The doctrine, tactics, plans, and policies discussed do not reflect current or planned U.S. Army doctrine, tactics, plans, and policy. Nor are the characters depicted in the story based on any people, living or dead. Any similarity between the characters in this book and real people is purely coincidental. There are many who will find fault in some of the actions and decisions made by the characters. Some of the weapons effects and employment are equally open to criticism. I apologize if my use of literary license, which is free and frequent, is offensive to some.

Politics and strategic and operational plans are not discussed in detail except where they are important to the story and its characters. Thus the reader should find himself, like the characters of the book, limited to the immediate and narrow world in which they live, lacking a full understanding of the "big picture."

Times used throughout the story are local times. All events are sequential.

All unit designations depicted are fictitious, but their organizations and equipment allowances are, in general, in accordance with current tables of organization. All information on weapons effects and characteristics as well as information on Egypt, Libya, and Germany are from open source materials available to the general public. The author does not have, nor has he ever had, access to contingency plans concerning operations in the area discussed in this book, nor has he participated in simulations concerning that area of operations. The scenario depicted is pure fiction.

PROLOGUE

No man is fit to command that cannot command himself.

—WILLIAM PENN

**Prince Frederick, Maryland * 2335 Hours,
25 October**

Except for the whine of the computer's fan, the house was quiet. The man seated at the computer desk, staring at the small screen of his Macintosh SE, was in his early forties. His close-cropped hair showed little sign of the gray that plagued his wife. Dressed in a well-worn gray VMI sweatshirt, casual slacks, and white crew socks, Major (Promotable) Scott Dixon's five-foot-ten frame was casually sprawled in his chair. The only visible motion was his hand moving the computer's mouse as he scrolled the letter on the screen.

It was a short letter, less than a page, but it was without doubt the most difficult he had ever written. In the fine tradition of military writing, it began with a reference to the letter he had received from his personnel manager at Armor Branch that afternoon: he expressed his gratitude to the man for taking the time to confirm Dixon's decision to turn down command of a tank-heavy task force in Germany.

Dixon's response, drafted and redrafted three times, was short, almost curt, but Dixon couldn't think of any other way to put it. "I have no need to reconsider my decision. Based on my performance during the war in Iran, I do not feel that I am qualified, or capable, of command. Coupled with family con-

1

cerns and personal aspiration, command of a task force is not in my best interests.'' In that single, short paragraph, Dixon knew he was putting an end to his career. There would be no more promotions, no more challenging duties. Instead, he would fall by the wayside, diverted into backwater jobs and duties that required little responsibility and less thinking.

Satisfied, Dixon printed the letter. While he waited for the printer to finish, he picked up another letter, which he had printed earlier that evening. It, too, was set up in official Army format. But as difficult as his letter turning down the chance for command had been to write, the one in his hand had been even more so. It was his resignation.

Holding it at arm's length, Dixon reread it. Its contents were formal, copied from the example shown in the regulations. No, it wasn't the contents or the style that Dixon had difficulty with. It was the end result. Though he was willing to forgo command and accept the chain of dead-end jobs that that decision would yield, he was not sure he was ready to leave the Army. His wife, Fay, was ready: she took every opportunity to tell him so. But he was not.

Like an accountant balancing a ledger book, Dixon had mentally listed all the pros and cons of staying in and leaving. That approach, however, was too transparent, too simplistic. For Dixon, there was something to being a soldier that transcended the simple addition and subtraction of debts and assets. In his heart he knew it was time, but still he could not bring himself to leave the Army.

Without further thought he crumpled the letter of resignation between his hands. Leaning back in his chair, he turned and tossed the ball of paper toward a wastepaper basket in the corner. It bounced off one wall, then the lip of the basket, then landed on the floor. It would remain there for two days, untouched and forgotten.

1

When the animals gathered, the lion looked at the eagle and said gravely, "We must abolish talons." The tiger looked at the elephant and said, "We must abolish tusks." The elephant looked back at the tiger and said, "We must abolish jaws and claws." Thus each animal in turn proposed the abolition of the weapons he did not have, until the bear rose up and said in the tones of sweet reasonableness: "Comrades, let us abolish everything—everything but the great universal embrace."

—Attributed to WINSTON CHURCHILL

Southern Sudan * 1400 Hours, 1 November

Three officers, a Sudanese major followed by two Americans, emerged from the two-room hut that served as headquarters for regional defense force, a small force consisting of two understrength infantry companies. The tall, black major—the force's commander—paused, straightened his lanky frame, then led the two Americans toward a waiting helicopter, walking with a casual, easy gait. Even the wave of his right hand as he acknowledged the salute of the two guards posted at the door of the hut was casual and unhurried. Part of his easy manner was for show, an effort to impress the American officers that all things would be done in his time. But part was due to the fact that he really was in no hurry. The war he and his men were waging against the communist guerrillas had been in progress when he joined the Army and would no doubt continue long after he returned to the hands of his God. He therefore found it difficult to understand why the Americans were always in a hurry, setting deadlines and rushing about. Battles, after all, couldn't start until both sides were present.

The two American officers following him were a study in contrast. The first lieutenant was as tall and as black as the Sudanese major, to whom he served as an adviser, but, unlike the lanky major, he had wide shoulders and a narrow waist. He wore a set of faded and well-worn battle dress—BDUs for short. The edge of a folded map protruded from the pocket on his right thigh, while the top of a spiral notebook wrapped in plastic popped out of the left thigh pocket. The other pockets of his BDUs bulged too, to varying degrees, hinting of more hidden cargo. Hanging from a web belt was a well-worn government-issue holster for his M1911A1 .45 pistol, an ammo pouch, a lensatic compass, and a two-quart canteen. His uniform was topped off by a well-molded green beret worn at a rakish angle. He walked with a purposeful gait that hinted at a swagger. At twenty-four years of age, First Lieutenant (Promotable) Jesse Kinsly was the very image of the field soldier, a warrior leader.

The other American, last of the three men to emerge from the hut, was Lieutenant Colonel William V. Dedinger. The colonel's attire left no doubt that he was a staff officer who neither belonged to the remote military post nor had any intention of staying. His BDUs were clean and appeared new. Despite regulations to the contrary, they were starched, with neat, sharp edges, and the pockets were ironed shut. The colonel didn't even carry a pen in his left breast pocket. His BDU cap, neatly blocked, was centered on his head, with the brim coming down and lightly touching the frame of his aviator sunglasses. Like the pilots of his helicopter, he was armed with a .38 pistol, which he carried in a highly polished shoulder holster under his left arm. The only other equipment Dedinger carried was a large black leather briefcase.

The appearance of the colonel and his briefcase was both scorned and dreaded by the men of Kinsly's Special Forces A Team. "Never trust an officer who takes a briefcase to the field," Kinsly's team sergeant, Sergeant First Class Hector

Veldez, always reminded Kinsly when Dedinger arrived from Cairo. It didn't take Kinsly long to learn what Veldez meant.

Dedinger was the operations officer for the 2nd Corps (U.S.) (Forward), located in Cairo. Part of the 3rd U.S. Army, which itself belonged to the Rapid Deployment Force, 2nd Corps (Forward) was a planning headquarters only, manned by a skeleton staff. The bulk of the corps headquarters was in the States, along with all the troops belonging to it, ready for deployment in the event of an emergency.

Ostensibly, the mission of the 2nd U.S. Corps (Forward) was only the planning of training exercises in cooperation with various countries in the Middle East. In a crisis, it would conduct military operations until the full corps staff was deployed to Egypt. In the past year, however, a new mission had been added. The Iranian conflict two years earlier had driven home the importance of Soviet air and naval bases on the Horn of Africa. From there, the Soviet Union presented a threat to the Middle East, Central Africa, and the Indian Ocean. Translated into practical terms, from the Horn of Africa, the Soviets, or their surrogates, were in a position to interrupt the flow of oil and mineral resources from the area.

In an effort to deny the Soviets free use of the Horn of Africa and to keep Soviet-sponsored covert operations from subverting Ethiopia's neighbors, the United States had initiated covert operations in Sudan and Ethiopia. Code-named Twilight, this operation involved a number of Special Forces, or SF, teams operating in central Sudan. These teams assisted a number of groups, including Sudanese government forces, Eritrean insurgents, and Ethiopian guerrillas. The immediate goal, and the one briefed to Congress, was the preservation of the current government in Sudan. The long-range goal, more of a hope and seldom discussed, was the restoration of a pro-Western government in Ethiopia.

Dedinger, as the operations officer for 2nd Corps (Forward), was responsible for the activities of the SF teams—planning their operations and coordinating them with Air Force and Navy operations. He produced and issued orders to the teams for their operations and received reports on those operations.

Based on those reports, he assessed the situation and revised plans as necessary, resulting in new missions and orders. He coordinated transportation and resupply, evaluated the wounded, and arranged for replacements where necessary. The black briefcase, used to transport the written orders for the A teams in the field, was Dedinger's main weapon.

A man whose career was on the fast track, Dedinger enjoyed his role. Based in Cairo, Dedinger spent a great deal of time bouncing between Atlanta, Georgia, where the 3rd Army had its headquarters, Washington, D.C., and the Sudan. Dedinger had a great deal of "face time" with the senior staff of the Army. If it weren't for the fact that his boss expected him to personally issue the orders and receive reports from the A-team commanders in the field, Dedinger would never go out into "the bush," as his section referred to the Sudan. At this stage in his career, if he wanted to stay on the fast track, it was critical that he do exactly what was expected of him.

Dedinger was painfully aware of how tenuous that position could be. Though he had managed to survive a successful task-force command in Germany, he had not served in Iran. This alone threatened to knock him out of the lead in his race for promotion and brigade command. The war in Iran had put a severe crimp on his well-laid career plans. Not long after that conflict, rumors began to circulate that any lieutenant colonel who had served in Iran, especially as a task-force commander, would be a shoo-in for full colonel and selection for brigade command, the final stepping stone to the stars. The first promotion board for full colonel after the conflict seemed to confirm that rumor. Though he was angry that the war in Iran had changed the rules of the game, Dedinger was nonetheless determined to get his brigade.

While the pilots of his helicopter prepared for takeoff, Dedinger paused for a moment to remind himself of his career goals. His current job meant that he spent a great deal of time in Washington, a fact that could not help but increase his chances of making it to full colonel. As he looked around at the dry, parched landscape and the motley collection of mud huts, one thing was certain: the eagles of a full colonel wouldn't be found here.

The crew chief of his helicopter gave Dedinger the signal that they were ready to go. Feeling the need to give some final order or advice before leaving, Dedinger turned to Kinsly, ignoring the Sudanese major, as he had done during most of the just-concluded meeting. "Remember, Lieutenant—time is everything, and you don't have a lot of it."

Staring at the colonel, Kinsly tried to understand why he had just said that, but couldn't. He simply replied, "Yes, sir, no need to worry."

The Sudanese major also looked at Dedinger, then at Kinsly. He wondered why it was so critical to attack the airfield at Gondar, Ethiopia, on the date designated, or, for that matter, on any particular date. The planes and helicopters had been there for months and would still be there when his unit got there. Perhaps he had missed something in the discussions. If he had, Lieutenant Kinsly could explain after the pompous American colonel had left.

Satisfied that all was in order, Dedinger saluted Kinsly, turned, and trotted into the swirling dust storm created by the helicopter's blades. Once in the aircraft, he secured his seatbelt, stowed his black briefcase securely under his seat, put on his flight helmet, and made an intercom check with the pilot. Ready, he told the chief pilot to pull pitch whenever the crew was ready. Leaning back, he closed his eyes and prepared to enjoy the long flight back to Cairo via Khartoum.

Five kilometers to the north, the whine of the helicopter's engines alerted a small band of guerrillas: their hours of patient waiting were, they hoped, about to pay off. Holed up in hiding near the compound since the previous night, the guerrillas—members of the SPLA, the Sudanese People's Liberation Army—had waited for the helicopter that was due to land at the compound that morning. They would have struck had it not been for a last-minute turn by the pilot—instead of flying in a straight line from the north, he had made a wide approach from the south before landing. To make sure that another miscalculation didn't ruin their chances, the detachment commander bribed a young boy tending a flock of goats to go down to the army compound and see which way the American helicopter was pointed. The boy returned with the news that it was pointed north. Though there was no guarantee that the pilot wouldn't alter his course after takeoff, the guerrillas could only be in one place. Deciding that where they were was as good a place as any, they waited until the helicopter's engines began to crank up.

The man selected to be the gunner opened the shipping container and carefully lifted the cover, raising it up and over the SA-7 surface-to-air missile. The missile was well traveled. Manufactured in the Soviet Union, it had been delivered to the Ethiopian army years ago. Unused, outdated, and replaced by an improved surface-to-air missile, it had been passed on to the SPLA, which the Ethiopians were supporting. It had but one more trip to make—this one under its own power.

Training on the employment of the missile had been almost nonexistent. Since the instructions supplied with the missile were in Russian and English, all the gunner and the commander knew about it had been passed on to them verbally. Its internal workings, what would happen when it was fired—even whether or not, stored for who knows how many years, it would work at all—these were a mystery.

Hoisting the missile onto his shoulder, the gunner popped the fixed sights, one near the front and one in the center, into the upright position. Supporting the launcher with his left hand, he carefully wrapped his right hand around the trigger grip and turned in the direction of the army compound to watch for his target to appear.

He didn't have long to wait. Out of the swirling cloud of dust that rose from the center of the army compound, the unmarked helicopter appeared. Doing as he was told, the gunner looked along the open sights, centered the helicopter, and began to follow it. Applying a slight amount of pressure with his right hand, he pulled the trigger back to its first position. A red light came on, just as the Ethiopian instructor had said it would.

Momentarily distracted by the appearance of the light, the

gunner allowed the helicopter to fly out of his sight picture. He quickly corrected his error, bringing the muzzle of the launcher around until the helicopter once again appeared to be perched on his sights. As he continued to maintain his sights on the helicopter, he watched for the red light to turn green. Once it changed colors, he pulled the trigger all the way in and braced for the explosion.

The initial reaction of the missile, however, was a surprise. There was dull explosion as the booster charge kicked the missile out of the launcher. As they watched the missile emerge from the launcher and hang in the air for a second, both the gunner and his leader thought it had been a dud. But their anxiety was replaced by joy when the sustainer motor ignited and kicked the missile out, accelerating it to Mach 1.5. Relieved that he had done nothing wrong, the gunner lowered the launcher and watched as the missile raced to catch the departing helicopter.

"JESUS CHRIST! Missile, seven o'clock—headed right for us!"

The scream from the crew chief startled Dedinger. He lurched forward and looked to his right, then corrected himself and looked to the left. The copilot was also looking left, as was the crew chief.

Recognizing the danger, the copilot barked to the pilot, "Jerry, bank right and take it down, *now!*"

The resulting violent maneuver threw Dedinger back against his seat and blocked his view of the incoming missile. The crew chief was also thrown off balance. Barely hanging on, he regained his balance, then lunged forward toward the open door in order to track the incoming missile.

"Where is it? Can anyone see it?"

For a second, no one answered the pilot. The crew chief spoke first. "I lost it. Colonel, look out the right door. I can't see it from the left side."

Dedinger was about to shift position when the impact fuse made contact with the side of the helicopter's main engine and set off the five-and-a-half-pound warhead. The resulting detonation caused a violent jolt, giving the occupants just enough time to realize that they had been hit before the catastrophic explosion engulfed the helicopter, its crew, and its sole passenger.

Kinsly stood there for the longest time, watching the bits and pieces of the helicopter rain downward. The main frame and the heavier fragments fell as part of a huge fireball that reminded him of a great burning meteor. Following the fireball, small, light pieces floated downward, each trailing a thin wisp of gray smoke against the harsh blue sky. There was nothing Kinsly could do. The Sudanese major had already turned away from him and run off to rally his men to pursue the assailants. The odds of catching them were slim to nonexistent, but they would try.

Unnoticed, Sergeant Veldez came up behind Kinsly. "Well, sir, looks like we need to get a new colonel."

Stung by the callousness of Veldez's remark, Kinsly turned on his heels and faced Veldez. "Sergeant, I don't appreciate that kind of humor. I don't give a damn what you thought about that man—he was one of us and now he's dead."

Veldez, startled by his lieutenant's response, was about to respond but stopped when he saw the anger in Kinsly's eyes. They stood there for a moment, Kinsly enraged and Veldez not knowing how, or if, to respond. He had fucked up. Everyone reacted to death differently. Veldez's efforts to soften the harsh reality of their stock-in-trade, death, were not appreciated by Kinsly. Kinsly's approach was proper, dignified. Each man had great regard for the other as a soldier; they understood each other's position on most issues, and respected it—most of the time. It was a rare occasion when Veldez overstepped his bounds.

Kinsly waited, staring at Veldez as he allowed the tension of the moment to ease. Veldez responded by coming to attention. "Sir, permission to take the team out and recover the remains of the crew and Colonel Dedinger."

Relaxing his stance, Kinsly turned his head in the direction where the helicopter had disappeared. A pillar of black smoke rose in the sky. He studied it for a second before turning back to Veldez. "Take your time, Sergeant Veldez. It will be a while before we can get them out."

"Will you be coming with us, Lieutenant?"

Kinsly considered the question. It would be so easy to say no. Veldez could handle it. There was no need for an officer to accompany the recovery party. Kinsly had no great desire to see more charred remains; he had seen enough of them in Iran. But it wouldn't be proper for him to stay behind. He was their leader. It was expected. It was the American way—leaders sharing the shit details as well as the good deals. Besides, he had to recover Dedinger's briefcase or, failing that, at least confirm that it and its contents were destroyed. "Yeah, I'll be going. But first I need to report. Have Terrel crank up the radio." Looking at his watch, Kinsly considered the time difference between the Sudan and Washington. When this hit the Pentagon, someone, no doubt, was going to have a great Monday morning.

The Pentagon, Alexandria, Virginia * 1036 Hours, 1 November

As he wandered along the seventeen and a half miles of corridors of the Pentagon, affectionately known as the Fudge Factory, Major Scott Dixon couldn't make sense of the excitement generated by the report of a training accident. For the past hour and a half, he had been bounced from one office to another, hand-carrying a sealed folder that, as far as he was concerned, dealt with nothing more than a routine occurrence. In each office, he handed the folder to the secretary or an aide, who immediately whisked it into the general's office. Five minutes later, the secretary or aide was summoned back into the presence of the unseen general to retrieve the resealed folder. Each time it was a little fatter and had a new routing slip attached to it. Except for a perfunctory hello, no one spoke to Dixon or asked him any questions. In effect, Dixon was a highly paid mailman.

On normal duty days, Dixon was the operations officer for one of five duty teams that manned the Army's Operations Center round the clock. Reports of serious training accidents were only a fraction of the dozens of operational reports and messages concerning the daily status of the Army units and operations in the field handled by Dixon and his enlisted assistant. It was his task to ensure that the reports and messages were routed and handled properly. He or his assistant would check the addressee and make sure that the incoming report was in the proper format and that all information needed by the action agency was included. That done, they would verify that the final product was routed to the appropriate agency or that the proper actions required by the situation were initiated. In the case of a message concerning the death of a military member, Dixon's responsibility ended with an annotation in the duty log and the routing of a copy of the message to personnel, so that notification of the next of kin could begin. Only when such an incident had an impact on operations or held the potential for future problems did Dixon become involved.

From the beginning, everything concerning this notification of the death of a lieutenant colonel and the crew of a UH-60 in the Middle East was wrong. The initial message was a FLASH-OVER RIDE message from the chief of the Office of Military Cooperation, or OMC, in the Sudan addressed directly to the office of the deputy chief of staff for operations, with an information copy to the chief of special operations. That alone was enough to arouse Dixon's interest. The content of the message was even more extraordinary. Classified top secret, it simply stated:

1. CARDINAL WITH AIR CREW DOWN RETURNING FROM BRIAR PATCH BASE.
2. ALL ON BOARD KIA.
3. TWILIGHT 33-07 DELIVERED.
4. NO COMPROMISE OF TWILIGHT OR TWILIGHT 33-07.

Never having heard of Twilight, Cardinal, or Briar Patch Base, Dixon flipped through his briefing book to make sure that he hadn't missed something. Finding nothing there, he quick-referenced his listing of contingency plans and their code names. He found nothing there, either. He was about to turn the message over to the full-colonel team chief when a second FLASH-OVER RIDE message, this one from the Office of Military Cooperation in Egypt, came in, referencing the message from OMC Sudan. The first paragraph of the message from OMC Egypt ordered that the initial message from OMC Sudan be disregarded and destroyed. The second paragraph announced that Lieutenant Colonel William V. Dedinger, 176-44-9238, and the crew of a U.S. Army UH-60, names currently unavailable, were killed in an accident at 1208 hours ZULU (1406 local) during a routine training flight. The third paragraph simply stated that the cause of the accident was unknown and currently under investigation.

Befuddled by the two messages, Dixon took both to Colonel James Anderson, the watch officer, his immediate superior. Anderson was seated at his desk, leaning back in his chair, talking on the phone. Waving the hard copies of the two messages, Dixon signaled that he had something hot. Anderson wedged the phone between his shoulder and his ear and continued to talk while reading the two messages. Where Dixon's reaction to the messages had been confused, Anderson's was electric. In a single movement he bolted upright in his chair, hung up the phone without so much as a goodbye, and was out of his seat, headed for a small cubicle where selected contingency and operational plans were stored.

Dixon was now *totally* confused. It was apparent that indeed there was something going on that he had not been made privy to—a suspicion that was reinforced when Colonel Anderson emerged from the cubicle with a sealed folder sandwiched between two yellow-and-white Top Secret cover sheets. Handing the package to Dixon, Anderson told him to get it to the chief ASAP. Dixon looked at the folder and at the simple handwritten note on a routing slip that addressed the folder to the Deputy Chief of Staff for Operations and Plans. "PRIORITY—EYES ONLY," in bold letters, was the only message written on it. Looking at the folder, then at Anderson,

Dixon asked, "Am I supposed to know something about this or provide anyone with additional information?"

Anderson's reply was about what Dixon expected. "Scotty, you're not to talk to anyone about this or leave this package out of sight until everyone who needs to see it has had an opportunity to do so. When they're done with it, bring it back to me. Clear?"

Scott gave him a crisp "Roger, out" and left without further delay, still befuddled, but confident that at least Anderson had a handle on whatever it was that had happened or was happening.

Thus began Dixon's odyssey through the halls of the Pentagon. First stop was the Deputy Chief of Staff for Operations and Plans. From there, he was directed to carry the folder to the Deputy Chief of Staff for Special Operations. Next came the Vice Chief of Staff for the Army, followed, in turn, by the Chief of Staff of the Army, the Vice Chief of Staff of the Joint Chiefs, the office of International Security Policy in the Office of the Secretary of Defense and finally, routing to the Office of the Secretary of Defense.

No doubt, Dixon thought as he moved along the corridors, there was something unique about this lieutenant colonel who had died. And odds were, based on the initial report from the OMC Sudan, that the accident had not taken place in Egypt, as the second message stated. He was even willing to bet that the "accident" hadn't been an accident. Beyond that, Dixon had nothing. Finally resigning himself to the fact that he would never be able to figure out what Dedinger had been up to, he let his mind move on to other, more mundane things as he wandered the halls of the Pentagon.

The first thought to cross his mind was more of an observation. For the better part of the morning Dixon had been playing errand boy. It never occurred to him to be indignant or feel any degradation that he, a promotable major, had been given such a menial task. He reflected on that thought for a moment. Had someone told him three years earlier to do what he had been doing all morning, Dixon probably would have told him where he could route his folder. Then Dixon corrected himself: there would've been no "probably"—he *would* have told the offending superior where to stick it.

But that was a long time ago, during a time when he was full of piss and vinegar, confident in himself as a soldier, his abilities to make things happen, and a career that was well charted and firm. Iran had changed all that. He had started that war—now commonly referred to as "the Iranian conflict"—as the S-3, or operations officer, of Task Force 3-4 Armor, a tank-heavy combined-arms maneuver task force stationed in Fort Hood, Texas. His task force had been with the first heavy maneuver brigade to arrive in Iran. Its arrival coincided with the first major crisis for U.S. forces in the war, allowing almost no time for the full acclimation of the men or proper organization of the brigade for combat. They had literally gone straight from the docks in Bandar Abbas into combat. Within seventy-two hours of arrival, the lead elements of his brigade were moving to establish defensive positions along the Soviet main axis of advance. Five days later, they were in contact with the lead Soviet combat units. The brigade, and Task Force 3-4, had remained in contact for another twenty-four days. On the twenty-fourth day, the task force again faced the main Soviet effort, the last Soviet offensive in Iran.

That battle was also the last for Task Force 3-4. Though the actual combat lasted less than forty-five minutes, when it was over, the task force had ceased to exist as a fighting force. Dixon, the senior officer alive and unwounded, had managed to halt the Soviets in his sector through a series of counterattacks. The initial defense and counterattacks that followed, however, had cost him two-thirds of the personnel in the task force and attached units. It was a month before the unit was ready to be committed again. Even then it was only a shell, with less than 75 percent of authorized personnel. Not that it mattered. The "conflict" had shifted into its "political" stage then, with an armistice separating the combatants. That lasted for six months—long enough for Dixon's psychological scars to begin to fester.

Traumatic as battle and its immediate aftermath had been, it wasn't until he was preparing to return his task force to the

United States that Dixon realized that the real war, the war within him, was only beginning. Memories and thoughts that he had been able to push aside to a dark corner of his mind now came forth. While most of the men in the task force greeted the prospect of returning to "the world" with unbounded joy, Dixon found himself gripped by a formless and overpowering apprehension. In the beginning he didn't see it for what it was, for it crept upon him like a shadow. First he lost his ability to concentrate. By the time the unit closed into its final staging areas at its port of embarkation, Dixon was unable to deal with even the simplest problems. And along with his difficulty to deal with the problems of command came violent mood swings. Fits of depression were suddenly displaced by unexpected outbursts of rage.

Unable to control himself, Dixon withdrew within himself. He did so in part in an effort to protect his subordinates from being the objects of an undeserved eruption of rage. He also realized that he needed to sort himself and his feelings out before he returned home. His last days in Iran were spent in almost total isolation as his attempts to muster enthusiasm about going home were met instead with fear and apprehension for the future. Finally, on the last night in country, the last piece fell into place.

In the quiet darkness of his tent, it all came back. The images of war, dormant and all but forgotten for six months, burst forth. In his mind's eye Dixon began to relive the final battle. The dream crept over him like diesel-and-artillery-generated smoke. For a moment there was nothing; he could see nothing in the white, manmade fog. He could hear, however, what he could not see. Above the idling engine of his own tank, Dixon could hear the squeaking of tracks on drive sprockets and the straining of engines as other armored vehicles moved about in close proximity. The noises they made ebbed and flowed like waves on a shore. Some of the sounds were familiar, like the whine of a Bradley fighting vehicle making a sharp turn. Others were not, since they came from Soviet armored vehicles.

The crack of a tank cannon firing, followed by the screeching of metal ripping metal not more than a hundred meters from where he sat, finally convinced Dixon he had to move. Sitting there waiting to be found was worse than blundering about in the smoke. Barking out a short order, he instructed the driver to move out. The M-1 tank lurched forward, rolling in the direction of what Dixon thought was the east. Since leaving his initial position and submerging himself and his tank in the manmade smoke, he had lost his orientation and what little command and control of the battalion he had had when he gave the order to counterattack.

As his tank rolled forward, an object moving out of the smoke to his flank caught Dixon's attention. Instinctively he turned—and froze in horror. Less than twenty meters away, the muzzle of a Soviet 125mm tank cannon emerged from the smoke. Transfixed, Dixon watched as its gaping maw slowly turned toward him. Panic, helplessness, and unbridled fear seized him. The Soviet tank cannon grew nearer and larger. He was going to die, and there was nothing he could do to stop it.

He closed his eyes for the briefest of seconds, then opened them again. It was gone. The Soviet tank and its main gun were gone. So was the smoke and the tank he was riding. Instead of on a battlefield, he found himself in a dark tent, in bed, and alive. The nightmares had begun. And they were destined to continue, a constant reminder that he, a commander who had so freely committed his men to battle, was alive while many of those who had so willingly followed him were not. The question of whether he had been right or wrong never figured into the equation. All attempts to rationalize that what he had done had been right failed to bring even a modicum of relief to his troubled mind. Unable to come to grips with himself, Dixon couldn't make the transition from war to peace.

Dixon hadn't been the only casualty of the war in his family. His wife, Fay, with little warning and no preparation, had suddenly found herself facing the prospect of losing her husband. Plans built on the promise of twenty years in the Army followed by retirement on half-pay, a home in the country, and a second career were in jeopardy. For the first time in her life, Fay Dixon was helpless, unable to do anything to save their once precious vision of a happy future. At first Fay banded together with other wives of the Task Force's officers and NCOs in an effort to present at least the appearance of normalcy. That pretense, however, came to an abrupt halt shortly after the first battle.

Military sedans, each bearing an officer, a chaplain, and, whenever possible, the wife of the senior officer in the unit, began to make their rounds, delivering the dreaded message: "I regret to inform you that your husband was killed in action." In short order, the appearance of any type of military vehicle in the military housing area where Fay lived brought fear to the wives. Soon, the moving vans appeared, removing the shattered remains of broken families while the military sedans weaved in between them, carrying the dreaded message to more wives and families.

Dixon's reunion with his family was a cold event, almost totally bereft of emotion. For Dixon, the war continued. He had lost all confidence in himself and his abilities as a soldier and destroyed forever any illusions Fay had about the future.

So Dixon's almost aimless wanderings throughout the Pentagon that morning were symbolic of his passage through the last two years. Though eventually he would get someplace, it didn't matter to him. Until such time as he was able to pull himself together, to bury his ghosts and to breathe life into a marriage that was on a holding pattern, Dixon was content to pass the time doing what he was told, within the secure bosom of the same Army that once had been home to the same men who now peopled his nightmares.

Fort Campbell, Kentucky * 1035 Hours, 1 November

Bob Mennzinger brought his car to a stop across the street from the duplex where his old-time friend Jerry Eller lived. The duplex was modest in appearance, a simple one-story brick home that looked, and was in fact, exactly like the others that surrounded it. It was, as Jerry once said, "a place to hang your hat between flights." Looking about, Mennzinger didn't see the Army sedan that was supposed to meet him. He mumbled a curse under his breath while he considered his next move. The first thing that came to mind was swinging around the block to his own quarters and changing out of his flight suit into a clean set of BDUs. While he was doing so, he could call the unit adjutant and find out where the notification team was. The thought that they might show up while he was gone was overridden by his desire to postpone what he had to do for as long as possible.

Though Jerry Eller no longer belonged to his unit, Mennzinger felt a sense of obligation to be with Betty in her time of need. Snatched up by the Department of the Army four months early and reassigned to a special general-support aviation detachment in the Middle East, Jerry Eller had seemed to drop off the face of the earth. As it was an unaccompanied tour, better known as a hardship tour, his wife and their six-month-old son had been given the option of remaining in quarters or moving back to his or her hometown. Betty Eller had decided to remain at Campbell, living in her own home rather than moving in with her mother and risk suffering round-the-clock advice on how to raise her son. As the unit commander and a personal friend of Jerry's, Mennzinger made sure that Betty felt like part of the unit family. He had told Jerry before he departed that he would do whatever was necessary to make the separation easy for Betty. But the news that Jerry had been killed in a helicopter crash in Egypt—how could he make *that* easy?

He was about to pull away when Betty, her baby riding on her hip, emerged from the side door of the house and headed for the car parked in the driveway. Mennzinger watched for a moment, pondering his next move. As Betty opened the car door, he threw his car door open and called out to get her attention. "Betty!"

Surprised, she turned, then smiled when she saw Mennzinger. "Bob, what are you doing home so early?"

Getting out of his car, Mennzinger straightened out, wiped his sweaty palms on the side of his flight suit, then began to cross the street. "Betty, I need to talk to you."

Despite Mennzinger's hesitation and tone, Betty continued to smile. "Sure, Bob. Only let's go inside—the baby will catch a chill. And besides, I don't want the neighbors to see me conversing with a strange man in the middle of the day. You know how rumors get started—a wife with a husband overseas entertaining men in the middle of the day is sure to get a rise out of someone!"

Betty's attempt to joke with him wasn't making his task any easier. He had lost friends in combat in Iran, but that had been different. They had been at war, in a combat zone. And Mennzinger didn't have to face the families afterward. Most of the time he hadn't even seen the bodies. It had been so clean, so impersonal, so quick. This was entirely different. For a second, Mennzinger thought that facing antiaircraft fire had been easier. The dread of telling Betty was so overpowering that it all but crippled him. Death had come quickly for Jerry. He was beyond pain and suffering. But that thought was small comfort, for Betty's own pain was about to begin. Mennzinger continued to look at her, standing there with a quizzical look on her face as he struggled for the right way, any way, to tell her that she would never see her husband again.

The awkward silence was broken by the appearance of a military sedan pulling into the driveway behind Betty's car. She turned and looked at the sedan, watching while the unit's chaplain got out of the passenger side. The chaplain looked at Mennzinger, then at Betty. Assuming that she already knew, he simply said, "Betty, I'm sorry. Is there—"

A shrill "NO!" cut him off. Clutching her baby to her breast, her face contorted in horror, Betty yelled again, "No! No! It's not true. It can't be!"

Before either man could move, she turned and ran to the door of her house, fumbling with her keys as she tried to open the door. All the while she kept yelling over her shoulder, "Go away—go away!" When she finally managed to open the door, Betty dashed in and slammed it behind her, leaving Mennzinger and the chaplain standing where they had been, wondering what to do next.

Washington, D.C. * 0736 Hours, 2 November

The camera opened with a wide-angle shot of a studio decorated to look like the typical middle-American home, then slowly zoomed in on two people seated in overstuffed chairs. They appeared to be having a casual conversation, which continued until the camera had closed in on them. On cue, the two people, co-hosts of this morning show, nonchalantly turned to the camera and flashed big, toothy smiles. The woman, dressed in a radiant yellow-and-black dress, beamed a bright and cheery greeting: "Good morning to those of you just joining us."

The man's smiling face now changed, on cue, to a serious stare. "Two years after the shooting stopped," he began, "the debate over whether we should have become involved in the conflict in Iran rages on in the chambers of Congress. Defenders from the Right claim that we had no choice but to intervene in the region militarily in order to protect our national interests. To have allowed the Soviets to gain control of the Strait of Hormuz would have been, in the words of Republican senator George Ryan of Maryland, 'tantamount to surrender.' Critics from the Left, on the other hand, contend that U.S. interests were never endangered, that the decision to send troops into Iran was a knee-jerk reaction that almost led to Armageddon.

"Today we have with us in our Washington studio one of the most vocal critics of that conflict. A veteran, Representative Ed Lewis was a battalion executive officer in a Tennessee National Guard unit at the time. His unit fought in the final campaign that stopped the Soviet push to the gulf and brought them to the negotiating tables. Today he continues to fight, not in Iran but in the chambers of Congress, and not against the Soviets but against the dangerous involvement of the United States in alliances and covert military operations." He turned to his left as the camera panned out, showing him facing a man of forty-two, in another overstuffed chair.

"Congressman Lewis, in a very short time you have become the spokesman for many antiwar and antimilitary groups in this country. To what do you credit this distinction?"

Turning to face the camera, Lewis canted his head before he

spoke. "Well, for one thing, I have seen war and what it can do. Any sane and responsible person who has survived the horrors of war should, and must, do everything in their power to keep such a thing from happening again. My success, if you care to call it that, in leading the fight to reduce the size of our military and avoid unnecessary involvement in affairs that are not our country's concern is based on my belief that until someone takes a meaningful step in that direction, we will continue to live with a sword hanging over our heads."

The host asked his next question. "There are those who insist that the Soviet reductions that continued even after Iran are merely symbolic, that the Soviet Union retains forces far beyond its stated needs for self-defense."

Lewis smiled. "Someone has to make a first move, symbolic or not. America has yet to make a meaningful response of any kind. Until we do so, I can't blame the Soviets for not making real, substantial reductions in their forces."

"Congressman, the Pentagon claims that it is currently unable to contain any further expansion of the Soviet Union given its current troop levels and that any reductions would mean that somewhere, something would have to give. Your critics claim that your proposals are tantamount to unilateral disarmament, with no guarantee that the Soviets will reciprocate in kind. How do you propose to protect our national interests without a military capable of enforcing our policies overseas?"

Looking back to the camera, Lewis smirked. "You make it sound as if we are still at war. And that is precisely the kind of attitude that I am fighting to put an end to. The Pentagon has been a major player in determining our foreign policy for far too long. Additionally, the cost of maintaining a large military has resulted in a national debt that has been an incredible drain on our economy for years. Until the military is reduced to a manageable size commensurate to our nation's needs and budget, this nation will always be in danger of war. Strict control of the military and its budget, along with drastic reductions in troop strength, are the only means we have available to ensure that we maintain peace in our time and allow for the reduction of our national debt. Someone has to make the first move. The

Soviets have on numerous occasions stated publicly that they would match our reductions man for man, weapon for weapon. We, the United States, must have the courage of our convictions, to take that step.''

Back-Channel Message from Commander in Chief, CENTCOM, to Chief of Staff, U.S. Army * Date/Time Group 021345Z Nov (1345 Hours GMT, 2 November)

In reference to your message concerning the death of LTC Dedinger, I see no need to curtail current TWILIGHT operations. There was no compromise in either Egypt or the Sudan. Recovery of his and the helicopter's crew has been accomplished.

The necessity to replace Dedinger with a top-notch man at the earliest opportunity is not only critical to TWILIGHT but also to the upcoming BRIGHT STAR exercise. I have already submitted a list of possible replacements to Bill Neibert at PERSCOM. He promises fast action.

Of greater concern than the recent accident, as regrettable as it was, is the impact of further budget cuts on TWILIGHT operations; I see no way that we can continue to carry on at the current level of operations if those cuts are put into effect. I will not be able to continue to divert operational and training funds into TWILIGHT without seriously degrading operational readiness in other areas, in particular the Gulf, and, specifically BRIGHT STAR, as it is *currently* planned. As to your question concerning the value of TWILIGHT, I have read all the intelligence reports and analyses generated by my people here and your people in Washington and disagree with them. While TWILIGHT will not help the guerrilla forces we are supporting win, it is keeping the other people from winning and, equally important, from spreading conflicts across the borders. Like the South African STRIKER operations in Angola, TWILIGHT is causing the Soviets and their surrogates to commit personnel and resources to defensive operations, leaving them very little for cross-border agitation, support of Sudanese insurgents, and offensive operations. We must continue. The only question is at what level and what program will become the bill payer for TWILIGHT.

Total U.S. military personnel directly involved in TWILIGHT operations remains at 1,500. In my opinion, that is sufficient at this time. This figure includes the ten Special Forces A teams currently deployed and two preparing for deployment. To date, no U.S. military personnel have been involved in military operations that fall within the South African sphere of influence. We do, however, exchange critical intelligence that concerns Soviet-backed operations and movements.

Soviet response to TWILIGHT operations has been minimal. We have seen some increase in force levels. The no-bullshit strengths I have are; Angola: 2,800 Soviet and 15,000 Cuban; Ethiopia: 3,000 Soviet and 20,000 Cuban; Libya: 1,600 Soviet and 9,000 Cuban; Mozambique: 750 Soviet and 2,000 Cuban. An additional 900 Soviets, 2,500 Cubans, and 1,800 Warsaw Pact personnel are spread throughout the continent. I believe the Reds will continue to downplay their role in Africa so long as they can do so without losing any more face or ground. All bets are off, however, if they perceive that one of their client states is about to go down the tubes. After they took a beating in Afghanistan and Iran, the last thing the Soviets can afford is another defeat, real or apparent, even if it involves one of their proxies.

Herein lies the danger: how much and how hard do you want me to push? I can keep the bastards off balance and from spreading conflicts with what I have, given our current budget. If, however, our operations, or those of our client states, become too successful, the Soviets may simply say "Screw public relations" and throw in their combat troops or Cubans. There are sufficient Soviet and Cuban personnel currently deployed in Africa, if pooled, to present a combat force capable of defeating any standing African army, outside of the South Africans and possibly the Egyptians. Please keep that in mind the next time you talk to The Man.

I would not have presented you a problem without a solution. My people tell me that if we cut the Army's ground component of BRIGHT STAR by one brigade, and transfer funds saved there to TWILIGHT operations, we will be able to carry on with TWILIGHT at current levels for the balance of this fiscal year without dipping into other funds. Currently, the 16th Armored Division is scheduled to deploy with two of its armored brigades and one brigade, reinforced, from the 11th Air Assault Division. We can, in my opinion, accomplish the same training, vis-a-vis deployment, and the same political goals, by deploying only one armored brigade and one reinforced air assault brigade under the control of the 16th Armored. As this is a no-notice deployment exercise, and we have not yet finalized the exercise plan or our troop list with the Egyptian government, we will lose no credibility with any foreign governments or the public. The other option is cutting the Marine brigade. That, however, would be very unpopular, with both the Marines and the press. You know how the media loves seeing Chesty's boys wading ashore. Makes good copy.

Regards to the wife and family. Hope your oldest is having a better plebe year at the Point than you and I did.

Robert Horn
General, U.S.A.
CinC, CENTCOM

2

Guerrillas never win wars but their adversaries often lose them.

—CHARLES W. THAYER

Gondar, Ethiopia * 0330 Hours, 12 November

The journey from Kassala in the Sudan to Gondar, Ethiopia, had been a hard one for Kinsly and his men. In eight days they had covered the 150 kilometers, or 92 miles, straight-line distance from the drop-off point north of Gallabat on the east bank of the Atbara River on the border of Ethiopia. The march had been uphill all the way, with the drop point being a thousand feet above sea level and the target, an airfield at Gondar, a little more than seventy-five hundred feet above sea level. Carrying weapons, a full combat load, and three weeks' rations while traveling only at night over broken and rocky terrain in a hostile country had been no easy feat. But they had done it—and without a single mishap or contact of any kind.

Kinsly had been concerned about the men, his own and the Sudanese. He shouldn't have been—they were tough and ready. Each American Green Beret in Kinsly's A Team, Kinsly included, was a volunteer and a veteran of either the war in Iran or antidrug operations in Central and South America. Some, like Sergeant First Class Hector Veldez, were veterans of both. The Sudanese, now clad in shoddy, faded uniforms similar to those of the Eritrean rebels, had been toughened by an unending guerrilla war. Despite an appearance that reminded Kinsly of men on the verge of starvation, in a fight they were, man for man, every bit as capable as Kinsly's own.

What really bothered Kinsly during their quiet march toward the Ethiopian airfield was the realization that he had lost faith in himself and what he was doing. When he had volunteered for Special Forces, he had done so for the simple reason that he wanted to be on the cutting edge—out in the boonies, making things happen. Special Forces, he had been told, would make a difference. "We go in when the war is small," Dedinger had told him during his initial in-brief, "and we keep it small." While there was some merit in what the colonel said, eight months in the Sudan, training and advising a counterguerrilla unit, had convinced him not only that he was in the wrong place but that he was there for all the wrong reasons.

The glamour of special operations, training "indigenous" personnel to defend themselves and being where "the action" was, had faded in the harsh conditions, rank poverty, and confused political situation of the Sudan. The savage civil war that had no discernible beginning and no foreseeable end completed the ravage of southern Sudan. It didn't take Kinsly long to realize that the Sudanese had been killing each other before he came and would no doubt keep on doing so after he had left. The Sudanese government itself was walking a picket fence, attempting to keep the communists out of power without seriously offending their powerful neighbor to the south or the Soviet Union, backer for both Ethiopia and the Sudanese rebels in southern Sudan. In the midst of all this, the most Kinsly and his men could do was to make the killing process slightly more efficient.

Even had he been able to reconcile himself to the absurdity of the military situation and his role in it, Kinsly was unable to accept the pitiful conditions to which war and famine had reduced the country's population. His middle-class upbringing had done nothing to prepare him for working and living with a people so stricken with perpetual famine, drought, and war that it left them teetering on the edge of survival. As hard as he tried, Kinsly had difficulty embracing the people he was expected to help.

Nor could he turn off his emotions or harden himself to the suffering that surrounded him, as SFC Veldez did. It was the children that got to him. Every child between the age of three and five reminded him of his own daughter. In the beginning he had tried participating in civil assistance operations, projects designed to help the "indigenous" population and win their hearts and minds away from the communists. But that didn't last long. One day, while helping his team's paramedic inoculate children, he saw a young girl, not more than five, sitting alone under a lone tree that was as malnourished as the child seeking its shade. Kinsly squatted down and tried to strike up a conversation with the girl while she waited patiently to be seen by his team's medic. His efforts were for nought. The girl's only response was to stare at him with large, vacant, unblinking eyes. Her face was a frozen mask of despair.

Determined to bring some joy to this poor creature's existence, Kinsly told the girl he had a surprise for her. Returning to where his team had dropped their rucksacks, he retrieved a roll of caramel candy he had been saving from his rations. Walking back, he hoped that she would be able to chew the sticky candy. His concern was unnecessary. As he neared the tree, he noticed that the girl had not moved since he had left her. Her large, vacant eyes continued to stare unseeing into the distance. Nothing he had experienced before or since haunted Kinsly more than the image of that little girl's body, lifeless and alone. The death of that innocent young girl, more than anything else, summarized the stark despair and bankrupt future the country faced. From that day on, Kinsly stopped volunteering and kept to himself, attempting to survive by isolating himself from everything not connected with the military aspect of his mission.

The operations they conducted as part of Twilight helped. "Twilight" was the name given to raids designed to keep the Ethiopians and their Soviet advisors off balance and reduce their backing of the Sudanese communists. These raids allowed Kinsly to maintain the illusion that he was doing something useful and soldierly, but even they seemed at times to be of questionable value. Though the idea was sound, Kinsly saw no indication that Twilight operations were having any effect. Like every other aspect of his team's mission, these Lilliputian efforts were pinpricks that solved nothing, ended nothing.

In quick succession, explosions ripped open the large fuel tanks, shattering the silence of the night, bringing Kinsly's mind back to the task at hand. Thousands of gallons of burning aviation fuel, spilling out of ruptured containers, bathed the airfield in a shimmering light. Hours of crawling about in the darkness, clearing a lane through a mine field and cutting through two barbed-wire fences, were over. Kinsly didn't need to cue the commander of the Sudanese guerrilla assault team he was with. They were already up and headed for the helicopters parked along the runway in protective revetments. Now it was time for action—quick, violent action.

The colonel who had planned the operation and had given Kinsly's Special Forces A team the mission figured that they had less than twenty minutes from the beginning of the attack before the Ethiopians could muster their ready reaction force and mount an effective counterattack. In that time, the guerrilla band that the A team was working with had to take out some twenty helicopters and six MIG fighters as well as their maintenance facilities and support equipment. The fuel storage tanks and trucks, which served as the trigger for initiation of the attack, were already gone. Barring any unforeseen complications, Kinsly was sure they could do it.

In an instant, Major Grigori Neboatov, senior Soviet advisor to the battalion of infantry guarding the airfield at Gondar, was awake, off his cot, and on the floor. His reactions were not the results of training; they were the instincts of a veteran, a man who had survived in combat living long enough to learn how to survive. He lay on the floor for a moment, motionless and listening. After the initial detonations, there had been a great spasm of automatic and semiautomatic fire in the distance that had lasted five, maybe ten seconds. Then, five seconds of silence. When the shooting started again, it came in random bursts. The echoing gunfire was not from Russian-made weapons. The explosions had not been an accident, and the gunfire was not friendly. They were under attack.

Satisfied that he was in no immediate danger, but not wanting to take any unnecessary chances, Neboatov rolled across the floor to where his clothes and pistol hung on the back of a chair. Fumbling with his clothes, he continued to listen to the sounds of battle outside. There was still no return fire from his people. That meant that the Ethiopian soldiers on duty had been taken out in the initial explosions or in the volley fire that he had heard immediately after the explosions. The enemy, therefore, was there in strength and within the perimeter of the airfield itself.

With pants, boots, and pistol belt on, he pondered his next move. If the enemy had been clever enough to cover and eliminate the troops on duty, they no doubt would have the barracks covered with automatic fire. A burst of machine-gun fire not more than fifty meters from where Neboatov lay confirmed his suspicion. With measured bursts of twenty-five to thirty rounds, the unseen machine gun, sited to cover the front of the troops' and the officers' billets, began to rake the troop billet next to the one where Neboatov and the other officers were. Knowing that the uninsulated wooden walls of his building didn't offer any cover, he decided it was time to move.

In a single bound, Neboatov sprang from the floor, leaping over his cot and through the door of his room, grabbing an AK assault rifle that stood propped next to the door as he went by. Without stopping, he continued across the hall, smashing through the thin wooden door of the room across from his. Once in the room, he flopped back down onto the floor and looked around. The window facing the rear was open, and the Cuban captain, Neboatov's assistant, who occupied the room was gone. Assuming that the Cuban had already made good his exit, Neboatov pushed himself up off the floor and made for the window. Wanting to get out of the dark confines of the building and into the open where he could at least defend himself, he threw himself out of the window head first, hoping as he did so that there wasn't anyone or anything on the other side prepared to bar his way.

As Kinsly and the demolition teams ran, random shots from all about them began to ring out. The Ethiopian Army guards on duty had recovered their wits and were beginning to return fire against the attackers. The odds, however, were momentarily against them. Too few guards had survived the initial fire fight. Those that had were separated and silhouetted against the burning fuel tanks. The attackers, emerging from the darkness, were ready, massed and determined. The Ethiopian guards who managed to fire got off only one or two bursts before they were cut down by the assault team. This process was made even easier for the assault team since many of the guards, rather than dropping to the ground and assuming a good prone position before firing, stood fully exposed while they blazed away into the darkness at their still-unseen assailants. The Ethiopians sealed their own death warrant: this both appalled and pleased Kinsly. Such stupidity, he thought, all but guaranteed his success. Though he saw a couple of the Sudanese soldiers go down, more by sheer accident than by accurate and aimed fire, their loss did not deter the follow-on demolition team. The Sudanese were used to losses and death. They were professional soldiers. It was, and for many of them had been since their birth, a way of life.

Once the assault team, charged with the task of clearing away the guards, had finished that part of its mission, it moved on to prepare to repel the counterattack force. Immediately behind it came the sappers with the demolitions. Kinsly dropped back and joined the sappers. Organized into four three-man teams, they dispersed among the parked aircraft. Each team followed the same procedures; while one man stayed on the ground to provide security, two climbed up onto the aircraft, one on either side. Once up near the aircraft engine, the two men pulled blocks of C-4 plastic explosives, with fifteen-minute delayed-action detonator fuses already stuck into them, out of pouches dangling from their sides. Pulling the cord that initiated the fuse, they stuck the blocks of C-4 into the air intakes of the helicopters' engines and jumped down, and the man who had been standing guard put a big X on the nose of the aircraft with a piece of chalk. The sapper team then ran down the line of aircraft until it found one that did not have a chalked X on its nose. As before, two of the sappers climbed up and went about their work.

Kinsly followed the sapper teams. He counted the aircraft marked with X's, making sure that none had been bypassed and looking to see if any of them carried new equipment or antennas he had not seen before. He also recorded in a little green notebook any numbers or tactical markings painted on the aircraft. All this data would be turned over to the military intelligence people later for their review and consideration.

In a gully behind the billets, Neboatov found the Cuban captain organizing the Ethiopian soldiers who had made it out of their billets. The captain was talking, or, more correctly, yelling, at an Ethiopian officer. Coming up from behind, Neboatov put his hand on the shoulder of Captain Angel Torres. "Captain Torres, how many men do you have?"

Torres turned his head toward Neboatov while holding his right hand up to the Ethiopian officer, indicating that he was not yet finished with him. "Major, I was in the process of trying to get a firm grasp on that now. I believe we have about thirty armed men and a dozen or so without weapons."

Turning to his right, Neboatov looked at the soldiers lining the sides of the ditch. They were in varying stages of dress and, despite what Torres had just reported, only about one in three was armed. But Neboatov's growing despair turned to delight when he spied one of the soldiers grasping an ancient American-made 60mm mortar. A smile on his face, he turned back to Torres. "Take that man over there with the mortar and as many rounds as you can into a position where they can take the flight line under fire. I'll organize this rabble here into a counterattack force."

Torres interrupted. "But we don't know for sure where they are. We should recon first while we consolidate our available forces."

Neboatov wasn't used to debates with subordinates, especially in combat. "You idiot, why do you think the enemy is here? They are after the aircraft. If we wait and dress up our lines and prepare a proper, well-staffed plan, the enemy will destroy every aircraft and be gone before we act. Now get that mortar into position. Give me five minutes, then start lobbing shells into the center of where the aircraft are parked. Watch for me and the enemy, adjusting your fire as necessary. Clear?"

Torres was about to say something, then thought better. He knew it was pointless to discuss tactical matters with a Russian once he had made up his mind. He looked at Neboatov one more time, shook his head, then went about gathering up an ad-hoc mortar team.

From several hundred meters to his rear, Kinsly heard the familiar thud of a mortar round being spit out of a mortar tube. As his people did not have mortars, that could only mean that the Ethiopian army counterattack was about to get under way. Instinctively, Kinsly hunched down, waiting for the impact of the first mortar round. That round landed among the helicopters that had not yet been rigged for detonation. Standing upright and turning back to look, he couldn't make sense of that. Either the mortar crew was firing wild, not knowing or caring where the rounds went, or they knew where the sappers were and were attempting to keep them from destroying the aircraft still untouched. Either way, it was time to leave.

The thumping sound of three more mortar rounds being fired and the report of a pair of heavy machine guns firing from the same general vicinity brought Kinsly back to the immediate situation. Turning and running down the line, Kinsly continued to count aircraft rigged for demolition. He had counted sixteen when someone on the perimeter of the airfield gave three loud blasts on a whistle, the signal to leave. Though they were not finished, his commander had determined, as Kinsly had already, that it was time to cut and run while they could. The mortar and machine-gun fire would soon become effective. Once that happened, the Sudanese would be pinned, unable to move and easy prey for a counterattack.

As if to underscore that point, a mortar round impacted not more than fifty meters from where Kinsly stood. The blast caught him off guard and knocked him down. For a moment he lay on the tarmac, collecting his senses and checking for wounds. Finding none, he raised himself up on one elbow and looked in the direction of where the round had impacted. A MIG-23 fighter had been hit and was now burning. In the light thrown off by the burning aircraft, three lifeless forms in ragged brown uniforms could be seen sprawled about the aircraft. One of the sapper teams had been taken out.

Getting up on his hands and knees, Kinsly crawled over to and behind a revetment. From there he watched as the remaining sapper teams moved away from the aircraft and headed back into the darkness in the direction from which they had come. Close behind them came the assault team that had been providing protection for the sappers. As the assault team came up even with Kinsly, he left the cover of the revetment and joined them. At a trot, he moved across the airfield, flanked by the soldiers he had helped train. Every twenty or thirty meters he would turn, running backwards, to see how closely they were being followed. On one of these looks back, he saw three figures dart out from between two buildings and set up a machine gun near the revetment he had just left. They were about to fire when the fuse in the C-4 planted in a helicopter nearby went off. The blast, followed by secondary explosions caused by the detonation of fuel and rockets on the helicopter, showered the machine-gun crew with shrapnel, killing or wounding all three. By incredible luck, the demolitions began to go off just as the counterattack force was moving into position to engage the withdrawing Sudanese, thus discouraging the Ethiopian soldiers from pressing their attack and allowing the Sudanese to withdraw.

Once outside the barbed-wire fence that had been set up to

keep intruders out, the guerrillas quickly reformed and took a head count. In the darkness Kinsly called out to his NCOs. Each in turn answered Kinsly with a simple "Yo."

From down the line Sergeant Veldez called out to Kinsly. "Looks like we got everybody, sir."

Looking back onto the airfield, Kinsly could see several lifeless forms sprawled about on the runway—the Sudanese that had been cut down in the initial assault and withdrawal. He looked at them for a second, then turned back to the direction from which his commander's voice had come. "Yeah, I guess everybody that's going is here. Let's move it."

Without further comment, the attack force formed up into a loose column and began to move back into the shadows.

The exploding aircraft, spewing scraps of aluminum and burning fuel in every direction, had been more than enough to destroy the fragile organization of Neboatov's counterattack force. The rough skirmish line that he had formed and led forward disappeared. All hope of catching the attackers was abandoned as he and anyone else still alive scurried for cover. Flattening himself onto the concrete, Neboatov looked about for cover. Spinning himself about on his stomach like a great top, he turned around and crawled back to the safety of a revetment. Once he reached it, he propped himself up and caught his breath.

As the explosions began to subside, Neboatov dropped back into the prone position. The mortar fire had ceased. So had the small arms. Carefully, very carefully, he stuck his head around the revetment toward the runway. In the flickering light of burning aircraft and fuel, Neboatov could see a trail of bodies spread out on the runway. The trail disappeared into the darkness. Looking to his right, he could see that several aircraft were still intact. Pulling his head back, he sat upright again and pondered his next move. Though they hadn't saved all the aircraft, they had saved some, and, in the process, killed some of the attackers. And best of all, he thought, he was alive. That in itself, he thought, was a victory.

Prince Frederick, Maryland * 1945 Hours, 12 November

While their wives were putting the final touches on dinner, John Heisman gave Scott Dixon the high sign to move into the living room out of earshot of his wife, Annie, and Fay Dixon. There Heisman turned to Dixon. "Jesus, Scott—I haven't seen that much ice since the last time I saw the movie *Titanic!* You and Fay haven't said two words to each other since you got here. Is she *that* upset about the orders?"

Scott moved over to a large overstuffed chair and plopped down into it before he answered. "Upset?" he said in a glum, expressionless manner. "I wish she was only upset. Livid is more like it. And it's not just the orders." Scott leaned forward toward Heisman to emphasize his next point. "Actually, Fay took it quite well, considering." Dixon took a drink, then continued. "Did you know Fay had been out job hunting?"

John nodded his head. "I found out tonight, just before we got here. Annie warned me the situation here might be a little tense."

Glibly Dixon shrugged his shoulders. "Well, tense it was and tense it is." Easing back into the chair, he added, "Fay was not a happy camper when I brought home the wonderful news that I had orders for Egypt."

Three days after he had run around the Pentagon handcarrying the messages concerning the "accidental" death of Lieutenant Colonel Dedinger, Dixon had been notified by Personnel Support Command, or PERSCOM, the Army's personnel management center, that he was about to receive orders assigning him to Egypt as the chief of staff of the 2nd Corps (U.S.) (Forward). Several quick calls and a few inquiries into the possibility of getting out of the assignment yielded nothing. When the Deputy Chief of Staff for Operations and Plans called him in and told him that he had been hand-picked for the job, Dixon resigned himself to the inevitable and prepared for the worst part: telling Fay.

Surprisingly, Fay took the news well. Instead of horrified and outraged, she was calm and noncommittal. She was, in fact, too calm and too noncommittal—a reaction so far out of character that it threw Dixon. The house in Prince Frederick, once owned by a famous writer, was to have been their last: Fay and Scott had agreed that this was it, the end of the line. Though the commute to Washington, two hours every day, was hard on Scott, that sacrifice was his way of showing Fay that he meant what he said.

It was a year before Fay finally was able to settle back into a comfortable relationship with Scott and believe that he meant what he said about finishing his twenty where they were, then leaving the Army. His decision to decline command of a task force finally convinced Fay. Happy, she had begun to dig her roots deep into the community. The house was redone, top to bottom. The children were enrolled in every program that Fay could find and the best private school in the area. And, unknown to Scott, Fay began to prepare herself for resuming a career in TV news. Scott didn't find that out until he hit her with the news that he was under orders for Egypt. "Well, I guess that shoots my job with CBS in the ass, doesn't it?" was Fay's only response, and the first he had known that she had been out seeking employment. It was hard to tell which of them had been more surprised. Fortunately, there had been no fighting, no verbal thrashing—which, as Scott told John, not only came as a shock but aroused his suspicions.

In the kitchen, Annie was pumping Fay for information. Fay, for her part, was being very selective about what she provided. Though she knew that with Scott leaving the next day, the odds were that he wouldn't get any information via Annie or John, Fay wasn't taking any chances.

Before marrying Scott, Fay had been a successful field producer. Together with her college roommate Jan Fields, who had opted to go the reporter route, she had achieved a couple of remarkable coups. Young, ambitious, and willing to take chances, the two of them dug into stories other reporters and producers wouldn't touch. In a couple of cases, it had almost cost them their jobs; but in the end they had earned themselves a reputation, a joint nickname—"the Terrible Two"—and healthy salaries to go with it.

Then Scott Dixon came into Fay's life. They met while doing a story on the introduction of a new tank into the Army's inventory. The tank was reputed to have many problems and couldn't meet specifications. Because it was a dirty job and very touchy, the Terrible Two were sent to tackle it. The Army also prepared for battle, selecting a young, self-confident cavalry captain to escort the two female media types and charm their pants off. In the case of Fay, Scott Dixon did just that. In short order, Fay turned her back on a promising career and on her best friend, despite Jan's efforts to get her to listen to reason. They parted, still friends, but each pursuing divergent goals. Jan continued her career, roaming the world in search of news, while Fay became the good Army wife.

It wasn't until Fay was applying for a position with the CBS news office in Washington, D.C., that she got in contact with Jan Fields again. Though Fay had seen her on TV, and those appearances had provided the impetus for Fay to apply for a job, Fay had not tried to contact Jan. Now, however, since she was once again entering the world of TV news, Fay would be able to deal with Jan as an equal again. So Fay fired off a long-delayed letter to Jan care of the World News Network Middle East Bureau in Cairo. To her delight, Jan's response was rapid and positive. In an hour-and-forty-five-minute phone conversation initiated by Jan, the two college roommates caught up on twelve years and promised that they would get together again soon, just like in the old days.

So when Scott came in and announced that their lives were about to be uprooted again, Fay didn't bat an eye. While Scott had taken away her shot to work with CBS in Washington with one hand, he was setting up an opportunity, at the same time, for Fay to reenter the world of TV news at the side of an old and trusted friend. Fay resolved that this time nothing—not Scott, not the Army, not heaven or hell—would stand between her and the realization of her dream.

As Annie filled the bowls with salad, she said quietly to Fay, "Well, are you?"

Fay, just finishing taking the baked chicken breasts from a cookie sheet and arranging them on a plate, looked Annie in the eye. "What would you do? After all, nothing has changed. I may have to beg and wait till hell freezes over before I can find a decent job in Egypt, but I'm going to do it."

"Does Scott know?"

"He knew about the CBS job." Fay paused, her expression softening as she let her arms fall to her side. "You know, I think he was really sorry that he screwed up my chance for the job with CBS."

"Does that surprise you? After all, Scott still loves you, doesn't he?"

Fay was tiring of Annie's probing. Signaling that Annie had overstepped her bounds, Fay picked up the plate with the chicken breasts on it. "Well, let's serve 'em while they're still hot."

15 Kilometers West of Gondar, Ethiopia *
0730 Hours, 12 November

For miles around one could see the lone and ancient tree perched atop a jagged rock ledge. The tree, its gnarled roots grasping the gray soil that gave it support and life, was surrounded by hundreds of square kilometers of windswept hills and gullies. The ledge and the tree therefore served as a reference point for travelers, human and animal, who traversed this part of northwestern Ethiopia. The tree also served as a home and resting place for migratory birds in need of a place to rest on their annual journey. The pale morning sun this morning greeted a flock of such birds that had been drawn to the tree the night before. Quiet chirping and an occasional flutter of wings were the only sounds that could be heard.

Suddenly, as if on signal, the birds sitting in the lone tree paused in their chatter and became still. Some of them turned their heads slightly in an effort to better identify the danger they sensed, rather than saw or heard. Not waiting to find out its source, the birds took to wing as one in a frenzy that bordered on panic. Predators that had moved up near the tree under cover of darkness and now lay hidden in the rocks were startled by their sudden flight. Fearful that they had been discovered, the predators tensed up, ready to strike in any direction. Only when the last of the birds had flown from earshot and stillness returned to the rocky ledge did the predators relax, but only a little: they knew the birds had been spooked by something— something big. Perhaps that something was their prey. Minutes later this assumption was confirmed when the morning silence was again broken. The slow, distant rumble of many heavily burdened trucks could be heard. As the trucks drew closer to the lone tree, the sound of gears grinding and the laboring of the engines became distinct.

In the early morning sun, the line of twenty trucks and half a dozen jeeps moved slowly west from Gondar, along the dirt track that followed a gorge that cut into the mountain like a scar. Dust rose and hung about them in the morning calm. The pace of the trucks and their lack of proper dispersion infuriated Major Neboatov. The column was moving too fast to provide proper detailed recon ahead and too slow to enable it to reach a position from which they could cut off the force that had assaulted them several hours before.

Immediately after the fighting at the airfield had ended, a lively debate had begun. Neboatov knew that the guerrilla force would disperse at dawn. Time therefore was critical. He insisted that a force of two battalions, moving along separate routes, move immediately to intercept the enemy before they slipped back across the Sudanese border; there was always the outside chance that they could get into position before the guerrilla force made it to safety or dispersed. Such a bold stroke might succeed. But there was a great deal of indecision on the part of the Ethiopian regimental commander. A former guerrilla with years of experience fighting the former government, he had never made the transition to waging a counter-guerrilla war. And even Neboatov's assistant, Captain Torres, sided with the regimental commander.

Thus, instead of striking out with all available forces and

speed, the regimental commander had reported to army headquarters in Addis Ababa and requested instructions. For hours
nothing was done, either in Gondar or in Addis Ababa. When
instructions were received, at 0435 hours, they were a compromise. The battalion to which Neboatov was attached as an
advisor was to move out at dawn by truck in pursuit of the
attackers. Incensed by the half-measure, Neboatov contacted
the senior Soviet advisor in Addis Ababa. He submitted his
own report and recommendation, stating that the battalion, cut
to two-thirds strength by the attack, was in no shape to move.
Furthermore, his report pointed out, using such a small force to
chase the enemy was pointless. He never received a response,
other than acknowledgment that his message had been received. Frustrated, Neboatov decided, against his better judgment, to go out with the column. Though it would accomplish
nothing, at least he could vent his frustrations in the field.
Anything had to be better than sitting around doing nothing and
accomplishing less.

As was the normal practice, Neboatov and Captain Torres
were in the fourth vehicle. The guerrillas were in the habit of
mining roads and trails. In the early days too many Soviet and
Cuban advisors had been lost to this practice. To reduce this
wastage, an order was issued that advisors would not travel in
the lead vehicles. Though this reduced casualties among the
advisors, it lowered the esteem in which the Ethiopian forces
once held their fellow socialists. Neboatov, a combat veteran,
understood the need for leadership and the effects it had on
morale. When he arrived, he ignored the order. The effect was
immediate and beneficial. The officers of the battalion he was
assigned to accepted him but shunned Torres, who insisted that
it was important that they follow the order. The result was that
the Ethiopians openly snubbed and looked down upon Torres
while Neboatov was held in high regard. Neboatov made real
headway with the Ethiopians and established a relationship
based on trust and respect. This hard-earned rapport was threatened, however, when he received a reprimand from Lieutenant
Colonel Lvov, his immediate superior. It didn't take a great
deal of intelligence to figure out that Torres had reported Ne-

boatov's violation through his own channels. Neboatov never forgave him.

Torres, now slouched down in the back of the jeep, was asleep. The initial excitement of assembling the battalion and moving out was gone. The tedium of the trip, the unchanging scenery, and the effects of lost sleep began to dull Neboatov's senses. Rather than give in to the urge to sleep, as Torres had, he studied the terrain and kept track of their progress, calculating the time it would take to arrive at various critical points along their route. There were precious few features on the terrain that he could use for reference. Running his finger along a map, he followed the winding goat track they were on. The map showed a hairpin turn at a rocky outcropping just ahead, where the goat trail came out of the gorge they were in. The place had a name, but Neboatov could not pronounce it. He knew that it had something to do with a lone tree and that everyone used the place as a reference point. Neboatov sat up in the seat and tried to look ahead for the rocky ledge, but the lead vehicles and the dust they kicked up frustrated his view. It was not until he felt the jeep begin to climb a steep incline that he realized they were at the turn.

On top of the ledge, the predators that had been startled when the birds had taken wing listened to the advance of the trucks. Unlike the birds, they did not flee. Instead, they slowly eased themselves into position and prepared to strike. Even the drone of a pair of attack helicopters patrolling the road in front of the column of trucks did not bother them. In silence they waited for the first vehicles to come over the crest of the ledge and move past the lone, empty tree. They would strike only when they were ready; they would not be rushed. Their leader patiently watched and waited. He watched as the first vehicle of the convoy passed the tree and continued without halting or slowing. He relaxed, watching as the second, then the third vehicle reached and passed the tree. As the fourth vehicle reached the lone tree, Sergeant First Class Hector Veldez, one of the hidden predators, raised his M-16A2 automatic rifle to his shoulder and, in a booming voice, ordered his men to fire.

Without thought, Neboatov reacted to the first crack of rifle fire and the choke of mortar rounds being fired. Looking neither left nor right, and not bothering to gauge the speed of the jeep, he threw himself out of the vehicle, flattening out on contact with the ground and rolling toward the tree. Hitting a large, serpentine root that rose a foot from the ground, Neboatov stopped, scrambled to the other side of the root, and rolled over onto his back. For a moment he lay there, listening to his heart pound in his chest, gasping for breath. He watched bits of leaves from the tree above detach themselves and flutter down on him. The sound of his breathing was soon obscured by the crescendo of battle unfolding all about him. The bits of leaves were fragments that had been chipped off by stray bullets.

Rolling back over onto his stomach, Neboatov slowly raised his head and peered over the root. The first six vehicles of the convoy were stopped and burning or overturned. His own jeep was ablaze; its driver lay next to it in a pool of blood. Captain Torres hung half out of the jeep, his body engulfed in flames. From the far side of the road, figures rose up from hidden positions and began to move toward the vehicles. The line of attackers advanced swiftly, staying crouched low to the ground, their rifles at the ready. They were going to move to the edge of the knoll and fire down onto the remainder of the column, now halted and under fire from other hidden assailants.

Neboatov had to move; in a few minutes the attackers would be at the tree. Slowly, he crawled back, away from his covered position behind the root. But his efforts attracted attention. An enemy soldier, not twenty meters from Neboatov, shouted and turned toward him. Jumping to his feet, Neboatov drew his pistol and fired two quick shots; both hit their target. For a second he watched the man twirl about and fall to the ground. The enemy soldier's hat flew off, revealing straight black hair and the white face of Sergeant Veldez. "Americans! They're being led by bloody Americans!" The sound of rounds from other enemy soldiers hitting the tree near Neboatov reminded him of his plight. He turned and, followed by a hail of bullets, ran back down into the gorge, where he assumed the survivors of the column would be forming.

Despite the fact that he was in grave danger, he surveyed the scene before him as he ran. Many of the trucks that had not made it up the side of the gorge were also burning. That meant that there were enemy forces hiding along the edge of the gorge as well as on the rock ledge. When he reached the rocks and boulders, however, the scene before him was ripped apart as plumes of fire and dirt exploded before Neboatov's eyes. Mortars. The concussion of a near miss sent him sprawling. He lay there for a moment, trying to decide if he was hit. He gasped for breath; his mouth was dry; sweat dripped from every pore. But he was alive. A sharp pain in his shoulder when he began to move told him he was hit. But he was alive. Propping himself up slightly, he found that his injury was not a crippling wound. Ready to continue, he got onto his hands and knees and crawled behind a boulder, guided by the sound of AK assault rifles returning fire.

The first Ethiopian soldiers he came across were dead. He paused by one body, holstered his pistol, and took the AK assault rifle from the dead man. He then emptied the dead man's ammo pouches of magazines and stuffed them into his belt. Better armed now, Neboatov continued. After passing several more dead Ethiopians, he came up behind an Ethiopian who was lying prone behind a mound of dirt. The noise of Neboatov's approach startled the Ethiopian soldier; he spun about and prepared to shoot. "Don't shoot! Friend!" Neboatov yelled in broken Amharic. The soldier paused, then turned around again, continuing his random firing. Neboatov had no idea what the man was shooting at; but at least someone was returning fire.

Slowly Neboatov began to collect whatever Ethiopians he could find and organize them. He even came across a captain and a lieutenant, to whom he assigned a section of the small defensive perimeter that was beginning to take shape. In the midst of this, the beating of blades announcing the approach of the escorting attack helicopters could be heard above the din of the fire fight. For a moment Neboatov allowed himself to breathe a sigh of relief. Salvation. Surely the motley American-led guerrilla band would be no match for the heavily armed MI-24 Hind gunships.

Kinsly and his men, however, were ready. They too heard the approaching helicopter gunships. On cue, two Sudanese soldiers emerged from their concealed positions. They removed surface-to-air missiles from their containers and stood up, facing the direction of the gunships. As the helicopters bore down on the knoll, the Sudanese gunners casually shouldered their weapons, activated the infrared seekers of the missiles, and waited for the tone that would tell them the missiles' heat-seeking guidance systems were locked onto the approaching gunships. Once he had a tone, each gunner let fly his missile.

The relief Neboatov had felt when he heard the approaching gunships was short-lived. From the far side of the knoll, two pillars of flame and smoke raced toward the approaching gunships. In an instant Neboatov knew what they were. In horror he watched the missiles intercept the gunships. The first missile appeared to hit the lead gunship head-on, causing the helicopter to erupt into a ball of fire. The second gunship banked sharply in an effort to evade the oncoming missile, but it too was hit. The missile impacted on the engine just below the blades. The resulting explosion separated the blades from the helicopter, letting the fuselage fall away to the ground like a rock.

For a moment the ground fire died down; it was almost as if all the combatants had stopped in order to watch the destruction of the helicopters. The respite did not last long. Encouraged by the destruction of the enemy aircraft, the guerrillas doubled their fire and began to press their attack home.

This new attack, however, was met with stiff and organized resistance. Leadership and organization among the Ethiopians were beginning to take effect. Sensing that the time was right,

Neboatov led a small counterattack force he had formed around the flank of the attacking guerrillas. Using his limited command of Amharic and hand and arm signals, he ordered his counterattack force to hold its fire until it was within twenty meters of the enemy.

Slowly the Ethiopians moved forward among the boulders and gullies. When he could clearly hear the enemy leaders issuing orders, Neboatov signaled his force to stop. Carefully he raised his head. To his immediate front he could see a lanky black officer directing several of his men. Lowering himself down, Neboatov looked to the Ethiopian soldiers to his left and right. They were in a rough scrimmage line. Raising his gun above his head to signal the beginning of the attack, Neboatov waited until he was sure the word had been passed down the line. When he was ready, he stood up, cut down the guerrilla officer with a burst of fire and yelled "Charge!" in Russian.

Kinsly sensed, more than saw, that the tide of battle was beginning to shift. To his right he could hear a maelstrom of small-arms fire. To his left, where the bulk of the Ethiopian force had been pinned, there were only random shots. To his immediate front there were only burning trucks and motionless bodies hanging from them or sprawled between them. Even before Sergeant Johnny Jackson came crawling up to him, Kinsly knew that the Ethiopians had shifted over to their right and were counterattacking.

"Thirty, maybe forty Ethiopians deployed on line came into our flank and began to roll up the second platoon," Jackson reported, huffing. "We were able to reorient, but not before losing the major and half a dozen men."

Rather than being energized by the report, Kinsly suddenly was overwhelmed by exhaustion. It was as if he were an inflatable pool toy from which someone had just released the air. They had been on the go for the last twenty-four hours. The accumulated stress—the exertion of a thirty-kilometer march, two major engagements, the unending chain of life-and-death decisions—momentarily paralyzed Kinsly. Jackson knelt there watching his leader and waiting for an order that Kinsly was unable to give. Enough, Kinsly thought. We've had enough. This shit has gotta stop. We've had enough.

The firing from the right began to diminish but did not stop. From the left, a Sudanese lieutenant came up to Kinsly. "Do we attack, Lieutenant Kins-lay?"

Kinsly turned to the Sudanese. It wouldn't end unless he did something. The killing would continue with or without him. They had accomplished what they had set out to do. The airfield, its fuel dump, and the defending company had been hit, and the only force capable of interfering with their withdrawal back to the Sudan had been badly mauled. The Sudanese had gained no ground that they could hold, nor could they totally destroy the enemy. They had, however, carried the war into the enemy's country. So long as the communists were busy fighting in their own country and unable to control it, they would have no time to bother Sudan. That, at least, was what everyone hoped. It was now time to cut losses and withdraw while they still held the upper hand. There would be another day, another battle. There always was.

Drawing in a deep breath, he ordered the Sudanese lieutenant to pull his platoon back from the left and establish a firing line one hundred meters to their rear. The platoons on the left and in the center, he told him, would break contact and withdraw to the rally point through his platoon, in that order. Once both platoons were through, he would disengage his own platoon and move back to the rally point by bounds. Turning to Jackson, he ordered him back to the second platoon on the left to prepare it for withdrawal. Kinsly himself would move over to the hidden mortar position and direct the crews to lay down a suppressive fire to cover the withdrawal of the second platoon. He told Jackson that when the mortar rounds began to impact, he was to pull out the second platoon.

As Jackson began to leave, Kinsly grabbed his arm. "Is the major dead or wounded?"

"Wounded, real bad."

Kinsly thought for a moment. "Bring him along when you pull out."

Jackson was about to protest but decided against it. There

was no need to remind Kinsly that from the beginning the standing orders had been that the wounded were left behind. After all, Kinsly himself had put that word out. The lieutenant, Jackson reasoned, had a damned good reason for countermanding his own order.

Neboatov crawled up and down the thin line of Ethiopian soldiers he was trying to get to counterattack. As he did so, he encouraged them, getting them ready to make one more rush forward. A sudden volley of mortar rounds that impacted right in the middle of their line stopped Neboatov's efforts. All hope of pushing forward and finishing the enemy dissolved as the surviving Ethiopians, exhausted by exertion and fear, scattered for cover. Seeing no hope for regaining control of the situation, Neboatov rolled into a shallow depression and squeezed himself between two rocks. The sudden volley of mortar fire and lifting of enemy small-arms fire could only mean that the enemy was breaking off and retreating. All he could do was wait till the mortar fire lifted and it was safe to come out.

Tired as they were, both Americans and Sudanese fell back at the double, jogging the two kilometers from the ambush site to the rally point. At the mouth of a gorge, Kinsly stopped to count the men as they passed him. He looked each man in the eye as he went by. Some smiled broadly, proud of their achievements. Others, content merely to have made it that far, gave him a simple, almost sheepish smile. A few, barely stumbling along, just looked through him as if he weren't there. Physical and mental stress had taken their toll. As a fighting force, they were temporarily finished, at the end of their rope. Kinsly also watched as two of his A Team moved by him carrying the body of Sergeant First Class Veldez. The body was wrapped in a poncho spotted with dark red stains where the blood had seeped through. Kinsly felt nothing as the pair of Green Berets moved into the covered assembly area and lay the body down. It was a shitty end for a man, but not an unforeseen one. Like everyone else, Veldez hadn't wanted to die; but he had known, as every member of the A Team knew in his heart and soul, that death was part of the contract, part of the price some pay for being a soldier. For Sergeant First Class Hector Veldez, the bill had come due.

Last in were Jackson and two Sudanese soldiers. They were bringing in the lanky Sudanese major on an improvised stretcher made from two rifles and two field jackets. Kinsly looked in the major's eyes as he went by. Odds were he wouldn't make it; but for some reason Kinsly felt compelled to give him the chance. Perhaps, if they were lucky, they could get the major back to the Sudan alive, where he could die among his own kind. Veldez hadn't had that opportunity. Maybe, Kinsly thought, he could make up for that with the major.

He stayed for a minute after Jackson and his carrying party had passed, looking for more men to come stumbling over the rise. But none came. All who were coming back were there. Seventy-two men out of the one hundred and six that had started out twenty-four hours ago had made it.

The firing died away slowly. Neboatov paused, but only for a moment. There was much to do. He needed to reorganize the force, gather and tend to the wounded, and, of course, report. Of three hundred and fifty men who had left Gondar that morning, fewer than one hundred were combat effective. Scores of wounded and many dead were scattered about. All hope of catching the enemy was gone.

Neboatov moved among his men, directing the reorganization of his force and the establishment of a defensive perimeter and ensuring that the wounded were tended to. Years of training and battle experience in Iran had taught him well. Though his mind was numb from the shock of battle, his actions were almost mechanical. He ignored the dead. They could do nothing and were beyond help. Even when he looked at the wounded, he did so through the eyes of a combat leader. Every time he saw a wounded man, Neboatov paused and studied him and his wound to determine whether he could fend for himself and fight if necessary.

That the Ethiopian soldiers, both dead and wounded, were

men with families did not enter the equation. There was no time for such thoughts. Besides, Neboatov knew from experience that if he allowed himself to view the carnage laid out before him from a personal standpoint, he would go crazy. He had seen other officers who had let their guard down. Eventually, they had cracked under the strain of guilt, compassion, and pity. A good commander, Neboatov told himself, had to prepare himself, mentally as well as physically. If this meant that he had to steel himself against even the slightest emotion in order to maintain his sanity and proficiency, so be it.

Despite his mental preparation, however, he was not totally devoid of emotions and fear. His experience also told him he had been lucky—extremely lucky: he had survived. But nothing more. There was no glory, no honor, no gains. Only death and the chance to fight again, and again, until one day he led one too many charges. In his mind he knew how it would end.

Tripoli, Libya * 1035 Hours, 12 November

The traveler was blinded momentarily as he moved from the bright day into the dark corridors of the former palace. His escort was a dirty, heavily armed member of the Islamic Guard. The young man, carrying a Russian-made AKM automatic rifle slung over his shoulder, a 9mm PM pistol in a hip holster, two RGD-5 hand grenades hanging from web straps, and enough ammunition stuffed in ammo pouches to supply three men, led with long, swaggering strides. Muhammad Sadiq was always amused by the young men who loved to show off by arming themselves to the teeth. As he followed, Sadiq smiled and thought to himself, This young lion would be easy to find in the desert. One would only need to follow the clanging of his weapons for the first two hours, then the trail they would leave as he discarded them for the next two.

Sadiq was led into a large outer office guarded by two other members of the Islamic Guard armed in a manner similar to his escort's. Across the room was a huge double door that went from ceiling to floor. Two more guards were posted in front of it. These guards, however, were regular army, whose appearance and bearing were in stark contrast to the Islamic Guardsmen's. Their uniforms fit and were freshly pressed. Their rifles, glistening and clean, were held across their chests at a forty-five-degree angle. The web gear they wore was clean and neat, and contained only two ammo pouches, neatly boxed and arranged. The contempt they held for the young Islamic Guardsman showed in their eyes as Sadiq and his escort approached. Undeterred by their silent rebuke, the young man walked up to them with the same swagger with which he had moved through the corridors, and announced in a gruff and booming voice that an important visitor from Egypt was here to see Colonel Nafissi.

Without a word, the soldier on the left stepped to the side and opened the huge door. The Guardsman also stepped aside and motioned toward the door with his hand. "You may enter." The young man, full of self-importance, no doubt thought that Sadiq had been waiting for his permission to enter. As Sadiq walked past him, their eyes locked. In the young man's eyes, Sadiq saw himself as he had been twenty years before. Sadiq slowed for a moment; then he went in.

A short, squat man in the uniform of an air force colonel sat behind a desk in the center of the room, scribbling madly on a pad. He did not take note of Sadiq until it pleased him to do so. When he finally acknowledged Sadiq's presence, he did so with great flourish and feigned surprise. "Ah, my friend! May the Prophet be praised for returning you to our presence so soon! Come, have a seat, and some dates. You must be exhausted and weary from your journeys."

Colonel Nafissi, the second-most-powerful man in Libya and nominal commander of the Libyan armed forces, stood and moved around the desk. He motioned Sadiq to a pair of chairs that flanked a table bearing a tea service and a heaping bowl of fruit. After they seated themselves, Nafissi poured tea for them before he began to talk.

"There is much being discussed. Each day the news from Egypt grows more alarming. The talk that the Americans plan to put troops there is disquieting to many. Your rapid return was unexpected and adds to our concern. What news do you bring us that requires you to travel at such risks?"

Sadiq sipped his tea. How strange that we should prefer the company of the godless Russians in our own lands over the Americans, he thought before answering Nafissi. "Yes, there is much changing in Egypt. They are making another great lunge toward the west—a lunge in which few find comfort, as it is believed to be taking them away from Islam."

Nafissi's ears perked up, as Sadiq knew they would. Any problems in a neighbor's country offered, in Nafissi's mind, a chance for the forces of Islam—under his control, of course— to strike. Nafissi, like his fellow colonel who ruled Libya, had aspirations of power and expansion that far exceeded his country's meager ability. Sadiq knew that had Libya been blessed by Allah with the surplus population that was the bane of Egypt, North Africa would be far different. The sway of Libya's green banner and its brand of Islamic fundamentalism would have united the Arab states—or, more likely, Sadiq thought, brought about total desolation. But Allah had been wise (and the world fortunate), giving Libya only enough people to allow its leaders to obtain the status of a fifth-rate power. That, however, did not stop the dreams, aspirations, and covert machinations that they hoped would someday lead to greatness and importance for their country and, of course, themselves.

Continuing, Sadiq told Nafissi what he had seen and heard in Egypt. After several minutes, he paused for a moment, then got down to the reason for his trip back into Libya. "It is my belief that our opportunity to strike is near." Sadiq let this statement hang as he casually took a sip of tea, ensuring that he had Nafissi's full attention before he continued. "God willing, and if we take advantage of the opportunity he has given us, we can convince the people that their leaders are corrupt and have opened the door for American imperialism to enter Egypt and trample them into the dust as the British had done." Again, Sadiq paused and took a sip of tea. Although Nafissi was trying hard to hide his displeasure at being so toyed with by Sadiq, he maintained his composure and listened attentively with a feigned air of casual indifference.

Sadiq was enjoying himself. Putting his teacup down, he leaned forward, his eyes narrowed to mere slits, his face set in a frown. In a whisper, he continued. "Within three weeks the Republican Brigade deploys to the desert for maneuvers. An American unit, whose equipment is already in storage in Egypt, will be alerted and transported to Egypt to practice their war deployment procedures. That unit will join the Republican Brigade during the brigade's training—"

Anxious to get to the point, Nafissi interrupted. "Yes, yes, we know that. How will that bring about the fall of the Egyptian government?"

Sadiq paused momentarily to ensure that Nafissi's outburst was at an end. Sadiq fought back the urge to smile; he had him. "The presidents of both Egypt and the United States will visit that training. They intend to allow the world to see them and their soldiers side by side, 'friends in peace, comrades in war,' as the American secretary of state likes to say. Can you imagine the crisis and distrust that would result if the two 'comrades' were struck down while they were in the presence of Egyptian forces?" Again Sadiq paused, watching the wheels in Nafissi's mind turn as he considered his proposal.

The possibilities that such a strike would bring excited Nafissi. He tried to conceal it, but his excitement overcame his façade of self-control and feigned indifference. "There would be a great deal of security. Do you believe that they would allow another assassination such as the one that brought down Sadat? How do you propose to penetrate the wall that the army will build around the two presidents?"

In control, Sadiq sat back, folded his hands under his chin, then opened them as if they were a door while he spoke. "We will walk through an open gate and slay them at our convenience. The risks are high, yes. But the results! Think of the repercussions and acquisitions! The Americans will see a country that has lost two of its own leaders at the hands of its own soldiers—the same soldiers responsible for the death of America's president. What will become of their friendship and trust? And in Egypt, the turmoil will provide the Brotherhood with fertile ground in which to plant the seeds of Jihad against the corrupt and ineffectual Western-oriented rulers.'' Sadiq became animated. His eyes wide and fixed on some imaginary object, he held the index finger of his shaking right hand pointed toward the ceiling. ''And this will come when the Republican Brigade is out of Cairo.''

Relaxing slightly and softening his expression, Sadiq turned to Nafissi. He rested his elbows on the arms of the chair, settled back, and folded his fingers together in front of him. A slight smile lit across his face. ''Yes, we risk much. But great rewards belong only to those willing to take great risks.''

Again there was a pause while Nafissi considered what Sadiq had said. ''Do you really have the key to this gate you believe will be open for you?''

The confident smile on Sadiq's face grew ever so slightly. ''Yes, I have the key.''

''Who?''

Knowing that knowledge is power and not wanting to lose control of the plan, Sadiq merely smiled. He had Nafissi's attention. ''You need not trouble yourself with such trivial details, my friend. You only need to give me the weapon that, God willing, will bring an end to the corrupt government that has been a plague in my land.''

Trusting Sadiq less than Sadiq trusted him, but sufficiently intrigued with the man's plan, Nafissi smiled as he held up his cup of tea in a salute. ''Yes—God willing.''

3

For the first time I have seen "History" at close quarters, and I know that its actual process is very different from what is presented to Posterity.

—From the World War I diary of GENERAL MAX HOFFMAN

On Interstate 64, Illinois, 50 Miles East of St. Louis, Missouri * 1745 Hours, 14 November

For the first time in days the sun broke through the thick, leaden clouds that had cast a pall across the land. Though it provided little warmth, and the glare caused him to squint, Staff Sergeant Jonathan Maxwell welcomed the sun's appearance. It was a good sign—a sign that perhaps not all was darkness and gloom.

Holding the wheel of his three-year-old red Chevy Berretta with his left hand, Maxwell reached down between his legs with his right hand and readjusted his seat. Four hours on the road were taking their toll. Though he already knew that he would need to stop for fuel before he reached St. Louis, he glanced down at the fuel gauge anyway as soon as he had settled into his new driving position. With a slight adjustment to the car's visor, he was ready to continue his trek west, back to Fort Carson and home.

The prospect of getting back home was welcome. While the three-month master-gunner course at Fort Knox was a good one, it had been hard on the family—especially since it followed almost three months of field duty, including a trip to the

Mojave Desert and the National Training Center. Maxwell looked forward to spending the holidays with his family.

The prospect of rejoining his unit, Task Force 3-5 Armor, however, was far less inviting. Although it once was regarded as the best combined-arms maneuver task force in the 16th Armored Division, a change of command and a few too many times as the lead element during major brigade and divisional exercises had worn both the leadership and the troops thin. While the training and duty were no less demanding under the new commander, it had been different under the former commander, Lieutenant Colonel Andrew A. Stevens. Under Stevens, the leadership of the task force, from the task-force commander on down, had been both positive and inspiring. Stevens never made his people do anything that didn't pass his "so what?" test: simply put, any order, any task, any training, any mission had to have a purpose, a reason—if it didn't, either the event didn't happen or Stevens would do his damnedest to get out of it. This resulted in a boundless confidence between leadership and troops. In addition, Stevens understood that there were times when "the 80-percent solution" applied. He realized that excellence in everything was a dream few mortals could realize. In some areas, "good enough" had to do if the overall mission of the task force was going to be accomplished.

That feeling of confidence and common sense, however, was fleeting. Lieutenant Colonel Vince Vennelli changed all that. Though the new commander was intelligent and technically proficient, his vanity and arrogance hamstrung his ability to work with people. He came into Task Force 3-5 Armor like a tornado. His twin mottos of "No mission too hard, no task too trivial" and "Excellence is our standard" were an about-face in policy for a unit that was used to sanity and rationality. The quiet, understated professionalism of Stevens's regime was replaced by a boastful and blustery pride that had little to back it, adding to the alienation between the task-force commander and his men.

Though Vennelli was difficult and far from being a desirable commander, most of the NCOs in the unit could have tolerated him had he been slightly more astute in his handling of them, especially those who had seen service in Iran. Maxwell, a gunner during that war, was proud of his service in Iran. There he had learned many hard lessons about his vocation in the only classroom that mattered to a soldier—the battlefield. In the final days he had participated in the pivotal battle of the war north of Hajjiabad. During that fight he had had two tanks shot out from under him. His tank commander, the task force S-3 or operations officer, had assumed command of the task force and led the survivors in a series of desperate counterattacks, which stopped the enemy and earned the S-3 the Congressional Medal of Honor. Maxwell walked away with a Silver Star for saving the life of the S-3, and a Purple Heart for the smashed knee that he got in the process. It therefore came as a shock to him, and to others like him, when Vennelli, who had never left the States during that war, told the officers and NCOs of Task Force 3-5 Armor, "You had better forget all that horseshit you learned in Iran and start training to standards."

Ever conscious that he had yet to prove himself in battle, Vennelli went out of his way to discredit those who had. Veterans or not, most of his men could not understand their commander's attitude. But right or wrong was not in question. He was the commander, the Man. Thus, the task force was torn into two camps. Heading the one side were the veterans, and most of the NCOs who believed that they knew what soldiering was all about and had the credentials—scars, campaign ribbons, and medals—to prove it. Rejected and scorned by the very man who should have been using their experience, they, and their adherents, kept to themselves and did what was necessary to get by.

On the other side, led by Vennelli, were some of the officers and NCOs who, like him, had not been in combat. Many of them, tired of hearing about how the vets had done it in Iran, actually welcomed Vennelli's changes. Others, lacking the wisdom to know who was right or the courage to stand for what they believed was right, took the easy out, saying nothing and doing exactly what they were told. It was a no-win situation. In the end, it was the task force that suffered. Morale dropped as bickering between the rival factions and the resulting drop in overall unit readiness made Task Force 3-5 Armor an unpleasant environment.

A flash of light broke Maxwell's train of thought and brought him back to the here and now. The sun, its brief appearance over, had set, and drivers were turning on their headlights. Maxwell reached over and switched his on, noticing while he did so that the low-fuel indicator was flashing. The thought of returning to the unit had effectively canceled any joy the late-day sun had brought. Now it was gone, just like his fuel. Twisting in his seat, Maxwell felt a slight pressure in his bladder that told him it was time for a pit stop. With St. Louis coming up fast, it wouldn't be hard to find a gas station and a McDonald's.

Looking at his watch and without giving it much thought, Maxwell decided that he would drive straight through to Fort Carson. He loved to surprise his wife. His only concerns were (a) that the kids could be shuffled off to the neighbors for a few hours; (b) that he would be able to do something about his surprise after driving all night; and (c) that it wasn't that time of month.

Cairo, Egypt * 0325 Hours, 15 November

There was no escaping the nightmare. Even worse, there was no predicting when it would steal its way into his sleep. Awakened by it, Dixon brought his hands to his face and covered his eyes. It never changed. The images were always as sharp in his mind's eye as they were that day in Iran. Sometimes the images slowed down for a particular horror, almost as if his mind wanted to study in detail, over and over again, certain aspects of that battle. At other times the nightmare whirled by with the speed of a roller coaster.

It always started the same. The swirl of the white, artillery-generated smoke slowly became laced with oily black smoke pouring from unseen tanks and armored personnel carriers burning somewhere out there. Shadowy figures of armored fighting vehicles emerged from the smoke, some friendly, most hostile. The screams of fire commands, his own fire commands, echoed in Dixon's ear. At that point his body would begin to tense up and rock, as if it were reacting to the recoil of the main gun and the bucking of the tank as it rolled over the broken ground and plowed through the smoke.

Once the nightmare had grasped him, there was no escape. Sweat soaked the sheets as he relived the death of his battalion. There appeared the image of a burning American M-2 Bradley on its side, its hatches blown open by the explosion of the ammunition stored inside, its dead crew scattered about it. For a second it came into view; then it vanished. Close to him, a man, his uniform on fire, was running in circles, thrashing his arms wildly in the throes of death. Dixon heard the distinct crack of a Soviet T-80 tank cannon firing from somewhere in the smoke. There were no logic, no pattern, no control—and worse, no escape from the random killing and destruction, either then or in the nightmare. It was everywhere, and seemingly unending. Death that day had been swift and sudden—a point that the nightmare hammered home every time and never allowed Dixon to forget.

Dixon never screamed, never became violent. He would only lay there as his mind raced along like a runaway train. When Fay was with him, she would wake him gently, ever so gently. When he was alone, as he was tonight, he merely rolled and tossed until the nightmare passed, its images disappearing into the hazy shadows of his subconscious. There they would wait patiently, ready to creep back into Dixon's dreams.

He took his hands from his eyes and opened them. He lay there for a moment, listening to his own breathing as it came in short, rapid gasps. He began to shiver as the cool night air hit his body, now soaked with sweat. Still, he did not move. His first conscious thought this morning, as it always was after the nightmare, was the same: I'm alive. It was a dream. I'm alive. And, as always, that thought brought an immediate feeling of shame and guilt, for he could never forget that he, the man who had ordered and led the attack that day, was alive, while many of those who had obeyed and blindly followed were not.

Finally free of his sleep, Dixon began to orient himself to his surroundings. The only noise in the room was that of the air conditioner. He rolled his head to one side, his eyes falling on the lit figures of the digital clock he used for travel. It was still too early in the morning to get up, but he knew he had no choice. The wet sheets he was wrapped in were becoming uncomfortable, and he was suffering from jet lag. Further sleep would be impossible. Besides, there was always the lingering fear that if he went back to sleep, the nightmare would return.

Reaching over, Dixon felt around for the switch to the light on the nightstand. His fingers fumbled about until he turned it on. Once his eyes had adjusted to the light, he threw his legs over the side of the bed and sat up. The room was cold: the air conditioner had been adjusted during the hottest part of the day. Mechanically he rose from the bed and moved over to the window. He opened the curtains and stood there motionless, looking out from the sixth story of the Sheraton down onto the Nile. He gave no thought to the fact that he was clad only in a white T-shirt and boxer shorts. His mind was elsewhere, wandering aimlessly, stopping only momentarily to focus on a random thought before discarding it and moving on. Since Iran, Dixon's life had been like that, aimless and almost random—no fixed points to grasp, no pattern. Aimless, random, loose.

The serenity of the Nile flowing to the sea began to calm his troubled mind. Dixon stood there transfixed, watching. The three-quarter moon shone brilliantly off of the glassy surface of the river as it slowly wound its way through the sleeping city. For a moment there were no thoughts, only peace, as he allowed himself to become enmeshed in the scene before him. As he stood there and watched the gentle river, all thoughts of war slipped away. How fortunate you are, Dixon thought as he looked down on the water. You know your place and have a purpose. All you must do is follow the river banks and you will find your goal. I envy you. No thoughts, no dreams, no worries, no fears, no yesterdays, no tomorrows. Only now, only here. You know a peace I never will.

Dixon felt a shiver. The moment of peace was over. His

thoughts left the river and turned to the day ahead. There would be a great deal to do and many people to meet. Most of them would ask the same questions he had been pelted with so many times before. And those that didn't ask out loud would do so in their minds. So few understood, really understood, that he could not answer them even if he wanted to. For, like his nightmare, the answers to their questions were locked away somewhere in the dark corners of his mind, mixed and twisted with the horrors of the past and the uncertainty of the future.

Cairo * 0345 Hours, 15 November

Along the river bank a lone figure moved. His steps were mere shuffles, his pace halting. Though he was wrapped in the robes of a fellah, even at night it was clear that he was no peasant. The erect carriage and square shoulders belonged to a soldier— or, more correctly, to an officer.

Lieutenant Colonel Ahmed Hafez often came to the banks of the Nile when he wanted to think. When he was a boy, he and his friends had spent many happy hours playing along the banks of the ancient river. And when he was a young man growing up in the turbulent 1960s, Hafez had turned to the river for comfort and peace. It was a place where he could reflect on the troubles of the day. As he wandered along its banks that morning, he could not remember a time when he had been more troubled, more confused. Even the mighty Nile could not wash away the thoughts that befuddled his mind that night.

After evening prayers at the Mosque of Sultan Hassan, Hafez had been approached by Muhammad Sadiq, a childhood friend and a member of the Brotherhood of the Book. Hafez had once belonged to the Brotherhood, during the years following Egypt's defeat at the hands of the Zionists in 1967. Wounded and captured during the rout across the Sinai, Hafez had felt betrayed by an incompetent government and its leaders, to whom he had pledged his loyalty and had so freely offered his services. The swiftness and totality of their defeat, compounded by the supreme arrogance of his country's enemy, came as a shock to the young Hafez. Rather than being welcomed or comforted by his countrymen when he was exchanged, he was scorned for the shame the army had brought down on the once mighty Egypt.

In his moment of supreme despair, his friend Sadiq and the Brotherhood offered a solution to the woes that seemed to plague Egypt. Unquestioning belief in Allah, strict adherence to his Word, and total devotion to the True Faith seemed to provide Hafez something that he needed then—a reason for carrying on and the hope of a better life for his country. Believing that the government and its inept leaders had betrayed the Egyptian people, Hafez threw himself into the arms of the Brotherhood with complete and careless abandon. At that moment in his life, there was only one answer, one way: that of the True Faith.

Like all things, that too changed. His enthusiasm for the Brotherhood waned. Time, the great healer, passed; and with its passing, a new, dynamic leader came forward and brought Egypt out of despair and shame. Hafez's mind, educated and trained to analyze the world around him, soon began to dissect the Brotherhood. He asked questions and searched the dark corners of the Brotherhood, which reminded him of the places where they met. Like a thunderclap, it dawned upon him that he had surrendered his loyalty to a cause that was not founded in the Word of the Book but, instead, in the same petty politics that had brought so much misery to his noble country. The leaders, most of them, were not wise and holy men driven by God to save Egypt but only humans like himself. Unlike him, they had the vision of power in their eyes. They wished to rule Egypt and remold the government into one that fit their image. True, their visionary government was based upon strong and uncompromising Islamic faith. But Hafez wondered if such a government was right for Egypt, the mother of all civilizations. A devout Muslim, Hafez was nevertheless an Egyptian, the product of a civilization that spanned four thousand years.

The discovery that the Brotherhood was being manipulated by people from other countries was the final factor in turning

Hafez away from it. True, the Brotherhood preached unity throughout the Islamic world. Hafez, however, had seen that unity coming from common consent from each nation, willingly given by its people when they saw that belief in Islam offered them the only true way. The thought of working for a foreign power against his own nation was repugnant to Hafez. Unable to wholeheartedly embrace or support such men, he eventually rejected them and their cause. Again, as he had been after the '67 war, he was lost and cast adrift. Though he never officially broke with the Brotherhood, he never went back.

Fortunately for Hafez, the army left little time for him to ponder his fate or drift about. After the death of Nasser and the ascent of Anwar Sadat to power, the army, and Egypt, changed. During Sadat's "corrective revolution," the army began to prepare for the day when it would strike to defeat the Zionists and retake Sinai. Reorganizing and reequipping the army, coupled with intensive training, absorbed Hafez's time and energy. As a brigade staff officer responsible for plans and training, he threw himself into his tasks with an enthusiasm and energy that soon came to the attention of his superiors. It did not matter that his efforts were those of a desperate man trying to escape his problems by submerging himself totally into his job. What mattered was that they were rewarded by his selection to command a tank company, a company that he trained and ultimately led into battle in 1973. His skill as a soldier and ability as a leader resulted in two stunning victories over Israeli tank units, a medal for valor, and a wound sustained during a desperate counterattack at a place called Chinese Farm.

Returning to his home village to recover from his wounds, he was welcomed as a hero. Though he knew, as most of his fellow officers did, that their victory was not complete and that retention of the bridgehead across the channel was tenuous, they had nonetheless done what the world had least expected—defeated the Israelis in open battle. For the first time since the Crusades, an Islamic army had defeated a non-Islamic army in battle. While the significance of this was lost to most of the world, it gave Egypt a new beginning, a beginning that Hafez was part of.

Again Hafez's life changed. Marriage to the daughter of a wealthy merchant from his home village was followed by selection for advanced military schooling, promotion, attendance at the American Command and General Staff College, and, finally, selection to battalion command in the Republican Guard Brigade. These successes gave him a satisfaction and security in purpose that had escaped him in his youth.

Into this secure world that Hafez had built, Sadiq, an image from his troubled past, came like a thief in the night. Into Hafez's ear Sadiq poured the poison of discontent and hate, thinly veiled as the Word. "The Brotherhood, and Islam," Sadiq said, "need your help." The apparition from his past frightened Hafez. Instead of sending Sadiq off, however, as his conscience told him he should, he stayed and listened.

"The time has come," Sadiq had whispered, "to sweep away the temporal government that tears Egypt and its people away from the bosom of Islam and the teachings of the Book. The new caliph has come. Like the sun rising in the east, he is spreading the word as Muhammad had done. We are but his soldiers, serving the will of God." The thought that Sadiq was serving another country was numbing. Rather than protest and end the discussion, Hafez had sat in silence, listening to the words of treason flow from the mouth of his "friend." "My brother, we are but instruments in his hands. We can only submit to his will. Prepare yourself for the day. When it is time, I will find you."

Like a shadow, Sadiq had moved back into the night before Hafez could reply. That had been days ago. Since that meeting Hafez had had to refight the age-old battle he had fought many times before. Who was he? Was he, as Sadiq had said, nothing more than an instrument in the hands of God? Was he a soldier who owed loyalty to no man but only to his nation? Or was he something else—something more important?

Hafez stopped. His wanderings had taken him away from the river and out of the city. To the west, across the flood plain, he could see the outlines of great pyramids of Giza, the symbol of four thousand years of Egyptian civilization. They were ageless, unchanging. For a moment Hafez focused his thoughts on them. Alexander the Great had passed in their shadows and disappeared into history. They had been there for a thousand years before the first Roman took that name. Muhammad and his early followers had driven past them in their drive to spread the word of their new True Faith. Behind them the Turks and the British had come and, in their time, had gone, like the others.

Still the pyramids stood, looking down on the events of man like great spectators. Hafez was mesmerized by them. Thousands of years ago his ancestors had built them with little more than their bare hands, their minds, and their muscles. The pyramids were more than monuments of stone to rulers long since dead. They were an ageless symbol of the first civilization of the Western world—a civilization that never passed from existence, as so many other civilizations and empires that had viewed them had. And Lieutenant Colonel Ahmed Hafez was the product of that civilization. He was an Egyptian. At that moment he could not explain what that meant. He did not fully understand how that would, or could, help him in his current dilemma. But he knew that his heritage, symbolized by the pyramids, was important, perhaps critical.

Headquarters, U.S. Office for Military Cooperation, Egypt, Cairo * 0825 Hours, 15 November

Dixon entered the outer office of the deputy for plans and operations of the Office of Military Cooperation, Egypt, and approached the desk where a female sergeant E-5 sat fingering through the early-morning distribution dump. Dixon stood there for a moment and waited for her to notice. When it was clear that she either did not notice him or was ignoring him, he set his briefcase on her desk and announced, "Sergeant, would you inform Colonel Wilford that Major Dixon is here for his 0830 meeting."

The sergeant looked up. Dixon's announcement was not a request; it had been an order. It took her a moment to comprehend that—just enough time for Dixon to notice her look of annoyance before it turned into a polite smile. "Yes, sir, of course. Would the major have a seat?"

Her efforts to shoo him out of her space failed as Dixon simply replied in the negative and continued to stand in front of the desk, waiting for her to execute his order. Seeing that the sooner she got him in to see Wilford, the better, she buzzed the intercom and, without waiting for a response, announced, "Sir, your 0830 appointment is here."

There was a noticeable hesitation before Wilford told her to send him in. The sergeant gave Wilford a short "Yes, sir," flipped off the intercom, and looked up to Dixon. "Sir, the colonel will see you now."

Without so much as a "thank you," Dixon took his briefcase from the sergeant's desk, stepped back, and entered the open door of Wilford's office, stopping three feet in front of his desk. Coming to a position of attention, Dixon saluted and announced his presence. "Sir, Major Scott Dixon reporting as ordered."

The man in front of Dixon returned his salute, then stood up and leaned across the desk as he extended his right hand. "Welcome to Egypt, Dixon. Glad to have you." Wilford paused, then added, "I was under the impression you had already been promoted."

Dixon stepped forward to shake Wilford's hand. "I was hoping I would be. It will be a while before that happens. The rate of promotion really slowed down after the latest round of budget cuts." Even though Wilford was bent over, Dixon had to look up in order to look into his new superior's eyes—eyes that were already studying him as if he were a newly discovered microorganism. The fact that he was taller than Dixon seemed to please Wilford. It was a natural reaction. Some senior-ranking officers are more comfortable when they are taller than their subordinates. The handshake was also meant to be a gauge of the new man. Dixon extended his hand and prepared for that test. If it was a firm grasp, he would respond with an appropriate amount of firmness, just enough to show that he could take it. If it was merely a quick cupping of the hands, Dixon would respond in kind, withdrawing his hand as soon as it was polite to do so. If it became a tug of war, Dixon was prepared to hold his ground without challenging the superior. Fortunately, it was a simple pressing of the flesh followed by an invitation to take a seat.

When both men were seated, Wilford started. "Your new duty position calls for a lieutenant colonel. One of the first things we need to do is see that you get frocked. You won't get a light colonel's pay, but it will make your job a hell of a lot easier. Egyptians take their rank seriously."

Leaning over, Wilford flipped the intercom. "Debbie, could you scare up some coffee for the major and me?"

The sergeant responded with a short "On the way," neglecting to add a "sir." Dixon waited for Wilford to correct her. When he flipped the intercom off without doing so, Dixon began to deduct points from the imaginary score card that he had already opened on his new boss.

Wilford continued to take the lead in the conversation, asking Dixon if his flight had been on time and his hotel accommodations were satisfactory. Dixon, his guard up, simply responded to Wilford's questions with a short, perfunctory "Yes, sir" or "Everything is fine, sir" or "No, sir, no problems, sir." When the sergeant came in, she handed both men a cup of coffee and left, closing the door behind her.

For several moments both men sat in silence, taking short sips of their coffee and eyeing each other. Wilford's scrutiny made Dixon noticeably uncomfortable, especially since Wilford's stare always came back to the ribbons on Dixon's chest—or, more correctly, the top ribbon. Above all the other multicolored ribbons, almost all of which were standard for a man with as much time in the Army as Dixon had, sat a simple light-blue ribbon randomly speckled with tiny white stars. In his entire twenty-two-year career, Wilford had seen only two other men wearing that ribbon, both of whom had earned it in Vietnam. As much as he wanted to avoid doing so, Wilford could not help staring at the light-blue ribbon, which represented the Congressional Medal of Honor. Dixon had been awarded that medal for his actions at Hajjiabad, the day he had assumed command of the task force after his colonel had been killed.

Feeling uncomfortable and wanting to get on with the business at hand, Dixon broke the silence. "Sir, I was told in Washington that you would provide me with all the details of my duties once I arrived."

Wilford, intently staring at the ribbon, was caught off guard by Dixon's question. He blinked, looked Dixon in the eye, and paused for a moment before answering. "Yes, I have no doubt they told you that. Tell me, Major, how much do you know about Egypt?"

Dixon looked down into his cup of coffee. "Well, sir, to tell you the truth, not a whole hell of a lot—only what I could get out of the area study book and a couple of travel guides and books. There wasn't enough time, or so I was told, to send me to all the neat courses I needed to fully learn about the country and its people. I didn't even know how to say 'thank you' to the bellboy for carrying my luggage up to my room yesterday."

Wilford thought about that for a moment. "I should have figured as much. Exactly what were you told concerning your duties?"

"I was told that I would be the chief of staff of the 2nd U.S. Corps (Forward) and that you would provide me with all the necessary details. Since I had so little time to get my affairs in order, and everyone at 3rd Army who was connected with this project was on temporary duty someplace, I decided to wait until I arrived to get a full briefing, from the man who was actually in charge. Which brings me to the next point. Who exactly, sir, will I be attached to and report to?"

Again Wilford hesitated for a moment before speaking, considering his answer. "That, Major, is difficult to answer. The 2nd Corps (Forward) belongs to the 3rd Army. As such, there are certain reports that you will be required to submit directly to 3rd Army with information copies to me. In areas concerning in-country activities, exercise planning, and most operations, you report to me with information copies to 3rd Army. For certain, selected operations, you report to me only."

Without thinking, Dixon quipped, "Well, that certainly clears that up."

Ignoring Dixon's remark, Wilford droned on. "We are about to complete the prepositioning of equipment in Egypt for use by U.S. forces in an emergency. Up until now, no country in the region has allowed the United States to establish a permanent presence. Whenever we have conducted exercises here, we have had to bring everything we needed for the exercise and take it away when we were finished. As you know, that is a very expensive way of doing business."

Dixon was tempted to feign surprise at the last comment but decided against it. No sense, he thought, in completely pissing off the old bird.

"Furthermore, in a real emergency, our ability to move everything we need into the area is, at best, still questionable, despite the buildup in the nation's sea and airlift capability. Unfortunately, too many people walked away from the Iranian conflict with the wrong lessons."

For a moment Dixon's mind went blank. It always did when someone referred to the war in Iran as a "conflict." Like a knee-jerk reaction, Dixon thought to himself, It was a fucking war, you asshole.

Pushing dark thoughts out of mind, Dixon listened to Wilford's continuing dialogue. "The whole project is a shoe-string operation, officially labeled as a means of saving money by leaving a division set of equipment in place for the units coming over here as part of the Bright Star series of exercises. We, and the Egyptians, have been working hard to convince everyone that this is nothing more than a cheap way of running those exercises. The 2nd Corps (Forward), part of that operation, is a planning headquarters with minimum manning, much like the 9th Corps in Japan. It will have the responsibility for the administration and inspection of the equipment and ammunition storage sites here in Egypt as well as planning and coordinating all U.S. ground operations in the Middle East."

Dixon interrupted. "How successful, sir, have we been in selling that line to the other Arab states and the Russians?"

"Not very, I'm afraid. Our friends in DIA tell us that the Soviets have been working on a similar training and deployment exercise to counter our Bright Star series. They call it Winter Tempest. To date, they haven't done anything beyond planning and opening discussions with Libya, Iraq, and Syria. But that is not important, at least not to you. What is important is the fact that we now have a viable presence on the ground here and can do something with very little notice."

"What heavy units are tagged for deployment to this part of the world?"

"As with all contingencies, Major Dixon, that depends on exactly what the situation is and what's happening in the rest of the world. If the Rapid Deployment Force is uncommitted, besides the 17th Airborne and the 11th Air Assault Divisions, the 52nd Infantry Division (Mechanized) comes here. If the 52nd is busy somewhere else, the 16th Armored Division is the next in line."

Dixon thought about that for a moment. The 52nd Mechanized Division had been badly mauled in Iran. In a one-on-one fight with a Soviet motorized rifle division, the 52nd had come off second-best. Its defeat resulted in the loss of most of the oil fields in southwestern Iran. On the other hand, the 16th Armored Division, though a proud unit, had not seen combat since World War II. Putting those thoughts to the side for the moment, Dixon continued. "By being here, if something happens—that puts us right in the middle of it, whether or not we want to be part of it. I mean, it's kind of like a marriage, for better and for worse."

Leaning back in his chair, Wilford hesitated for a moment before continuing. "That, Major, is very perceptive, and unfortunately true. We are, after all, dealing with a region that is not noted for its stability. In Egypt alone the Russians have been in and out twice in the last twenty-five years and we have almost been out once. During that same period there have been two major wars with Israel and a minor border conflict with Libya."

The word "conflict" again provoked a reaction in Dixon's mind. I wonder if the Egyptian tankers and commandos considered what they did in 1977 as minor, he thought.

"As real as that problem is, that is not your concern."

Impatient, Dixon asked, "Exactly, sir, what are my concerns and duties?"

Leaning forward and folding his hands on the desk, Wilford delineated in detail Dixon's duties and responsibilities. As the chief of staff for the 2nd Corps (Forward), Dixon's responsibilities were diverse. For the most part he would be a planner, working on contingency plans, training exercises, and coordinating future operations in Egypt. His other major area of responsibility would be as liaison with the Egyptian army units that would operate with American units during training exercises and, if necessary, at war.

His role concerning the prepositioned equipment, as Wilford explained, was minimal. For this Dixon was thankful. His primary task was to ensure that the plans his people developed matched what was available on the ground in storage. When it didn't, Dixon's small staff had to inform deploying units of what equipment they needed to bring to supplement the prepositioned stores. The development and implementation of a program of routine maintenance and services on the equipment in storage was not his duty. An Ordnance Corps lieutenant colonel was charged with that.

Even in storage, checks and services must be performed on the equipment. The 1973 Arab-Israeli war provided a bitter lesson in this. Equipment stored in Europe for U.S. forces had been taken out of storage and flown to Israel after staggering losses by the Israeli Defense Force. Unfortunately, some of the equipment had not been properly maintained. The recoil systems of self-propelled howitzers, for example, had not been exercised on a routine basis, and thus dry rot had been allowed to eat the seals. When the Israelis received the equipment, they sent it right into battle, only to have many guns blow out their seals after just a few rounds. It was therefore crucial that there be a system that kept the equipment ready and serviceable.

To operate the equipment storage sites, both U.S. military and Egyptian nationals were used. They secured the equipment, performed maintenance on it, and, when the time came, issued it to a unit deploying. Very few of the personnel were American. Each storage site, containing a brigade's worth of equipment, was commanded by a captain. He was assisted by four or five NCOs and a like number of enlisted personnel. The rest of his people were Egyptian under contract to the U.S. Government. A massive training program had been set up to train Egyptians in the proper care and maintenance of every type of equipment that a U.S. division processed.

In addition to the equipment storage sites, there was the need for the establishment and security of an ammo storage point, or ASP. The first shipments of ammunition were just beginning to arrive in country. The goal of the U.S. Army was to have thirty days of ammunition on hand for a reinforced division. This goal, as Colonel Wilford pointed out, would not be realized for several years. Budget cuts had slowed that program. For now, the Army had to content itself with two weeks' worth of ammunition in country, with contingency plans for emergency airlift of critical items if that became necessary.

There was a pause. Wilford hit the intercom. When the sergeant answered, Wilford merely told her to bring the Twilight and Pegasus files in. While they waited, neither he nor Dixon said anything. Though he had no idea what Pegasus was, Dixon felt a surge of excitement. He was finally going to get an opportunity to find out what the man he was replacing had been doing when he had been killed.

The sergeant gave him two thin folders. The Twilight folder was covered front and back with bright yellow-and-white Top Secret labels. The Pegasus folder was only Secret and therefore had red-and-white Secret labels. Each folder contained a summary of an operation in which Dixon would play a part. As he read each summary, his heart sank. Far from being a low-keyed and laid-back job, his new position put him in a virtual hot seat.

Twilight was the name given to covert Special Forces operations in Sudan and Ethiopia. A number of SF teams, operating out of central Sudan, were assisting both Sudanese government forces and Ethiopian guerrillas against Soviet-backed forces. At the time that the summary was written, there were twelve such teams in the field. Dixon's task would be to plan and coordinate their activities with the Air Force and Navy and to coordinate the resupply of team members and the evacuation, when necessary, of the wounded among them. His code name when operating under Twilight was Cardinal, the same code name Lieutenant Colonel Dedinger had been using when he died earlier that month.

As surprising as Twilight was, Pegasus was more so. For years the Army had conducted readiness exercises designed to test its ability to move troops from the continental United States to reinforce forces overseas or to potential trouble spots. Re-Forger (short for "redeployment of forces to Germany") for Europe, Team Spirit for Korea, and Bright Star for the Middle East were the oldest and best known. These were good exercises, but one of the chief criticisms of them was that they were planned and coordinated months in advance. Congressional critics charged that in a true "bolt out of the blue" scenario, U.S. forces couldn't respond in time. The war in Iran had come close to proving them right. One of the lessons the Army had walked away with was the need to improve the speed with which various units tagged with overseas contingency plans could deploy with no notice. Thus, Pegasus had been developed.

The concept was simple. Rather than stage elaborate, well-prepared-and-planned readiness exercises, units would be alerted with little or no notice for deployment. Pegasus was, in effect, a massive test to determine if the Armed Forces could meet their worldwide commitments. From the beginning, it was a controversial plan. Many in the Army felt that it would not be a true test, arguing that in the real world tensions would build up, allowing time to accomplish last-minute planning, mobilization, and deployment. One of the sharpest congressional critics, Congressman Ed Lewis of Tennessee, listened to those arguments, then simply asked, "Well, then, what about Korea, Grenada, and Iran? How much time did you have before you had to respond to them?" In the end, Congress drove its point home, stating that unless the military clearly demonstrated its ability to deploy in a timely manner, funds for more sea and airlift assets would be cut off.

Then there was the matter of the Helsinki Accord, which

required signatories to notify each other before conducting major military exercises. Meant as a means of preventing misunderstandings or tension when a potential enemy moved forces in preparation for a training exercise, the accord had been used selectively after the war in Iran. It had not been renounced by either the United States or the Soviet Union and was technically still binding. Both the United States and the Soviet Union used various means to sidestep the problem. The United States claimed that forces already in a theater did not count against the total until all forces were brought together, allowing it to initiate notification and initial movement within the period required for notification. In addition, Army and Marine divisions deployed with most, but not all, of their assigned brigades or battalions, bringing the total strength as near as possible to the limits of the accord. The Soviets opted for another method. They simply ran several small exercises in close proximity of each other, in both time and space, with the total personnel in any one exercise never exceeding that specified in the accord.

Under pressure from Congress, the Chairman of the Joint Chiefs of Staff directed that selected Army, Navy, and Air Force units would participate in no-notice deployment exercises, code named Pegasus. Those exercises, based on real-world contingency plans, such as ReForger, would commence with no advance warning to the units participating. Only those people who needed to coordinate with the host nation where the training would take place would know in advance. The Pegasus folder that Dixon was reading contained the concept of operation for the first Pegasus exercise to be held. The exercise was to be part of the Bright Star series, with a start date of 29 November, fourteen days hence.

When he finished reading the documents, Dixon closed the folders and laid them on Wilford's desk. Unconsciously, he wiped the palms of his sweaty hands on his trouser legs. "How many people know about these operations?"

Wilford thought before he answered. "Not many. Very few know about both. You, your G-2, and your G-3 will be the only ones on your staff that will know about both. Everyone else is to be on a need-to-know basis, and only with my approval. There will be little time for you to get your feet on the ground.''

"I assume, then, that they have the rest of the plan for the upcoming Bright Star exercise.''

Surprised by how poorly Dixon had been prepared, Wilford leaned back and thought for a moment, trying to find an easy way of telling Dixon that he was about to get royally screwed. There was no easy way. "Colonel Dixon, you have just read everything there is on Pegasus. If there was a plan for the exercise, it was in Dedinger's head and went down with him in the Sudan.''

"You mean we're going to plow on with this?'' Dixon responded, more annoyed than surprised.

"We are. That's one of the reasons you were rushed over here.''

The finality of Wilford's answer left no doubt that come hell or high water, Pegasus would happen. It also left no doubt that Dixon was the man on the spot. Seeing no point in pursuing that any further, Dixon moved on to his last order of business. With little to lose, he asked the question that had bothered him since receiving his orders: "Why me?''

Pausing for a moment, Wilford considered how to answer the question. He thought about handing him a line of bull, but quickly decided against that. Dixon appeared to be the type that would not fall for a song-and-dance. No, Wilford decided, I'll tell it like it is.

"Scott, despite the fact that you don't know shit about this country and its people, you were picked because the people in Washington thought you would be accepted.''

Dixon thought about that for a moment before he continued. "Accepted by who? And why am I more acceptable than someone who knows logistics? After all, this slot calls more for an officer with more time in plans, someone who understands joint operations, not to mention the area and the people. This is not a job for a lieutenant-colonel designee whose only experience above division level has been mailman in the Army's War Room.''

"The medal, Dixon—you have the medal. You happen to be

the only armor major who commanded an armored unit in battle and, as a result of your actions, won the Congressional Medal of Honor. You have no idea what that does for your credibility. Washington offered four fully qualified officers, none of whom were acceptable to the chief of the Military Assistance Group or to me. None of them made it to Iran while it was hot. One of them turned in his resignation as soon as he learned he was being considered. Another had never served a day overseas in sixteen years of active duty. Besides, the Egyptians asked for you by name. Apparently the Egyptian military liaison office in Washington did some checking on their own and came across you.''

"Then they also know that I declined command of a combined-arms maneuver battalion at Fort Carson and as a result I am a permanent fixture on the Army's shit list.''

Wilford looked at Dixon for a moment. He had avoided that subject intentionally. For the first time he felt anger. To be offered an opportunity to command a combat unit and turn it down was a concept foreign to Wilford, an officer who would have sacrificed anything for just such a chance. "Yes, I'm sure they do.''

For a moment there was a cold and uncomfortable silence as both men stared at each other, not trying to hide their mutual contempt. Dixon had been through this before. Well, Scotty me boy, he thought, so much for impressing your new boss with your tact and getting along with him. Fuck him! He doesn't understand and never will.

Wilford flinched first, looking down at some papers on his desk. "Well, I suppose you're anxious to get started. To help you get into the swing of things, it's been arranged to let you train with an Egyptian unit for three days in order to get you acclimated and familiar with the terrain and the Egyptian army. The unit you'll be with is a tank battalion of the Republican Brigade. They are conducting gunnery and small-unit tactical training west of Cairo, in the area that has been selected for Bright Star. The battalion commander, a Lieutenant Colonel Ahmed Hafez, is a veteran of the '67 and '73 wars and a graduate of CGSC. His English is quite good, and he has a full understanding of our system. That will be very useful to you as you attempt to learn theirs, evaluate the terrain, and get some exposure to the culture.''

Not wanting to spend any more time with Wilford than was necessary, Dixon limited his responses to a simple "Yes, sir, I'll do my best" or "That will be fine, sir." Even Wilford's inquiries into when Dixon's family would arrive and where he was looking for quarters were met with short, perfunctory responses. Until Dixon had a handle on his new assignment and had everything arranged, including living quarters, he planned to leave Fay and the boys in the States. The last thing he wanted to do was to drag his family into Egypt unprepared.

Without much ceremony the meeting ended. Dixon rose from his seat, walked up to Wilford's desk, and again saluted. Wilford's response was, at best, a wave of the hand.

It's going to be a long, hard tour, Scotty old boy, Dixon thought.

4

Man has two supreme loyalties—to country and to family. . . . So long as their families are safe, they will defend their country, believing that by their sacrifice they are safeguarding their families also.

—B. H. LIDDELL HART

Tehran, People's Republic of Iran * 1245 Hours, 17 November

Out of the corner of his eye, Captain Nikolai Ilvanich watched the young lieutenant approach the officers' table. He didn't recognize him as an officer within the regiment, and immediately he went on his guard. Ilvanich and the other company commanders of the 1st Battalion, 24th Airborne Regiment had just finished their lunch and were listening to Captain Korenev, commander of the 1st Company, tell a story about his latest bedroom adventure. No doubt Korenev expanded and added to the facts, adding great embellishments as he went along. Though Ilvanich was not really interested in Korenev's love life, at least Korenev had enough of an imagination to discuss something other than the counterguerrilla campaign in which they were currently involved. Anything was better than listening to Melnik, commander of the 2nd Company, puke up the latest party slogans.

As the young lieutenant came up to the table, Korenev saw him and stopped speaking. Aware that all eyes were on him, the lieutenant halted a few feet from the table and snapped to attention. Surveying the assembled officers before him, he asked if one of the captains present was the commander of the 3rd Company. Turning around in his chair to face the lieutenant, Ilvanich responded. "Your search is over, comrade. You have found Captain Ilvanich."

The lieutenant turned to face Ilvanich, rendered a snappy salute, and bellowed, "Senior Lieutenant Andrei Shegayev reporting for duty with the 3rd Company, 1st Battalion, 24th Airborne."

Ilvanich studied Shegayev for a moment and without returning his salute, told him to stand at ease. Shegayev responded by bringing his hand down and assuming a position of parade rest. "By any chance, Senior Lieutenant Shegayev, are you related to Lieutenant Colonel Pavel Shegayev?"

Shegayev looked into Ilvanich's eyes. "The colonel is my uncle, Comrade Captain." This surprised Ilvanich, and Shegayev saw it. "My uncle was the youngest son in the family, sort of a mistake my grandfather made late in life."

From across the table, Korenev chimed in. "Such things are mistakes only after the fact, Shegayev. At the moment, young Pavel no doubt was the last thing on their minds." The officers at the table, including Shegayev, laughed.

Seeing this, Ilvanich relaxed. It was a good sign. "Have you eaten, Lieutenant Shegayev?"

"I am not hungry, Comrade Captain. We were well fed on the flight coming in."

Standing up and recovering his hat, Ilvanich began to walk to the door, signaling with a nod of his head for Shegayev to follow him. As they walked away, Korenev yelled across the room, "Hey, Shegayev, if your uncle is in personnel assignments, write him soon and ask for a new job. Ilvanich is rough on lieutenants." Shegayev turned his head to see Ilvanich's reaction. There was none. Stone-faced, Ilvanich walked out the door.

Once outside, the two officers walked along a muddy path toward the company area in silence. Shegayev knew what Ilvanich was thinking. No doubt his new company commander suspected that he was KGB. Shegayev's uncle had tried to persuade his nephew to go to another unit for just that reason.

But young Shegayev was headstrong and determined to serve with the best. Begrudgingly, Uncle Pavel admitted that Ilvanich was the best airborne officer he had seen, and made the necessary arrangements for his brother's son to be assigned to Ilvanich's unit.

After several minutes, Ilvanich reached into his pocket, pulled out a pack of cigarettes, and offered one to Shegayev. Shegayev declined but waited until Ilvanich had lit his before speaking. "My uncle sends his regards and belated congratulations on your promotion."

Ilvanich turned his head toward Shegayev, cocked it to one side, and looked at the lieutenant for a moment. "Your uncle was very instrumental in my reinstatement as well as my promotion. Few officers who were captured by the Americans in Iran were reinstated; and I know of none who were promoted. Had your uncle not risked his own career, I would be working at the bottom of a mine in Siberia right now, had I been lucky."

Seeing an opening, Shegayev jumped on it. "My uncle thinks very highly of you. You saved his life and served both the party and Mother Russia well."

Ilvanich suddenly stopped, catching Shegayev off guard. "Tell me, Shegayev, are you also KGB, like your uncle?"

For a moment Shegayev looked into Ilvanich's eyes, trying to determine whether he should lie or simply tell the truth. Did he know, or was he guessing? Shegayev continued to stare into Ilvanich's eyes, but they told him nothing. They were dark and expressionless. There was no way of determining what was going on behind them. Trusting in luck, he opted for the truth. "Yes, Comrade Captain, I am KGB."

Ilvanich looked at him for a moment, then smiled. "Good. I am glad you decided to tell the truth. It is only natural that you would follow in your uncle's footsteps. Come, tell me how your uncle is doing."

With a sigh of relief, Shegayev turned and continued to walk with his commander, filling him in on his uncle's life. In front of the company orderly room, Shegayev stopped and asked how Ilvanich knew he was KGB.

"Your uncle is KGB. I've been told that it runs in the family. Besides, one night your uncle told me of a young and energetic nephew he had who had completed the initial KGB indoctrination and had opted to go in the army."

"And you don't mind that I am KGB?"

Ilvanich smiled again. "Why should I mind that you are KGB? My last deputy commander was KGB. While the state had enough confidence to reinstate and promote me, it wants to watch me for a while, just to be sure. Hence a KGB man is always somewhere in my unit."

Shegayev was visibly relieved. "I am glad that you know. It will make working for you so much easier."

The smile disappeared from Ilvanich's face. His eyes, dark and expressionless, sent a shiver through Shegayev. "Don't be so sure that this assignment will be easy. Hopefully your uncle told you everything about him and me, especially the incident at the oasis. While it is my sworn duty to defend the state and the party, in combat other things, such as the lives of the men, have a nasty habit of becoming more important than party slogans and adherence to rhetoric best left in Moscow. No, your job will not be easy. There will come a time when we will be in a very tight spot and something will happen that you—or, more correctly, the party—does not agree with. You will then have a hard choice to make. Hopefully you will meet that crisis better than your predecessor. His choice cost him his life."

With that, Ilvanich turned away and walked into the company orderly room, leaving Shegayev standing in the street, confused and dumbfounded.

Moscow * 0830 Hours, 18 November

Though they could not see him yet, the click of heels on the marble floor alerted the guards that someone was approaching from a connecting corridor. The guards could normally guess the number and rank of visitors. The rhythm of this visitor's pace was steady, and the meaningful stride told them that the person in these boots had purpose and self-assurance—

definitely an officer. The sharpness of the footfalls indicated a big man. Straightening his stance, one of the guards whispered, ''A colonel.''

From around the corner, a Soviet officer turned and continued toward the door where the guards stood. The early morning light was streaming into the corridor at a sharp angle through the windows on one side; the approaching officer disappeared at regular intervals as he moved from the sunbeams into the shade, then reappeared as he moved back into the sunbeams. Bracing themselves to salute, the guards faltered for a moment when the officer stopped, lost from sight in the sunbeam in which he stood. Leaning forward and squinting, the guard on the right saw him standing at one of the windows, looking out onto the courtyard below. Confused, the two guards glanced at each other but did nothing.

At the window, Lieutenant Colonel Anatol I. Vorishnov stood lost in thought as he looked down into the courtyard of the Kremlin. Soldiers, diplomats, politicians, bureaucrats, and couriers plowed through the freshly fallen snow and scurried about below him as they sought to get out of the cold. Even in the worst of weather, the business of the Union of Soviet Socialist Republics had to be carried out. As he watched the comings and goings of those who ran the nation, Vorishnov's thoughts turned to the meeting he was about to enter. Though surprised to be summoned to the Kremlin for another briefing, Vorishnov was prepared.

Working as an area specialist in the plans and exercise section of STAVKA, the Red Army's General Staff, Vorishnov had been instructed to do a quick study on the feasibility of deploying and operating an independent tank corps in the Libyan desert. With less than four days to produce a finished product, Vorishnov had been forced to cut many corners from established staff procedures. When he was unable to find exact information, he made assumptions and duly noted them as such. But this did not bother Vorishnov. Despite the fact that he had just graduated from the Frunze Military Academy as the top graduate of his class, a year in Iran before attending the

Frunze Academy had taught him that the "norms" for procedures and operations as taught seldom match their practice in
the real world.

He had also learned, however, that there were those who
choose to ignore reality, hiding instead behind accepted doc-
trines and procedures. In peacetime this was normal: no one
takes any unnecessary chances with one's career. Regulations
and doctrine provide convenient hiding places for the timid and
unimaginative. But Vorishnov, like many of his compatriots,
had assumed that once war had broken out, peacetime practices
would end. He expected that commanders and their staffs
would do what was necessary to accomplish the mission, even
if it meant taking risks and going against accepted doctrine. It
therefore came as a shock to Vorishnov that all too many
officers had continued to carry out their duties in Iran as if they
were still taking part in a peacetime exercise.

He was not alone. This revelation had come as a shock to
most of the veterans of the Iranian war. And this was not the
only shock that had greeted Vorishnov. Vorishnov began that
war as the deputy of a tank battalion belonging to the first
operational echelon of the Southwestern Front. As such, his
unit was frequently in combat and often in the lead. When the
battalion commander was killed in the closing days of the war,
Vorishnov had assumed command of the unit. He and the
remains of his battalion stayed in Iran as occupation forces
after the signing of the armistice. Only his selection for attendance at the Frunze Military Academy saved him from a longer
tour in Iran.

Vorishnov's joy in leaving Iran was short-lived. Returning
to the Soviet Union, Vorishnov discovered that he and his
fellow veterans were not only unwelcomed but despised. It was
at the train station in Kiev, en route to Moscow, that Vorishnov
came face to face with this reality. Waiting in line to pick up
his ticket for the remainder of his journey, Vorishnov noticed
an old man with a cane staring at him. The old man had several
military medals on the lapel of his jacket collar—obviously a
veteran from the Great Patriotic War. For a moment, their eyes
met. The old man's eyes were cold and hostile, his stare cutting

through Vorishnov like a knife. Though Vorishnov could not understand why, he shrugged it off and turned away.

The old man, however, would not be put off. Hobbling up to Vorishnov, he took his cane and smacked Vorishnov's right arm. Reeling from the unexpected blow, Vorishnov turned to face his assailant. Standing a head taller than the old man, Vorishnov kneaded his sore arm with his left hand and told the old man he was crazy. The old man, his face contorted by hatred, looked up at Vorishnov. "I may be crazy, but at least I am not a traitor."

Vorishnov was taken aback by the old man's statement. By now the people in the immediate area had stopped what they were doing to watch the confrontation. Trying to soothe the old man, Vorishnov forced a smile. "Grandpa, I am not a traitor. You are confused. I am a veteran of the war, just like you." Reaching out, Vorishnov lifted one of the medals hanging on the old man's lapel. "See, we even share the same award."

Instead of ending the confrontation, Vorishnov's action made it worse. In a stroke that surprised everyone with its speed, the old man raised his cane and smacked Vorishnov's hand down and away from the medal. "I SHARE NOTHING WITH COWARDS WHO BETRAY THE MOTHERLAND!" the old man yelled at the top of his lungs. His eyes narrowed, and standing on his toes, the old man leaned forward and shoved his face into Vorishnov's. "You lost the war to those pigs the Americans. You have betrayed the party, socialism, and Mother Russia. You should have died in battle clutching the colors of your regiment rather than surrendering them to our enemies. You are a filthy traitor. You are scum!"

By now a considerable crowd had gathered to witness the confrontation. Looking about, Vorishnov searched for a sympathetic face, an ally, a way out. But there were none. Even two militiamen stood back, returning Vorishnov's pleading gaze with a cold stare. Unable to find help and realizing he was on his own, Vorishnov replied to his attacker.

"Old man, you are crazy. The 68th Tank Regiment never lost its colors. We broke the Iranians at Mianeh. We were the first to enter Tehran. We crushed them at Qum and wiped out their last division at Yazd. When we faced the Americans, we crushed them at Harvand and fought them to a standstill at Kerman. Half of my men are buried in unmarked graves in that forsaken country. I am not a traitor. You are a fool!"

The old man stood there for a moment and looked at Vorishnov. Then he began to shake with uncontrolled anger. Repeatedly yelling "Traitor!," the old man raised his cane to beat Vorishnov. Prepared now, Vorishnov easily parried the blow but could not prevent the old man from grabbing his medals. Vorishnov's effort to break away resulted in the loss of his medals, as the old man refused to let go of them. Only then did the militia intervene—and then on the side of the old man.

While one militiaman calmed the old man down, the other pushed Vorishnov to one side. "Comrade Colonel, we discourage such acts of violence here. This is not Iran and you are not dealing with scum."

Insulted, Vorishnov reminded the militiaman that he was dealing with a lieutenant colonel in the Red Army. The militiaman laughed. "Do not try to impress me or anyone else here with that, Comrade Colonel. You and your kind left any respect you may have deserved in the Iranian dirt. We have no time here for those who are incapable of defeating capitalist mercenaries." Turning to the window and grabbing a ticket, the militiaman threw it at Vorishnov. "Go—go to Moscow and see if they will tolerate incompetent fools like you who led their sons to slaughter."

As disturbing as the confrontation in Kiev had been, it was not nearly as shocking as the attitude he met at the Frunze Academy. Rather than taking a cool, hard look at what had happened in Iran in an effort to correct deficiencies in their military system, the staff of the academy went to great lengths to find fault with those who had failed to follow prescribed doctrine and procedures. Day after day Vorishnov and the other veterans of Iran were subjected to lectures that explained away failures or the misconduct or poor leadership of one commander or another. Even their fellow students would have little to do with those who had served in Iran. While most of the Iranskis, as they were called, bit their tongues, some could not. One young lieutenant colonel of tanks, whose face was disfigured by scars he received when his tank had burned, was especially bitter and harsh with those who degraded the Iranskis. He often argued with the instructors and lecturers, referring to them as paper soldiers and fools. For a while he was tolerated. But he soon overstepped his bounds when he began to openly attack the party for not fully supporting the soldiers on the front line. Two days after those outbursts began, he was gone—''reassigned,'' according to the class leader.

For his part, Vorishnov held his anger. Instead of rejecting or fighting what was being said, he went along with the teaching. He did more than conform: he sought to excel. Despite the fact that he was an Iranski, he won the grudging acceptance of the academy's faculty and staff as his grades and his standing in the class remained at the top. Unlike his fellow Iranskis, he never lapsed into arguments about the tactics or techniques that were being taught. He never used his experiences in Iran as justification for an answer that the instructor claimed was wrong. Instead, Vorishnov approached his studies as if he were a newly commissioned junior lieutenant. Only in this manner did he survive. In the end, fewer than a quarter of the Iranskis finished the course.

That success, however, had been costly. Though he told no one and continued to do his assigned duties, inside he was cold. It was as if his very life spirit had died. His efforts to hold back his anger and hatred had killed that spirit. It didn't happen all at once; he didn't even notice at first. But slowly he felt himself change as his attitudes and views on life and the army turned. It was his wife who finally opened his eyes. A patient woman and a good soldier's wife before the war, she knew something was troubling her husband. But he refused to let her into his inner world. Efforts to comfort him were met with cold rebuffs. Unable to lash out openly at the army and those who looked down on him, he took out his frustrations on his wife by denying her his love and attention. In the end he lost her. She left, forcing him to face his past and his future on his own.

Looking down at the people in the courtyard of the Kremlin,

he wondered if they too were simply hollow shells, spiritless men going about the task of running a faceless nation.

Stepping back from the window, Vorishnov straightened his tunic, turned toward the door where the two guards stood, and continued down the hall. As he approached the guards, they stood at attention but continued to bar the door. Stopping two paces from them, Vorishnov flashed his pass and announced, "Lieutenant Colonel Vorishnov to see General Uvarov." Stepping to one side, the guard on the left opened the door and allowed Vorishnov to enter the outer office.

At a desk across the room sat a lovely young woman. Vorishnov was taken aback by her. Not only was she not in uniform; her manner of dress, hair style, and makeup were totally out of character for a military secretary. There was even a vase of fresh flowers sitting on her desk. Her soft, flowing brown hair fell loosely about her shoulders and framed a face that showed a quick smile and bright blue eyes when she looked up at Vorishnov. "Comrade Colonel, the general will see you now," she said as she pointed a pencil toward a double door to her rear. Though he tried not to, Vorishnov continued to stare at her as he went by and opened the door to the general's office.

Upon entering the main office, Vorishnov was confronted by Colonel General Iriska Uvarov. He was leaning on the front edge of his desk, arms folded, and deep in thought as he gazed at a large map of the world that covered an entire wall of his office. Uvarov was a young man for a colonel general. His face showed few wrinkles, his short-cropped hair no gray. Although he was as tall as Vorishnov, Uvarov was slim. Stopping several paces from the general, Vorishnov considered the man before him as the general continued to contemplate the map.

Uvarov was one of the few men to emerge from the Iranian war with his career enhanced. Commanding a motorized rifle division in the 28th Combined Arms Army, Uvarov had been detached from the 28th Army and given the mission of creating a diversion in the western mountains of Iran to draw American forces away from the main effort. The operation didn't unfold as planned. The 28th Army, the main effort, failed to break through the Americans and reach the Strait of Hormuz. Uvarov, on the other hand, not only succeeded in diverting considerable forces from the main battle area; his division mauled the American 52nd Infantry Division, secured the oil fields in Iran's southwest, and actually reached the Persian Gulf. During the American counteroffensive in the closing days of the war, Uvarov's division, though decimated and nearly isolated, not only held its ground but, through aggressive counterattacks, made some gains. For his performance Uvarov was promoted and became a military advisor to the Politburo.

Although Vorishnov knew the general was aware of his presence, the general did not acknowledge him or change his stance. Not knowing what else to do, Vorishnov clicked his heels and saluted. "Lieutenant Colonel Anatol Vorishnov reporting as ordered, Comrade General."

Instead of returning the salute, Uvarov continued to stare at the map and mused, as if to himself: "We have an interesting problem to solve, Comrade Colonel. It seems that the Americans feel the need to demonstrate that they can deploy an armored division from the continental United States to the Middle East in less than five days."

Vorishnov, bringing his arm down from his unreturned salute, thought about the general's comment for a moment before replying. "With their prepositioned equipment, they can do that, Comrade General, and there is nothing we can do to stop them."

For the first time since Vorishnov had entered the room, Uvarov turned away from the map and looked at him. A slight smile lit across the general's face. "You have done your staff work well. Unfortunately, you are correct. We cannot stop them from conducting this peacetime deployment exercise." Pushing himself up from his reclining position, the general started to walk about the room as he continued. "We can, however, discredit that achievement by demonstrating that we also can move forces to any trouble spot on short notice."

Vorishnov was not surprised. He had worked on the contingency plans to do so, though he never thought that anyone would seriously consider executing them. To commit the Soviet Union to such a provocative move seemed foolhardy, especially since it would be almost impossible to maintain a clear line of communications with them by sea or air once they got there. Without thinking, Vorishnov blurted out, "Putting Soviet ground forces in North Africa would unsettle the balance of power the two superpowers enjoy in the Mediterranean. A simple unilateral blockade by the American 6th Fleet—one that the Black Sea Fleet had no hope of lifting—would be enough to isolate our troops."

Turning toward Vorishnov, Uvarov raised an eyebrow. "You think the United States would try to stop us?"

Vorishnov was astonished by Uvarov's question. "Of course, Comrade General. The Americans would never allow us to introduce ground forces in Libya without demonstrating the ease with which they could isolate them. Our move to discredit their achievement would lead to an effort by them to do likewise. It would be a peaceful confrontation, but a confrontation nonetheless. To allow us free rein would, in their opinion, unhinge the entire balance of power in the Middle East—not to mention the threat that our forces would create to NATO's southern flank. To place ground forces in such a situation would only lead to another—" Vorishnov was about to say "defeat" but stopped short. Despite what he knew to be the truth, he could not openly admit to himself that they had been defeated in Iran.

"'Defeat,' Comrade Colonel? Another war that the Red Army cannot win?" Turning away from the window, Uvarov moved to his desk and plopped himself down into the overstuffed leather chair that sat behind his desk. "No, I do not believe so. Though the possibility of another Iranian disaster is very real, even if the Americans wanted to do something, they won't. They are just as jaded by their experience in the last war as we are. No. This operation will be a simple exercise in world diplomacy. Remember: the purpose of the Red Army includes more than the defense of the Soviet Union. Military power is a means for communicating our interests to the world, building prestige and reassuring friends. When it so suits the United States, they use their military for the same purpose. In this case, Bright Star is a demonstration of their desire to keep peace in the region and assure all pro-Western nations there that they, the United States, can come to their aid when necessary. We, with Winter Tempest, will simply show that we also have our own interests and friends there and that we are capable of assisting them in their time of need.''

Uvarov let that little lesson in geopolitics sink in before he continued. As if to reassure Vorishnov, he repeated himself. "In this case, the United States will do nothing about our operation, even our use of the airfield in the Sudan. They will conduct their exercise, watch ours, move their 6th Fleet here and there, and, in the end, accept a new status quo—one that recognizes that we are both capable of rapidly moving forces to our respective areas of interest—and leave it at that.''

There was a long pause. Sensing that the general was allowing him the freedom to speak his mind, Vorishnov abandoned all caution. "If the general is referring to the popular antiwar and disarmament movement that is sweeping through the United States, then those who believe that such sentiment will prevent positive action by the United States are wrong. As in Iran, the United States will act, invoking their policy of containment.''

Uvarov allowed himself to sink deeper into his chair as he studied Vorishnov. For a moment Vorishnov feared that he had misread the general and had overstepped his bounds. Then the slight smile returned to Uvarov's face. With a sweeping motion of his hand, he signaled Vorishnov to take a seat. Pressing a button on the intercom, he ordered his secretary to bring them tea before he continued. "I am pleased to see that I was not wrong about you, Anatol Vorishnov. You are both intelligent and practical. Nor are you afraid to speak your mind—truly a rare commodity these days. I could see that in the manner with which you wrote your report.''

Uvarov paused when the door opened and his secretary entered the room carrying a tray with two cups, a pitcher of tea, and bowls with sugar and cream. Vorishnov watched the secretary as she moved with the ease and lightness of a cloud. Despite his best efforts, he could not take his eyes off her. When she served him his cup of tea, she looked into his eyes and smiled. Vorishnov, overwhelmed by the woman's beauty and presence, was flustered and unable to utter a simple "thank you" as he took the cup from her. As if she knew how he felt, she simply smiled, nodded her head, and turned away. Even while she was leaving the room, Vorishnov's eyes remained locked on her, as if he were tracking a target.

When the door closed, Uvarov waited a second until Vorishnov turned around to face him. "Yes, Anna is quite stunning. Her father commanded an airborne regiment in Iran. He was killed in action during the final push to the gulf." Uvarov let out a sigh. "I shall miss her when I go to Libya. Fortunately, she will be able to stay on here and serve my replacement." Chuckling, Uvarov winked. "And I hope she serves him as well as she did me."

Vorishnov did not catch Uvarov's last comment. He was still sorting out his thoughts as he suddenly realized what Uvarov had said. "Excuse me, Comrade General—you said when you go to Libya. I do not understand?"

"Understand, Anatol Ivanovich? There is nothing to understand. The Politburo has decided that we will—correction, we *must*—match the introduction of American forces in the Middle East. I have been selected to organize and command the combined independent tank corps manned by Soviet troops and a combined arms army consisting of two Cuban and two Libyan divisions. Your plan for Winter Tempest, using forces currently stationed in Ethiopia, Angola, Mozambique, and our other client states, supplemented with personnel from a few additional units, is not only workable but will be quite effective. The use of excess equipment that the Libyans have purchased but cannot man, as your study points out, will allow us to converge the personnel necessary to form the tank corps and Cuban divisions rapidly and without drawing too much attention to a single source or along a single line of communications. Aeroflot, a civilian airline, will have little difficulty with overflights. Using the bulk of the Libyan army as a covering force to screen our deployment, we will be able to form the corps and divisions, deploy them, and tell the whole world that we, unlike the Americans, are abiding by the Helsinki Accord.

And finally, the use of the airfield at Al Fasher in the Sudan is brilliant. The premier likes that part of the plan. By doing so, we honor the desire of our friends in Libya by not establishing anything that looks like permanent facility in Libya. Aircraft can do all their refueling at Al Fasher, away from the long arm of the U.S. 6th Fleet. Fighters operating from Al Fasher will be able to cover the air corridor. Best of all in the eyes of the premier, we will be able to remind the Sudanese government of their vulnerable position. Our national interests will have been served by demonstrating that we are willing and able to stand by our commitments, that the Red Army is capable of striking anywhere, anytime, and that we are the dominant power in the Horn of Africa.''

Vorishnov sat and looked at the general. For a moment, the two men stared at each other, each waiting for the other to talk. Finally, Vorishnov had to speak. "Comrade General, I hope that you have read the entire study. Yes, I do believe that we can muster the necessary manpower in Libya to form a Soviet independent tank corps and two Cuban divisions. And yes, I did point out that, given the current deployment of Egyptian forces and their national policy, only three divisions would be available to oppose a Libyan operation.''

Vorishnov paused for a moment. Up to this point what he had said was reasonable and acceptable. What he wanted to say, what he *had* to say, however, might not be acceptable. But he had to say it. After all, he had already stated his reservations in his study. If he were to be condemned for an unacceptable position, there was ample evidence against him in the paper the general was now thumbing through.

Vorishnov drew in a deep breath, then continued. "While the maneuver units can be formed from the prepositioned equipment, combat service support equipment, units, and materiel will be insufficient. In the area of trucks alone, the entire inventory of trucks in Libya is insufficient to sustain any additional divisions in combat in the Western Desert. Even if there were sufficient trucks to haul the supplies necessary to sustain combat operations, the ammunition they would need to haul is limited. At best, there is sufficient ammunition in country to support eight days of offensive operations. Trucks and ammunition are only the beginning. Properly equipped maintenance units will be lacking. Even if we manage to form them, the stockage of spare parts that will be needed to repair what breaks down through normal wear and tear and battle damage is insufficient." Vorishnov stopped for a minute to let what he said sink in, then decided to finish. "In short, our deployment exercise would be seen for what it is—a paper tiger. The Western Alliance knows we could not win a protracted conflict in Libya."

Uvarov sat at his desk, slightly slumped down, looking at Vorishnov's study. Without looking up, Uvarov slowly muttered, "Yes, I have read the entire study and, for the most part, I concur with your conclusions. If there was a war in Libya, we would face major problems. The operational plan, drawn up by STAVKA and supported by your deployment plan, however, provides the basis for nothing more than a military tour de force, a demonstration that the news media of the world will record and report on. The pacifist movement in America and Europe is quite strong. They will see Russians in Libya and Americans in Egypt and ask themselves, 'What's the point?' Fears of another confrontation between the superpowers could very well cause the governments of both Europe and the Middle East to think twice before they trust American military power. The threat does not have to be real—it only needs to *appear* real."

Vorishnov looked down at the floor. He heaved a slight sigh. Softly he mused, "Then it is already decided. We will go into Libya." Sensing that Uvarov himself did not support the plan, Vorishnov looked up at him. "Is there no way to change their minds?"

Shaking his head from side to side, he indicated that there was not.

After several minutes of a cold and strained silence, Uvarov stood up and walked to the window and looked out. "Don't be so depressed. Remember, this is only a simple peacetime maneuver, not the end of the world. In the end, the worst that will come of this is a couple of hundred cases of sunburn, a thousand of diarrhea, and four or five burned-out jet engines.''

Uvarov stopped and looked at Vorishnov. ''Besides, this is an important day for you. Though I shouldn't tell you this, when you return to your office you will find orders reassigning you to Group of Soviet Forces in Germany. There you will assume command of the 2nd Tank Battalion of the 2nd Guards Tank Regiment stationed in Stendal. Congratulations on your assignment.''

Vorishnov was floored. When he had been assigned to the African desk of STAVKA's plans section, Vorishnov thought his career was over. To be selected to command a guards tank battalion in Germany was an award, a step up the promotion ladder. As Vorishnov sat there, mulling over the news just given him, Uvarov turned away from him, then paused. Almost as an afterthought, he called over his shoulder, ''You have twenty-four hours to complete the troop list for Winter Tempest. M day is 29 November. Our first units will arrive in Libya by M plus three, and all personnel will be in country by M plus ten. We must be ready for commitment to battle by M plus fifteen. Once you have turned that over to Colonel Gaponenko, my chief of staff, and it is deemed acceptable, you will be told that you have seven days in order to report to your new assignment.''

Vorishnov, overwhelmed, said nothing. Seeing that Uvarov was finished, Vorishnov stood. ''One final question, Comrade General. The name of the operation—why Winter Tempest?''

Uvarov turned back to Vorishnov. ''Why not? Isn't that what we are about to stir—a winter tempest?''

The name was familiar to Vorishnov and just about every officer in the Red Army. He was about to point out that the last operation that had been so named had been a dismal failure, but didn't. He had already pushed his luck too far. Still, why anyone in STAVKA would want to name any operation ''Winter Tempest'' was beyond him. Coming to attention, Vorishnov clicked his heels and saluted. ''Permission to leave, Comrade General.'' Uvarov dismissed him with the wave of his hand and a nod.

As he left the general's office and entered the outer office, Vorishnov noticed Anna putting on her coat. Pausing for a moment, he helped her. Anna gave him a timid smile and thanked him as she grabbed a tattered string shopping bag stuffed with a dozen rolls of toilet paper. Desperately wanting to talk to her, Vorishnov casually commented that she had been quite fortunate in her shopping. Anna smiled again. "Yes, Comrade Colonel—fortunate for myself and a friend in the Ministry of Tourism. I queued up for the paper last night while she went looking for shampoo. She just called. She found a really good buy—East German shampoo."

Vorishnov folded his arms and, like a father interrogating his teenage daughter, asked, "And I suppose you're on the way there now to make your trade?"

Playing the game, Anna replied, "But of course, comrade. If I don't hurry, my friend may find someone who has something far more attractive than toilet paper to trade for."

Vorishnov smiled. "True. But I doubt if your friend could find someone that had something as vital as what you have. After all, we all know that any job is never complete until the paperwork is finished."

Anna laughed at Vorishnov's off-color joke. For a moment, Vorishnov forgot the task that awaited him. The pleasure of entertaining this lovely young girl was far too enjoyable. "May I escort you to the subway, Comrade Secretary?"

"It would be a pleasure, Comrade Colonel."

Gorky Park, Moscow * 1045 Hours, 18 November

As Anna trudged through the snow not yet cleared from the narrow path, her thoughts kept turning to the colonel of tanks who had walked her to the subway, and to her own father. Her father had been a brave and kind man, not unlike the colonel of tanks. Anna's mother, a simple woman from a small farm in Belorussia, had worshiped him. News of his death, as hard as it was for both Anna and her mother to bear, was not nearly as hard on them as the public reaction to the Soviet defeat. Rather than being consoled by family and friends in their time of need, they were shunned. Public condemnation for the misconduct and failures of the commanders in Iran proved to be too much for Anna's mother. Less than a year after the war was over, Anna's mother was dead. Left without a family and treated as an outcast, Anna decided to take her revenge. Any system that, in the name of the revolution, so easily threw its youth away in a war and then so callously turned its back on those left behind, deserved to be punished.

That what she was doing was treason never occurred to her. The occasional passing of information that came across her desk to her "friend" in the Ministry of Tourism was the only way Anna could strike back at the system that had claimed her parents. She never accepted money and never asked what became of the information. Just the thought of doing something to hurt the faceless bureaucrats that ran the country was reward enough.

Up ahead, a female voice calling her name brought Anna's thoughts back to the matter at hand. On a park bench, a tall redheaded woman, well dressed and tastefully made up, waited. It was important to dress properly when dealing with Westerners. Like Anna, she had a string bag, only hers was filled with shampoo. As Anna approached, the redhead stood up and called out, "You've got it—good! Look what I have." The redhead held up a bottle of shampoo. "From East Germany."

Like an excited schoolgirl, Anna ran up and took the bottle, cooing and gibbering. Putting the bottle on the bench, Anna reached into her string bag and pulled out four rolls of toilet paper. "Here, four rolls for one bottle."

The redhead insisted that three rolls were enough, but Anna insisted. After a few minutes of haggling, the redhead gave in. Anna reached in and pulled out the four rolls of paper—the ones stuffed with copies of Vorishnov's deployment plan and a hand-scrawled note listing the M-day sequence.

From across the way, two militia officers watched Anna and the redhead go about their business. "The redhead is a fool. Imagine, not only did she not hold out for a fifth roll, she fought to take less. If I caught my wife doing that, I would make her use old copies of *Pravda* to wipe her ass for a week.''

The second militia officer, cupping his hands and blowing into them to warm them, sighed. ''Women, haggling over shampoo and toilet paper. We should have such worries.''

Slapping his friend on the back, the first militia officer laughed. ''Don't begrudge them their role. The next time you take a crap, try hard to imagine where you would be without the paper. Perhaps then you will be more tolerant.''

Laughing, the two militia officers turned away as they went about their business, leaving the women to finish theirs.

Cairo * 0915 Hours, 20 November

With little more than a phone call and twenty-four hours' warning, Dixon was informed that his family would be arriving in country on the seventeenth of November. In a flash, all his well-laid plans and ideas of properly preparing his wife and two boys for life in Egypt were trashed. Instead of staying in the States until after the upcoming exercise was over, Fay Dixon had unilaterally decided to come early so that, as she explained in the phone call, they could spend the holidays together.

Dixon had just overcome the effects of jet lag and started finding his way around. He had returned from four days in the desert the day before and had not begun any serious efforts to secure proper quarters for the family, check on schools for the boys, or even find out where the other American families went shopping for food. Such mundane chores had been low on Dixon's priority list. Fay's appearance changed that.

In a beat-up secondhand Volkswagen van with no shocks, bought from a sergeant assigned to the Office of Military Co-operation in Egypt, Dixon went to the airport to pick up his family. This turned into an ordeal in itself. Dixon was not ready for the chaos and pandemonium that characterizes Cairo traffic. If there were traffic laws in Egypt, they were not in evidence in Cairo. It took him less than ten minutes to become disoriented and an additional fifteen to become totally lost. Efforts to get directions from a traffic policeman were frustrated by Dixon's ignorance of the language and the policeman's half-hearted efforts to establish some semblance of order to the traffic. In desperation Dixon stopped in front of a first-class hotel and hired a taxi to lead him to the airport. Though the Egyptian really did not understand Dixon's plan or logic, thirty Egyptian pounds bridged the communications gap. After a drive through the city in what resembled a high-speed chase, the taxi finally led him to the international terminal.

Exasperated and already in a bad mood, Dixon rushed into the arrivals terminal and began to look for his family. He was over an hour late. Even taking into account the long wait for customs, Fay and the boys would no doubt be waiting somewhere. As he moved through the crowded terminal at a pace just short of a trot, Dixon looked to his left and his right. It wasn't until he heard a familiar voice yell "Daddy!" that he slowed. Turning in the direction of the voice, Dixon looked for Fay. The first person he saw was his older son rushing at him in a dead run. The younger boy was immediately behind his brother. In their usual manner, the two boys plowed into their father with the finesse of a nose tackle taking out a quarterback.

Dixon stooped down and hugged his boys, then looked up to search for Fay. "Where's your mommy, boys? Did she send you here all alone?"

This made the two boys laugh, the older one calling his daddy silly.

"Well, fine welcome for the loyal wife," a slightly indignant voice called out. "Less than ten days have passed and you don't even recognize your own wife."

Looking up at the woman speaking, Dixon blinked his eyes, then thought to himself, Shit, she's done it again. Instead of the familiar freshly scrubbed face framed in long hair with soft curls, the woman standing in front of him had short hair swept back over ears that had long gold loops dangling from them.

Her face was made up like a cover girl's. Dixon stood up, looked the woman in the eyes, and casually said, "Excuse me, ma'am, I was looking for the mother of my children. You haven't seen her, have you?"

Fay's eyes narrowed and her nose scrunched up just before she hit him in the arm. "That's a fine way to greet your wife after a twelve-hour ordeal on a plane with your sons."

Dixon looked at her for a moment before speaking. She wore a loose white cotton blouse, a long tan skirt, and white low-heel pumps. He didn't recognize the outfit, but that didn't mean anything. Fay was always mixing and matching clothes in an effort to stretch her meager wardrobe. "No doubt the plane trip was far less exciting than the sneak attack by the marauding clippers and blow dryer that hit you."

Folding her arms in a defiant stance, Fay looked to one side and, more to herself than to him, started talking. "I knew it—I knew he wouldn't like it. My mother told me, and as always she was right. Ten days and all I get is 'Hi, why did you cut your hair?' Girl, you've been married too long."

"Fine! Great! Then why the hell did you do it?" Dixon asked, puzzled.

Fay smiled as she fished in her purse. "I'll tell you later, dear. Now, Gunga Din, go fetch the bags. Here are the claim checks."

It wasn't until they were in the van headed for the hotel that Fay let the other shoe fall. In the midst of a casual conversation on how everyone at home was doing, Fay said matter-of-factly, "Guess who's in Cairo?"

Knowing that he was being set up for something, Dixon took the bait. "No—who?"

"Jan Fields."

Like a thunderclap, the reason for Fay's new look struck Dixon. There was an awkward silence. Dixon knew what was coming and prepared himself for it as Fay, looking straight ahead, continued. "Jan is the WNN's chief Middle East correspondent and Cairo bureau chief. She was so excited to hear that I was coming to Egypt—"

"And it just so happens she needs a producer," Dixon added dryly.

Fay turned to Dixon and stared at him. He could see that she was angry. He realized that he shouldn't have said what he did, but it was too late to take it back. Fay continued, her voice curt and determined, "As a matter of fact, she does need a field producer. And I have already applied with WNN."

"Don't you think you should get yourself and the boys settled first before you go out job-hunting?"

"Scott Dixon, we've discussed this many times before. We both agreed that as soon as the boys were in school and the opportunity offered itself, I would go back to work."

"As I recall, we discussed this, but I don't remember any agreements. Fay, I'm starting a new assignment, we're in a foreign country, and it's going to be a while before you get your bearings. There'll be time. Cairo has been here for a while. Besides, I think you should check things out in the Army community, sort of find out what's happening—"

Fay knew where the conversation was headed and didn't like it. It was her turn to interrupt. "Oh, yes, of course. I forgot. I need to find out what's expected of good little military wives and whose ass I need to kiss."

Dixon was becoming impatient, trying hard to fight back his building anger. For the most part he did. Still, he let Fay know that he was displeased by slamming down on the brakes a little harder than he needed to as he swerved through the Cairo traffic. Each time he did so, it threw Fay and the boys forward. Finally unable to contain himself, he turned to Fay while they waited at a stop light. "Damn it, Fay, you know what I mean. You're not an hour in country, you don't have any idea what's going on or what life is going to be like for you and the boys—and yet you've already decided you're going to go out and get yourself a job with Jan. Be reasonable."

Fay, angry, also turned to the attack. "I'm tired of being reasonable. I've been reasonable for eleven years. I've done everything you wanted and what was expected of me. It's not like you have a career you need to worry about anymore," she added cattily.

Fay's last comment cut deep and she knew it. Dixon turned to her but said nothing. The fire in her eyes told him she was not sorry in the least for what she had said. And the most damaging part was that she was right. The rest of the trip to the hotel was in silence. In his mind Dixon cursed himself for picking a fight in front of the boys and on Fay's first day in country. Well, Scott my boy, he thought, you sure have become an expert at fucking things up. Thank God the sofa in the hotel room is comfortable.

5

Nothing can excuse a general who takes advantage of the knowledge acquired in the service of his country, to deliver up her frontier and her towns to foreigners. This is a crime reprobated by every principle of religion, morality, and honor.

—NAPOLEON BONAPARTE

Fort Carson, Colorado * 0355 Hours, 29 November

It was as if Vennelli had been waiting all night for someone to call him. The phone's first ring had not stopped before he was up and reaching for the receiver. When he had it to his mouth, he simply said, "Colonel Vennelli."

"Sir, this is the staff duty officer. Brigade has just notified us that an emergency redeployment exercise has been called."

Without hesitation Vennelli, commander of Task Force 3-5 Armor, began to fire a series of questions at the duty officer, most of which he could not answer. Realizing that there was little to gain by playing a thousand questions, he instructed the young officer to make sure that the alert notification system was in effect and find out whatever he could from Brigade or Division. Vennelli glanced at the clock, made some quick calculations in his head, and ended his conversation by instructing the duty officer to notify all commanders and staff that there would be a situation update briefing at 0500 hours.

Vennelli hung up the phone and sat in the darkness for a moment thinking. From the other side of the bed, his sleepy wife rolled over and touched his hand. "Trouble at the battalion?"

Vennelli took his wife's hand, leaned over her, and kissed her gently on her forehead. "Yes and no. We've been tagged for an EDRE this morning. Nothing to be concerned about."

Still not fully awake, his wife asked if that meant he would miss dinner again. Vennelli thought for a moment before replying that he would call her from the office once he knew more. He already suspected that he knew the answer but decided not to worry his wife so early in the morning. Everyone in Congress and the Department of Defense was hot to trot to see if the units from the States could make it to equipment storage sites in Egypt in days, instead of the weeks it had taken during the Iranian conflict. If they couldn't, there'd be hell to pay, and more cuts in the defense budget.

Leaving his wife to drift back to sleep, Vennelli carefully got out of bed, went into the bathroom, and closed the door before he turned on the light. Though time was important, the commanders and staff would not be at task force for a while; he had time for a proper shower and shave. As he shaved, he considered the operation, the excitement within him building as he did so. He was finally going to be given the chance to show what he could do. There was no doubt in his mind that he had the right stuff—that he would have a successful command, earn his eagles, command a brigade, and eventually get his star. It was all preordained. His command of a tank-heavy task force was nothing more than a stepping stone, another benchmark toward his ultimate goal. Though Vennelli was not at all content with the current state of affairs in the task force—in particular the attitude of the Iranian veterans—he would prevail. He always had. Those who did not get with the program, his program, were as good as gone. Perhaps, he thought, this exercise would provide just the opportunity he needed to cut away some of the malcontents and dead wood. Once they were gone, he could get down to the serious business of training for war.

Fort Campbell, Kentucky * 0615 Hours, 29 November

The opening of the door to the company orderly room and a loud "Company, a-tennn-hut!" followed by "At ease" announced the appearance of the company commander. From his office, First Sergeant Andy Duncan could see that the commanding officer of B Company, 1st of the 506th Airborne, was in his PT uniform. The CO was looking about the room, filled with soldiers in desert camouflage battle dress. He had a quizzical look on his face. Turning to one of the assembled platoon sergeants, Duncan simply stated, "Looks like the Old Man didn't get the word. There'll be hell to—"

Duncan's comment was cut short as Captain Harold Cerro stuck his head in the doorway of the First Sergeant's office. "First Sergeant, could I see you in my office?"

Duncan slowly got up from his chair, picked up his clipboard, and followed Cerro to his office. He was followed by the tune of a funeral march being hummed by the platoon sergeants. Duncan knocked on the open door of Cerro's office. Cerro flopped down into the chair behind his desk, then told Duncan to come in and close the door. Duncan did so, sat down in a chair across from his commander, and waited for a moment before he spoke. Cerro had his feet up on his desk and was leaning back in his chair, staring at the ceiling and twiddling his thumbs in his lap. "Sir, the CQ called as soon as we got the word, but your wife said that you had already left."

There was a moment of silence. Then Cerro let out a sigh, took his feet off his desk, and swung around to face Duncan. "I know. That's what I get for living so far from post. You remember what the battalion commander said—'One more time and I'll move you into the BOQ, stud.' "

Duncan chuckled. "He wouldn't dare. The last thing he needs is the Italian Stallion running around on post at all hours without adult supervision."

This made Cerro laugh. "Okay, First Sergeant, what have we got?"

Both Cerro and Duncan were veterans of the Iranian war. Though only twenty-five years old, Cerro was commanding his second company. His first had been in Iran, where, as a second lieutenant, he had assumed command of his company when the commander and the executive officer had been killed in action. In that war he had made two combat jumps and earned the

Distinguished Service Cross and the Silver Star. Duncan, serving in a light infantry division, had also earned a Distinguished Service Cross, a Bronze Star with V Device, and a Purple Heart.

Looking down to his clipboard, Duncan began to brief his commander. "We were alerted for immediate deployment thirty minutes ago. Our exact destination has not been announced yet, but we were told it would be an out-of-country deployment and to be prepared for desert operations. Units from Fort Carson and Fort Bliss have also been alerted. Smart money says Egypt."

"Good guess, First Sergeant. No doubt the President's visit there and completion of the prepositioning of equipment for that armored brigade at Carson have something to do with this. Besides, we war-gamed a conflict in Egypt last month." Cerro thought for a moment, then shook his head. "Yeah, it's Egypt." For a moment both men looked at each other, saying nothing but thinking the same thing: Shit, not the desert. Anywhere but the fucking desert.

Standing up, Cerro went to the wall locker he kept in his office and began to pull out the appropriate uniform, underwear, boots, and socks. "What have you got for status, First Sergeant?"

While Duncan continued to brief him, Cerro dressed. He didn't hear half of what Duncan said. His mind was flooded with concerns and random thoughts—uppermost a feeling of dread.

Fort Carson, Colorado * 0510 Hours, 29 November

First Sergeant Terrence B. Walker, nicknamed Walkman, burst into the orderly room of A Company, Task Force 3-5 Armor. Walker was mumbling to himself—his practice when things were fucked up. Staff Sergeant Maxwell, until that moment the senior NCO present, stood up from the first sergeant's chair and moved out of the way as Walker moved around to take his seat. Only after he sat down did the first sergeant survey the room and acknowledge Maxwell's presence.

"Okay, Jon, what the fuck happened?" Walker grunted, looking up at Maxwell. "Why the hell did it take the CQ over an hour to initiate the alert notification?"

Maxwell, clipboard in hand, sat down and cocked his head to one side. "Top, about the worst thing that you can imagine. The CQ wasn't here, and the CQ runner was asleep in his room." Maxwell waited for this to sink in. Walker, fighting back his urge to slam his fist on the desk, sucked in a deep breath, then let it out accompanied with a long "Shiiiit!" Turning back to Maxwell, he said, "Well, are we on track now?"

Knowing that Walker was in no mood for long stories or explanations, Maxwell just nodded and told him that he had personally ensured that everyone had been notified. For the first time the first sergeant relaxed a bit. "You got any coffee made yet?"

"Sure, Top. On the way." Standing up, Maxwell moved toward the coffee maker. As he poured the coffee into a white styrofoam cup, Walker asked Maxwell how he'd been able to get in so soon.

Maxwell didn't answer until he had passed the cup of steaming coffee over to Walker and had resumed his seat.

"I came in just as the duty officer arrived down here to find out why no one was answering the phone in the orderly room."

"Couldn't sleep again?" Walker, looking at Maxwell through the steam of the coffee, asked in a low, cautious voice.

In a whisper Maxwell, hands folded between his knees, eyes riveted on the floor, simply said, "No, couldn't sleep."

"The leg again, Jon?"

"Yeah, Top. It's the leg."

Walker looked at Maxwell for several seconds. "You gonna be able to deploy?"

A smile lit across Maxwell's face. "Sure, Top. You think I'd let you and the Old Man face Vicious Vinny on your own? Besides, this company needs some kind of adult supervision."

Walker chuckled. Though there was much to do and they

were already behind the power curve, they'd make it. A Company was a good company, with a corps of solid NCOs that could make things happen. "Talking about Vinny and the Old Man, did the Old Man make it to the command and staff meeting on time?"

Maxwell looked up. "Yeah, he did. I imagine by now Valiant Vennelli, the Electric Wop, is ripping the captain a new asshole."

For the first time Walker laughed. "You can bet on that. And if we don't get our asses in gear, Vinny will stick his cattle prod up our bung holes. So, what's our current status, Jon?"

Referring to his clipboard, Maxwell began to brief Walker on who was present, platoon by platoon.

Fort Campbell, Kentucky * 0945 Hours, 29 November

With the initial battalion briefing over and operations order in hand, Bob Mennzinger sauntered on back to his company orderly room. There he would be able to sit down, reread the order, digest everything in it, his notes and what he heard in the briefing, and begin to develop his own company operations order. Walking into the open orderly room, he was greeted by half a dozen pairs of eyes. George Katzenberg, his senior flight warrant, nicknamed "the Cat," asked what they were all wondering: "Well, yes or no—do we self-deploy to Egypt?"

Mennzinger didn't answer. Instead, he walked over to the coffee pot, tucked his copy of the operations order and notebook carefully under his arm, took a cup from a stack of styrofoam cups next to the pot, and slowly began to pour himself some coffee. As he did so, everyone watched him and waited for an answer. Turning to the assembled group, he lifted his cup in a mock toast and announced, "Gentlemen, I give you a toast to the United States Navy. Briefing in thirty minutes." With that he took a small sip, turned on his heels, and went into his office.

From the corner of the orderly room, one of the younger

aviation warrants looked around. "Now what the fuck was that supposed to mean?"

Staring at Mennzinger's closed door, the Cat answered to no one in particular, "That means, sports fans, that we self-deploy." Standing up, he stretched. "Unless y'all have a bladder of steel, I'd recommend you lay off the coffee. Damned few pit stops where we're goin'."

With a small map of the route spread in front of him and the order in his left hand, Mennzinger went over the deployment phase again step by step. Whenever he had a question or wanted to make a note for his own company order, he jotted it down on a pad of yellow lined legal paper. The plan for the deployment phase was deceptively easy. Deployment would commence at 1300 hours ZULU, or 0800 hours local time, on 30 November. Selected elements of the Combat Aviation Brigade (CAB for short) of the 11th Airborne Division (Air Assault) would commence deployment from Fort Campbell, Kentucky, to a training area just west of Alexandria, Egypt. The entire 1st of the 11th Heavy Attack Battalion, which included Mennzinger's attack helicopter company, was committed to participate in the unannounced emergency deployment and Bright Star exercise. That battalion, equipped with eighteen AH-64 Apaches, thirteen OH-58C scouts, and three UH-60 Blackhawks, would lead off the deployment. Other elements of the CAB that would follow the 1st of the 11th were the 3rd of the 11th Assault Battalion, equipped with forty-five UH-60 Blackhawks reinforced with six CH-47D Chinooks, and one troop of the 2nd of the 14th Air Cavalry Squadron, equipped with four AH-64s and six OH-58C scouts. All aircraft capable of self-deployment, including the six AH-64s of Mennzinger's company, would fly over on their own. Only those aircraft with short legs, such as the OH-58Cs, would be broken down and transported by Air Force C-17 transports.

The actual deployment was broken into seven segments, or hops. An AH-64, equipped with four 230-gallon external fuel tanks and carrying no ordnance, was capable of flying one thousand nautical miles with a forty-five-minute reserve.

Therefore, each hop had to be equal to or less than one thousand nautical miles. Flying the traditional, northern route into Europe during winter was risky and would entail long detours around countries that normally denied overflights by U.S. military aircraft. To reduce weather interference and long detours, the deployment plan that would be used called for a straight shot across the Atlantic. A combination of land bases and aircraft carriers for refueling would put the aircraft self-deploying in Egypt in just under sixty-four hours. To assist in the navigation and back up the helicopter's own Doppler navigation system, the Air Force would deploy E-3 Sentinel airborne warning and control systems, or AWACS aircraft. The E-3s would track the deploying helicopters and vector them to where the carriers were.

For the deployment, all aircraft self-deploying would be divided into groups, each group having four aircraft, with no less than two transport helicopters in each group. The reason for that organization, as the commander of the CAB explained, was twofold. First, the aircraft carriers along the way could easily handle the refueling of four Army helicopters, at thirty-minute intervals, without interfering with the routine operations or the primary mission of the carrier. Second, the transport helicopters were distributed among the groups in pairs in case one or more of the aircraft in a group had to ditch over the sea. One of the transport aircraft would be able to recover the crew of the downed helicopter. The reason for a minimum of two transport helicopters per group was a hedge against the odds, chances being slim that both transport aircraft in one group would go down. Though no one seriously believed they would lose any aircraft, the operations plan was covering all possibilities.

The route would require forty-nine flying hours total. The first hop would be the easiest, Fort Campbell to Fort Bragg in North Carolina for a thirty-minute refueling stop. The unit had made that trip twice in the past year for training. From Bragg, the next hop would take them over the ocean to Bermuda for another thirty-minute refueling. The third hop was the real challenge. From Bermuda, the aircraft would fly almost due east to a rendezvous with the carrier USS *George Washington* near the 45th west meridian. While the theory of operating Army helicopters off Navy aircraft carriers had been practiced, the tests had been limited and well planned. This operation was the largest application of that capability. Little coordination, other than the exchange of radio frequencies and the location of the carriers, had been provided for. On top of that, due to the deployment schedule, many of the helicopters would be making their first carrier landing during the dark. Mennzinger considered that for a moment, trying to figure out how he could put it in a positive light when he briefed his own men.

After the carrier refueling, the rest of the operation would be relatively simple. The fourth refueling stop would be Lajes Field in the Azores, followed by a twelve-hour stopover at Gibraltar, the fifth stop. Where the sixth refueling stop would be was still in question. The Italian government, as of the time of the battalion order, had not given its permission to use Sicily as a refueling stop. The Navy, therefore, was prepared to have a second carrier positioned south of Sicily to provide an alternate refueling point in case the Sicilian stop fell through. From Sicily, the aircraft would fly into Alexandria, Egypt.

Mennzinger paused for a moment and looked at his notes. Simple—the whole plan was simple. All that was required to make it work was a few thousand people from three different services, two aircraft carrier groups, and a couple hundred thousand gallons of fuel to be at the right place at the right time. He looked at his watch. He could hear his pilots gathering in the orderly room. There was a great deal to do. Everyone would be anxious to run his aircraft up three or four times to make sure everything was in working order and that the external fuel tanks weren't leaking out of their filler caps. If time permitted, Mennzinger also wanted to go over to Kyle Lake and rehearse recovery procedures, just in case one of his aircraft went into the ocean. Standing up, Mennzinger looked down at his notes and thought for a moment. Rather than hold up the works and prepare the perfect plan, he decided to brief the deployment and wait on doing any planning for the actual in-country exercise in Egypt. Hell, he thought, Once we're there, we can finesse that part of it.

There was a knock at the door before the first sergeant opened it and stuck his head in. "Sir, everyone's here."

Looking up at the first sergeant, Mennzinger smiled. "Okay, Top, I'll be right with you. Oh, and Top—tell 'em to lay off the coffee."

Cairo, Egypt * 1310 Hours, 29 November

The increase in security at the airport and throughout the capital did not surprise Sadiq. With the announcement of the visit by the American President and rumors of short-notice joint U.S.–Egyptian military maneuvers to coincide with the visit, everyone would be on his guard. How unfortunate, Sadiq thought as his cab passed a group of police unloading barriers from a truck, that they decided to close the door after the serpent entered their house.

Planning and preparation for the operation had gone quickly and exceedingly well. Colonel Nafissi had decided almost immediately that there was insufficient time to prepare an Egyptian assault force. Instead, he insisted that a Libyan commando unit, which just happened to be ready for just such an operation, conduct the assault. It didn't take Sadiq long to realize that Nafissi had been planning and preparing for this operation. Sadiq's news had only given them the time and provided the catalyst for pulling the trigger.

Secrecy was uppermost in everyone's mind. Only those people who needed to know were told what was to happen. Sadiq doubted if even the leader of the revolution knew what was happening. The commandos who would be executing the operation themselves were given the plan one phase at a time: first, their instruction for infiltration into Egypt and a rally point. At the rally point, they would be given the route to and location of their assembly area. There they would be told of the nature of the operation but not the target or the time. In this manner, if someone was accidentally captured, he would be unable to provide much in the way of useful information. Even Sadiq did not know the whole plan. He knew what he had to: that the commandos, dressed as military police and riding in jeeps, would approach the position where the two presidents would be. The jeeps would go to the reviewing stand, one to either side. Once there, the commandos would simply get out and kill everyone in the stand.

Because of the need to get close to the reviewing stand, the operation could not be an all-Libyan affair. Support was needed from sympathizers within the Egyptian military. That was the single greatest concern Nafissi had concerning the operation. Security would be extremely tight. The memory of the assassination of President Anwar Sadat was always foremost in the minds of Egyptian security forces. To allow a second calamity such as that would be disastrous to the regime. If the American President were also killed, it would be cataclysmic. Sadiq, however, was adamant that he could make the necessary arrangements that would allow the Libyan commandos to get within striking distance. As he told Nafissi repeatedly, he had people in the right places who could make things happen. One of those people was Lieutenant Colonel Hafez.

While the taxi wound its way through the crowded streets of Cairo, Sadiq reviewed the plan in his mind. Three Egyptians, himself included, and five Libyans would make the attack. They were to be dressed in uniforms of the Egyptian military police and using two Soviet-built jeeps painted as MP vehicles. Two actual Egyptian MP vehicles would be diverted at the last minute to secure a crossroad far from the scene of the attack by an officer sympathetic to the Brotherhood. The two jeeps with the assault team would assume the mission of the real Egyptian MPs, driving through all the check points and right up to the reviewing stand where the two presidents would be. Once they were there, resolute hearts, grenades, and automatic rifles would be all that was needed.

Nafissi had liked the plan. It was like him—simple, direct, brutal. Looking at his watch, Sadiq decided that he had enough time to visit his favorite mosque before meeting with Hafez.

Leaning forward, Sadiq told the driver to go to the Mosque of Hassan near the Citadel. Sadiq always enjoyed praying there, mere meters from police headquarters. It was, to him, the ultimate challenge.

Cairo * 1325 Hours, 29 November

The newsroom of the World News office was sheer panic and pandemonium, and Fay Dixon was loving it. A joint news release from the Egyptian Ministry of Defense and the Ministry of State early that morning had announced the impending visit of the President of the United States and the conduct of unannounced joint military maneuvers involving the United States and Egypt. Since then there had been a scramble to gather everything that would be needed to cover the story and provide background information.

Arrangements had already been made to fly in two additional camera crews from WNN's London and Paris offices. Press passes and security badges for all the members of the camera crews and support people had to be obtained from the Egyptian military. Interviews with the U.S. ambassador, briefings by the military attaché, Egyptian military officials, and such had to be set up, shot, edited, and beamed back to the States by satellite. This process always required more time than was available. This was where Fay Dixon came in. She was responsible for developing the concept or angle that Jan would use in her news story. Once Jan approved, Fay put the production together and made sure everyone was doing his or her job. Far from being a simple producer, Fay had become Jan's assistant and the number-two honcho in the office in fact if not in name. Once the tape had been shot, it was Fay who reviewed it and pieced together news stories that would address the preparation leading up to the visit and the maneuvers as well as the actual thing. There was much to do and very little time.

That she had the job at all was more than a simple matter of luck. Through Jan's efforts, her former field producer disappeared almost overnight. Though he was due a promotion and reassignment back to the home office in the States, the speed with which Jan made it happen amazed everyone in the office. It shouldn't have. Jan had a way of moving heaven and earth to get what she wanted. In this case, she wanted the old producer out and her friend in. Nothing, not even the home office, could stop her.

Since her arrival in country and her assignment as Jan's field producer, Fay had been on the run. With Jan's help, she had secured an apartment in a neighborhood populated mainly by Americans and Europeans. They were mainly business types that Scott did not care for and refused to have anything to do with. Not that he was ever home. As always, Scott was gone from sunup to well past sundown, doing whatever it was he did. As far as getting the family settled in, that was left to Fay to handle. Other than a few handouts that weren't of much value, Scott gave her no guidance or advice, assuming that she would be able to sort it out on her own.

And, as always, she did. Taking the advice of the people from the WNN office, Fay enrolled the boys in an exclusive school catering to the Europeans instead of the one used by most of the American embassy staff, something that sent Scott ballistic. He was opposed to sending the children to a non-American school, isolating the boys from their own kind. The fact that his boys wouldn't receive any American history didn't help matters. Fay was prepared for Scott's disapproval but not for the viciousness of his attacks.

Though she suspected that his new assignment contributed to his dark moods, she didn't care at the moment. She was finally realizing her dream of many years—to be back in a newsroom with the flurry of activity and the rush of events. She was among the first to see the news that would shape the world, and she had a hand in shaping it. The mere thought of that was intoxicating. For the first time in years she felt completely and fully alive. The hours were long, the work stressful at times; but all in all it was wonderful.

To add to the bargain, Fay once again was working with Jan. Though they had kept in touch over the years, their worlds had drifted apart since Fay's marriage to Scott. Fay was all but chained to house and home: her life was one of dealing with children, doing laundry, running errands, performing all the pressing little duties expected of an officer's wife and playing substitute father to the children in place of the real one, who seemed always to be away from home at the wrong time. While Fay had been enjoying the so-called benefits of married life, Jan was romping around the globe, earning her spurs as an international reporter in Lebanon and Africa. It was in Africa that she really made her mark. Fortune smiled on her one day when, traveling with guerrillas, she happened across a village that the government forces, with the support of the Soviets, had hit with chemical weapons. The gruesome scenes of dead mothers clutching their dead children, cut down in mid-stride, were seen across the world. Jan appeared before both the U.S. Senate and the U.N. That story made her a star overnight. Along her way to stardom, Fay moved to the backwaters of her life. Until now.

Jan's entry into the newsroom was always like an event. She liked it that way. Returning from a late lunch, she strutted into the newsroom with a determined, businesslike pace. Those who were so privileged to be able to greet her as "Jan" received a smile or a nod of the head as she went by. The lesser lights of the staff addressed her as Miss Fields and received nothing in acknowledgment.

Jan stood a full-figured five foot six: while not heavy, she was slightly heavier than she cared to be. Fortunately, she was well proportioned and carried herself well; her size 10 outfits complemented her figure. Her oval face, framed by long brunet hair, was pretty in a girl-next-door sort of way. What made a difference between Jan Fields and many other bright young female news reporters was that she had the knack of being at the right place at the right time and knew what to do. She was always able to gauge the people she interviewed and to get what she wanted from them, using charm, wit, and a disarmingly casual manner. Her admirers called her intelligent and brilliant; her detractors jealously referred to her as lucky.

Walking over to Fay's desk, Jan flashed her award-winning smile as she greeted Fay, then let it fade into a worried frown. "Fay, we have a beast of a problem. I have an interview with the U.S. ambassador in less than an hour and then a Colonel Wilford immediately after that. I really don't think we'll be able to put together a piece in time for the late news in the States."

Fay glanced at her watch and thought for a moment, then answered very matter-of-factly. Turning a yellow legal pad around so that Jan could see, Fay showed her a draft schedule and explained each event, using a pencil to point to each as she discussed it. When she had gone down the entire schedule point by point, Fay looked up to Jan and stated, in her simple, efficient manner, "So long as I can have the material in hand by three o'clock, no problem. We have a bird at four o'clock with thirty minutes feed time."

Sitting on the edge of Fay's desk, Jan leaned over, smiling again. "Great! You don't know how good it is to have you back where you really belong. We're a great team."

Fay smiled. "I wish Scott understood that. I know he doesn't like this, but so far he hasn't said a thing."

Jan and Scott Dixon never did see eye to eye, except when they were fighting. She never forgave the last of the Neanderthals, as she referred to Scott, for taking the best field producer she ever had. Besides, despite the fact that she associated with military types frequently in pursuit of all the news worth making into news, she had no use for them. They were hard to interview, seldom provided information of any value, and often restricted themselves to a simple "yes" or "no" or "I'm not at liberty to say." She talked to them—or, more correctly, used them—only when absolutely necessary. Politicians, always anxious to get their faces in the news, were far better sources of information, even if they seldom fully understood what they were talking about. The interview with the ambassador, therefore, would be followed by the military interview. The ambassador would tell the story, and the segments with Colonel Wilford would add credibility.

"Doesn't your husband work for this Colonel Wilford, Fay?"

"Jan, you can forget about that angle. Scotty doesn't even tell *me* what he's up to, let alone telling you." Fay leaned forward and whispered, "Although he did tell me that he will be working with an Egyptian unit during this exercise and has to present a briefing with an Egyptian tank battalion commander. As a matter of fact, you may run into him at the embassy. He'll be there this afternoon for a briefing on the visit." As an afterthought, Fay added, "And Jan, if you do see him, though he's been a real shit lately and deserves it, try not to gouge out his eyes in public. He always sulks so whenever you two get into it."

Jan Fields, with a wicked smile across her face, replied, "Fay, would I do that to poor Scotty?"

Without batting an eye, Fay replied, "You know damn well you will." With that, they laughed and went about their harried pursuit of news and truth.

American Embassy, Cairo * 1405 Hours, 29 November

Despite the best efforts of the air conditioner, the briefing room was fast becoming hot and stuffy. At the front of the room, a young captain was going over the plan for the upcoming maneuvers and the President's visit with the aid of hastily made viewgraphs and an overhead projector that could not be focused properly. Dixon, who had developed the overall plan for the exercise and had initiated the coordination, had lost control of the project once the exercise had been announced and the bulk of the Corps staff began to deploy to Cairo. The captain doing the briefing was the protocol officer from 3rd Army, responsible for coordinating visits to military units and briefings, answering questions concerning the VIPs, arranging their transportation, and all the nitty-gritty chores that go with the care and feeding of VIPs. A lack of details and the captain's inability to answer even the simplest questions convinced

Dixon that many of the people involved in running the exercise had been told of it only after the units had been alerted that morning. That opinion was reinforced as he watched briefer after briefer come forward and develop their portion of the plan right then and there.

The captain's briefing, sketchy though it was, at least provided him with a warning order that he was to present a briefing during a live fire demonstration. On a draft agenda for the VIPs, marked "Secret" at the top and bottom, that had been handed out to everyone entering the briefing room, Dixon stumbled across a one-hour slot labeled "Combined Arms Live Fire Exercise: Relief of air assault forces by Egyptian armored units." Under the column that named the briefers, LTC Hafez and LTC Dixon were listed. Hafez's battalion was listed as the force that would relieve B Company, 1st of the 506th Airborne. This exercise was at the end of the visit to the maneuvers on 7 December. It was to be the grand finale. Because Dixon had been working with Hafez, it had been decided to attach him to the Republican Brigade temporarily as a liaison officer for the duration of the presidential visit. Dixon, wanting to watch the procedures used by the incoming units to draw equipment from the combat equipment site, and work in the corps headquarters as he should, had protested; but his protest had been overridden. What made sense in the long run was not important at that moment. Putting on a good show overrode all appeals to common sense and sanity. Dixon therefore spent all morning handing off his notes and plans to another lieutenant colonel, who had just arrived from McDill Air Force Base.

When the captain reached the portion of the briefing that addressed the live fire exercise, Dixon asked several questions but got few answers. In Dixon's initial proposal for the exercise, there had been no joint live fire; he had considered that type of training too hard to put together on such short notice. Not that it couldn't be done. The training benefit that would be derived from doing so would be minimal, he pointed out, versus the expenditure of resources. But his protests were in vain, and the decision was made to put on a really grand live fire show-and-tell for the VIPs.

Once the decision was made, however, no one pushed that part of the exercise much beyond the concept phase. When all was said and done, no one had a firm grasp on what was going to happen or how the exercise was going to go down. Instead, responsibility for that exercise, as well as the briefings to go along with it, was passed to Dixon and Hafez—Dixon was reminded of the old adage that people who ask questions usually get asked to find the answer.

Tuning out the rest of the briefing, Dixon began to consider the problem and formulate a plan and several options. With a little luck he could catch Hafez and discuss the options with him as soon as the briefing was over. Dixon had met Hafez twice and had done some training with his unit. He was impressed with both the unit and its commander. As Hafez had a good command of the English language and was a graduate of the Command and General Staff College at Leavenworth, Dixon saw no major problems with putting the briefing together. The exercise was a different story. Piecing together a combined-arms live fire exercise requires a great deal of planning, coordination, and preparation, not to mention resources. The use of forces from two different armies and an air assault company that wasn't even in country yet complicated the matter. They had eight days in which to pull it together. The sooner they came to an agreement on the concept of operation, the faster they could concentrate on pulling in all the resources and units needed in order to put on, as Colonel Wilford said, "a good show."

Dixon's calculations and gloomy thoughts were interrupted by a tap on his shoulder. He turned, his eyes meeting the impassioned eyes of the Marine corporal who had tapped him. Without saying a word, the Marine extended his right hand, which held a brown shotgun envelope. Dixon took the envelope, whispered a short "Thank you" to the Marine, and then turned back to the current briefer. Half-listening, he absentmindedly opened the envelope. There was a single-page message attached to a yellow routing slip signed by his intelligence officer. Turning to the message without reading the slip, Dixon looked to see who its originator was, then read the body of the message.

The message had been given a FLASH precedence and sent from the Office of Military Cooperation in Sudan. Its first paragraph blandly announced that Soviet forces, with the permission of the Sudanese government, would begin using the airfield at Al Fasher for deployment of a force of unknown size from Ethiopia to Libya commencing 1 December. The second paragraph stated that U.S. military personnel, at the request of the Sudanese government, would be restricted from operating within three hundred miles of Al Fasher for the duration of the Soviet deployment exercise. For several seconds Dixon wasn't aware that his reaction to the message, sprinkled with four-letter expletives, had halted the briefing in its tracks.

Southern Sudan * 1530 Hours, 29 November

Sergeant Johnny Jackson stuck his head into the room where Kinsly sat on the corner of his cot, writing out a response to a message he had just received. The room, barely big enough for two cots, served as a communications center for the team. Jackson coughed to gain Kinsly's attention. "Sir, the major's here to see you."

Kinsly looked up in surprise. "He's up out of bed?"

Jackson shook his head in the affirmative, then stepped back to allow the lanky Sudanese major in. Kinsly rose and greeted the major, offering him the only chair in the room. Still weak from his wounds, the Sudanese major shuffled over to the chair and seated himself.

"Sir, I am glad to see that you are able to get up and around. I hope this is a sign that you will recover soon."

The major did not respond immediately. Kinsly watched him. He was in distress—a distress that was not the result of his wounds. Without saying a word, Kinsly knew that the major had come over personally to inform him that the Soviets were in the Sudan with the permission of his own government. Kinsly already knew that, but he did not let on to the major that he did. To do so would only make it harder on the man.

Without looking at Kinsly, the major told him that due to political necessity, his government had favorably considered a Soviet request to use selected facilities in his country. Furthermore, the major continued haltingly, he had been ordered to inform Kinsly that he and his A Team were to be restricted to the immediate area of the compound during the period when the Soviets were in the Sudan. At the end of his speech, the major looked up at Kinsly. "You must understand, my friend, we have little choice in this matter. As much as it pains me to do so, I have little choice."

Kinsly put his hand on the major's shoulder. It was the first time he had ever touched the man. "Sir, I understand. We each have our duty. Regardless of what happens, however, our friendship will survive."

Looking into Kinsly's eyes, the major smiled. "Yes, our friendship will survive."

Cairo * 1945 Hours, 29 November

As before, Sadiq pulled his friend Hafez into a dark corner of a small mosque. Hafez had debated whether or not to go to the meeting. How easy it would have been to call the police and inform them that Sadiq, a wanted man for years, was in Cairo! But there was no way he could do that without involving himself. The question of how he, a colonel in the Egyptian army and a battalion commander in the Republican Brigade, had come upon information concerning a known terrorist and fugitive from the law would surely be asked. Even if Hafez could come up with a good explanation, there was always the danger that Sadiq would break under interrogation and implicate him in the plot and reveal his earlier dealings with the Brotherhood. Seeing a greater danger in not doing so, Hafez decided to cooperate, but with open eyes. Somehow he had to find an honorable solution to the problem that faced him. There had to be a weak point in Sadiq's plan that would allow him to escape without losing face, or worse.

Sadiq was confident and quite pleased with himself. "All is going well. The assault party is in place and preparing for the day when we, together, will strike down those who would tear us from the bosom of Islam and the True Faith."

Hafez was nervous. Sadiq actually was involved in something, something that was going to happen soon. But he saw a possible opening through which to escape. "If all is ready, then what need do you have of me? Surely your people are more qualified than I?"

Smiling, Sadiq reached out and grabbed Hafez's shoulders with both hands. He believed Hafez's plea was one of humility, not an attempt to back out of the plot. "No, my friend, you are very important. Without you, all will fail."

Hafez felt his heart sink. He stood there for a moment, half of him wanting to strike down the traitor who stood before him and run, the other half fascinated by the unfolding mystery and anxious to learn more. Curiosity won out. "What possible role could you have for me?"

Letting one arm fall to his side, Sadiq half-turned and leaned over to whisper in Hafez's ear. "Your tank battalion will be part of a demonstration on December 7, the last day of the American President's visit to the maneuvers."

Hafez felt himself go stiff. He had learned of this only several hours ago, when Colonel Dixon of the U.S. Army had approached him with the mission and several courses of action. The agenda and timing of the visit were secret. How had this terrorist found out so fast?

Sadiq continued. "Both presidents will be on a covered platform, where they will view the insertion of an American company from Egyptian helicopters. These Americans will dig in and defend against a fake attack. U.S. war planes and Egyptian artillery will fire in their support. At the end of the demonstration, a company from your battalion will break through an imaginary force and join the Americans. Some time during that demonstration, when all eyes are looking forward, two

Egyptian army jeeps carrying my men dressed as military police will approach the rear of the platform. Men from your companies not participating in the demonstration, deployed in a defensive security arch around the rear of the platform, will allow these jeeps to pass. My men will do the rest.''

There was a moment's silence while Hafez waited for more. But there was no more. That was it: simple, direct, quick. Hafez looked at Sadiq. "What about the presidential security at the platform? They will cut your men down before they get out of their jeeps. Anyone not expected will be suspect and stopped."

Sadiq smiled. "But these men will be expected. Additional escort vehicles and personnel will be on hand in case the two presidents are unable to fly out from the observation site. The real military police will be diverted en route and our military police inserted. All you must do is keep your men from examining the jeeps closely, merely waving them on. The presidential security teams will see the military police jeeps approach, watch your men wave them through, and turn back to watch for other threats. Once my men get within fifty meters of the platform, nothing can stop them.''

Again there was a moment of silence. Hafez's mind was racing a mile a minute in an effort to discover a flaw that he could use to dissuade Sadiq from carrying out his plan. Failing that, he found himself rationalizing, in reality he would have nothing to do with the actual assassination. Neither he nor his men had to pull a trigger. All they had to do was turn a blind eye to the two jeeps, both obviously belonging to the military police, and do nothing. To do so would be so natural, so innocent. Turning to Sadiq, Hafez continued to question him. "And what am I to do when the shooting starts? You cannot expect me to stand there like stone and do nothing."

Straightening up, Sadiq grasped Hafez by both shoulders. "The two presidents will fall with the first volley. When that happens, you will do your duty."

"You expect me to fire on your men? To strike them down?"

For the first time Sadiq's face went expressionless; his eyes narrowed. "Yes! I expect you to kill them, and they expect to die. They are ready to become martyrs in the struggle against the infidels and the nonbelievers. As we have learned many years ago, there is no greater privilege than to die for Allah.''

Shaken, Hafez nevertheless managed to collect his thoughts. "Yes, yes, my friend. So true, so true. All is in the hands of God.''

Tripoli, Libya * 1955 Hours, 29 November

There is always the tendency for planners and leaders at every level to meddle with a plan right up to the last minute. This tendency is not all bad in that few plans take everything into account. Variables not considered during the initial stages of planning have the nasty habit of popping up at the most inconvenient times. These variables can unhinge the whole operation if the commander on the ground lacks the training, flexibility, and agility of mind to deal with them. There comes a point, however, when the planners and leaders removed from the scene must leave well enough alone and allow the commander on the ground to do his job. The most successful commanders learn this early, which is why they are successful. Colonel Nafissi would never be a successful commander.

Nafissi was not only a commander but a man concerned about power, always seeking to gain and control it. Such men are reluctant to relinquish or delegate that power. In a system where virtually all power rested in the hands of a select few, to do so would mean competition and, possibly, a threat. While Nafissi was confident in the plan, he was always mindful that the world of international politics was an ever-changing sea of sand. He was unwilling to trust or delegate his power to someone who was less attuned to the politics and strategy of the cause.

His desire to retain tight control of the operation was also based on a basic distrust of his Egyptian "brothers." Though the operation was supposed to be Egyptian, it was not. The Brotherhood, like most clandestine organizations in Egypt, was infested with Egyptian security agents, making security impossible. Nafissi's distrust of his Egyptian brothers was also based on a deep conviction that they were not as dedicated to the cause as they should be. Though they all professed to the same beliefs and goals, the Egyptians carried an air of superiority borne of a cultural heritage and centuries of identity as a nation. Libya could never match either. It bothered Nafissi that some of the Egyptians who claimed to be working for the establishment of fundamentalism often confused the goals of Islamic fundamentalism with those of Egyptian nationalism. They could not be fully trusted.

Hence the reliance on Libyan commandos. Because most of the commandos were Libyan, Nafissi insisted that the assault team maintain communications with Tripoli. Again, an inbred desire to retain tight control over everything overrode common sense. He understood that there existed the danger that an electronic signal could, and probably would, be intercepted. But he considered that risk to be negligible from his viewpoint, and therefore acceptable. Should the timing not be right, he wanted the ability to cancel the attack. The parameters or conditions that would cause him to do such a thing were not clear in Nafissi's own mind. Still, he felt much better that he had some control over the operation and could influence it. Periodic status reports from the commandos and final clearance to conduct the attack would be given by Nafissi alone. After all, what use is it to be a commander if one cannot command?

To date, all had gone well. The commandos had gathered at the designated rallying point. There the equipment and weapons were ready and waiting. They had conducted several rehearsals and even had driven most of the route twice in a civilian van. With nothing to do until the commandos made their final clearance check with him, Nafissi began to consider the possibilities of what would happen if the raid failed. One of the first considerations was retaliation by either Egypt or the U.S.—or both. The American raid of April 1986 was still a sore point, especially for air force personnel. That raid was far more damaging, in the eyes of world politics, than the Egyptian incursion of 1977. Though he counted on the presence of

Soviet forces in Libya to act as a deterrent to retaliation by either Egypt or the United States, no one could be one hundred percent sure what would happen if the plot failed or was traced back to Libya.

Therefore, as a belated thought, Nafissi had the commander of Air Defense Command report to him on the current status of air defense. Not satisfied with his report, Nafissi ordered him to personally ensure that all was in order, in particular the systems covering the Cyrenaica, the eastern part of Libya. When asked the cause of his concern, Nafissi merely stated that he wanted to watch the maneuvers being conducted by the Americans and Egyptians closely, just in case they were using them as a cover for an attack on Libya. Though that story was nothing more than a means of keeping the commander of the air defense forces from becoming curious, Nafissi failed to appreciate the chain of events he set in motion.

Cairo * 2210 Hours, 29 November

Stretching, Dixon got up from his desk and walked over to the window. He was tired. The day had been a long one, one that didn't seem to have an end. For a moment he looked out the window. He was not ready to deal with the rush of events that was overwhelming him and his family. Little had gone right since he had been ripped from his nice, safe job in Washington and thrown into the middle of a tempest. Instead of preparing for retirement in Maryland, he found himself in the Middle East, preparing to face a potential international crisis. Instead of bringing his family back together and healing the wounds the war in Iran had opened between himself and Fay, he found the gulf between them widening daily as she struck out on her own, leaving him to muddle about on his own, dealing with his own problems as best he could.

As bad as his domestic problems were, the internal strife was worse. In the Pentagon, he was a highly paid paper shuffler, many times removed from the decision-making process. In

Egypt, however, he was again faced with the prospect of ordering men into dangerous situations.

Dixon paused in mid-thought and corrected himself. "Prospect" was a bad word—the wrong word. He was *in fact* ordering men into combat. Returning to his desk, he reread the message he was about to send out. Bypassing the Office of Military Cooperation (Sudan), the message would go directly to a newly promoted captain by the name of Kinsly. The message was an order that directed Kinsly to disregard all previous instructions to avoid the area around Al Fasher. Instead, Kinsly would take his A Team to Al Fasher by the fastest means available, place the airfield and any facilities used by the Soviets at Al Fasher under observation, and report any and all information on the units moving into and out of Al Fasher. The order was in direct violation of the official agreement between the United States and the Sudan that the United States would do nothing that would result in confrontation with the Soviets.

Dixon considered the order one more time. He didn't like the last paragraph. The bulk of the message enumerated the information that Kinsly's team was to gather. In the second-to-last paragraph, Kinsly was told that he could use whatever means he saw fit to accomplish his assigned mission. Then, in the last paragraph, Dixon added that Kinsly wasn't to take any unnecessary chances. Was Dixon using double-talk? Or was he sidestepping an unpleasant task and instead abdicating responsibility for deciding what was right and proper to some poor sap of a captain stuck in the bush?

Sliding the message into a folder, Dixon closed his mind to the matter. He didn't know, nor was he in any condition to sort out, what was right and proper. At that moment all he knew was that, like it or not, he had to issue that order and, for better or worse, trust that the man receiving it would act appropriately.

6

A man who has to be convinced to act before he acts is not a man of action. . . . You must act as you breathe.

—GEORGES CLEMENCEAU

Southeast of Al Fasher, Sudan * 0535 Hours, 1 December

A sharp buzz in his left ear woke Captain Ilvanich. Opening his eyes, he looked to his right and saw that the noise had been the intercom's buzzer. The crew chief of the Ilyushin 76 had already picked up the phone and was talking to someone in the cockpit. Unable to hear both sides of the conversation, Ilvanich looked around, all the while wondering how much further they had to go.

"YOU MUST BE VERY USED TO THIS BY NOW!" The shout came from Lieutenant Shegayev, who was sitting across the aisle from him, a nervous smile on his face.

Ilvanich had no doubt that Shegayev had been awake and staring at him the whole trip. He was nervous. It would be Shegayev's first jump with the unit. Ilvanich considered the young KGB officer across from him. I suppose I looked just like him two years ago, he thought. He considered harassing the young officer but decided against it. There still was the possibility that they would meet resistance at the airfield. There was no point in making things more difficult for the young political. Instead, Ilvanich just grunted, "Yes, one becomes used to this."

The crew chief hung up the phone to the intercom and turned to Ilvanich. Speaking loudly, slowly, and exaggerating his pronunciation so that he would not be misunderstood, the crew chief relayed to Ilvanich the message he had just been given by the pilot. "No jump. We will land you. We are twenty minutes out."

Relieved that there would be no jump or fighting, Ilvanich unsnapped his seat belt and stood up. As he did so, all eyes turned to him, waiting to hear the news or his orders. When Ilvanich announced that they were to remove their parachutes and prepare for an unopposed landing, a murmur of relief could be heard up and down the row of paratroopers. Everyone save Shegayev smiled and instantly began to shed the heavy parachutes that cut into their arms and legs. Noting Shegayev's disappointed look, Ilvanich bent over and whispered, "Have faith, my friend. I have great faith that the party will provide another opportunity for us to die a grand and glorious death for the motherland."

Shocked by Ilvanich's remark, Shegayev stared at him, ashen. Ilvanich, pleased that he had gotten the young officer's goat again, stood upright and smiled a sinister smile, winked, then continued to watch his men as they removed and stored their parachutes under their seats.

Over the Atlantic Ocean near the 45th East Meridian * 0035 Hours, 1 December

"Better look sharp there, Andy. Someplace down there is an aircraft carrier that has fifty-eight hundred pounds of fuel and a clean latrine waiting for us."

"Head, sir. Sailors use heads, not latrines. You go around asking those swabbies where the latrine is and they'll mess with you till you piss your pants."

Mennzinger laughed. "First, Andy, it wouldn't be the first time I pissed my pants. And second, if those yahoos fuck with me, I'll whip it out and piss all over their nice clean floor, or deck, or whatever they call it." After eight hours of being cramped into the gunner copilot seat, flying in total darkness over the monotonous ocean, Mennzinger was looking forward to stretching his legs, even if it meant landing on a carrier in the middle of the night. With nothing better to do, since it wasn't his turn to fly, he decided to scan the area to see if there was anything about. Seeing nothing on the screen displaying the pilot night-vision sensor, or PNVS, he leaned down, put his head up to the multipurpose sight, and switched on the target acquisition and designation sight. Once he had a good picture, Mennzinger began to scan the area to the front of the Apache, looking for a hot spot that would be the carrier.

Warrant officer Andy Post, Mennzinger's pilot, spotted the first ship before Mennzinger did. Post announced that he had a contact on the right. Automatically, Mennzinger traversed his sight over, centered the hot spot in his thermal sight, then increased the magnification. The thermal sight, detecting heat sources and translating them into a visible picture, displayed the image of a ship. The image, however, was not a carrier: there was no flat deck. "I think that's an escort, Andy. Try contacting the carrier. If that doesn't work, we'll try the E-3 Sentinel."

Flipping to the designated frequency, Post called the carrier. On his first try, the carrier's flight control responded and informed them that they were twenty miles out and on course. With an air of triumph, Post announced, "See, what did I tell you! Right on the money."

"Before we start congratulating ourselves," Mennzinger shot back without a pause, "let's see if we can put this bird down on the deck of that carrier in one piece, and soon."

"Your wish, sir, is my command."

Al Fasher, Sudan * 1735 Hours, 1 December

The early-morning sun, streaming into the window of the Aeroflot Ilyushin 86 jet, scanned the faces of the passengers like a spotlight as the aircraft turned and began its approach into the airfield. The sudden flash of the sun and the steep banking of the jet woke Neboatov from his fitful sleep. A major of artillery seated next to him was turned sideways and staring out the window. "Huh," the major grunted to no one in particular. "Will you look at this! I doubt if they've ever seen this much activity in this pisshole of a country. No doubt we're going to find ourselves asshole deep in really big operations this time."

Curious, Neboatov stretched, then turned to look out the window himself. The scene before him was, as the artillery major had stated, most surprising. Lined up on the runway below them were four Red Air Force Antonov AN-124 transports and six Ilyushin Il-76 transports. Interspersed between the oversized military transports were several smaller civil aircraft, mostly Ilyushin 86s with Aeroflot markings, like the one they were on. Farther down the runway were a number of fighter aircraft—MIG-29s by the look of their tail sections. Between the aircraft, personnel were scattered, some obviously ground crews, others passengers lined up or in small groups waiting for embarkation.

The major of artillery turned toward Neboatov. "There's enough transport down there to move more than two thousand troops in a single lift. Whatever is up is certainly big."

Neboatov nodded, then turned away from the window. All the Soviet and Cuban advisors, including Neboatov, had been picked up and whisked away before dawn without warning. They suspected that some type of major operation was at hand. Exactly what, no one could imagine. The sight of the large number of aircraft at an isolated airfield like the one below them and the magnitude of the activity there confirmed their beliefs while at the same time baffling them. Closing his eyes, Neboatov began to go over the possibilities. Airborne assault? That would explain the transports. But he ruled that out quickly: the openness of the operation would negate the surprise factor. No doubt by now every rebel unit in the country was alert and preparing for such an operation. Mass reinforcement? Possibly; the Ethiopian forces had been taking a beating in the last six months. The stepped-up efforts of the insurgents, backed by the United States, again threatened to topple the Marxist regime in Ethiopia. Perhaps Moscow was putting forth a great effort to crush the rebels in one mighty push. That was possible—but not likely. Moscow was trying to reduce its commitment in Africa for the second time in ten years. Advisors who had been killed or wounded in the last three months had not been replaced. A sudden reversal of policy did not make sense. Then there was the often discussed possibility of withdrawal. Perhaps an agreement had been reached in the protracted peace negotiations and it was time to leave. That possibility was the least likely: if they were withdrawing, there would have been no need for the great rush or the secrecy. All the Soviet and Cuban advisors had been instructed to carry only what they would need for a short trip—no extra clothing, ammo, or personal gear.

Regardless of the operation, the unit Neboatov advised would not be ready. His battalion, badly mauled in the ambush earlier that month, was still at less than 70 percent strength in personnel and less than 50 percent in heavy weapons and essential equipment. Training of the replacement personnel had barely begun. It would be months before the unit was ready for field operations. Other than simple guard duty, it would be murder to commit the battalion to battle. Suspecting the worst, Neboatov began to categorize the reasons for leaving his battalion out of the upcoming operation, regardless of what it was.

Upon landing, Neboatov found out that he could have saved himself a great worry. He and the rest of their group were shocked to find out that they were not in the desert region of Ethiopia but in western Sudan. That information was provided by an air force captain who greeted the group of advisors with whom Neboatov was traveling. To a man, everyone in Neboatov's group turned this way and that, looking for telltale signs of a struggle. But there were none. On the contrary, upon closer examination they saw Soviet officers and personnel working with their Sudanese counterparts, who were still armed. Confused, they followed the cheerful and bouncy air force captain to an open hangar near the airport's main administration building, mumbling among themselves as they went. The hangar was already crowded when Neboatov's group arrived. Soviet paratroopers, with rifles held at the ready, were posted at the door as guards. A young lieutenant of paratroops—probably KGB, Neboatov thought—checked the ID of each of the new arrivals against a list before he was allowed to enter the hangar. The procedure, standard whenever a classified briefing was about to be given, heightened everyone's curiosity and Neboatov's apprehensions.

Once past the guards at the door of the hangar, the new arrivals, unable to find any seating, simply pushed their way in and stood against the back wall. Many of those seated turned to see who the new arrivals were, just as those in Neboatov's group examined those who were already there. No one, apparently, had any idea what was going on. Neboatov recognized several other advisors. Judging from the sheer number of Soviet and Cuban officers present, he decided that whatever was about to happen, it involved just about every unit in northern, central, and eastern Ethiopia.

The babel of hundreds of conversations came to a sudden halt when a voice called the auditorium to attention. Everyone jumped up and locked himself into a rigid position of attention. From the front of the hangar, the click of several boots reverberated on the concrete floor. A different voice called for the assembled group to be seated. As the audience took its seats, the guards at the doors closed and locked them.

The speaker, a colonel of whom Neboatov had never heard, began the briefing by announcing that the officers assembled were now assigned to the newly created North African Front under the command of Colonel General Uvarov. Starting with a brief overview of the current military situation in Libya, the briefer discussed, with the aid of slides, how troops from the Soviet Union, Iran, Angola, and Ethiopia—in particular, combat forces—would be moved to equipment-storage sites in Libya, where they would draw equipment, be reformed into combat units, and then be moved to an area west of Tobruk, where they would form the second operational echelon for the combined Soviet-Cuban-Libyan exercise. The briefer then lapsed into a discussion of political matters and a lecture on the threat American exercises in the area created, to the party and

Mother Russia. After the initial five minutes, few details were covered. Neboatov wondered particularly how Soviet forces had managed to gain access and use of an entire airfield in Sudan, a country that was actively supporting guerrilla groups trying to bring down Ethiopia. He had no doubt, however, that when the time came, someone would tell him. The Red Army was notorious for waiting until the last minute before telling a person what he was to do.

At the completion of the briefing, the Soviet and Cuban officers filed out of the hangar and were led to an area set up to feed the mass of troops and air crews. The meal was rather bland, a stew with some vegetables, meat, and potatoes. Neboatov found a seat across from two colonels and began to eat his meal and listen to their conversation. The first colonel was a general staff officer and obviously part of the organization that was running the deployment exercise. He was explaining to the second colonel, a new arrival like Neboatov, how the Soviet government had "convinced" the Sudanese government to allow Soviet forces to use the airfield at Al Fasher. It was, as he put it, "in their best interest." "You see, Lysenkovich," he stated, as if he were lecturing a student in political science, "the ambassador simply told the Sudanese president that it would be far better to allow us the temporary use of selected facilities in his country now than to face the possibility of losing those same facilities for good."

The second colonel looked at him skeptically. "And I suppose he simply agreed, with no protest."

"Yes!" the first replied triumphantly. "He is no fool. He and his entire government know that they stand to lose the entire southern portion of the Sudan to the rebel forces we back. They are hanging on to it by a string—a string supplied by the United States. It would not take a great deal for us to escalate the civil war in the south. They know it, and the Americans do also. Our efforts have achieved an equilibrium—one that could easily be upset, since in reality the Sudan is not considered an area of vital interest to the United States. When the civil war starts to get too expensive, in men and dollars, for the United States, the Americans take their string away and

134

leave the Sudanese to their fate, just like Vietnam. The Sudanese know this. So the President of the Sudan made the best possible choice of two bad ones. He has gambled that we will come, use the airfield for three weeks, then go away and leave him to go about running this forsaken land."

The second colonel paused. "Will we, at the end of three weeks, simply walk away from here, as you said?"

The first colonel shrugged his shoulders. "Who knows. Much can happen in three weeks."

Neboatov, quietly eating his meal and listening, wondered if the first colonel was simply being mysterious, as many general staff officers like to be, or if he knew of other, bigger plans for the airfield at Al Fasher. Regardless, Neboatov found himself wishing that the new operation he and the hundreds of others about him were embarking on would come and go without a hitch. At age thirty-five, he had had more than his share of adventure.

Cairo * 0735 Hours, 5 December

To Fay, the last seven days had been like a dream. In fact, she had to stop every now and then and look around, trying to convince herself that it was all true. Whether it was preordained, as Jan liked to say, or simply good luck, Fay was in the middle of the biggest news story of the day. And if that wasn't enough, in short order Fay and Jan found that, despite the long years between the time they last worked together and today, they had not lost that special magic that made them a great team. Like in the old days, their minds were as one. Fay's ability to predict what Jan wanted and needed astounded everyone in the office and allowed them to put together a package in half the time it had taken before.

Jan, ever conscious that the news limelight now focused on the Middle East was fleeting, was thankful to have someone at her side who could make things happen. With Fay tending to the technical side of the story and setting up the next series of stories, Jan was free to go out and develop leads and do a lot of on-the-scene shooting. Every minute of satellite time Fay could beg, borrow, or steal was filled with Jan's story from "the scene of the newest East-West confrontation."

Blowing into the office like a storm, Jan dropped her coat on a chair without looking where it fell, reached out to grasp a proffered cup of coffee without seeing who gave it to her, and headed right for Fay's desk. "Fay, what have you got for me today?"

Looking up and over her reading glasses, Fay smiled. "Well, I see you survived the President's reception last night."

Jan made a face of mock despair, looked up at the ceiling, and put her right hand over her forehead, palm facing out. "It's a nasty job covering receptions, but someone has to do it." Dropping her hand, she rushed up to Fay, grabbed her shoulders, and swung her swivel chair around. "Fay, you have to save me. It's a jungle out there!"

Unable to restrain herself, Fay broke out laughing. Jan followed suit. The rest of the staff in the office pretended to ignore them as the Terrible Two laughed hysterically.

Finally able to gain some degree of composure, Fay picked up Jan's schedule for the day. "If you feel up to it, my love, you have an interview with Congressman Lewis at 0830 in his suite at the Sheraton Nile."

Jan's eyebrows arched and her eyes widened. "A suite? Well, the junior representative from the state of Tennessee certainly knows how to travel when he's looking for facts. Do you suppose some of those facts are hiding in that suite?"

Fay got a stern look on her face. "Now, Jan, be kind to that dear man. He's news. If you play him right, he may come up with some good lines we can splice in with the official garbage we're getting from the military affairs officer in the embassy."

"I'll try to remember that, Mother," Jan said, laughing.

Continuing, Fay briefed Jan on the rest of the day and on projects in the works and gave her a rundown on what she had been able to get from the Soviet and Libyan news releases on their exercises west of Tobruk. As a last item, Fay reminded her that she had to be back from her luncheon appointment in time to catch a copter to the training area for a recon of the site where the presidents of the United States and Egypt would view the live fire demonstration.

The reminder caused Jan to pause. "Isn't Scott going to be there?"

"Yes, he and an Egyptian colonel are responsible for pulling that part of the show together," Fay responded too matter-of-factly.

Jan noticed the change in Fay's voice: there was trouble at home. Fay had mentioned something about Scott opposing her working, but she dropped the matter within days of returning to work. Now every time Jan mentioned Scott's name or home, Fay became very quiet and quickly tried to change the subject. "Is there anything you want me to tell Scott if I see him?"

Fay looked up at Jan. The look in her eye was now cold and unnerving. "Yes, if you would be so kind. Remind him that if God and country could spare him for a few hours, his family would enjoy the presence of his company." There was a long pause before she continued. "Now, when you return from the desert . . ."

Cairo West, Egypt * 1415 Hours, 5 December

The platoon sergeants called the raggedy collections of men to attention as First Sergeant Duncan emerged from the tent that served as the command post for B Company, 1st of the 506th Airborne. Duncan placed himself in the center of the formation, twelve paces to the front, came to attention, and called for the company to fall in. When the men in the ranks stopped their shuffling, Duncan called for a report. Starting with the first platoon, each platoon sergeant rendered his report, yelling out either "Present" or "All accounted for." Finished with the formalities, Duncan called for the formation to stand at ease, then announced the duty schedule for the rest of the day and the personnel who would be on detail the next day. The schedule for that afternoon, like that of yesterday afternoon, and the afternoon of the day before, and every afternoon since they had been in country, would be cleaning and maintenance of weapons and gear followed by an inspection commencing at 1600 hours.

Like the rest of the men in the company, including the Old Man, Duncan was looking forward to the end of this exercise. It had been nothing but a pain in the ass for him since it began. Things got off to a bad start right from the beginning of the unit's deployment. Upon landing, B Company had been detached from the rest of the battalion and told it had a special mission. For the briefest of moments, the prospects of doing some kind of gee-whiz special operation made up for the sudden deployment exercise so close to Christmas. This momentary boost in morale, however, was quickly dashed when their company commander, Captain Harold Cerro, returned from a meeting and informed the men that they were going to participate in a combined arms live fire demonstration involving their company and Egyptian units. Though Cerro and the rest of the leadership endeavored to make the most of their task, the excitement and energy that the men of the company had begun with back at Fort Campbell had slowly worn away. Mindless, lock-stepped drills and careful rehearsals for the set-piece demonstration in the desert were not what the young soldiers were interested in. By the evening of the third, fights between platoons were becoming common as men began to seek an avenue to vent their frustrations and excess energy.

The first sergeant, ever inventive and ready to meet any challenge to unit discipline and threat to cohesion, stepped in and introduced measures designed to discourage lax performance and in-fighting. Always trying to solve his own problems in-house, Duncan organized the B Company Rifle and Hiking Club. Anyone not performing to standards or involved in a fight was automatically "nominated" for membership to the club by his platoon sergeant. Starting on the evening of the third, the "nominees" met in front of the company CP tent at sunset in full combat load and marched out into the desert. The first sergeant himself set the pace and led the men. After marching five kilometers, they would stop and dig a proper individual fighting position. This position was inspected and measured by Duncan to ensure that it was in accordance with standards set down in the field manual before it was covered in by the man who dug it. When everyone was done, the group would march five more kilometers, then repeat the digging-and-inspection process—the first of four repetitions. When they returned, the men would have to clean their weapons and gear and stand at full inspection by Duncan before they were allowed to catch what sleep they could. Normally this was precious little, as everyone was up early, preparing for the next day's training and round of rehearsals.

Though Cerro was against such "additional training" as a means of motivating the malcontents and lazies, he could see no other solution. He and the other officers in the company were heavily involved in the planning and coordination for the exercise and had little time to deal with minor breaches in discipline. They depended on Duncan and the platoon sergeants to deal with them. Time was pressing, and the men who had failed to respond to other, more positive leadership techniques had to be brought back into line. Though morale was still low, the fights stopped and the men performed. Besides, Duncan knew what he was doing. He had earned his Distinguished Service Cross for leading the remnants of his encircled platoon through 120 miles of enemy territory, fighting all the way and maintaining unit cohesion. That Duncan himself led the additional training sessions each night did much to end all debates and bitching, from both officers and enlisted men, on the matter and techniques he used.

In the shade of the platform where the two presidents would watch the demonstration, Cerro and his officers listened to a critique of the morning's rehearsal. Also present were Egyptian and U.S. officers from the artillery units, the relieving tank company, and other elements participating in the exercise. The two officers doing the critique were an Egyptian and an American lieutenant colonel. When Cerro had met the lieutenant colonel named Dixon, he was struck by the feeling that he had seen or met him before. That, however, seemed highly unlikely, since Dixon was an Armor officer and Cerro made it a point to stay away from treadheads.

As Dixon went through the points that had been missed or messed up that morning, Cerro tried to place the name or face. Suddenly it dawned upon him. Dixon had come out of the last war as one of its most decorated officers. Reaching back into his memory, Cerro recalled an article that recounted Dixon's deeds and awards, which included the Congressional Medal, two Silver Stars, and a Purple Heart. Though pleased that he had finally solved that mystery, Cerro wondered why Dixon was here in Egypt and not in some high-speed job getting ready to be a general. With a reputation like his he had to be a shoo-in.

His thoughts were interrupted as Dixon introduced the two civilians who would be in charge of security at the site. One was a tall, light-haired American who wore sunglasses and an open-collared white shirt. The other was an Egyptian, as short and dark as the American was tall and light. The two looked like a regular Mutt-and-Jeff routine—and as they got into their briefing, that analogy began to apply more and more. The two security agents interrupted each other frequently, holding quick, impromptu discussions in front of the assembled group whenever one said something with which the other disagreed. In no time at all it seemed that neither of them—much less the soldiers they were briefing—really understood how security would be handled. In the midst of a discussion, as if to highlight the confusion, a white van with a World News Network sign taped to the right side of the windshield rolled up to the pair as they bickered. A shapely, good-looking female reporter hopped out, went over to the American security man, and asked if this was where the presidents would view "the tank battle." The American soldiers began to cheer and whistle.

Seeing that the situation was totally out of hand, Dixon stepped forward, yelling "At ease!" Hafez, also taken aback by the confusion, followed suit and called for the Egyptian officers to be silent. With calm restored, Dixon turned to face the two security men. "Gentlemen, you no doubt have an important job to do, and I am ready and willing to assist you in any way possible. First, however, I recommend you figure out what it is you need, then tell Colonel Hafez and me what it is you want. We will, in turn, brief the troops and make it happen."

Turning to Hafez, Dixon asked, "Sir, is that agreeable with you?" Hafez shook his head in agreement, then barked something to the Egyptian security man that could only be an order or a rebuke, or both. The Egyptian security man looked at Dixon and agreed, backing away and pulling his American counterpart with him. The American security man, obviously unhappy with being spoken to in such a manner by a green suiter, turned to Dixon and stared at him eye-to-eye for a moment. Dixon, meeting the silent challenge, put both hands on his hips, jutted his head out slightly, and returned the stare. Seeing that his attempt at intimidation had failed, the American security man joined the Egyptian. Together they went to their vehicle, where they sulked and talked for a few moments before they departed. No doubt, Dixon thought, he'd hear from them through "official channels."

Turning to the female reporter, Dixon folded his arms, forced a smile, and let out a sigh. "Ms. Fields, what a pleasure it is to see you again. Your pursuit of truth and/or a news story has taken you a little off the beaten path. May I ask what you are doing here and how you managed to clear the security checkpoints?"

Imitating the stance Dixon had just used with the security man, Jan put her hands on her hips and stared at Dixon. Rather than being intimidating, however, her posture was provocative. "First off, Colonel Dixon, the news and the truth are one and the same."

Dixon let out a slight "Ha!" making Jan visibly angry.

"Second, Mr. Colonel, I have a right *and* the permission to be here." She pulled out a pass and a copy of the agenda of the visit listing where journalists were permitted. She flashed both inches away from Dixon's nose. Jan wore a coy smile and spoke sweetly. "I'm the reporter drawn from the media pool to cover this event. Guess you sort of lucked out, Scotty dear."

To her surprise, Dixon grabbed the agenda and examined it. As he read the agenda, an exact duplicate to the one he had that was marked Secret, he began to shake his head. "Where did you get this?"

"At a press conference this morning in Cairo. The American ambassador held a briefing for the press. How lucky for the American people that there are a few government officials who believe the press and the American public have a right to know."

Dixon continued to shake his head. He turned to Hafez, handing him the pass and paper. Hafez looked at them, then up at Dixon. "This will make security very hard. We cannot guarantee the safety of our presidents if everyone knows of their exact schedule."

Dixon was slightly taken aback by the colonel's comment. While the security was far looser than Dixon had wanted, Colonel Hafez's statement seemed to be one of fact, not mere concern. "Colonel Hafez, I too am concerned, but I am sure there are measures being taken to ensure the entire maneuver area is secure and entry is limited."

A concerned look on his face, Hafez tilted his head. "Yes, no doubt you are correct. But still, we must voice our concerns to our commanders. I, after all, am responsible for manning the outer security perimeter. It is not very good to have so many knowing where our presidents will be and when. Perhaps they can make some changes in the schedule and not come here."

Without waiting for a response, Hafez turned, called to several of his officers and stepped off smartly, leaving a slightly flabbergasted Dixon to figure out what he was up to.

"What's a matter, Superman, someone tuggin' on your cape too hard?"

Dixon turned to Jan, her defiance now turned to a smile, a mocking smile.

"No, it's just been one of those days. Two days to go and everyone suddenly is getting nervous and wants to change things." He turned his head and looked in the direction of the Americans still waiting in the shade of the bleachers. The Egyptians had all left. "Well," he continued, turning back to Jan, "since you know so much, there's no harm in introducing you to the star of this performance—Captain Cerro!" he called out to a man a few feet away.

Cerro came up to Dixon, saluted, and reported.

"Captain," said Dixon, "I'd like you to meet Ms. Jan Fields, the hottest little TV reporter this side of the Nile. Jan, Captain Harold Cerro, commander of B Company, 1st of the 506th Airborne, Air Assault."

Though Jan was displeased, to say the least, with the manner in which Dixon introduced them, she saw a great chance to get some interviews with the people who would be participating in the exercise. Turning on her charm, she began to fire questions at Cerro about his unit, its mission, and the demonstration.

Cerro hesitated, turning to Dixon with a worried look. Dixon knew the question. Nodding his head, he indicated that Cerro didn't need to worry about what he told her; Ms. Fields was clear. Satisfied, Cerro began to answer her questions in a careful and deliberate manner.

Dixon walked away to wait until they were finished. For a moment, he felt bad about handing Fields off to Cerro—but only for a moment. He knew that had he stayed, eventually he or Fields would have taken a cheap shot, pissed the other off, and began a fight.

When Jan finished with Cerro, she walked over to where Dixon was sitting, going over a briefing book and making notes. "I'm finally going to be able to get the last of the Neanderthals on tape. What a treat!"

Dixon looked up at her and smiled. "Sorry to disappoint you, but that's been changed. Seems like someone decided that the presidents deserved higher-paid briefers than Colonel Hafez and I. This morning we were replaced by the commander of the U.S. brigade that's deployed over here and the commander of the Republican Brigade. The only thing Colonel Hafez and I have to do is make sure that everyone is in their places with bright smiley faces on the seventh."

Jan frowned. "What a shame! I was so looking forward to listening to you try to answer Congressman Lewis's questions. That would have been a wonderful experience."

Dixon looked up. "Lewis? What the hell is that little communist doing here?"

Seeing that Dixon was surprised, Jan decided to have a little fun. "Communist? The distinguished congressman from the state of Tennessee would beg to differ with you on that. He happens to be a war hero and a leading spokesman for quite a few groups concerned about America's international policy and disarmament."

Closing his book and getting up, Dixon skewed his face into a frown. "He's a fucking communist. He took that war-hero image and used it to get elected. As a distinguished member of Congress, he's done more damage to the military's recovery and buildup in one year than the KGB could possibly hope to do in ten. That rotten little shit should get an Order of Lenin for his efforts."

Enjoying the fact that Dixon was pissed, Jan continued to egg him on. "Didn't you two serve together in Iran?"

Looking down at the ground, Dixon thought for a moment, deciding whether or not to answer. Then he thought, What the hell. "Yeah, we sort of served together. He was the XO of a National Guard battalion from Memphis that was ordered to move forward to counterattack and relieve my battalion, which was surrounded. The Soviets had broken through us earlier in the day and ripped us apart. Intelligence reports given to the National Guard unit before they attacked mentioned a Soviet recon battalion. Lewis's unit expected only scattered and light resistance from depleted Soviet units. They were unprepared for an encounter with a full tank regiment that the Soviets had moved forward after nightfall. The two units, Lewis's and the Soviet tank regiment, had a meeting engagement in the dark which neither expected or were ready for. They fought for eight hours." Dixon paused. His eyes were blank and staring into the distance. His face showed no expression. "When it ended, it was a draw—a draw that cost the Guard unit over 60 percent casualties. Lewis knew most of the men that had died and took it hard. A lot of people in Memphis did too. It was one of those things, you know—friction of war. You will never have one hundred percent intelligence in war, especially when someone breaks through like the Soviets did. There were bits and pieces of units all over the place, many of them out of contact with their higher headquarters. That things happened the way they did shouldn't have been a surprise.''

Dixon paused again. Jan saw he was lost in his story, oblivious to the world around him. She also saw in his eyes that what he was recounting was painful. Suddenly, for the first time, she felt sorry for Dixon. She had seen what wars did to people. Though she had never had to pull a trigger or order others to do so, she had little doubt that it had to be difficult. What she saw in Dixon at that moment was a man who had had to do both and had found the experience shattering.

Dixon continued. ''But Lewis didn't see it that way. He blamed the Army for sending his unit, a Guard unit, forward to be sacrificed to save a 'regular Army' unit. When he got home, he demanded an investigation into the conduct of the battle, then the war in general. His efforts gained in popularity in Memphis, which was stunned by the loss of so many of its citizens. When the congressman from that district attempted to fend off the investigation, he signed his political death warrant. Lewis was elected in his place and took his fight to the Hill, where he enlisted the support of every radical liberal against rearmament he could find in the House and Senate.'' Standing up, Dixon sighed, looked out to the horizon, and mused, ''And to good effect. We're no better off fighting the Russians today than we were three years ago.'' Turning to Jan, he let a faint smile light across his face. ''But why am I telling you this? You're the one with her finger on the news.''

''Can I quote you on this?''

Giving her a dirty look, Dixon didn't answer. Instead, he changed the subject. ''I'm getting ready to head into the cantonment area. Do you know your way back?''

Seeing the change in Dixon's mood and tired of her game, Jan thanked him but told him she and her crew needed to survey the site for the best camera angles and location for the mikes. Without so much as a wave, Dixon climbed into his vehicle and roared away in a cloud of dust.

Cairo West, Egypt * 1915 Hours, 6 December

Colonel Hafez took evening prayer alone in his tent that night. In the stillness of the early evening, he prayed hard. First he prayed for guidance, then the wisdom to make the right choice. Finally, he simply asked God to see him through the next day. He ended his prayers by placing his fate in God's hands.

Finding no answers and little comfort in prayer, Hafez turned his attention to preparing himself for the next day. First he cleaned his pistol, taking care to ensure that all parts were clean and functional. When he was finished, he loaded a full magazine, chambered one round, and put the pistol in his holster. Finished with that, he laid out his uniform, checking the ribbons, the insignia of his rank, and his crests.

Satisfied with that, he turned to his last chore, a letter home. For the longest time, he considered not writing anything. What was he to say? What could he say? He still did not know what he would do when the moment came. His attempts at writing a letter showed this. After writing three paragraphs, he stopped and tore it up. It sounded like a suicide note. His second letter was no better. After two paragraphs it sounded like a press release from a radical Islamic group. Hafez tore it up too.

Unable to concentrate, Hafez left his tent and walked out into the desert. He wandered for the better part of an hour, pondering what he would tell his wife and sons. Again, his indecision confused the issue. Finally, his mind muddled and confused, Hafez returned to his tent, sat down, and started to write his wife a simple love letter. In his expression of love, written in flowing prose, he found escape from the troubles he faced.

It was past midnight before he finished.

The Western Desert, Egypt * 0255 Hours, 6 December

The signal and electronic traffic from Libya was anything but routine. Since midnight, the search radars of air defense units across the border from Egypt had been fully operational. All the Egyptian collection and monitoring stations strung across western Egypt were alert and actively collecting information on the type of signal, the strength of the signal, the direction of the signal, and the number of active emitters. This information was relayed to the headquarters of the Western Military District. There electronic warfare intelligence officers received and processed the information by putting the pieces together like pieces of a mosaic. This mosaic provided them with a clear and accurate picture of the air defense capability of the Libyan forces facing them.

Each type and model of radar has its own distinct signature. The Egyptian electronic warfare officers, trained to distinguish the radars and assisted by computers, had no problem identifying, classifying, and counting the radar units in use. With this information, they were able to study the coverage of the search, or surveillance, radars used to find and identify incoming threats. From that study, gaps in radar coverage could be found. The target acquisition radars used to guide surface-to-air missiles onto targets were also found. When the target acquisition radars were activated to illuminate, or "paint," Egyptian aircraft on patrol over Egypt's Western Desert, they were identified and located. From that information, the location of the actual surface-to-air missile launchers, slaved to the target acquisition radars, could be determined and classified.

The windfall of intelligence was welcome but, at the same time, troublesome. When informed of the activity, the commander of the Western District asked the inevitable question: why? Except in time of national emergency, the Libyans had never activated all their systems as fully as they now were. What was motivating them to do so puzzled both the commander and his chief of intelligence and led to a lively debate. While the maneuvers currently being conducted would prompt the Libyans to increase their vigilance, they could not account for such an all-out effort. Concerned that there was more involved than a simple test of the system or paranoia over the current maneuvers, the commander ordered his intelligence chief to double his collection and monitoring of

Libyan command and control nets. If they were equally active, perhaps they could provide a clue as to what the Libyans were up to.

Just prior to 0300 hours, a series of short, encrypted burst transmissions were recorded on a high frequency normally used for command and control. Because they followed a pattern similar to those used by Libyan forces before, and since the point of origin of the initiating signal was near Tripoli, the recording was sent on to headquarters for analysis. A hasty analysis forwarded by the intelligence officer at the collection and monitoring station indicated that the second station, though not accurately located, appeared to be somewhere to the east, possibly within Egypt itself. It would be another twelve hours before this recording and its hasty analysis were received and reviewed by electronic warfare officers at the Western Military District headquarters. Six more hours would lapse before another copy, recorded at a different collection and monitoring station, provided enough data to accurately pinpoint the transmission. Its location was just west of Cairo.

Cairo West, Egypt * 1545 Hours, 7 December

The distant beating of helicopter blades through the hot desert air announced the arrival of the Egyptian helicopters. Cerro stood, adjusted his gear, and called out, "Mount up!"

The men began to stir, standing up, like their commander, and adjusting their gear. Cerro turned and surveyed his company, already divided up into small groups and spread out at fifty-meter intervals off to one side of a dirt landing strip. In less than a minute, the Egyptian MI-8 helicopters would touch down, one on each of the international orange panels staked into the ground opposite each of Cerro's small groups. On signal from the crew chief of each helicopter, the groups of soldiers, crouching low to avoid the helicopter's blades and the driving sand thrown up by the blades, would sprint out to the helicopter and climb in. Once the last man was in, each helicopter would, in its turn, lift off, circle to the west, and form up into formation. The drill that B Company, 1st of the 506th Airborne was about to execute had been practiced, and practiced, and practiced, to the point where the helicopter crews and the soldiers could do it in their sleep in the middle of a moonless night. As with all such exercises, the men looked forward to doing it this time, for they knew that, regardless of the results, it would be the last time they would have to do it. This was, after all, show time.

As Cerro watched, he counted the helicopters. There were ten choppers, enough for his unit and two backups just in case one or more experienced a maintenance failure en route to the pickup zone. If there was a maintenance failure between the PZ and the landing zone, one of the spare helicopters would touch down, police up the squad of soldiers, and join the assault. This contingency had been practiced several times and had actually occurred once during one of the many rehearsals.

As soon as the lead helicopter touched down and the side door slid open, Cerro was on his feet and headed for the aircraft, his command group behind him. They were in a hurry. The sooner they were in the helicopter, the sooner they would be out of the manmade dust storm being kicked up by the helicopters. As before, each man scrambled for his seat, buckled in, and clamped his weapon between his knees with the muzzle pointed down. The Egyptian crew chief watched as each paratrooper did so, ensuring that each man was in his place and secure. When the last man was in and set, he turned toward the pilot, gave him the signal that all was ready, then strapped himself in. The whole process, from touchdown to skids up, took less than thirty seconds.

Once in the air, Cerro could relax. For the next five minutes there was nothing he could do to influence anything. He and his company were at the mercy of the helicopter pilots. It was their job to get them where B Company needed to go. Once they were on the ground again, there would be a flurry of activity— a scramble as men deployed and the initiation of the live fire exercise. Cerro, like his men, looked forward to the end of this exercise. Its completion would be the signal to begin preparation for redeployment.

As if on cue, the helicopters bearing the two presidents, their entourage, and the security personnel responsible for the immediate security of the VIP party touched down on the landing pad marked with three orange panels in the shape of an H. Unlike the helicopters dispatched to pick up Cerro's company, these helicopters immediately began to shut down their engines. No one approached until the huge blades of the Mark II Commandos stopped spinning. Thus the VIPs would not be peppered by the sand that pelted those awaiting them on the ground.

From a distance Dixon watched in amusement. The show no longer belonged to him or to Colonel Hafez. Other officers, "better" suited to handle such matters, had been flown in and were now in charge. Both Hafez and Dixon, relegated to secondary roles, sat in an Egyptian army jeep behind the platform, out of sight and, if all went well, out of mind. Their purpose now was to monitor, via tactical FM radio, the progress of all the various elements participating in the demonstration. From here on in the operation was supposed to happen automatically in accordance with the master time line, just as they had rehearsed it. If, however, something went wrong, if someone missed his cue or was delayed, Hafez or Dixon would be able to react and issue appropriate instructions to recover from the error.

Dixon watched Jan Fields and her TV crew jockey for position to his right. They too had rehearsed. Their movements shadowed those of the VIPs, who, ever mindful of the press, dutifully ignored the TV crew with their best profiles showing. Once the presidents were in place, the briefings began. One camera crew taped the briefings, given in Egyptian and English, and the reaction of the VIPs. To one side of the platform, where there was a view of the action, Jan Fields stood with a second camera crew. That crew would tape the actual demonstration and Jan as she made comments. Hundreds of feet of videotape would be shot and turned over to Fay Dixon. Her task, to be done in a matter of hours, would be to oversee and direct the cutting and splicing of the tape and commentary into a nice, neat, and meaningful twenty-second news blurb that told an important, world-shaking story.

The screech of four jets, two Egyptian Mirage 2000EMs and two American F-16s, followed by the rumble of bombs impacting several thousand meters from the platform, announced the beginning of the demonstration. Even before the last of the reverberations of the explosions had ceased, the beating of approaching helicopter blades could be heard from the southwest. At the same instant, Dixon heard the distant rumble of artillery, followed by the impact of their high explosive shells. Looking at his watch, he turned to Colonel Hafez. "Well, it's show time."

Hafez acknowledged Dixon's comment with only a nod and a faint smile before he turned away and scanned the vehicle parking area. Dixon watched for a moment as Hafez continued to glance from the vehicle parking area to the road leading to it. He seemed to be nervous, jumpy and on edge, almost as if he were looking for something. But for what? Everything seemed to be in place. Hafez's men, located in pairs along the road at a checkpoint leading into the vehicle parking area and at strategic points overlooking the whole area, were up and alert. The four fighter-bombers had come and gone. Dixon monitored the order to lift and shift the artillery fires to the next target given by the fire support officer to the gun batteries. The first wave of helicopters was about to touch down and disgorge their human cargo. The tank company commander who would rush forward and relieve the paratroopers was on the radio, awaiting his cue. All seemed to be in order. The operation was unfolding as planned and rehearsed. Dixon could not understand why the colonel was so tense.

He was about to lean over and ask Hafez what the problem was when he caught a glimpse of movement along the road leading to the parking area. He settled back into his seat and turned to watch the dust cloud that grew on the horizon. For a moment, Dixon couldn't imagine who that could be. He glanced around to the front and watched as several of the security personnel accompanying the presidents also alerted to the approaching vehicles. One of them cocked his head to one side to speak into microphones to report the sighting.

Dixon turned back to watch the approaching vehicles. Picking up a pair of binoculars, he focused the lenses and trained them on the lead vehicle. They were jeeps. Since no U.S. units in country had the old style jeeps, these had to be Egyptian army. Dixon continued to track the jeeps as they came closer and clearer. As they turned toward the platform, a momentary glimpse of a blue light and white markings was enough to identify them as military police. Okay, Dixon thought, the standby escort in case the presidential party has to travel by land. A quick scan of the parking area showed that there were no MP vehicles there. In all the last-minute confusion, no one had double-checked to see if the backups were on station. Well, no harm done. They were here now. No wonder the colonel was so uptight, Dixon thought. He's probably the only guy that noticed they were missing.

Turning to talk to Hafez, Dixon stopped. Expecting to see a relieved man, Dixon was surprised to see Hafez get out of their vehicle, his face frozen in a dark, solemn mask as he watched the two jeeps continue their approach. It dawned upon Dixon that something was wrong—but what? What the hell is going on? Dixon's attention was diverted by a call on the radio from the American artillery officer, who announced that one of the guns had just had a hang fire and they were unable to clear the gun.

The moment was here. There would be no more delays, no more lies, no hiding. Colonel Hafez had to decide, right now, in the next thirty seconds, if he was a patriot or a—or a what? If he allowed the Libyan commandos to perform their tasks, what would he be? A martyr? A traitor? A rebel? What?

As he watched the jeeps approach the checkpoint at the parking area, he saw one of his men begin to lift the pole barrier to prepare to allow the jeeps to enter. Suddenly Hafez was incensed. The order he had issued to all of his men was that all vehicles and personnel entering the area were to be stopped and checked. Those were his own orders, and now his men were about to violate them. In his moment of crisis, it hit Hafez that the one thing he would not be if he allowed the Libyans in was a soldier—a soldier trained to obey and defend. In a flash he reached into the vehicle, grabbed the hand mike that was being used for administrative command and control, and called the sergeant at the checkpoint. Without waiting for acknowledgment, Hafez ordered him to close the pole barrier and check the identity of all personnel in the two jeeps as he had been ordered to.

Holding the hand mike to his mouth, ready to broadcast his next message, Hafez stood there and watched. He could see the sergeant call out to the soldier at the pole barrier. There was a moment of confusion, then hesitation before the soldier dropped the barrier down and unslung his rifle. The lead jeep, expecting to be waved through, had to break fast, fishtailing as it came to a stop in a cloud of dust just before the barrier.

The squeal of the jeep's brakes caused Dixon to turn his head in the direction of the checkpoint. He glanced at Hafez, who stood with the radio mike to his mouth, staring in the direction of the checkpoint. Dixon, not knowing what was happening, also turned and watched the checkpoint. The sergeant there approached the lead jeep while the soldier who had been opening the barrier stood to the other side, rifle at port arms. The sergeant could be seen stooping over and sticking his head into the jeep as if to talk to the passenger in the front seat.

The unexpected muzzle flash, the image of the sergeant's body flying backwards, and the belated crack of rifle fire totally bewildered Dixon. *"Colonel, what the fuck is going—"*

Dixon was cut short by a volley of fire from the second jeep, which cut down the soldier standing at the barrier. The first jeep gunned its engine, then literally jumped forward, crashing through the pole barrier. Without hesitation, Hafez threw down the radio hand mike, drew his pistol, and began to run toward the vehicle parking area, waving and calling to several of his men to follow him.

Dixon grabbed the hand mike on the American control net, called out the code word that an emergency was in progress, and, like Hafez, drew his pistol and began to run in the direction of the two jeeps, now approaching the platform at full tilt.

In the excitement of the moment, Dixon's call over the radio was missed by most of the people on the net. At the artillery battery, all attention was turned to processing the next fire mission, which for a peacetime operation was close. Cerro and his men, in hastily prepared positions, watched as ten Egyptian tanks rolled from around the side of a hill and deployed into line, firing over their heads as they went. Only the Air Force forward air controller caught the call; but, wanting confirmation, he called for Dixon to repeat the message. Dixon, now gone from the radio, failed to respond. Unfamiliar with the habits of Army types, the Air Force major let it drop. Besides, with two F-16s rolling in for an attack in less than sixty seconds, he didn't have the time to mess with the administrative control net.

The VIPs and the other spectators watched and listened as the two brigade commanders explained in detail the drama unfolding before them, blissfully unaware of the one developing to their rear. All except Representative Ed Lewis. The crack of an AK assault rifle firing to his rear caused him to start. Craning his neck around, Lewis attempted to determine what was going on. No one had mentioned anything about Egyptian infantry, the only ones armed with the AK-47, participating in the demonstration. The only thing the Egyptians should have been firing at that time was tanks. Almost instinctively Lewis knew something was going on, but he couldn't determine what it was.

Turning back to the front, he noticed the colonel next to him giving him a strange look. He was about to ask him about the firing but decided not to. The firing had stopped. If something was wrong, there were people paid to handle it. Besides, no one else seemed to be excited. The last thing Lewis wanted was to make an ass of himself in front of so many Army types.

Instead, he watched the Egyptian tanks, now visible from the platform for the first time.

Jan was looking into the camera, commenting on the amount of training and coordination that an exercise like the one then occurring required. The popping of small arms fire from the parking area was masked by the crash of impacting artillery rounds behind her. In the middle of one of Jan's sentences, one of the British camera crewmen turned and yelled, "Jesus! Those bloody bastards back there are really killing each other!"

Angry that someone had interrupted her shot, Jan was about to lash the offender with a stream of obscenities when she saw Hafez and Dixon, pistols drawn and followed by Egyptian soldiers, running away from the platform. With her view masked by a slight rise, she called out, "What's going on down there?"

There was no response. The camera crew, veterans of Northern Ireland and Lebanon, had already turned and were running toward the unfolding drama, cameras rolling. They did not answer Jan. She stood there for a second before it dawned upon her that something big was going down. She wasn't sure what was happening but ran to join the camera crews anyhow, driven by one thought: ASSASSINATION ATTEMPT ON THE PRESIDENT OF THE UNITED STATES. FILM AND STORY BY JAN FIELDS AT ELEVEN.

Once through the barrier, the two jeeps separated, one headed for each side of the platform where the two presidents, still unaware of the danger they faced, continued to watch the demonstration. Dixon saw Hafez peel off and head for the jeep on the left, the one that had been the lead. Dixon veered off to the right and ran for the second one. As he did so, it suddenly dawned upon him that he had no idea what he intended to do. One man and a pistol against a jeep full of terrorists did not seem like an even match. Without stopping, Dixon glanced over his shoulder to see if he was being followed.

To his relief, there were two of Hafez's men coming up

behind him. Dixon waved his pistol toward the second jeep and yelled to them in Arabic, "COME—FOLLOW!" At least he hoped that he had said that. The effect was immediate as the two soldiers quickened their pace in an effort to catch up with Dixon.

Confident that he now had enough firepower to do something, Dixon locked all his attention onto the approaching jeep. The scene before him now began to unfold in slow motion. The images that ran through his mind were like a series of snapshots instead of a steady stream of events: the glare of the sun on the jeep's windshield, the arm holding an assault rifle out of the passenger side of the jeep, the flash of that rifle firing, the cloud of dust and flying dirt. They all flashed through Dixon's mind as he rushed to place himself and his two followers between the jeep and the platform to his rear.

Satisfied that he and his two Egyptian soldiers were in as good a spot as they were going to get, he stopped. His two followers came up to his side and also stopped. No sooner had they done so than rifle fire from the jeep cut down the soldier to his left. Dixon knew it was time. Do or die. He lowered his pistol and then, in English, yelled "Fire!"

The surviving Egyptian soldier to his right did nothing. Shit! Dixon thought. How do you say "shoot" in Arabic? He had no idea. Nor did he have any more time to think. The jeep was less than one hundred meters away and closing fast. All he could do now was fire himself and hope the Egyptian soldier would follow his lead.

Holding his pistol with both hands, Dixon stood before the onrushing jeep, feet spread shoulders' width apart. Fifty meters. Dixon, blinded by the glare of the sun off the jeep's windshield, aimed at where he thought the driver should be, then began to fire. After his second round the Egyptian joined in.

Dixon never did find out who actually killed the driver. The body had both 9mm and 7.62mm bullets in it. What did matter was that the driver, hit several times, cut the wheel and rolled the jeep, killing all on board. Even as the jeep tumbled and rolled, Dixon remembered, he continued to follow it, firing into the wreckage. He fired until he had emptied the magazine of his Beretta. His Egyptian companion also fired until he had expended all thirty rounds in his AK-47. When he had done so, the two of them merely stood there, aiming their empty weapons at the wrecked jeep. Past them rushed security men and other soldiers. It was only after one of the American Secret Service men at the jeep shouted out that all the terrorists were dead that Dixon let the arm holding his pistol fall to his side. Suddenly winded and shaking from the burst of activity and rush of adrenaline, Dixon turned to walk away from the jeep. Instead, he walked right into the lens of a camera.

Their eyes locked together for a moment. Neither Hafez nor Sadiq spoke. What was there to say? Pinned under the overturned jeep, Sadiq stared at his former Brother, now holding a pistol to his head. He had lost. He had lost everything. He closed his eyes as he felt himself slipping into unconsciousness. Then he realized that he had not lost all. At least he had his soul. In a few seconds he would be a martyr. All that he had done, he had done in the name of God, the one God, the true God. And now, as always, he was in the hands of his God. With his last breath he called out ''Allah Akbar, Allah Akbar''—God is great, God is great.

Sadiq never heard the report of Hafez's pistol. Nor did he feel any pain.

7

The urge to gain release from tension by action is a precipitating cause of war.

—B. H. LIDDELL HART

Headquarters, CENTCOM * 2130 Hours, 7 December

The staff officers that comprised the core of the CENTCOM crisis action team, or CAT, were used to dealing with situations that suddenly cropped up out of nowhere. The assassination attempt on the two presidents was no different. Although they were supported by the most sophisticated intelligence network in the world, the officers' ability to project what would happen in the future was still, at best, guesswork.

Information gathered from many sources is dumped on a handful of people every day, three hundred sixty-five days a year. These people, called analysts, have the task of sorting through the glut of data they are given and putting together an intelligence summary that can be used by those who make the plans and decisions. The problem is that there is a tremendous amount of raw data available. It is impossible for a small group of people, let alone one person, to see and digest all the information available. Therefore, a system of screening and compartmenting this information as it comes in is used. Some of it is never forwarded because it does not fit an established criterion. Some, because it concerns only one military service or is gathered and used by nonuniform intelligence agencies such as the CIA and FBI, is sent to that service for handling. Even after the initial screening and sorting takes place, the analyst must still pick those items that he deems to be important based on the current situation as it exists or as he projects it will be. The final product, a summary at best, is based on many factors: the nature of the situation, the training and experience of the analyst, his personal biases and view of the world, and the information and guidance given to him for sorting through the data.

General Horn reviewed the revised intelligence summary, less than two hours old, and clearly saw, through 20-20 hindsight, how they had missed calling this one. With so many of the limited intelligence assets in the region oriented on the Soviet deployment and the joint Soviet-Cuban-Libyan exercise, one seemingly insignificant man easily slipped by. The report started with a summary of sightings of a known Egyptian extremist, Muhammad Sadiq. A terrorist who had learned his trade in Lebanon, Sadiq had become a prominent leader in the pan-Arabian fundamentalist movement and, with connections in the Egyptian military, was considered to be a dangerous man. He was spotted in Tripoli, Libya, on 12 November after being out of sight for six months. The CIA tracked him: he was next seen in Cairo on 15 November, then on 29 November at the international airport in Rome, transferring from a plane just arriving from Tripoli to one headed for Cairo. After that, he fell out of sight again until today, when his body was identified by the Egyptian military at Cairo West. The CIA had shared this information with the Egyptian Government but not with CENTCOM, since it was a CIA and FBI matter that did not concern the military.

The next item in the summary described the increased readiness status of Libyan air defense search radars. Both the U.S. 6th Fleet and the U.S. Air Force operating out of Italy had monitored the increased activity by Libyan air defense not associated with the Soviet-Libyan exercise and forwarded their findings, separately, to the U.S. European Command; sanitized versions of the summary were provided to the Italian military, but not the Egyptian military. Because this information was strictly military in nature, it was not immediately passed to the CIA.

The final item, provided by the Egyptian military, identified three of the terrorists killed in the aborted assassination attempt as Libyan. Evidence to corroborate this claim, including a picture of one of the men standing with the Libyan head of state, was enclosed.

There was no doubt in General Horn's mind that the Egyptians were doing their damnedest to build a case against Libya. He had four questions that needed to be answered, and he put them to his crisis action team. First, why were the Egyptians building a case against the Libyans? Second, what would the Egyptians do if and when they blamed Libya? Third, what immediate actions, if any, should U.S. forces in the region take? Fourth, what actions, if any, would the Soviet and Cuban forces in Libya take?

Though there were no immediate threats to the American President or to U.S. forces, the presence of U.S. forces in Egypt and Soviet/Cuban forces in Libya were factors that complicated the entire situation. If the United States unilaterally withdrew its forces, it might send a false signal to both the Libyans and other terrorist groups, as well as to the Soviets. In doing so, it would present the image of a nation easily frightened by acts of terrorism and willing to abandon a friend. Such a move would also allow the Soviets a free hand to use its forces to influence the situation as it saw fit. Finally, if the Egyptians retaliated and the U.S. forces were left in place, it would appear that the United States was sanctioning the actions of Egypt—actions that the United States might not be able to control—and was prepared to back Egypt, even if it meant confrontation with the Soviets. Any way he and his staff looked at it, Horn came up with a no-win situation for the United States, unless both the Americans and the Soviets could defuse the situation and quietly draw down their own forces simultaneously.

Horn put the summary down, leaned back in his chair, and turned to his operations officer. "Jim, where is the President now?"

Opening a folder that contained a revised itinerary, the operations officer looked at his watch, then down the list. "He should be having dinner with the ambassador right now. The Egyptian president was to have been in attendance but excused himself."

His face still expressionless, Horn turned to his intelligence officer. "What about troop movements? Any reported activity on either side of the border in the Western Desert?"

The intelligence officer replied without referring to his notes. "Movements? No, not yet. But the entire Western Military District is on full alert, with the rest at a higher state of readiness. Air Force personnel have been recalled from leave. In addition, six guided missile boats and one frigate left Alexandria less than two hours ago. Libya has taken similar measures. Forces involved in the joint Soviet-Cuban-Libyan exercise have stood down and commenced redeployment to assembly areas south and west of Tobruk. Right now, each side has only a handful of aircraft and vessels in position and ready to pounce. We do not, however, have any indication that they will. Neither side appears to be really ready to do anything substantial."

Leaning forward, Horn continued his interrogation of his intelligence officer. "Okay, Edgar, I want your no-bullshit best guess what you expect to see happen in the next forty-eight to ninety-six hours."

For a moment there was silence. Then the intelligence officer answered, carefully considering his words. "I expect that the Egyptians will begin by building a case against the Libyans via the media. The photos and information on Sadiq provided to us is just the beginning—probably an attempt to get us to help spread the hue and cry. While the PR campaign is building, the Western Military District will be quietly reinforced, probably from units of the 1st Army. When world opinion has been sufficiently whipped up in their favor, the Egyptians will move."

The intelligence officer stood up and walked over to a map on the wall. Picking up a wooden pointer hanging from a string next to the map, he continued, pointing to the locations as he spoke. "I expect some type of limited retaliation, much like what the Egyptians did in 1978. I see ground forces striking out at the Kufra Oasis and occupying it for several days before withdrawing. In the north, I see a combination of ground attack and commando operations aimed at destroying or damaging the oil fields at Sarir, Awjiah, Natora, Gialo, and Harash. We can expect naval operations along the coast, either limited landings or perhaps commando operations, aimed at destroying the refinery at Tubra, which we call Tobruk. It will take the Egyptians five days to stage their forces, four to five to do what they want, then three to pull back and dig in on their own side of the wire fence." Putting the pointer back onto its hook, the intelligence officer turned to Horn. "If we see no movement of 1st Army units in the next forty-eight hours, odds are the Egyptians will do nothing. If, however, they begin to move, the first crossing of the border will occur within ninety-six hours from that time."

Horn thought about that for a moment. "Why the 1st Army? Why not the 2nd Army? That's Egypt's best equipped and best led."

The intelligence officer pointed to Israel on the map with his finger. "Despite the Camp David agreement and years of peace, Israel is still seen as Egypt's greatest and most immediate threat. If the retaliation against Libya is only going to be a punitive raid, then it would be foolish, militarily and economically, to expose their rear by removing forces from the Sinai and moving all that equipment the entire length of Egypt. It would be much cheaper and put far less wear and tear on the equipment if units of the 1st Army are used. Also, the combat service support for the units in the Sinai are all layered to support operations in the east, not the west." The intelligence officer paused for a moment to allow Horn to consider what he had just said. "Having said that, if there is a sudden flurry of diplomatic exchanges between Egypt and Israel before Egypt begins to move any of its forces, then we may see movement of units from the Sinai to the Western Desert. That movement would mean a major war, not just a raid."

"Tell me, Edgar, what are the odds that Egypt will go into Libya with the aim of ripping that little shit's heart out?"

"Almost none. Simply put, unless we provide them with tremendous amounts of logistical support, or they are willing to mortgage their entire economy, Egypt lacks the ability to over-run Libya. Besides, there are the Soviets. The Soviets don't have to lift a finger to stop the Egyptians. If they simply sit astride the coastal road—say, there at Ayn Al Ghazalah—with the forces they currently have in country, they'll keep the Egyptians from moving any further west."

With a nod Horn signaled to the intelligence officer that he was finished.

For a moment there was silence in the room while the CAT staff considered what the intelligence officer had just said. This silence was broken by the operations officer. "General, if the Egyptians do move, what do we do with our people in country? They are right there, sitting between Cairo, where the 1st Army units will move from, and the border. Do we pull the plug and run, or stand fast?"

Leaning back into his chair, Horn stared at the ceiling and considered that question before answering. Without turning his gaze from the ceiling, he mumbled, almost to himself, "That, my boy, is a political decision—one that's going to be made by someone with more horsepower than you or I, thank God."

Sitting upright in his chair, then standing in one motion, Horn brought the meeting to an end. There was much that needed to be done. Although his staff didn't know it yet, the chairman of the Joint Chiefs of Staff had given him a warning to be prepared to fly to Egypt with a small staff to assume control of a military operation if the National Security Council opted for one. Until that happened, all he and his people could do was wait and watch.

Cairo West, Egypt * 2145 Hours, 7 December

The tension that hung in the air in the 3rd Brigade's assembly areas was oppressive. While details concerning the assassination attempt were at best sketchy, the proximity of the brigade to the incident and the involvement of American forces in the attack caused a great deal of excitement. The exercise was terminated and the entire brigade was ordered to move back into assembly areas. Once there, the troops were placed on full alert. Orders went out that no Egyptian personnel, military or civilian, was to be allowed into a U.S. area unless in the company of a U.S. Army officer. Even then, the U.S. officer had to identify himself and have his identity verified by the unit intelligence officer.

As he walked back from chow to the area where his platoon was located, Staff Sergeant Maxwell was pelted with questions from his men. Were they going home? Were they going to be issued more ammunition? What had really happened? Was the U.S. at war? And if so, against whom? A veteran of the war in Iran, Maxwell knew that a lack of information bred fear; rumors and imagination ran wild. They were at the lowest end of the information chain, a tank crew was on the cutting edge. Maxwell knew that it was not that the higher-ups wanted to keep the men in the dark. The problem was that since only so much can go down, at each level the information is refined, strained, and reworked, and by the time a tank commander hears something, only that information necessary to accomplish the given operation is provided. Even in the task force in which he had fought during the Iranian war, Maxwell was seldom told anything other than to move to such-and-such a place and orient to a certain direction. There was definitely no information glut in Maxwell's platoon.

As he came to the last tank position, the man on guard challenged him. After giving the proper password to the soldier's challenge, Maxwell walked up to the young man and asked if he had seen or heard anything. Private Willie B. Graddy from Atlanta, Georgia, shook his head, said no, then asked what he should be looking out for. Maxwell sighed, then simply responded, "Anything or any person that don't speak or understand English. And if they do but speak it with an accent, let me know."

Graddy, half seriously, asked if that included Sergeant Yermo. Maxwell, fighting the urge to whop the soldier up the side of the head for being so stupid, simply replied no, that did not include Sergeant Yermo. Graddy, he knew, was confused, nervous, and concerned. None of them knew for sure what was happening or what the next day would bring. It was, Maxwell said to himself, Iran all over again.

The crunching of sand under boots caught Maxwell's attention. He moved up next to Graddy, putting one hand on Graddy's shoulder and signaling him to be still with the other hand. The two men stood motionless, staring into the darkness, watching and listening. There was silence. Whoever had been moving was now also stationary. Taking his hand from Graddy's shoulder, Maxwell slowly reached down, unsnapped his holster, and carefully drew his pistol. With his arm bent at the elbow and the pistol pointed up, Maxwell carefully cocked the pistol's hammer with his thumb as he continued to scan the darkness. Taking his cue from his platoon sergeant, Graddy brought his M-16 up to the ready and flipped the safety to fire.

From the darkness a voice thundered, "Okay, bang! You're both dead. Now I get to send your miserable bodies back in a flag-draped box." The voice belonged to their task force commander, Lieutenant Colonel Vennelli. Releasing the hammer of his pistol back to the safe position, Maxwell put the pistol back into its holster and awaited an ass chewing—something that, according to the men of the task force, was Vennelli's favorite sport. Maxwell didn't have long to wait.

"It doesn't do us a damned bit of good having guards posted if a goddamn blind elephant with a roaring case of hemorrhoids can come crashing in here without being challenged!" Maxwell grunted. For some reason Vennelli thought he was funny. Maxwell didn't mind being corrected when he was wrong. He didn't mind being dumped on when he had screwed up. He did, however, get bent out of shape when those above him used ridicule and mockery as a means of correcting their soldiers. He felt his men were good soldiers and should be treated as such. He also believed that the men in his platoon were just that—men, men who deserved to be treated better. Unfortunately, that philosophy was no longer in style in the task force. It was almost as if every officer in the unit wanted to top the task force commander in the number and severity of ass chewings. There were a few exceptions, but very few. Vennelli's foul mouth and abusive manner, coupled with an ego that could fill a county, had made working for him during this operation a miserable experience.

For the next five minutes Maxwell and Graddy endured a tongue lashing that did nothing but give Vennelli the satisfaction that somehow he was doing his job of beating his unit into shape. When he was finished, Vennelli turned and walked into the darkness. Graddy watched him disappear, then turned to Maxwell. "What a shithead."

Barely able to contain his own anger, Maxwell looked at Graddy. "Regardless of what you think, soldier, that man is your superior ranking officer. I will not have men in my platoon calling officers shitheads. Is that clear?"

Confused, Graddy stuttered for a moment. "But, Sarge, that man—"

Cutting him off, Maxwell continued. "No buts! The man is an officer and he is our commander. You will not call him 'shithead,' 'moron,' 'idiot,' or anything else other than 'sir' in my presence. Is that understood, Graddy?"

Graddy shook his head. "No, I don't understand, Sarge, but I'll do what you say."

"Good. Now carry on." Turning, Maxwell began to march off, thinking over and over that Graddy was right—the man was a shithead. Then Maxwell stopped, turned back to Graddy, and called out, "And for Christ's sake, challenge anything that moves. If it don't answer, shoot."

Cairo, Egypt * 2201 Hours, 7 December

The staff of the WNN Cairo Bureau, standing in front of a bank of TV monitors, watched copies of the news story WNN and five news teams from other networks had fed back to the States. Half a dozen national news programs in the U.S. would be opening their nightly news broadcasts with the footage of the assassination attempt that Jan Fields and her British camera crew had taped less than seven hours before. All the news commentators, faces fixed in grave masks of concern, spoke in deep monotones of how terrorism had again raised its ugly head. Fortunately for their viewers, they cut quickly to the tape, which all dubbed "dramatic and harrowing" after warning their viewers that the clip contained scenes of violence. In quick succession, Jan Fields was plastered across all the TV monitors in the room.

The clip started with her introduction and selected shots of the VIPs arriving, the live fire exercise as it progressed, and an occasional comment by Fields. Suddenly, in the middle of one of her comments, the scene became blurred as the camera was jerked away from the exercise and Fields toward the rear of the reviewing stands. When the camera stopped and refocused, it did so on two Egyptian army jeeps charging for the reviewing stands. The scene was jumbled as the cameramen ran closer. Despite the distortion, however, the TV viewers could clearly see two figures, one dressed in the camouflage uniform worn by the U.S. Army, pistols drawn, run toward the charging jeeps. These figures, followed by Egyptian soldiers, stopped and began to fire at the jeeps. A zoom to the jeep on the left showed a terrorist hanging out of it, firing his automatic rifle. The camera remained fixed on this jeep until it made a sharp turn to the right, then rolled over several times.

Not waiting for it to stop, the camera jerked over to the jeep on the right. The second jeep continued to charge. Panning back, the camera caught three men standing in the path of the jeep. Focusing in on them, the camera watched as one of the three was thrown back by the impact of rounds hitting him. The other two, one of them the man in the U.S. Army uniform, leveled their weapons and began to fire. Like the first jeep, the second one suddenly jerked to one side, then rolled over. The camera stayed on it for a moment before panning back and forth from one jeep to the other as more soldiers ran up and searched the wreckage. There was a slight pause; then the tape continued. This time the man in the American uniform was in front of the camera, the rank of a lieutenant colonel visible on his collar. He was still panting as if he had just finished a run. In his right hand, ready for use, was his 9mm pistol. He glanced from side to side, looking at one jeep, then the other, then toward the reviewing stands. When he saw the camera watching him, he waved his left hand in front of it, motioning it to cut. The camera crew did not leave him until he turned his back on it and walked away.

The crowd in the newsroom commented on or exclaimed at the quality of the camera work. Despite the speed of the action and the distance involved, the TV viewers could see everything, from the bloodstained body of the Egyptian soldier at the American colonel's feet to the colonel's name tag. Fay Dixon, however, didn't need exceptional camera work to be able to recognize her husband. She could have picked him out of a crowd of American officers wearing the same uniform.

She had overseen the editing of the tape before it was fed to the WNN home office. Even though she had reviewed it a half a dozen times already and knew every inch of it, every word, the image of her husband standing there, pistol in hand and a body at his feet, still sent a shiver up her spine. It was hard for Fay to relate the figure she had seen blasting away in the tape, killing real people, to the man with whom she shared a bed. Though she knew Scott was a soldier, and a veteran, Fay had always been able to conveniently ignore that aspect of her husband's life. The tape of the shooting, however, rubbed her nose in it. Inch by bloody inch ran past her eyes as she edited it, burning images in her mind of her husband placing himself in danger with seemingly careless abandon while taking other men's lives. Though she tried to be rational and professional about what she was doing, the fact that it was Scott bothered her as nothing ever had before.

Standing alone against the back wall, Fay watched the TV monitors and the rest of the staff. When the spot on the assassination attempt was finished, the monitors went blank. The WNN staff, as one, turned to Jan Fields and applauded. Watching them push and shove to get close to Jan, Fay felt real anger and hatred. What bothered her, however, was that she was unsure whom she was angry at. Was she mad at Jan for building a career on the death and misery of others? Or was she mad at Scott, for the casual manner in which he placed himself in harm's way?

She was still mulling over her feelings when Jan, breaking free from her admirers, came up, grabbed Fay by the shoulders, gave her a hug, and announced to the others that without a great producer like Fay, a reporter was nothing. Caught off guard, Fay looked about as the others in the room came up to shake her hand or give her a peck on the cheek. Jan Fields stood next to her, arm in arm and all smiles. For the moment, the concerns of the real world disappeared as Fay graciously accepted the warm regards of her fellow workers.

Tripoli, Libya * 2330 Hours, 7 December

The meeting of the General Secretariat had long ago degenerated into a screaming and shouting match as those who had been lukewarm about the operation heaped abuse on those who had pushed it. At the head of the table, the Leader of the Revolution sat calmly, detached from the melee in which his council was engaged. He watched without comment, as accusation and counteraccusation were flung across the table. At the far end, Colonel Nafissi also stood aloof from the fracas, watching the Leader of the Revolution and waiting for the other members of the council to wear themselves out. The only break in the marathon screaming match had come when the council stopped to view a television in the corner of the room. The news program they watched showed the same tape clip around the world. There was no need for Nafissi to become involved in the petty war of words. Those of the council who supported him were more than holding their own against those who supported the Leader.

For a moment Nafissi pictured the council as nothing but pawns in a great chess game between himself and the Leader. Everyone knew who had the power and who were the mouthpieces. There would be much shifting of power as a result of the failed plot. An astute politician had much to gain if he made the right moves and was ruthless. Nafissi was ruthless; no one doubted that. What remained to be seen was whether or not he could make the right moves.

Tiring of the squabbles, the Leader of the Revolution sat up and, with the wave of a hand, brought silence to the council chamber. "We have solved nothing. Were we in the desert, your hot air would have blown away all the sand. What we have not discussed is what we will do now. As we have seen, the Egyptians are building a campaign of hate and falsehoods against us. No doubt, once they have convinced the world that we were responsible, they will use this excuse to strike at us and destroy not only us but what we stand for. With the fall of Iran, we are the last true defenders of the faith. What we do is therefore critical not only to the survival of our people but also to all those who truly believe. As the chief of staff of the armed forces, what do you propose to do now, Colonel Nafissi?"

There was silence as all eyes shifted from the Leader of the Revolution to Nafissi. All waited to see if Nafissi would pounce and attack, defending his decision directly and giving the Leader a retort, or ignore the comment about the "failure" and bide his time. Nafissi thought about his options, carefully guarding against any show of emotion. Deciding that now was not the time or place, he did not push. Instead, he simply reported the status of his military forces and what actions he had taken to safeguard the state and the council against retaliation by the Egyptians. "We continue to maintain our vigilance in the Western Desert. Air defense forces are fully alert and interceptors on standby. A flotilla of missile boats has been dispatched from Tobruk to find and shadow Egyptian naval forces that were reported headed west toward our territorial waters. If the Egyptians begin a buildup of forces in their Western Military District, we will implement our mobilization plans."

As if watching a tennis match, all eyes shifted back to the Leader of the Revolution to see what he would say next. The two antagonists, their eyes locked, considered their next move. The Leader spoke first. "And if the Egyptians do strike, how far do we let them go? You know as well as I that we cannot do any more than delay the Egyptians if they wish to attack in force."

Nafissi leaned back and smiled. ''Yes—alone, we cannot stop them. But we are not alone.''

''The Soviets have no desire to commit their forces. Their ambassador has already informed me that their ground forces are being withdrawn into assembly areas where they will wait for redeployment.''

Nafissi continued. ''The Russians cannot be allowed to leave. They have on many occasions pledged their support. While none of us can, in our hearts, forgive them for what they did to our brothers in Iran, we must overlook that in our time of crisis. Instead, we must do as the Egyptians themselves did: use them. When it fits our need, we will invite them in, take their equipment, and accept their advisors and troops. When it no longer suits our needs, we will send them home. Right now, we need them. So long as they are here, the United States will restrain the Egyptians. Even if Soviet ground and air units do not actively participate in combat, the Egyptians dare not confront them. We must keep the Soviets here, regardless of whether they help us or not.''

''How do you propose we do that, my friend?''

Pointing to the television in the corner, Nafissi smiled. ''The American and European media is already doing that for us. We must play upon the Soviets' fear of losing influence and face in this region and world. So long as the American forces are in Egypt, the Soviets must stay. So long as the Soviets stay, the Americans must stay. With their forces near at hand, any confrontation will be limited in size of forces used and area of operation. With American forces west of Alexandria and the Soviets west of Tobruk, their mere presence will ensure that the conflict remains limited and controllable.

''The Europeans will also assist us in limiting the war. Fearful that any type of confrontation involving the U.S. and the Soviets will end their cherished glasnost, they will exert pressure on the U.S. to defuse the confrontation. With luck, if the Egyptians are foolish enough to attack, we can avenge the defeats we suffered in 1977 by meeting whatever limited force they use to retaliate head-to-head, on equal terms. A defeat in open battle for the Egyptian forces, regardless of how small the force, would open the doors for a campaign to discredit their government. In the ensuing chaos, opportunities would abound.''

The Leader of the Revolution thought about Nafissi's proposal. ''Why would the Russians continue to support our efforts? While we may be able to fool some that what happened in Egypt today was not our doing, the Russians know. Besides, there is the chance that the Americans will come to the aid of the Egyptians. The American President, after all, was nearly assassinated. They have attacked us in the past for less. It would be all too easy for the American fleet in the Mediterranean to lock out further Russian support. Their Air Force will throw a shield over us that no one will penetrate. Under that shield, we, along with the few combat troops the Russians care to sacrifice, will wither away like leaves before the winter wind. How do you propose we neutralize the Americans?''

''We attack the Americans in their own homes through television. There are many antiwar factions in the United States. Properly manipulated, the Americans will be far too divided to take effective action.''

''What you propose, Nafissi, is playing with the devil. If we misjudge, as your people did today, we will be finished.''

Again ignoring the remark about failing, Nafissi continued to smile. ''It is only through great challenges that great things are achieved. Mohammed was only one when he came out of the desert. But he conquered much because he had a pure heart and the fire of the True Faith in him. Egypt is a house of sand. We can scatter it before us and establish ourselves as the rightful leaders of the Arab and Islamic world. Let the Egyptians strike the first blow. Let them pound their chests in feigned righteous indignation. In the end, we will prevail because we are bold and we believe.''

Nafissi leaned back and waited. The members of the council who sat between him and the committee looked at one, then the other, waiting to see who spoke first. Finally, the Leader of the Revolution stood. ''There is much to do. We must go forth into danger with courage and a pure heart. With Allah as our guide, we cannot fail in our noble task.''

As the members of the council left the room, those who were followers of Nafissi looked into his eyes and saw the smile concealed from the rest. They, like him, were prepared to seize victory from the flames of disaster.

Outside, one of his supporters, a frown on his face, approached Nafissi, leaned over to him, and whispered into his ear. "What do we do, my friend, if the Egyptians do not oblige us and strike?"

In the half-moon, a huge smile shone on Nafissi's face. "Have no fear of that, brother. They shall strike. And if they hesitate, we shall encourage them."

Still not convinced, the supporter continued to badger Nafissi. "Encourage them? How?"

"In the night, who is to say which man cast the first stone? Even if foreign intelligence detects our little ploy, it will be our word against theirs. Most Westerners, especially Americans and Europeans, will choose to believe that which they want. If by believing their government, they place themselves in a position where they must do something that is dangerous or expensive, they will ignore it."

"How can you be so sure?"

Tiring of the stream of questions, Nafissi stopped. "My friend, during the 1970s, Americans spent millions trying to save whales and little white furry seals but didn't lift a finger to stop the slaughter of three million Cambodians. Do you really believe that the American public and its Congress will care what happens between two Arab countries?"

Finally convinced, the supporter also began to smile. "Yes, I see. You are right."

Nafissi, glad that the conversation was over, turned and continued to walk. He didn't care whether his man understood what was happening. Only he needed to.

8

When the situation is obscure, attack.

—GENERAL HEINZ GUDERIAN

Over the Mediterranean * 0230 Hours, 8 December

Banking slightly to the left, the pilot of the E-2 Hawkeye AWACS began the northbound leg of his orbit. Cruising at a speed of three hundred miles per hour and at an altitude of twenty-five thousand feet, the E-2 was monitoring air and naval activity off the Egyptian and Libyan coast. The aircraft commander was under strict orders to maintain a position at least two hundred miles from the coast in an effort to keep U.S. personnel and aircraft from becoming involved in a sudden flare-up. Even at that range, however, the APS-125 radar, linked to an advanced radar processing system, was able to monitor everything that flew or floated within a range of three hundred miles. That included a Soviet Ilyushin 76 Mainstay airborne warning and control aircraft operating to the west near Benghazi. Like the Hawkeye, it was watching and reporting.

Inside the Hawkeye, the crew of five went about their tasks. They were three hours into their current mission with sixty minutes to go before being relieved. Though the Hawkeye was capable of being refueled, allowing it to remain on station longer, the crew was ready for a break: unlike the earlier patrol, this one was boring, and their coffee had run out long ago.

After several near-confrontations between Egyptian and Libyan aircraft earlier in the evening, the level of activity had dropped off. Activity in the last three hours had been limited to a flight of two Egyptian fighters that scrambled from the airfield at Mersa Matruh and the sailing of several missile boats. Unlike before, the Libyans did not respond by scrambling their own aircraft. Even when the Egyptian fighters made a high-speed run toward the Libyan border, the Libyans did nothing. Watching the activity, the combat information officer commented dryly that perhaps the Libyans were finally settling down in an effort to defuse the situation. Since the assassination attempt, the leaders of the two countries had been waging a war of words, using the media of the Western world as their battleground. The crew of the Hawkeye didn't mind. So long as the leaders of both countries were throwing words and not making any major movement of troops, ships, or aircraft, the crisis would eventually peter out. It had happened before, and no doubt this incident would be no different.

Though it was not really their assigned task that night, the crew of the Hawkeye continued to track three Egyptian missile boats that had sailed from Mersa Matruh and four Libyan boats from Tobruk. All the boats had left their respective ports at approximately the same time. The commander of the Hawkeye passed that off as a simple coincidence, since their speeds and courses indicated that their departures were not related.

Leaning back in his seat, the radar operator tugged on the sleeve of the air control operator, who had nothing to control, and pointed to the green blips that represented the missile boats. "Five bucks says the Egyptians spot the Libyans first."

The air controller studied the screen for a moment, then said, "You're on."

Off the Coast of Egypt * 0235 Hours, 8 December

From his position on the bridge of the center missile boat, Lieutenant Commander Rashid, Egyptian navy, could see only

175

one of the other two boats in his small flotilla. Their course, which was due west, was taking them toward the imaginary line that divided the Egyptian coastal waters from those of Libya. All three boats were Ramadan class boats armed with four Italian-made Otomat surface-to-surface guided missiles. Two boats, including Rashid's, were running close to the shore. The third was out at sea, riding the line that divided the open sea, or international waters, from the territorial waters of Egypt. Only that boat used its search radars, and then only in short spurts. The idea was to have the boat at sea locate and report any targets to Rashid. If any Libyan patrol boats detected the radar of the Egyptian boat at sea, they would turn and head for it, exposing themselves to the two Egyptian boats running along the coast. Only when he was sure that the Libyan boats were committed and unaware of the two boats running the shore line would Rashid turn on his own search and acquisition radars. That, he reasoned, would surprise the Libyans and cause them to break off their attack.

When Rashid's small flotilla was less than fifty kilometers from Libyan waters, the commander of the boat at sea reported radar contact with four boats that he assumed were Libyan. Like the two Egyptian boats running along the coast, the Libyans did not have their search radars on. For several minutes Rashid maintained his course and speed as he listened to the reports from the boat at sea. After two minutes the electronic warfare operator on Rashid's boat reported that two, then four search radars had been switched on. The source of those search radars was the Libyan boats. They had detected the radar of the Egyptian boat at sea and were now attempting to get an accurate fix on its source. Still, Rashid maintained course and speed, tracking on a chart the locations of the Libyan boats as they were reported.

Calmly, the commander of the boat at sea reported that he had switched his radar on to continuous search and was commencing evasive maneuvers. As planned, that boat changed course from a westerly direction to one running to the northwest. This took the third boat out into international waters; and if the Libyans conformed to his maneuvers, they would expose themselves to flank attack by the two Egyptian boats running along the coast. An update from the commander of the third boat clearly indicated that the Libyans had changed course and were doing exactly as Rashid had expected and wanted. Deciding to wait until he was within twenty-five kilometers of the Libyan boats, Rashid continued to hug the coast and head east.

The calm reports of the third boat's commander were suddenly replaced by a shrill and excited report. The two lead Libyan boats had each fired a surface-to-surface missile at Rashid's third boat. Rashid immediately ordered the commander of the third boat to break contact and evade. His order was followed by several moments of nervous silence. When the radio crackled again, the commander of the third boat regained his composure as he acknowledged that he was executing Rashid's order and updated Rashid on the location, speed, and course of the four Libyan boats. Rashid relaxed slightly. For a moment he considered his next move. There was the off-chance that the Libyans had made a mistake when they fired. If that was so, to expose his two boats and threaten the Libyans from the flank and rear might trigger a nervous and undesirable reaction.

The momentary calm and Rashid's indecision, however, both ended when the commander of Rashid's third boat reported that two more missiles had been fired. The first two missiles could have been a mistake; the second two couldn't be. Rashid was now free to act. As he prepared to issue orders to his boats, the commander of the third boat reported that he was firing chaff. A follow-on report was cut short by static, then silence. Out at sea, in the distance, there were two quick flashes. Sixty seconds later, two muffled explosions could be heard above the hum of Rashid's missile boat's engines.

Over the Mediterranean * 0250 Hours, 8 December

Removed from any fear or danger, the crew of the Hawkeye watched the maneuvers of the Egyptian and Libyan missile boats. The air control officer was convinced that he had won the bet. The radar operator, however, claimed that the Egyptians had seen the Libyans first because the Egyptian boat at sea had changed course. They were in the midst of this debate when the appearance of two new blips caught the radar operator's attention.

"Holy shit! Those fuckers have fired!"

The combat information officer turned to the radar operator. "Who fired? And what did they fire?"

Now hunched over his screen and studying it intently, the radar operator thought for a moment, then responded. "Two surface-to-surface missiles have been fired, one from each of the lead Libyan boats. Correction—*four* missiles have been fired from the lead boats." There was a pause. The Hawkeye had gone silent except for the steady drone of the two engines. The radar operator continued. "The Egyptian boat at sea is taking evasive maneuvers. He is turning away from the Libyans."

A pause. "He's firing chaff. One missile has overflown the Egyptian."

Another pause. "The second missile has gone past the Egyptian." The radar operator watched the frantic maneuvers of the Egyptian boat as it tried to avoid the second pair of incoming missiles. Slowly, however, two of the blips, which represented the follow-on missiles, closed in on the boat; then one of them merged with it. "He's hit! One missile impacted." The radar operator paused. The second missile blip closed and merged with the Egyptian boat. "A second impact!" The cluster of blips where the radar plot of the boat and the two missiles had come together fluttered for a moment on the screen, then disappeared.

Sitting upright, the radar operator turned to the combat information officer. "Sir, the boat's been blown up. It's gone."

Off the Coast of Egypt * 0255 Hours, 8 December

Rashid stood motionless for a moment as he watched the glow on the horizon disappear. Attempts to raise the third boat by radio failed. It was gone. Turning to his executive officer, he told him to report what had happened to squadron headquarters at Mersa Matruh. He paused, then told the officer that he was preparing to attack the Libyans. All eyes turned to him for a moment. He stared back in turn before he issued the order to bring the boat about on a course that would take them to where the Libyans had been last reported.

When the second boat had turned to conform to the maneuver of Rashid's boat, Rashid looked at his chart, made a few quick calculations, then ordered his helmsman to change course slightly. Turning to the radar operator, he ordered him to stand by to switch on search radar on his orders. He ordered the weapons operator to arm all missiles and be prepared to launch, on his order, two missiles at the lead Libyan boat at ten-second intervals. Over the radio he told the commander of the second boat his intentions. Rashid ordered the commander of that boat to conform to his maneuvers and engage the trail of the Libyan boats.

After both the radar and the weapons operator acknowledged his orders, Rashid turned his back to them and looked out into the darkness. He waited several seconds before he ordered the radar on. All four Libyan boats appeared on the green radar screen in the first sweep of the radar. The weapons operator took the data, checked that the missiles were locked on target, and informed Rashid that he was ready to fire. Without a pause Rashid gave the order.

Outside, on the deck of the missile boat, the darkness was shattered by the ignition of the first missile's rocket motors and its eruption from its canister. A streak of blinding light against the blackness of the night trailed the missile as it arced up for a moment, then dipped down to skim along the surface of the sea just above the waves toward its invisible target. Silence and darkness had just returned when the second missile was fired, followed by the third, then the fourth, at five-second intervals. The other boat, now to the left, was visible briefly as it too fired its missiles. When all missiles were expended, Rashid ordered the two boats to turn back toward the Egyptian coast and head east.

Over the Mediterranean * 0300 Hours, 8 December

In morbid fascination, the crew of the Hawkeye watched the sea battle as it unfolded on their radar scope. The two surviving Egyptian boats, which had been hugging the coast, turned and ran for the Libyans. The attack against the Egyptian boat had taken the Libyans out to sea, away from the coast, leaving the Egyptians free to come up behind them undetected. Then the radar operator on the Hawkeye announced that the two Egyptian boats had cut on their radars. This brought no immediate reaction, almost as if the Libyans had not detected them. It was nearly a full minute before the Libyan formation began to turn about in an effort to reorient against the new threat. The commander of the Hawkeye, watching the action, dryly commented, "That minute's going to really cost them."

Like a sportscaster at a baseball game, the radar operator described the action to the rest of the crew. "The Egyptians are firing now, one missile from each boat." Five seconds later he announced two more missiles. "The Libyan formation has broken up. They're scattering, but the missiles appeared to be locked on."

After several seconds he began to record the hits. "First missile hit the Libyan farthest south. Second missile hit the Libyan in the east. Another hit on the Libyan in the south." There was a slight pause. "He's gone now. The Libyan in the south is gone. Must have blown up. Missile hit on the Libyan in the west. One missile has gone erratic—it's crashed halfway to its target. Another hit on the Libyan in the east. He's stopped in the water."

The rest of the crew was silent as they listened. Two hundred miles away, men were dying. The green blips, squares, and triangles identified by computer-generated numbers were boats, warships being torn apart by mindless missiles of silicon, wires, aluminum, and composite materials that sought their prey unerringly and struck without feeling, without remorse.

The green blips that represented boats might have been disappearing from the screen of the Hawkeye's radar scope, but for the Libyan sailors who had manned those boats the horror continued. Death by fire, mutilation, and drowning was still going on. The crews of the boats, some wounded, some on fire, were in the water, thrashing about in an effort to save themselves or a shipmate. Screams of pain and cries for help blended with the hiss of raging fires and explosions from unexpended ammunition on the derelict boats. While the boats remained afloat, their fires cast an eerie glow over the scene. When they sank, the survivors were plunged into darkness, a darkness that hid them from each other. In that darkness, where sky and sea merged, the cries of pain from the wounded turned to soft moans, then silence as their lives, like their boats, slipped away into oblivion.

The crew of the Hawkeye saw none of this. Defeat at sea left few traces, few survivors. After ten minutes, only the two Egyptian boats were still showing on the radar screens. The sailors struggling in the sea were too small to be detected by radar. They did not appear on the Hawkeye's scope. It was over, for now.

Cairo, Egypt * 1630 Hours, 12 December

From the Citadel, the view of Cairo is breathtaking. Jan Fields had hoped to shoot her report from one of the bridges over the Nile in central Cairo, but the police and the military kept interfering with her or blocking the camera crew. Attempts to secure permission or assistance from the Egyptian government through the American embassy to allow shooting at the bridges failed. Frustrated, Jan did the best she could. Besides, by the evening of the eleventh, the bulk of the Egyptian combat forces moving to the Western Desert had already passed through Cairo. Only occasional truck convoys now came through, and these were no substitute for tanks and personnel carriers being hauled on transporters to the front. Her attempts to go into the Western Desert were even more futile. Turned back twice at military checkpoints, Jan had to rely on official news releases made by the Egyptian government and on her own sources.

Even at the Citadel, police armed with automatic rifles were still in evidence, watching, intimidating.

Still, Jan had her sources and kept the reports coming. This evening, dressed in a khaki safari jacket topped with a red scarf, Jan faced the camera with Cairo and the setting sun to her back as she began her report.

"Five days after the aborted assassination attempt against the presidents of the United States and the Republic of Egypt, military preparations for retaliation against Libya appear to be reaching the final stages. Long convoys of tanks and armored fighting vehicles that jammed the streets of this city two days ago are now absent. The tapering off of military traffic here and at other crossing points along the Nile indicates that those forces that will be used against Libya are already in place in the Western Desert.

"The size of the ground forces Egypt intends to use is questionable. Despite years of peace that resulted from the Camp David accord, the bulk of the Egyptian forces remained oriented against Israel. Even in this crisis, it is believed that no more than four divisions have been moved into the Western Desert. If this is true, then the campaign Egypt is intent on launching is more along the lines of a punitive raid, very similar to those Egypt carried out against Libya in 1977.

"This theory, supported by most Western diplomats here in Cairo, is further supported by the failure of the Egyptian government to recall reserve forces or shift all major combat forces from the east to the west. Official news bulletins continue to emphasize the role Libyan terrorists played in the December seventh attack. What is missing now is the fervent rhetoric of December eighth and ninth, when the Egyptian leadership spoke of a war to crush the Libyan threat once and for all. Instead, the government spokesmen now speak of a measured response, aimed at punishing Libya, not destroying it. The word 'war' has been supplanted by 'retaliation' and 'punitive action.'

"Efforts by the Soviet Union and the United States to defuse the situation here have continued to snag on the issue of withdrawal of troops and air units from those two countries. Each is insistent that those forces will be needed to ensure the safety of their respective citizens and property in their client state. To date, neither country has been willing to make the first move.

"In the capitals of Western Europe, an official wait-and-see attitude has replaced the earlier condemnations that were leveled against Libya for its role in the assassination attempt. Publicly, European officials have repeatedly stated that this is a matter best left to the United Nations. The potential that this border skirmish could escalate into superpower confrontation, however, has led to low-keyed discussions between European leaders on how best they might assist in defusing the situation.

"Little has come out of Libya in the past few days. Reports that the Soviets are rushing in additional quantities of equipment and technical advisors have been difficult to confirm. Since air traffic from the Soviet Union across the Mediterranean has been near normal and the Soviets continue to use the airfield at Al Fasher in the Sudan, there seems to be little to substantiate those reports. In the words of Dr. Henry Millerent of the World Strategic Institute, the Soviets would have little to gain from backing Libya with other than token logistical support and advisors.

"Regardless of what the Egyptian government calls it and how the Soviets respond, what is certain is that in the next few days, the outcome of this conflict will rest with the men and equipment that passed through this city. From Cairo, this is Jan Fields for World News Network."

Jan held her stance until the camera crew gave her the high sign that they had finished shooting. Relaxing, she called out, "How long was it?"

The chief of the camera crew, the same British crew that had been with Jan on 7 December, looked at a stopwatch. "Two minutes, twenty-eight seconds, love."

"Damn," Jan sighed. "Fifty seconds too long. Well, Fay has her work cut out for her tonight." Pulling the mike off her safari jacket, Jan looked up. "Gentlemen, we have a deadline to meet. This tape needs to be edited and out in less than two hours. Let's get moving."

Headquarters, 2nd Corps (Forward) Cairo *
1730 Hours, 12 December

Turning off the television monitor, the operations officer turned to the general. "That tape is less than two hours old. NSA picked it up as it was being fed back to the U.S. from the World News people here in Cairo and thought we might be interested in a sneak preview."

Leaning back slightly, General Horn chuckled. "Jim, I wish I could get that kind of concise analysis from your people." The other officers in the room chuckled. "Where's she getting her information from? Is there a leak somewhere in Cairo?"

Colonel Ed Linsum, deputy chief of staff for intelligence of 2nd Corps, didn't look up at Horn. Instead, he continued to play with his number-two lead pencil, doodling on the yellow legal pad in front of him. "General, I wish it were that easy. Unfortunately, Fields is cleaner than Snow White. She just reads the tea leaves better than your average TV reporter."

"Well, Ed, find out what kind of tea she uses and buy some for your people." Horn waited for the laughing to stop before he continued. Sitting up straight and turning his smiling face into a deadpan stare, he signaled the start of serious business. "Okay, let's be different tonight and start with the current Egyptian order of battle and dispositions."

From across the room, Dixon watched and waited for someone to shoot a snide remark about his wife's role with WNN in Cairo. Since the beginning of the crisis, his boss, the same full colonel who had taken over the Bright Star exercise plan he had developed, had pulled him over twice to warn him about passing classified information to the media through Fay, even accidentally. The first time Dixon shrugged it off as simple stupidity on the part of the colonel for even thinking that he would do such a thing. The second time the colonel collared Dixon and addressed the issue, however, Dixon became livid. Shoving his face within inches of the colonel's and spitting as he talked, Dixon told the colonel either to produce evidence that he was doing so and relieve him or to back off. The colonel, completely taken by surprise, backed up two paces, looked at Dixon, then turned and walked away. Nothing was ever said about Fay, or the incident, again.

Dixon knew that there was no need for anyone to worry. He hadn't seen Fay since the night of the assassination attempt. Returning home to clean up and change his uniform, he had found Fay waiting for him. Instead of a hug and concern, he was greeted with a slap in the face. Reeling from the blow, Dixon pulled back in amazement and fell backwards over a chair and onto the floor. Fay, following up the blow, began to scream at him as he lay there. He was barely able to understand her as she babbled that he had lied to her, that he had gone back on his promise that he would never again put himself in a position of danger. All she ever had asked for, she said, was a live husband, not an American flag neatly folded into a triangle. He had no business, she yelled, throwing himself in front of that jeep full of terrorists.

Dixon, exhausted by the stress of his brush with death and by hours of dealing with the crisis, also snapped. Without thinking, he bounded up off the floor and rushed at Fay. Grabbing her by the shoulders, he began shaking her like a rag doll, screaming in her face to shut up. He was still shaking her and screaming when his younger son came out of his room. Neither Fay nor Dixon noticed the boy until he started hollering, "Mommy, Daddy, don't hurt each other! Stop it, please! Stop hurting each other!"

The sudden realization of what he was doing hit Dixon harder than Fay's slap. Releasing her, he stepped back and tried to collect his wits. The boy instinctively ran up to his mother and grabbed her leg, still hollering uncontrollably. Without saying another word, Dixon turned around and walked out. After that, he didn't return.

As he mulled over those dark images, he missed his first cue from the general. The chief of staff finally got his attention. "Colonel Dixon," he called out, grunting, "if you would be so kind as to join us . . ."

With pointer in hand, Dixon stood, stepped up to the operations map, cleared his throat, and began his briefing. "Sir, the Egyptian order of battle in the Western Desert is shown here.

Attached to the 1st Army, now headquartered in Matruh, are the 22nd Mechanized Division, reinforced with an artillery brigade, deployed south of Sollum; the 5th Armored Division, deployed west of Sidi Barrani; and the 14th Armored Division, reinforced with the 7th Mechanized Brigade, around Bir Bayly. The Republican Brigade, which we believe to be the 1st Army's main reserve and exploitation force, is located here, at Bir al Khamsa. In addition, an airmobile brigade has been moved from Alexandria forward to Siwa and the parachute brigade is on stripe alert in Cairo. These last-mentioned units are believed to be under the control of the Egyptian General Staff, not the 1st Army."

"Why do we think that, Scott?" Horn asked.

Dixon paused to think about his answer before he continued. "Command and control, sir. Once it's been launched, the 1st Army would be hard pressed to control the airmobile brigade, which we believe has Al Jagbub as an initial objective and the oil line from Sarir to Marsa al Harigah, west of Tobruk, as its secondary objective. That operation, more of a raid and diversion, would do little to support the 1st Army's main operation directly. Commitment of the parachute brigade, Egypt's one and only, will be a decision made at national level, and then only if the target is worth the investment of that valuable asset."

Horn considered Dixon's response. It made sense. It was logical. And it was probably correct. The only thing that bothered him was the last comment about the parachute brigade. Horn hated it when professional soldiers used terms like "valuable asset" and "investment." Stockbrokers and bankers used those terms to discuss inanimate objects. A parachute brigade was a living and breathing organism. It was populated by real people, soldiers. Those soldiers would have to fight and win or lose, perhaps die, regardless of whether their superiors made a wise "investment." Horn believed in calling it as it was. He was surprised that Dixon, normally quite blunt when it came to such matters, resorted to using those terms. But he decided to let the issue pass. This was neither the time nor the place to have a discussion

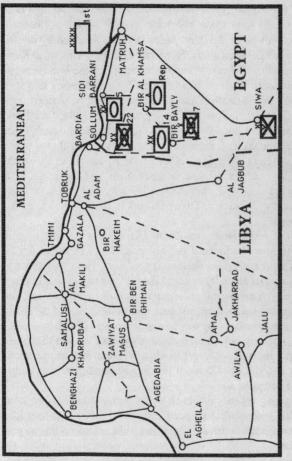

INITIAL EGYPTIAN DEPLOYMENTS

on semantics. No doubt, Horn thought, from his looks and actions, something was troubling Dixon.

With a wave of his hand he signaled Dixon to continue.

"We believe, given this posturing of forces, the Egyptians will strike west along two main axes of advance. The main effort will be by the 22nd Mech Division followed by the 5th Armored Division along the coastal road from Amsaad to Kambut and then Tobruk. A supporting attack by the 14th Armored in the south is meant to spread the Libyan defenses thin and, should the main effort along the coastal road be stopped, provide the Egyptians with a force postured to outflank the Libyans and drive onto Tobruk from the south via Al Adam. Once the Egyptians have secured Tobruk, in particular the oil terminal at Marsa al Harigah in the north, Al Jagbub in the south, and severed the oil line between Sarir and the coast, it is believed they will stop, declare the operation a success, and withdraw." Pausing, Dixon looked at Horn and awaited his response.

Once more Horn considered Dixon for a moment. Again Dixon was overlooking the obvious. The war would not be over until both sides decided it was over. Horn was about to ask Dixon if he really believed the Libyans would simply allow the Egyptians to roll in, occupy Tobruk, and then roll out again, but decided against that. No point in pounding Dixon into the ground. If he was having some type of personal problem, slapping him about in front of the staff wouldn't help. He made a mental note to get together with the chief of operations later and discuss Dixon in private. Perhaps there was something he could do.

Turning his thoughts back to the matter at hand, Horn studied the map while he sipped coffee. "Anyone have any idea when H hour is for the Egyptians?" he asked no one in particular.

When no one else provided the answer, Dixon responded. "We believe some time in the next twenty-four hours—forty-eight at the outside. All dispositions seem to be complete, including placement of combat service support units."

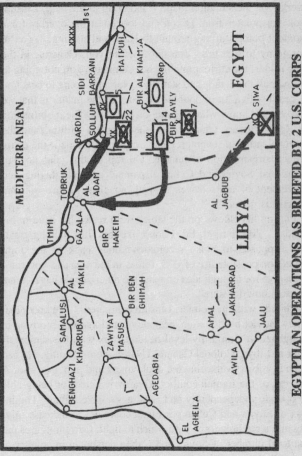

EGYPTIAN OPERATIONS AS BRIEFED BY 2 U.S. CORPS

Turning to the chief of intelligence, he nodded. "Ed, tell me what the other people think about all this."

As Linsum stood up, two of his people placed an acetate overlay on the situation map. Walking up to the map, Linsum took the pointer from Dixon and looked at the overlay for a moment before turning around to Horn and starting. "You're not going to like this. You have before you, General, in the blue folder, the current intelligence summary. I'm not going to go over all the details and statistics. Nor am I going to beat you to death with a lot of double-talk. Fact of the matter is that we really don't know what is going on in Libya. The mobilization of Revolutionary Guard units, the People's Militia, and the reorganization of several regular army units has made the entire prewar organization a muddle. On top of this, the flow of additional Soviet and Cuban personnel and the staging and movement of units leaves us with no clear picture of what exactly is going on."

Putting his elbows on the table, Horn rested his head in his hands. "You're right, Ed. I don't like this. Just fucking great. I'm supposed to make recommendations back to the Joint Chiefs on possible use of U.S. forces in the area and you can't even give me a rough idea on what the other people have. What do we know for sure?"

Playing with the pointer, Linsum continued. "We know that a new Soviet headquarters became operational this morning in Benghazi. It's an army-level headquarters with the senior officer in Libya, Colonel General Uvarov, commanding. He had been in Libya overseeing the deployment and joint exercise. A veteran of the Iranian conflict, Uvarov is noted for being able to operate independently and is an aggressive fighter. The influx of Soviet and Cuban personnel continues to increase, giving him a credible force with which to fight. Current figures put the total number of Soviet and Cuban personnel in country at seven thousand and eighteen thousand, respectively. Most of these have come from other African countries, explaining why there has been little increase in movement across the Med or Atlantic. The one notable exception has been the movement of a parachute brigade and a fighter regiment from Iran to Addis Ababa in Ethiopia.''

Surprised, Horn sat up. ''What are they up to?''

''Either they will reinforce the parachute battalion that is securing the airfield at Al Fasher or they will move into Libya and become an operational reserve for Uvarov.''

''The airhead, Jim—will the Soviets continue to use their airhead in Sudan? The time limit agreed upon by both countries is about to run out. Any chance of the Sudanese throwing the Russians out?''

Turning to the map, Linsum looked at it for a moment as if it would give him the answer. ''None, sir. If the Soviets demand they be allowed to use the airfield indefinitely, I believe the Sudanese will give in. They already have their hands full dealing with the Sudanese People's Liberation Army in the south and control very little of the southern region. They do not have the capability to throw the Russians out. Therefore, any attempt to resist the Soviet intervention would be, politically speaking, pointless. By giving the Soviets what they want, the government of Sudan at least keeps the hope alive that the Soviets will pull out when they are finished in Libya. If they resisted, the Soviets, using support of the SPLA movement as a pretext, would take whatever they want, permanently. In my opinion, given the remoteness of the region and the fact that it has practically no strategic value to the U.S., I believe the Soviets know they face no risks and will hold on to the airhead at Al Fasher as long as they need to keep their air corridors to Libya open.''

Again Linsum paused while Horn looked at the map and thought. ''Ed, see me after this. I need more info on the situation down there and some options.'' Turning to Dixon, the general pointed. ''Colonel, you come too. I may want your Special Forces people watching that airfield ready to go in and stir things up. I don't believe in giving anyone a free ride. That air corridor from Iran to Ethiopia to Libya is the biggest Achilles' heel I've ever seen. The only question is how best to sever it.'' Turning back to Linsum, he signaled him to resume the briefing with a nod.

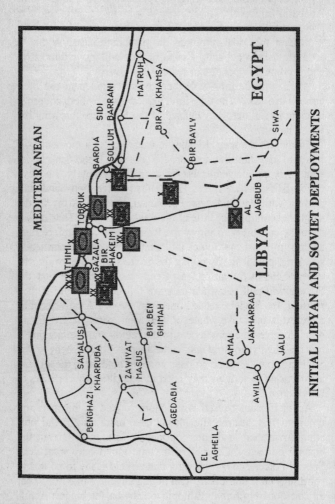

INITIAL LIBYAN AND SOVIET DEPLOYMENTS

"In a nutshell," Linsum continued, "this is the way I believe the Libyans will deploy." Using the pointer, he began to trace imaginary lines on the map. "Altogether, the Libyans have the equivalent of four divisions plus two brigades in Cyrenaica. Two brigades of Revolutionary Guards or militia have deployed along the frontier. They appear to be preparing to conduct covering force operations, delaying and channelizing Egyptian forces for as long as possible. This will buy units in the main defensive belt time to complete their preparations.

"The main belt is manned by a mix of regular army and Revolutionary Guard units equal to three divisions. Battalion and company strong points, called pitas, are being prepared in depth along likely invasion routes. These pitas, which are basically great sand forts, include bunkers, trenches, and firing ramps for tanks and armored fighting vehicles. They are placed in checkerboard fashion with overlapping fires. It will be a major drill to breach the main belt, requiring destruction or neutralization of several of these pitas by direct assault. The main belt extends from the sea south to Al Adam, then southwest to Bir Hakeim. West of Tobruk, there is a buildup of regular army armored and artillery units. These appear to be a mobile reserve, consisting of two brigades, ready to counterattack any force that makes its way through the main belt.

"The real question is the exact disposition of Soviet and Cuban units and their use. CIA puts their strength at two Cuban divisions, one tank and one motorized infantry, and a Soviet independent tank corps consisting of three tank brigades, a motorized rifle brigade, and an artillery brigade. I suspect that they will form a second operational echelon west of Tobruk. In that role, they have two possible missions. The first is to block the Egyptians from advancing any further west. Their mere presence will do this. To attack the Soviets and Cubans would broaden the war and invite further Soviet involvement in the Middle East, something the Egyptians do not want. The second mission for the Soviet and Cuban forces, if the Soviets opt for active participation, is to conduct a counteroffensive. After Libyan forces slow or stop the Egyptian forces in front of Tobruk and the Egyptian offensive has lost its momentum,

Soviet forces would be free to launch a counteroffensive. This mission would include the destruction or rollback of the remaining Egyptian forces in Libya and restoration of the original boundary.''

Linsum looked across the room to Horn. ''Pending any further questions, that's all we have right now, sir.''

Horn looked at Linsum for a moment before answering. ''No, Ed—not for you, thank you.'' Turning to the operations officer, Horn asked how the American troops in Egypt were holding up.

''Fine, sir, just fine. The only thing the commander of the 16th Armored Division requested were additional instructions and warning orders.''

''What kind of warning orders does he expect us to give him?''

Shrugging his shoulders, the operations officer responded. ''I guess he wants to begin preparing contingency plans in the event we have to commit his division.''

Irritated, Horn pointed his finger at the man. ''Please reiterate to him that his mission is to protect the equipment and ammo storage sites and, on order, evacuate American personnel from Egypt using the brigade from the 11th Air Assault Division. Beyond that, he has no mission. The President is under a lot of pressure, especially from that distinguished congressman from Tennessee, to pull those people out of there. If we did that, we would be giving the Russians the wrong message. Right now, protecting our bases and civilian personnel, as flimsy as those excuses are, are the only excuse we have to keep them on hand. Any hint that we are preparing to join the Egyptian attack into Libya would be dangerous, to us here and to the President back home.'' Cooling off, Horn lowered his finger. ''Ted, I want you personally to fly over to the division headquarters in the morning to ensure that they understand that. . . . Any other business before we adjourn?''

The chief of staff leaned over the table. ''Sir, one minor point. You were invited to attend the French ambassador's Christmas reception this evening. With the situation as it is, neither you nor the primary staff will be able to attend.''

Horn, annoyed by the need to maintain the appearance of normality when nothing was normal, contained his anger. "Well, what do you recommend? Can't offend the diplomatic corps, now, can we?"

The other officers laughed. The chief continued. "I recommend we send Colonel Dixon. He's known to most of the diplomats and is at this time quite a celebrity. His presence would more than cover your absence."

Everyone turned to look at Dixon. Dixon said nothing, but he could feel his ears begin to burn in anger.

Horn smiled. "Good idea. Probably would do Scott a world of good to get out of this hole and associate with real people." Turning back to the chief, Horn asked again, "Anyone else have any other pressing issues?"

When no one answered, Horn stood up and picked up the folder containing the intelligence summary. "Okay, that's all for now. Jim, give me half an hour to digest this summary, then see me in my office. Scott, you can see me about the Special Forces operations tomorrow. Be prepared to discuss the Sudanese situation in greater detail." Scanning the group, Horn thanked them and left the briefing room.

Bir Bayly, Egypt * 2145 Hours, 12 December

Pausing for a moment, Captain Hassan Saada stood erect in the ceaseless wind and checked his bearings. On such a night it was easy to lose one's orientation and wander outside the circle of tanks into the trackless desert. Saada's tank battalion, equipped with American-built M-60A3 tanks, was formed in a loose circle with a diameter of three hundred meters. As he returned from a final orders briefing at the battalion commander's post, located in the center of the circle, Saada's mind was cluttered with details of the upcoming operation and with personal fears that kept him from concentrating on the work yet to be done.

The operation, from his standpoint, seemed to be simple. Just prior to dawn on the thirteenth of December, his unit would cross the Egyptian-Libyan frontier and support the attack of a strongpoint. The strongpoint, manned by a reinforced infantry company, was little more than an outpost. Its purpose was to act as an early warning and cover the deployment of the main Libyan mobile forces.

What bothered Saada most about the operation was what would happen once they were in Libya. The purpose of the operation, as explained by his battalion commander, was to punish the Libyans. Saada could understand the need to do so. After all, terrorism, regardless of whether or not it was successful, still needed to be stopped. The Egyptian military was by far the best able to deal out that punishment. The use of the army, however, was, in Saada's mind, questionable. An air strike, much like those conducted by the Americans in 1986, was far simpler, quicker, and more spectacular. The air force would be able to do far more damage to Libya in one afternoon than an entire army division could do in two days.

Pausing for a moment, Saada wondered if his assessment was clouded by his apprehension about going into battle for the first time. Yes, he thought, how easy it would be for me to let someone else punish the Libyans. After five years of service, he had never been called forward to put his life on the line, to fulfill his obligation to his government and his people. His oath of service was a commitment that bound him to defend his nation and its people. It was, to him, a blood oath, one that required the ultimate sacrifice, if necessary.

For years he had enjoyed the prestige of being an officer. He had taken advantage of the pay and the benefits that came with his position and rank. Now, when his government was calling on him to meet his end of the contract, he was flinching, looking for a way out. Did that make him a coward? Or was it simply a human reaction to pending danger? Looking up at the crescent moon, Saada wished he had someone with whom he could share his fears and apprehensions. He wished he could talk to his father. He had always had the right answer when Saada was a boy. His father was a harsh man but a just and wise one.

But there was no father to turn to. There were no prayer leaders or fellow officers with whom he could talk. He was alone, in the cold desert night—alone, with all the fears and anxieties that young men experience on the eve of their first battle.

The French Embassy, Cairo * 2210 Hours, 12 December

Tiring of listening to the French ambassador's view of geopolitics and the role that the United States should be playing in the current Egyptian-Libyan crisis, and tired of allowing him to inspect her cleavage at close quarters, Jan Fields politely bowed out of the small circle gathered round him. She turned and slowly began to move about the crowded room, looking to see who was there and who wasn't. That was usually a good stress indicator. If all the principals of the Egyptian government agencies who had been invited were there, chances were that nothing was imminent. If, however, their deputies, or representatives of even lower rank, were there, then odds were that something was about to happen. From the looks of the crowd, including the diplomatic corps, all was as it should be.

As she approached the far side of the room, she glanced into a small side room where one of several bars was set up. Other than the bartender, the only person in the room was an American Army officer, leaning against the far side of the bar with his back to the door. Seeing the officer there alone suddenly made her realize that there was a decided lack of military types. A quick scan of the room revealed few uniforms. Deciding to follow a hunch, Jan walked into the room and approached the officer from behind.

The click of high heels on the marble floor and a whiff of perfume from behind him alerted Scott Dixon that a female was coming up fast at his six o'clock. Pushing off from the bar, he stood, tugged at the bottom of his mess dress jacket, and turned to see who the lady was. To his surprise and disgust, it was Jan Fields.

Jan froze in mid-stride when she saw who the officer was. For an awkward second, she stood there speechless. The last time she had seen Scott in the flesh was at the live fire demonstration, just after the assassination attempt. He had just finished making a grandstand play by gunning down a jeep loaded with terrorists.

When she and her camera crew reached him, he was standing there next to a dead Egyptian soldier. Dixon stood there like a statue, his legs shoulder-width apart, holding his pistol with both hands aimed toward the sky near his right shoulder. His eyes were riveted on the overturned jeep less than ten meters from him. In that instant he reminded her of a rattlesnake, coiled and ready to strike. Though Dixon was of medium height and build, he looked bigger than life. Only after two Egyptian soldiers reached the jeep and confirmed that its passengers were dead did Dixon relax his stance and turn toward Jan. When he did, she saw his face and looked into his eyes. What she saw in his eyes was haunting, almost frightening. The impassioned look, the deep dark eyes, and the hard expression etched on his face were like that of a great white shark, a natural killing machine.

"Well, if it isn't Madame Media. Correction—Mademoiselle Media. What brings you here this evening? A night off? Or are we trawling for a story?" It was obvious that Dixon was well past the feeling-no-pain stage and was in the process of hoisting his third sheet to the wind.

Recovering from her surprise, Jan put her right hand on her right hip, then put her left hand over it. She cocked her head back and shook it, tossing her long brown hair about in the process. "I was invited by the ambassador. We happen to be old friends. He helped me on several stories in Paris, and I provided him with some international TV exposure."

Dixon was about to make a snide remark about the type of exposure, but checked himself. Instead, he looked at her. Her stance was defiant but decidedly feminine. Jan's outfit was simple, elegant, and sensual. The black form-fitting sheath dress with long sleeves and an open V back that dropped to her waist accentuated all of Jan's best features. Her face, framed by her long hair and simple gold jewelry, radiated confidence and poise. Her eyes were alive and gleaming. They stood there for a moment, looking into each other's eyes, equally prepared to do battle or simply talk. Disarmed by her simple but striking beauty, Dixon offered her a drink.

Jan, too, was taken by Dixon. Standing there, well manicured and dressed in a form-fitting dress uniform, bedecked with gold braid and rows of miniature medals, Dixon was the image of the dashing cavalry officer who once had stolen Fay's heart. Rather than lashing out at him for what he had done to Fay, Jan simply replied, "Yes, I'd love one."

Bir al Khamsa, Egypt * 2305 Hours, 12 December

Lieutenant Colonel Hafez had few fears or apprehensions. He knew what was about to happen, and he was ready—ready to carry out his orders and do what he knew was necessary to restore his honor and pride.

In the mayhem that followed the assassination attempt, no one even suspected that Hafez had had anything to do with Sadiq or the plot to kill the two presidents. At least that was what Hafez hoped. Unfortunately, there was no way to be sure. Hafez had no idea who knew of his role in the plot. If the Libyans knew, then there was the possibility of revenge against him or his family. There was, of course, no way he could seek protection for his family without raising suspicion or telling the whole story. As before, Hafez found himself in a quandary with no good way out. No way but one—the only honorable way out for a soldier.

It had come to him slowly. At first Hafez was repulsed by the thought. It was against his training to seek death. Only live soldiers, able to fight and survive to fight again, served their nations well. Martyrs did little good in modern war. Death in battle, however, was an attractive solution. One attacked a man's loved ones as a way of striking at the man. If Hafez were dead, there would be little use in attacking his family. Besides, death in battle would be a means of purifying himself of the treason that he had encouraged and almost committed. Hafez was now convinced that it had been God that had decided for him on the seventh of December. Believing that, then, he had to regain God's favor by serving him one more time in battle—his last.

So Hafez faced the coming battle with the calmness of a man

who saw clearly what was to be and was confident in his decision. Commencing at 0615 hours the next morning, when the opening barrage would begin, Lieutenant Colonel Ahmed Hafez's life would be in the hands of his God.

Cairo, Egypt * 0125 Hours, 13 December

For the longest time Dixon lay next to Jan, watching her sleep in the pale light of her bedroom. She was on her stomach, her head lying on a pillow and turned toward him. Her long brown hair was piled on her back in a swirl of loose curls. In the light, with her makeup off, she had a wholesome, clean, and natural beauty that reminded him of a young girl's. Carefully Dixon placed his hand on her naked shoulders. Slowly he ran it down the center of her back, over her buttocks, and along the back of her thigh. The feel of her warm, smooth skin beneath his hand excited him.

Though still asleep, Jan was also becoming aroused. She let out a soft, low murmur, squeezing the pillow she held to her breasts. Carefully Dixon withdrew his hand. Rolling over to face the night stand, he looked at the clock. It was well past the time when he needed to leave. The next day would be a long one, and he needed at least a couple of hours of sleep before he reported back in. As much as he would have loved to work Jan back into another frenzy, it was time to go.

Backing out of bed, Dixon carefully negotiated the unfamiliar terrain of Jan's bedroom. As he was picking his way through the jumbled heap of clothes, sorting his from hers, he thought that he should feel at least a twinge of guilt or remorse for having slept with another woman. But he didn't. Perhaps, he thought, as he pulled his pants on, that comes later, in the light of day. Whether it came or not, however, didn't matter anymore. Standing at the bedroom door before leaving, Dixon looked at Jan one more time. He had enjoyed every minute of it and had no doubt that, given the offer again, he'd return.

9

Hit hard, hit first, hit often.

—ADMIRAL W. F. HALSEY

Al Haria, Libya * 0250 Hours, 13 December

"Come, come. You must come. Now."

Neboatov rolled over and tried to see who had woken him. But there were no lights on in the cramped bunker. Even though the Libyan was within arms distance, Neboatov couldn't even see the form of the man who had awakened him. But he could smell him. Until that day Neboatov had believed that no living creature on earth could smell worse than an Ethiopian soldier. The Libyans proved him wrong. Though he had never been close to a camel, Neboatov suspected he now knew what one smelled like.

His unseen comrade shook him again. "Come. You must come."

Pulling his arm from the Libyan, Neboatov grunted, "Yes, yes, I'll come," in Russian. Though not understanding, the Libyan let go of Neboatov's arm, scooted back, and said something in Arabic. Blindly Neboatov groped about, searching for his boots and field jacket. Still groggy from his odyssey from Ethiopia and less than three hours of sleep, he struggled to dress in the darkness. Once ready, he called out in English, "We go."

Again the Libyan called out, "Come, come."

Neboatov began to stand upright, forgetting that the bunker he was in was half a meter lower than he was tall. He hit his head on a crossbeam, resulting in a spectacular show of stars, followed by a stream of cursing in Russian. His guide, now visible in the entrance to the bunker, stopped, turned, and called something back in Arabic. Rubbing his head, Neboatov thought that the Libyan was no doubt warning him about the low ceiling. The Libyan waited at the entrance until Neboatov signaled that he was ready to continue.

Once out of the bunker and in the communications trench, Neboatov paused to see which way the Libyan had gone. He heard the crunching of sand under boots to his left and turned in that direction. As he moved along the trench, he was painfully reminded of the fact that he had only a vague idea of where he was and how this position was laid out. He had arrived only eight hours before, and he had spent all but one of them in either the command bunker or the bunker where he had slept. Though he had studied the diagrams of the old fort and the defensive positions that had been hastily dug in and about it, they followed no pattern and made little sense. That was what he was there for. His task was to advise a Libyan Revolutionary Guard infantry battalion and get the defenses of the old fort at Al Haria in order.

Upon reaching the command bunker, his guide stopped, opened a canvas cloth that covered the entrance to the bunker, and stepped aside to allow Neboatov to enter. The light of the command bunker blinded him. Instinctively Neboatov reached out with both hands and felt for the walls to either side of the entrance. Using them as a guide, he carefully felt his way forward and down with his feet, stepping down slowly every time he found a step. Even the steps were irregular, following no pattern. How, Neboatov thought, could he be expected to organize a proper defense with a unit that couldn't even build a set of simple steps?

By the time he had reached the bottom step, his eyes had readjusted to the light. In the dimly lit command bunker, he could see the commander of the battalion he was assigned to and several of the battalion's staff officers huddled about a small map pinned to the far wall of the bunker. Off to one corner was a young Soviet captain sitting next to a radio. There were three Soviet officers and two enlisted men with this battalion: Neboatov, two captains, and two radio men who also doubled as drivers. One captain and a radio man were awake at all times, manning the radio that was their link to the Soviet advisor group at the next-higher headquarters and monitoring what was going on. The Libyans did not like the idea of having foreigners in their headquarters, especially nonbelievers. They liked it even less since they had an independent radio net that they, the Libyans, did not control. Though it was standard Soviet practice to do so, it did little to diminish suspicions and promote trust.

Neboatov glanced over to the captain with a questioning look on his face. The captain responded to his major by shrugging his shoulders and shaking his head from side to side, indicating he had no idea what was going on. Unnoticed by the Libyans gathered around the map, Neboatov moved up to the rear of the group and stood there. He watched as one of the officers, holding a phone in his left hand up to his ear, marked several arrows on the map with a grease pencil he held in his right hand. The arrows, in red, were along the Libyan-Egyptian border and pointed west. He was obviously receiving a report from observation posts or recon units on the border.

The battalion commander, a skinny colonel named Efrat, with narrow, suspicious eyes, noticed Neboatov. In English, the only language that the two of them had in common, Efrat called out, "It has started. Egyptian recon units have crossed the border. They will be here by dawn."

On the Egyptian-Libyan Border North of Al Haria *
0630 Hours, 13 December

The roar of his tank's engine and the muffled ear phones of Captain Saada's helmet blocked the screech of outgoing artillery rounds. Even their impact was hidden by the great clouds of dust thrown up by the tanks of the lead company. Though he wasn't exactly sure what the opening battle of the war should have been like, he was sure it would be different. Since leaving their forward assembly area less than two hours before, however, the operation had appeared to Saada as nothing more than another training exercise. It was not at all what he had expected. Even the radio transmissions were calm, routine and unhurried, almost as if the battalion commander and staff were bored. After some reflection, Saada decided that this was good. It meant that all their training had been good and had prepared them for this moment, this event. They were ready. He was ready.

Standing up in the cupola of his tank, Saada turned sideways, grabbing the hatch with one hand and placing his other hand on the periscope sight for his machine gun in order to steady himself. Like an old sailor on the deck of a ship, his body automatically swayed from side to side in order to maintain balance as the M-60A3 tank bucked and pitched across the uneven desert surface. He leaned over slightly and peered into the dark and dust. For a moment, he could see nothing, not even the tail lights of the tank to his front. Reaching up, he keyed the intercom switch of his helmet. "Driver, what is your speed?"

Without unkeying his own intercom, Saada listened. He heard the click of the driver keying his intercom. He knew it was the driver for as soon as the driver had keyed, the sound of the tank's tracks grinding could be heard over the intercom. Each crewman's station on a tank had its own distinctive noise. From the gunner's station the whine of small hydraulic pumps and the chatter of the thermal sight's cooling system could be heard when he keyed his intercom. The loader's intercom normally picked up the squeak of the track as it was pulled up over the drive sprocket and the roar of the engine. The sound of wind whipping across the tank commander's small boom mike told the rest of the crew when Saada's intercom was keyed.

"Twenty-four kilometers per hour, Captain."

Without hesitation, Saada shot back, "What is on the odometer?"

The driver looked at his odometer and read back its current mileage. Saada, referring to a small scrap of paper on which he had recorded their mileage when they had rolled across the line of departure, made some quick calculations in his head. By subtracting the mileage they had on the tank when they crossed the LD from the current mileage, Saada could plot where they were on his map. After doing so, Saada looked at his watch, then looked around.

Still partially blinded by the dust and darkness, he caught only glimpses of the tank to his front, artillery impacting in the distance, and the blackout drive markers of the tank to his rear. Still, this, along with the reports coming over the battalion command radio net, was enough for Saada to confirm that all was well. In ten more minutes they would cross the border and begin to deploy into three company columns. In turn, the companies would move into platoon columns before occupying firing positions from which the tanks would support the infantry attack on a Libyan fort.

It would be a difficult and costly attack for the infantry. The Libyans had reinforced and expanded an old fort with new bunkers and firing positions for tanks. The whole defensive position was protected by many belts of barbed wire and land mines, both antitank and antipersonnel. The assault would need to be a deliberate, set-piece operation. Though many of the officers in Saada's battalion felt that it was a waste of time to stop and reduce the fort, they were not consulted before the plans had been made. In reality, it was not their place to pass judgment on the decision of the high command. For some reason, a reason that was known only to the planners, the fort had to be reduced. Those same planners had decided that Saada's battalion would play a part in that battle. Given the mission, Saada needed only to trouble his mind on how best to accomplish his assigned mission. The battalion's plan and his plan for the company were well thought out and sound. For the tank units, it would be little more than a long-range gunnery drill. For the infantry, the poor bloody infantry, supported by the engineers, it would be cruel and expensive.

Saada's momentary air of confidence quickly evaporated when the commander of the lead tank company reported contact with Libyan reconnaissance vehicles. The lead company commander's voice betrayed his surprise and excitement. Though he shouldn't have been surprised, he was. They had been told to expect contact with the enemy recon at, or soon after crossing, the border.

* * *

Recon elements, equipped with light armored vehicles, are descendants of the old horse-mounted light cavalry. Like the light cavalry units of old, modern recon units screen their own forces from the prying eyes of enemy reconnaissance units, while attempting to find the location and composition of the enemy's main force. Both missions require patience, stealth, and cunning carefully mixed with a touch of audacity. This mixture has always been hard to develop, for a recon commander who is too bold will find himself fighting and losing his own men instead of gathering information about the enemy. The opposite is also true. A recon commander who is too cautious will preserve his force but find out nothing about the enemy. That the lead company of Saada's battalion was being engaged by enemy recon vehicles meant that the Egyptian recon forces had failed in their mission to screen the main body and that the Libyans were winning the fight for information.

Saada automatically passed word to his platoon leaders to stand by for orders, telling them only that the lead company was in contact. Anticipating action, his first, Saada could feel his heart rate and breathing pick up. The cold wind that had cut through his field jacket a moment before no longer could be felt. He tried to calm himself by taking deep breaths but found himself almost hyperventilating. Wanting to do something, anything, Saada stood high in the cupola of his tank, leaned forward, and peered into the predawn darkness, trying to catch a glimpse of the battle now developing in front of him. The darkness and swirling dust, however, continued to defeat his efforts to see anything beyond the tank to his front. Frustrated, Saada lowered himself back down into the turret and listened to the auxiliary radio receiver set on the battalion radio net.

In contrast to the frantic company commander in contact, the battalion commander was calm but firm. The first thing of which he reminded his excited company commander was to use proper reporting procedures and to talk slower. His comment seemed to be more of a reminder than a rebuke. There was a momentary silence on the radio net before the company commander came back with a full report. The battalion commander's call had had the desired effect.

Saada, intently listening to the conversation on the radio, hadn't noticed that the firing had ceased. It was only after the lead company commander reported that the enemy had lost two vehicles and had broken contact that Saada looked up and scanned the area around him. To his rear the morning sun was just peeking over the horizon, casting a cold, pale light over the desert. The transition from day to night in the desert is quick, almost startling. The darkness in the west was already receding. Even with daylight, however, there was little Saada could see. The dust kicked up by dozens of tanks to his front still obscured his field of vision. About all he could see was two pillars of black smoke rising straight up in the calm morning sky, marking the two enemy recon vehicles destroyed by the lead company.

Follow-on reports confirmed that the enemy had indeed broken contact and had withdrawn. Saada was amused by the change in the attitude of the lead company commander. On contact with the enemy he had been near panic. After the battalion commander had calmed him, he had been all business. Now, the subsequent reports from the lead company commander were joyful, almost boastful. Saada wondered how long that would last. Until the next encounter with the enemy, no doubt. Of greater concern to Saada at that moment, however, was how he would handle his first battle. He looked at his watch and glanced at his map. In an hour he would have an opportunity to find out.

Cairo * 0710 Hours, 13 December

The offices and newsroom of WNN were already swarming with people running hither and yon with no apparent direction or purpose when Fay Dixon arrived. Every other person stopped when they saw Fay and asked the same thing, "Have you seen Jan?" Fay responded to them all with a simple shake of the head and a curt "No" as she rushed to her desk, thankful that she had arrived before Jan.

Even though everyone knew that Egypt was going to act, Fay was still taken aback. It was so unreal, so unlike anything that she had ever experienced. The excitement of the past week, the building tensions, and the sudden burst of action that morning animated Fay like a drug. Jan had once told her that working the international news scene gave her a rush that was better than sex. It wasn't until that moment that Fay believed her. But it was true. Amidst the chatter and chaos there was an electricity that ran through Fay and everyone about her.

As she seated herself behind her desk, her eyes lit across the photo of Scott and the children. Fay's taut face drooped into an unconscious frown as she stared at the photo. How desperately she wanted to share her excitement, her newfound happiness as a career woman, with Scott, the man with whom she had shared everything for twelve years. Now, however, at the single most important moment in her life, he rejected her. More correctly, he rejected her choice of jobs. To listen to Scott, it seemed that it was Fay who had betrayed their trust and bond. From the beginning, he had opposed her working at WNN and with Jan Fields. Everything that was remotely connected with her job was a point of irritation. The mere mention of Jan's name had been enough to darken his mood. Each new trapping that came with the job met with resounding disapproval from Scott. The Egyptian maid that tended the house and watched the boys when they were not in school, the apartment in the European quarter of the city, the Egyptian driver that took Fay to and from work every day—all met with a storm of screaming and swearing. Even the new wardrobe that Fay thought necessary caused Scott to throw a fit of rage.

Through it all, Fay had resolved to press on, convinced that Scott was overreacting and would eventually come about and see it from her viewpoint. That, however, never happened. The situation simply continued to deteriorate. The final act was rung down the night Scott returned from the fire power demonstration for the American and Egyptian presidents. Since then, especially at night when she was alone in her apartment, Fay desperately wished she could go back in time and pull back that slap. That she had done such a thing was as much a shock to her as it had been to Scott. How badly she wanted to see Scott and talk to him, reason with him as they had in the old days, the days before Iran. She had convinced herself that they were at the lowest possible point, that their relationship and differences couldn't get any worse. Fay was sure of that. Given time and some reflection, Scott would see the folly of what had happened, as she had, and come back. But that wouldn't be possible until the temporary insanity that was consuming not only them but the entire country had passed. And with the Egyptians now committed to a war, that day was on an indefinite hold.

A young man of twenty-two ("a mere boy," according to Jan) came storming into Fay's office. "Mrs. Dixon, here's the latest from the Egyptian Ministry of Defense."

Without a second thought she took her eyes from the photo of her family and turned to the office boy. "Who did the translation?"

Panting, the young man tried to talk while catching his breath. "No translations necessary—the statement—was in English."

Fay looked at him with a blank expression. While it was wrong to call Johnny effeminate, his fair complexion, slight build, soft voice, and refined manner would not impress Scotty. "Johnny, do you seriously expect me to put together a story based solely on Egyptian propaganda? Who's recording the Egyptian broadcasts and emergency radio nets?"

Stung by Fay's response, Johnny straightened up and thought for a moment. "I don't know, Mrs. Dixon. I can go find out if you want."

Throwing her head back, Fay fought back the urge to yell at him. Regaining her composure, she stood and headed for the door. "Never mind, Johnny, I'll go myself." Stopping at the door, she turned to the young man with his wounded pride. "What I really need you to do right now is find out where in the devil Jan is. She needs to be here pronto. Now get a move on and find her."

Luck had yet to favor Jan that morning. Though she had been notified early, a series of delays had beaten her every effort to make it to the office. If anything, it appeared to her that she was moving backwards.

Out of bed in a flash, Jan had grabbed the first clothing she came across. Looking about and seeing no sign of Scott or his clothes, she wondered how he had been able to slip out without waking her. In a single bound she covered the distance from her bed to the closet. She pulled out a silk-and-lace blouse and dress slacks, the first articles of clothing that flew into her hands. As she slipped on the high-heeled pumps she had worn the night before, she felt a momentary anger at Scott for slipping out as he did. To her surprise, she was not mad that she had slept through one of the biggest news stories of her life. Instead, she was mad because he had not been there when she awoke. How much, she thought, she would have loved to be roused by him in the early-morning light.

But there was no time for such idle thoughts. A war had just started. No doubt Scott was at his place of duty, and it was well past the time when she, the bureau chief, should have been at hers. Though she was dressed in clothes designed for an evening out, she was ready: she maintained a proper set of clothing at the office for emergencies such as this. There would be time to dress and put on her makeup while her staff briefed her. All was in order and under control—at least in the beginning.

Buttoning her blouse with one hand, she dialed the number for her driver. Half concentrating on pushing the small cloth-covered button through a hole a tad too small, Jan talked to the driver's wife in English, then hung up without waiting for a response and turned her full attention to forcing the button through the hole. Finished dressing, she grabbed her shoulder bag and flew out of the apartment and down to the street to wait for the car. Twenty minutes passed and the car did not show. Jan ran back up to her apartment and called the driver's home a second time. Again she got his wife; this time she spoke in Arabic and waited for an answer. In broken English the driver's wife explained that her husband had been taken by the army last night. What had he done wrong? Jan asked, confused. The driver's wife explained that he had done nothing wrong—sometimes her husband was a soldier. It finally sunk in that the driver was a reservist who had been recalled to active duty.

Cursing her luck, Jan threw her shoulder bag across the room and tried to call the news office. She could have someone there pick her up. But her efforts yielded nothing but further frustrations. The phone system was controlled by the government. Most lines were taken out of general use and reserved for official use. Those lines that were available were overworked. It wasn't until her fourth attempt that Jan finally got a dial tone. Even that was for naught, for the office number she dialed was busy. Twenty minutes of effort and three busy numbers added to Jan's irritation and frustration.

Realizing that the phone system had defeated her, Jan grabbed her briefcase and rushed out the door, slamming it behind her as she ran down to the street, where she hoped to find a taxi. But the taxis that were normally queued up and waiting for customers were nowhere to be seen. For a second she wondered if all the drivers in Egypt were reservists who had been recalled.

With no salvation in sight, she reached down to grab her shoulder bag as she prepared to run to a main street where there was bound to be a taxi. It was only then that she realized that her bag was not slung over her shoulder. It—and her apartment keys and her money—sat on the floor of her apartment, right where she had thrown it not more than half an hour before. In a fit she looked about her, then paused and thought for a moment. Totally frustrated, she clenched her fists, cursed, and stomped her right foot with just enough force to break the heel.

Stunned by this last piece of bad luck, Jan stood motionless, trying hard to decide if she should cry or laugh. Here she was, the hottest reporter in the entire Middle East, in the middle of the hottest story of the year. She was *almost* in the right place at the right time—almost, but not quite. Instead of being at the helm of the WNN news office, reading the latest news from the front and putting together a story that would be featured on the next news broadcast in the States, she was standing on a side street with no makeup on, her hair still knotted from sleep, dressed in slacks and a silk blouse, and standing off-balance with a broken heel. She was still standing there when Johnny drove up in a WNN van and saved her from herself.

To Jan's relief, Fay had the situation well under control when she came storming into the news office, shoes in hand. Someone from a line of faceless office workers shoved a cup of coffee into Jan's hand as she disappeared into her office followed by Fay and Johnny. Fay slammed the door and began to fill Jan in on what information they had while Jan frantically rummaged through the closet in search of the appropriate outfit for her broadcast. Never missing a word Fay threw out, Jan began to strip off her wrinkled evening clothes. Johnny, standing in the corner and prepared to take notes, turned beet red when he realized what Jan was doing. Turning away, he monitored as Fay continued to spew out information like a machine gun.

Stripped down to bra and panties, Jan draped the outfit she would wear over the back of an office chair and seated herself at her desk. Pulling out a drawer, she extracted a makeup mirror and kit and prepared to do her face. Before she started, however, she looked in the mirror, took a sip of coffee, and thought. Noticing that Jan had stopped and was concentrating, Fay stopped talking. Johnny, trying hard to make himself inconspicuous, looked at the two women and wondered what telepathic message had prompted Fay to stop. Whatever it was, he stood ready. For what he didn't quite know. But he was ready anyway.

Jan continued to sip her coffee and consider what look would be appropriate for a war story. Nothing flashy, nothing soft. The image had to be serious, almost harsh. Everything was important: her clothes, her makeup, the way she wore her hair, the way she spoke. Slowly Jan began to form a clear idea of the image she wanted to flash across the television screen. When she was ready, she dug out the appropriate cosmetics and went to work, as Fay began to throw out her ideas on how best to package the first story of the war.

Al Haria, Libya * 0750 Hours, 13 December

The traininglike atmosphere ended in a thunderclap for Captain Saada. Nearing the fort at Al Haria, Saada moved his company along a wadi. As they reached the position from which they were to support the final infantry attack, Saada ordered his tanks to move into their firing positions. The column of tanks halted for a moment before turning south to climb out of the wadi. Saada looked to his left and watched as the tracks of the M-60A3 tank next to his clawed at the soft, sandy sides of the wadi and slowly pulled itself up and onto the open ground beyond. The roar of the laboring tank engines almost masked a volley of antitank guns fired from beyond the wadi. The sound of the antitank guns, like the cracking of a whip, startled Saada.

In the twinkling of an eye, the tank he was watching was engulfed in a ball of fire. From every opening of the stricken tank, sheets of flame shot skyward. The tank had been hit by an antitank round. For a fraction of a second the flames died down ever so slightly. Then the tank shuddered as the warheads of high-explosive antitank rounds stored on board cooked off, setting off the propellant of the rounds next to them and stoking the flames to new heights.

"BACK UP! BACK UP! DRIVER, MOVE BACK!" Screaming into the boom mike, Saada braced himself and rocked with the motion of the tank as the driver hit the brakes, threw the tank into reverse, and began to move back into the wadi. Just as he straightened himself up, a fountain of dirt and sand rose before his tank and whipped him with a shower of sand. A near miss—an enemy antitank round had landed just short of his tank, raining dirt, not death, on him.

There was no time to reflect on his good fortune, however. A flash to his right caused him to turn just in time to witness the death of another one of his tanks. Saada reached up to the radio switch on the side of his helmet and yelled over his company command net for all tanks to move back into the cover of the wadi. His order was too late for yet another of his tanks: further down the line a third M-60A3 erupted into flames.

But there was no time to reflect on that. Over the auxiliary radio receiver, set on the battalion radio net, the battalion commander was calling Saada's radio call sign, demanding a report on what was happening. Saada was about to switch the frequency of the main radio in order to report when he noticed that his tank not only was still backing up but was in fact backing out of the wadi on the other side. Pushing the radio switch from the forward, or radio, position to the rear, or intercom, position, Saada yelled for the driver to stop. The driver, already shaken by the near-miss and the unexpected panic of his tank commander, did so without hesitation. Saada, with one hand on the radio frequency knob and the other on the intercom switch on the side of his helmet, was not prepared for the jolting stop. As the tank lurched to a halt, Saada was thrown back, then forward, smashing his face down with force onto the steel box that housed the sight for the tank commander's machine gun. Like a rag doll thrown against a wall, Saada went limp and dropped down onto the floor of his tank.

In excited gibberish, the loader yelled that the captain was dead. The gunner—a sergeant and the next-senior man on board the tank—turned to see what the loader was babbling about. To his surprise he saw Saada crumpled on the floor, blood everywhere. For a moment, the gunner, like the loader, believed that Saada was dead. Turning around and getting himself into a position where he could reach his commander, the gunner reached down and carefully turned Saada's head to look at his face. The loader fought back the urge to vomit.

A soft moan from Saada brought a sigh of relief from the gunner. His commander was alive but momentarily unconscious. Saada's nose was pushed almost flat; blood was spurting from his nostrils. There was a wide cut across his forehead from which blood ran freely. Below the neck, there appeared to be no signs of injury. To be sure, the gunner ran his hands down Saada's body, feeling for any unusual breaks or bumps and watching Saada's smashed face in case his probing caused pain. There were no other injuries. Having been in many fights, the gunner correctly figured that his commander was not in any great danger—at least from the injuries he had just sustained. The situation outside the turret, however, was different.

The gunner ordered the loader to help him move Saada into a position under the main gun. Once they had Saada in place, the gunner reached up, grabbed the edge of the tank commander's cupola, and pulled himself up into the tank commander's position. Once settled in, he plugged his helmet into the tank commander's radio-intercom jack. The earphones of his crewman's helmet blared in his ear. The radio was alive with reports from the platoon leaders of the company on the main radio transmitter and from other company commanders and the battalion staff on the auxiliary radio receiver.

The gunner listened for a moment. Though no one knew for sure what had happened to Saada, their company commander, the deputy company commander had already assumed command and was in the process of receiving status reports from each of the platoons. In turn, the deputy commander reported the company's status to the battalion commander. When there was a moment of silence on the company radio net, the gunner keyed the radio. Using Saada's radio call sign with an additional letter to identify himself as the gunner and not Saada, he called the deputy commander. Excitedly, and with apparent relief, the deputy commander asked if Saada was alive and needed assistance.

Looking down between his legs, the gunner saw the loader on the turret floor with Saada. Using bandages from the first-aid kit, the loader was carefully cleaning Saada's wounds. The gunner thought for a moment. He didn't consider evacuation, even though Saada was hurt. While fighting the tank with only three functional crewmen and a wounded man on board would be damned difficult, taking Saada out and trying to evacuate him in the middle of the battle could be more hazardous. Artillery, a very real threat since the Libyans obviously knew their location, could fall on them at any minute. A single volley of artillery in the confines of the wadi would shred anyone who was not under cover. The gunner replied that Saada could not fight but did not need immediate evacuation.

The deputy commander paused for a moment, then began to issue orders. The company, down three tanks and its commander, had yet to fire a single shot at the enemy. The Libyan fort, sitting two thousand meters from the wadi, still had to be taken. The infantry, now ready to assault, needed support if they were to succeed. Though he would remain with the company, braced upright in the gunner's seat as he passed in and out of consciousness, Saada's ability to influence anything was nil. A simple and almost stupid accident had taken him out of the fight just as effectively as a Libyan antitank round.

Al Haria, Libya * 0755 Hours, 13 December

The respite was only temporary. They had perhaps only five minutes, no more, before the Egyptians recovered from their first shock of combat, figured out that their initial barrage had not done its work, and came up with a new plan. When they did, they would carry the fort and the adjoining defensive works. Of this Neboatov had no doubt.

At the command observation post Neboatov lay on his belly behind a wall of sandbags, watching as a second Egyptian tank company maneuvered into position. The first tank company had blundered into the teeth of the antitank kill sack that Neboatov and one of his captains had set up that morning. In short order they had killed three M-60A3 tanks and caused the others to drop back into a covered position. They would have done more damage had the Libyans waited until the entire Egyptian tank company was out of the wadi and in the open. But the Libyans were nervous, inexperienced, untrained, and worse, poorly led.

After being summoned to the command bunker earlier that morning, Neboatov had sat without saying a word for two hours while the leadership of the Revolutionary Guard battalion debated what they should do. Unable to contain himself, Neboatov had pulled Colonel Efrat off to the side. Using a simple diagram, Neboatov showed that his antitank weapons were best deployed in depth and facing to the south and southeast to cover the most likely armor avenue of approach. Efrat, not understanding what Neboatov was talking about, shook his head in agreement. Turning to his assembled staff, Efrat ordered one of his captains to go with Neboatov and see that the guns and antitank missile teams were redeployed. Satisfied that he had disposed of the Russian for the time being, Efrat turned his back to Neboatov and rejoined the debate that was still ongoing.

Realizing that he had been summarily dismissed, Neboatov turned to the Libyan captain and attempted to explain what needed to be done with the antitank weapons, but the man understood neither Russian nor English. Looking around him, Neboatov saw that the second Soviet captain had entered the bunker. Deciding that the only way they would get anything done was to do it themselves, Neboatov called him over and quickly explained what he wanted done, then divided up the task between them. Using gestures and pointing to the diagram, he got the Libyan to lead them to the first antitank positions. Once there, Neboatov and his captain took over. They had labored until dawn, leading, pleading, and prodding the Libyan antitank gun and missile crews. Only the initial artillery barrage had stopped their efforts.

From behind, Neboatov felt a slight tug on his pant leg. Turning, he saw one of his captains looking up at him. "What is it, Dmitri?"

"Sir, Colonel Rakhia wants you to contact him immediately."

"Did he tell you what he wanted?"

"Yes, sir. He wants your assessment of the situation here before he orders us out of here."

Neboatov looked at the Libyan captain next to him for a moment and hoped that he really didn't understand Russian. He turned back to his own captain. "Did you tell him we wouldn't be able to hold for more than a few hours?"

The captain shook his head in the affirmative, then added, "Yes, sir. He knows that. That's why he wants us to leave. But he wants you to talk to him personally. He said that there's nothing more that we can do here. I believe he just wants to confirm that before he gives us permission to go."

Cursing, Neboatov began to shimmy his way back into the main portion of the trench, grumbling as he went. "If he knows we're finished here, why the hell didn't he just tell us to go!" Just as his feet hit the floor of the trench, the Egyptian shelling began anew. The Egyptian gunners had the range now and used that knowledge to great effect. The first volley impacted just to the front of the command observation bunker. Neboatov and his captain flattened themselves on the floor of the trench as a shower of debris and dirt came raining down.

The captain, a veteran of two years in Angola, looked up to Neboatov as they lay there. "Those shits don't waste any time, do they?"

Picking his face up from the floor of the trench, Neboatov looked into his captain's eyes. Though the young captain was trying to make light of their situation, there was fear and apprehension in his eyes. "Dmitri, welcome to your first real war. Be thankful that we are facing, as Colonel Rakhia said, a third-rate power."

This caused Dmitri to laugh. "Yes, Comrade Colonel, I guess there is much I should be thankful for."

A second volley of artillery impacted just to the rear of the command observation bunker, sending more debris into the trench. "Come, Dmitri, enough of this idle chitchat. They have us bracketed. The next volley will be right on the mark. Let us get out of here before we are buried. Our colonel is awaiting our call. Lead on."

The young captain pushed himself up off the floor of the trench, turned in the direction of the command bunker, and began to move along the trench in a low crouch. Neboatov also got up but turned to take one last look at the situation before he followed. The sight that greeted him caused him to hesitate. The Libyan captain whom he had been lying next to was on his back. His elbows were tucked into his sides, his lower arms upright. The hands were clutched and frozen like the talons of a hawk clawing at the sky. Blood ran down the faceless head in tiny rivulets into the sand.

Neboatov shook his head and simply muttered, "Luck, that's all it is—simple luck. You are dead and I am not." The screech of the next volley caused Neboatov to lower his body below the lip of the trench before turning toward the command bunk. He wondered how much luck he had left.

10

Over the Mediterranean, 200 Miles North of Tobruk, Libya * 0930 Hours, 14 December

Five minutes ahead of the main strike group, the Egyptian aircraft tasked with flak suppression began to climb in preparation for their final run-in and attack. As soon as they did, Libyan ground-based search radars picked them up. The radar warning receivers, or RWRs, on each of the Egyptian aircraft readily identified the search radars. Referring to the data provided by his electronic counter measure, or ECM, pod, the leader of the flight confirmed the radar type and its direction. He gave a curt order and slowly corrected his heading, flying directly to the source of the Libyan radar beam.

The personnel manning the Libyan ground-based radar weren't the only people watching the incoming Egyptian strike. Though the pilots of the French-built Mirage 2000EMs could not see them, the skies were alive with electronic signals. For some time the Egyptians' RWRs had been signaling them that the Russian Ilyushin 76 Mainstay airborne warning and control aircraft, or AWACS, flying to the west had been tracking them. These aircraft, manned and controlled by the Soviets, were still operating over Benghazi, three hundred miles away. The Ilyushin 76 itself posed no immediate threat. But its reports on the size, direction, and location of the Egyptian strike force via a downlink to a Soviet ground station were critical to the air defense network covering the Cyrenaica. The Soviet ground station transmitted the information provided by the Il-76 to its counterparts in the Libyan air defense command. The Egyptians knew of the Il-76 and its role. For now, they only monitored the Soviet AWACS, taking no direct action against any Soviet aircraft. To date the Soviets had not physically intervened in the conflict, and the Egyptians wanted to keep it that way.

Egypt's enemies were not the only ones watching the Egyptian strike. The RWRs of the Egyptian aircraft detected a search radar coming from the north. That signal belonged to an American E-3 Sentry AWACS flying out of Italy. The larger and more capable E-3s had been flown in to supplement the U.S. Navy's E-2 Hawkeyes still operating off the decks of the 6th Fleet's carriers. The Americans, like the Soviets, were watching and reporting. Though they were not directly linked into the Egyptian air defense command, as the Soviets were linked into the Libyan system, the information gathered by the Americans would eventually find its way into Egyptian hands.

From the northeast, at a range of two hundred miles, the signal of an American-built E-2 Hawkeye flown by the Israeli air force was also detected. Like the Americans, they were merely watching and taking notes. Unlike the Americans, who for the most part viewed the conflict with a mild interest, the Israelis knew that they had a vested interest in what was going on. Information gathered by the Israeli E-2 on this and other Egyptian strikes would be studied in great detail. The tactics, attack profile, and results would be analyzed and used in the training of Israeli pilots in preparation for the day when they would have to defend themselves against just such an attack, perhaps against the same pilots.

Finally, from the east, the signal of their own American-built E-2 was detected by the Egyptian Mirage 2000s. Loitering above Mersa Matruh, the Egyptian E-2 AWACS monitored the strike force and the response of the Libyan air defense to the impending attack. Shortly after passing through one thousand meters in altitude, the Egyptian controller aboard the E-2

Hawkeye reported Libyan aircraft on an intercept course with the Mirages. In a calm, almost casual voice, the air control officer on the Egyptian Hawkeye updated the Egyptian strike force on the posturing of eight Libyan MIG-25M Foxbats west of the strike force.

Armed with a combination of four Soviet-built AA-6 Acrid and AA-8 Aphid air-to-air missiles, the MIG-25Ms were interceptors, hunting for the Egyptians. Through the use of automated uplinks, the Libyan ground-based search radar now locked onto the approaching Egyptian aircraft and fed course, range, and altitude information directly to the pilots of the MIG-25Ms. In this way the pilots of the MIG-25Ms would be able to close with the Egyptian aircraft without switching on their own search radars, thus exposing themselves to electron countermeasures or worse. Instead, the MIG-25Ms would approach their targets, designated by the ground controllers, until the MIGs were within one hundred nautical miles of their targets. On order, they would accelerate, switch on their radars, and lock onto their target. At that range, the powerful onboard continuous wave, or CW, radar of the MIG-25M used to illuminate the target for the air-to-air missile would be able to burn through any electronic jamming the Egyptians might use to break the radar lock. When semiactive radar homing, or SARH, air-to-air missiles were locked onto the MIG's CW radar reflections bouncing off the illuminated target, the pilot fired. When firing a SARH missile, the MIG pilot had to continuously illuminate the target with the MIG's radar until the missile impacted. If radar lock was not possible, then the pilot had the option of closing with the target and using his two heat-seeking missiles. Because a heat seeker homes in on the hot spots of an aircraft, the pilot could break away once he had launched the missile.

The appearance of the MIGs was expected but still disquieting to the Egyptian pilots. The natural reaction for the pilots of the Mirage 2000s was either to turn and evade or to turn and attack the MIGs. This, however, was not their assigned task. Their targets were the search and acquisition radars of the ground-based air defense systems in and around

Tobruk. The MIGs belonged to a flight of American-built F-16 fighters.

Once he was satisfied that he had all the information necessary for the setup, the Egyptian air controller over Matruh began to issue orders. His first was to the crew of an American-built EC-130H electronic warfare aircraft. He ordered it to commence the jamming of the Libyan ground-based search radar that was providing data to the MIG-25Ms. Using power sources not available in smaller aircraft, the electronic warfare operator in the EC-130H found the frequency of the Libyan radar and switched on his jammer.

The reaction was predictable and immediate. The Libyan pilots, suddenly denied data from the ground station, panicked momentarily. They called for instructions, holding fast to the last course ordered. Two hundred miles to the southeast, in a bunker outside Tobruk, the radar operator at the ground station began to hop from one frequency to another in an effort to find one that was not jammed. One hundred and fifty miles further east, the EW operator on the EC-130H had also begun hopping frequencies, following the Libyan radar operator and frustrating his efforts to find a clear frequency.

The air control officer aboard the Hawkeye, satisfied that the ground station had temporarily lost control of the situation, next ordered the F-16s into action. Tracking the MIG-25s, he computed a plot that would allow the F-16s to intercept the MIGs well before they were in position to interfere with the Mirage 2000s. This information was passed on to the flight leader of the F-16s, who turned onto the intercept course and began to close at the prescribed speed.

Around the periphery of the electronic battlefield, the Russian, American, and Israeli AWACS watched as best they could, for the fight for the airwaves also affected their radars. On the ground, unable to find a clear radar frequency, the Libyan air defense commander ordered the MIG-25Ms to continue to close with the Egyptians and use their own radars to find and shoot down the enemy. Reluctantly, the Libyan MIGs continued to stumble forward, blindly, looking for the Egyptian Mirage 2000s somewhere to the east. The Mirages, on order from the controller aboard the Hawkeye, had changed both course and altitude, removing themselves from danger and clearing the way for the F-16s, now screaming in from the northeast.

Sure that he had to be within range of the Mirages, the flight leader of the MIGs ordered his pilots to activate their radars. This order assisted the four F-16s. Coming on line, they made a slight turn, accelerated, and drove for the MIGs. From the Ilyushin Il-76, the Russians attempted to warn the Libyan ground control officer of the impending attack.

The warning, garbled through translation from Russian to Arabic in the heat of battle, confused rather than clarified the situation. Only the last part of the message, stating that F-16s were attacking, came through clearly to the air defense commander at Tobruk. Taken by surprise at the sudden appearance of F-16s, he ordered the antiaircraft batteries to switch on their acquisition radars. The acquisition radars immediately illuminated the F-16s, the Mirage 2000s, and the MIGs. To the east, the EC-130H detected the new radars and began to jam as many of them as possible.

Seeing that time was running out, the F-16 flight leader ordered his aircraft to fire, then break off the attack. The Mirage 2000s, their ECM pods on, turned toward the active acquisition radars and began to launch antiradiation missiles at the Libyan radars. The MIG pilots, lost and confused, suddenly found themselves under attack from an unexpected quarter. Reacting to the new attack, they turned toward the F-16s and fired heat-seeking air-to-air missiles at their attackers. On the ground, the harried air defense commander, unable to get a clear picture of what was happening, ordered his surface-to-air missile batteries to open fire. The commanders of the firing batteries, also unable to sort out who was who, began to fire at any target plot that appeared.

At one battery, a Soviet advisor watched a surface-to-air missile race down its launch rails. Once free of the rail, the missile sprinted skyward, followed by a tongue of flame and a plume of white smoke. The young captain, who had served in the Red Army for six years without ever seeing a live missile launched, stood and watched in awe. When the missile was lost from sight, he turned to the Libyan captain commanding the air defense battery and asked what he had fired at. Still watching the sky where the missile had disappeared, the Libyan shrugged his shoulders. "I do not know. But wasn't it beautiful?"

In the American E-3 AWACS to the north, a young Air Force captain leaned back in his chair, his eyes growing bigger than saucers as he watched the melee to the south. Unable to make sense of the cluttered screen, he threw his hands up and turned to his commander. "Geez-us Kee-rist, sir! What a rat screw! I have no fucking idea what's happening down there."

Neither did anyone else. Dozens of missiles, launched from the ground and from aircraft, flew hither and yon. To further confuse the situation, the pilots, now under attack, began to launch flares to deceive heat-seeking missiles or fire small buffs of aluminum strips called chaff to deceive the radar lock of radar homing missiles. Some of the missiles—those that had actually been aimed at something—lost their intended target, found another, then lost it. Others, by luck or through a good setup, began to find their marks. Across the Mediterranean, sophisticated combat aircraft costing as much as forty million dollars apiece were blown out of the sky. Some, when hit, blew up in gigantic fireballs. Others, clipped by the pursuing missile, lost a wing tip or part of a tail section, causing the aircraft to spin wildly out of control. The antiradiation missiles fired by the Mirage 2000s also found their marks. These missiles began to take out Libyan ground radar sets and stations in and around Tobruk, blinding the Libyan air defense commander. Unable to further influence the battle, he sat in his bunker, wondering what to do next.

In the space of a few minutes the battle was over. After the great maelstrom, there was a momentary respite as air controllers began to take stock of what was left. The Egyptians were the first to realize that they had won. Based on information from the EC-130H, the E-2 Hawkeye over Mersa Matruh, and reports from the flight leaders, the air controller determined that the Libyan air defense had been temporarily neutralized and the MIG threat was gone. The main strike force had been untouched by the melee that had involved the MIGs, the Mirage 2000s, and the F-16s. Satisfied that all was in order, the air controller gave the go-ahead to the strike commander to commence his attacks.

To the northeast, a radar operator aboard the Israeli E-2 Hawkeye cursed and pounded his fist on his thigh in disgust. Having lost his bet that the Egyptians would be stopped, he shook his head, reached into his pocket, pulled out five Israeli shekels, and handed them to his grinning friend.

Tobruk, Libya * 0945 Hours, 14 December

The wailing of the air-raid siren drifted up from the city to the old Italian fort where Colonel Nafissi had established his forward command post. The concrete, steel, and sand complex insulated Nafissi and his staff from the sound of the air-raid siren as well as from the bombs that the approaching Egyptian aircraft would soon release on the port facilities and the nearby airfield and troop concentrations. The war Nafissi fought bore no resemblance to the one outside the bunker complex. Colonel General Uvarov knew this and felt uneasy sitting in the main briefing room next to Nafissi, listening to the morning update briefing. He was out of place and, as far as he was concerned, worse than useless.

Uvarov despised commanders who tried to run their battles through telephone lines from behind slabs of concrete. They neither saw nor understood what was really happening. The information they received was always old and filtered through layer after layer of staff officers and commanders. All too often, staffs of subordinate units told their next-higher headquarters what they thought they wanted to hear. Uvarov could never fight a war that way. He had to be there, up front, looking, listening, feeling. Many times in Iran he had made decisions or initiated a move based on what he had seen or after a brief conversation with a front-line commander. In a bunker miles from the front, it is impossible to gauge how much further one can push his troops or whether a report is fact or fantasy. No, Uvarov thought as he listened to the Libyan major's brief, this is not my kind of war.

Still, he had his instructions from Moscow and little choice but to obey. Officially, he had two tasks. As the senior Soviet officer in Libya, he was the chief military advisor to the leadership of the Libyan armed forces. As such, he had direct access to those military leaders and was free to render whatever advice and assistance he deemed necessary. He was assisted in this task by a structure of Soviet advisors who worked with Libyan field commanders at every level down to battalion.

His second task was that of commander of the North African Front. In reality, the North African Front was not really a front at all. A front, in the Red Army, normally consisted of two or more armies with attached combat and combat service support units such as engineers, signal units, transportation units, etc. At best, when all Soviet, Cuban, and East German ground, air, and naval personnel designated to fill out the North African Front were in place, he would have little more than a weak combined arms army.

Presently, the North African Front consisted of two incomplete Cuban motorized rifle divisions, a Soviet independent tank corps, a Soviet artillery brigade, a Soviet air defense brigade, two fighter regiments, one fighter-bomber regiment, and eight guided missile boats. All these were mustering in and around Al Gardabah. What worried Uvarov most was not what he had, pitifully little as it was, for a proper front. His concerns centered on what he didn't have. The combat support and service support units—in particular, engineers and helicopter units—were missing from his troop list, as were the transportation and supply units required to maintain his force in the field. These units, according to the plan, were to have been provided by the Libyans.

Even during the training exercise before the crisis, Uvarov had had surprise after surprise. Though he was prepared for the ordeal of dealing with the Revolutionary Council, he was not prepared for a lack of enthusiasm that bordered on apathy in the armed forces. Even as the Leader of the Revolution and his functionaries spoke of great, sweeping advances and preparations that would result in crushing defeats of the Egyptians, neither Uvarov nor his swarm of advisors saw any evidence of making those boasts realities. On the contrary, there was every sign that the Libyans were going to allow the Egyptians to overrun the Cyrenaica, the eastern desert area of Libya, and withdraw almost unmolested to the west. The best units of the Libyan forces, ground, air, and naval, were deployed west of El Agheila, preparing to defend the Tripolitania, the western desert. In effect, instead of backing up the Libyan army, Uvarov's North African Front was in front of the bulk of it.

As Uvarov became familiar with the situation and the personalities on the ground, he soon learned that Colonel Nafissi, the second-most-powerful man on the ruling council, had been charged with the defense of the Cyrenaica. For this he had been given a mix of regular army, Islamic Revolutionary Guard, and militia units. Air and naval support of this force was minimal despite the fact that the Libyans stood to lose many of their oil-producing fields and refineries. It wasn't until the chief of the Soviet KGB section in Libya briefed him that Uvarov understood. From the KGB Uvarov learned of Nafissi's role in the assassination attempt that had precipitated the crisis. He learned, too, that the naval incident of 9 December was also Nafissi's doing. The Libyan missile boats had sailed with orders to provoke a fight. The KGB theorized that Nafissi was trying either to embarrass the current Leader of the Revolution or win more popular support for himself. Regardless, it was well known that Nafissi meant to become the next Leader of the Revolution, at any cost. After meeting him, Uvarov had no doubt that Nafissi would do whatever he had to do in order to obtain his goal.

Looking about the briefing room, Uvarov casually studied the Libyan commanders and staff officers gathered there. They were a mixed lot. The regular army officers, in uniform, with rank and badges properly placed, at least gave the appearance of paying attention to the situation update. The leaders of the Revolutionary Guard and militia units, dressed in assorted shades of tan and khaki with no emblems, were not interested in the briefing or in what the regular army officers had to say.

They showed their disdain for the proceedings and for their army counterparts by sleeping, staring blankly at the ceiling, or carrying on a conversation with the nearest fellow Guardsman.

Uvarov himself did not listen to the briefing. He had little need to listen, as it was given in Arabic and, though he did have a translator seated behind him, Uvarov had already been briefed on the current situation by his own staff. Besides, much of what was said was old and clouded by half-truths or downright lies. Uvarov was appalled at how effectively the Libyans could delude themselves, creating elaborate fantasies that bore no resemblance to the actual situation on the ground. The map that the briefer used to update Colonel Nafissi showed Libyan units in positions that Uvarov knew had long since been overrun by Egyptian units. Some Libyan units still shown on the map had already ceased to exist.

After an earlier briefing, Uvarov had taken Nafissi to one side and pointed these problems out. As the translator told Nafissi what Uvarov had said, the colonel had a concerned look on his face. When the translator had finished, Nafissi thought about what Uvarov had told him, then smiled. Such errors were to be expected, he said simply. "After all," he told Uvarov, "there is a great deal of confusion in war. You know, fog of battle and friction of war. I wouldn't concern myself with a few minor discrepancies in one or two reports." After that, nothing could surprise Uvarov. At least that is what he thought.

As if to underscore this point, two staff officers, a Libyan followed seconds later by a Soviet, came into the conference room. The Libyan handed Nafissi a report concerning the air raid that was still ongoing from the commander of the air defense units around Tobruk. The Soviet officer handed Uvarov a similar report from the Soviet Il-76 AWACS. As he read the note, a broad grin lit across Nafissi's face. Turning to his staff and commanders, he triumphantly announced that eight aircraft had been brought down in the air battle. The assembled officers smiled and congratulated themselves on another victory over the Egyptians.

Uvarov, after listening to the translation of Nafissi's comments, read his officer's report. Surprisingly, the number of aircraft shot down was correct. Eight aircraft had been brought down. Not surprising was that Nafissi had neglected to tell his own people that six of them were Libyan—and of those six, two had been brought down by the Libyan ground-based surface-to-air missiles, fired indiscriminately. Turning to the officer who had handed him the message, Uvarov looked him in the eye questioningly. The staff officer merely shrugged his shoulders and looked down at the ground. What more could he say? Nothing that he could do would alter the sad state of affairs. Turning back to Nafissi, Uvarov locked eyes with the colonel. For a moment they stared at each other. There was no trust between them, no common ground for understanding—only distrust and contempt. After several seconds Nafissi smiled, turned back to the briefer, and signaled him to continue.

Like his staff officer, Uvarov knew there was nothing he could do, even if he had had the desire, which he didn't. It was still the Libyans' fight. For the moment the Soviets were spectators, a second-string team waiting on the sidelines. The situation he was in, politically, tactically, and logistically, was deplorable. Not only were the Libyans lying to the Soviets about everything from the tactical situation to supplies that needed to be delivered, they were lying to themselves. The best Uvarov could hope for was that the Egyptians would not venture beyond Tobruk. So long as the Egyptians remained east of the Gulf of Bomba, Uvarov's orders from Moscow were to keep his North African Front out of the fight.

Tiring of the briefing, Nafissi signaled an end to it. He stood to go, then stopped and walked up to the map at the front of the room with one of his commanders. For several minutes they discussed in hushed voices the disposition of some of the Libyan forces. Uvarov remained seated, watching Nafissi as he waited for an opportunity to speak to him. Uvarov turned to his aide and asked who the Libyan commander was. The aide replied that it was the commander of the Libyan artillery and rocket troops, a Colonel Radin. Nafissi, finished with Radin, began to walk over to the tall Russian general. Uvarov stood and was about to speak when a Libyan staff officer slid in between Uvarov and Nafissi.

Turning his back to the Russian general, the Libyan officer leaned over Nafissi's shoulder and whispered in the colonel's ear. As he spoke, Nafissi's face betrayed surprise, then agitation. When he finished, the staff officer stepped back and waited for Nafissi's instructions. For a moment Nafissi was lost in thought, troubled by whatever it was the officer had reported. Taking a deep breath, Nafissi stood erect, then turned toward Radin. Nafissi snapped at him, ordering him to report to him in his private office, then stormed out of the conference room, followed quickly by the staff officer and Radin.

To his translator Uvarov whispered, "Find out what that was all about."

Nafissi didn't even wait until the door to his office was closed before he turned on Radin, calling him an idiot and a fool, incapable of command. Puzzled by the sudden shower of abuse, Radin stood there dumbfounded. Though he, like Nafissi, was a colonel, he did not belong to the Revolutionary Council. Nafissi's authority and power far transcended that of an ordinary colonel. At that moment Nafissi was, by order of the Revolutionary Council, commander of all forces in the Cyrenaica. He had the undisputed power of life and death—a power he had already used to punish two commanders who had abandoned their posts without orders. So long as he carried out the tasks assigned to him by the council, no one would question his methods. By the same token, it was well known that if he failed, the council would have no reservations about punishing him in the same ruthless manner in which Nafissi himself dealt with those who failed.

Finished with his tirade, Nafissi walked around behind his desk, sat down, and waited for Radin to respond. Seeing that Radin didn't know what was going on, the staff officer came up from behind. "Colonel Radin, ten minutes ago we received word that a battalion of the 2nd Rocket Brigade was overrun at Kambut. All equipment, personnel, and munitions were lost."

As the shock of what he had been told began to sink in, the color began to drain from Radin's face. For several seconds he tried to think of something to say, some way he could disassociate himself from the calamity that had befallen one of his key units. But nothing came to him. A heavy, oppressive silence hung in the room as Radin's mind raced and stumbled over disjointed thoughts. Through the stupidity of one of his battalion commanders, not only had a critical unit been lost, but the contents of the warheads on FROG-7 rockets were no doubt now known to the Egyptians.

Impatient, Nafissi broke the silence by pounding his fist on his desk and yelling. "The order was to hold all surface-to-surface rocket brigades back, away from the frontier. If you remember, our plan—the one which you yourself developed—called for the initiation of chemical warfare only after the Egyptian forces were well within our own borders. There was no reason for that unit to be that far forward." Pounding his fist even harder, he repeated, "No reason."

Pausing, Nafissi let Radin consider his probable fate. Then, in a low and emotionless voice, Nafissi began to question Radin. "What type of agent did that battalion have?"

Turning to the staff officer, Radin asked what battalion had been overrun. The staff officer replied that it had been the 3rd Battalion. Turning back to Nafissi, Radin thought for a moment. "Nerve agent—persistent nerve agent."

Nafissi thought about that, then continued his questioning. "Are there any other rocket units east of Tobruk?"

Radin hesitated before he answered. "No, there are none east of Tobruk."

"Are you sure? After all, you had told me that none would be deployed forward, and somehow one managed to be where it should not have been."

"That is true, Colonel Nafissi—I had told you that. But the Russians, they became suspicious when none of our rocket units were moved forward to where they could strike into Egypt."

"So you moved a battalion forward to please the Russians!"

"No, not to please them—to keep them from becoming curious. After all, you said that you wanted no one that didn't need to know to find out about our plans. You yourself stated that secrecy was critical if we were to succeed in our plan."

Irritated, Nafissi stood up, leaned over his desk, and began to yell again. "So, to fool the Russians, you sent a unit with chemical weapons forward, right into the hands of the Egyptians! How safe, do you think, is our secret now? The Egyptians may not follow the true ways of Allah, but they have eyes and brains. Not only will they be ready for our chemical attack but they will no doubt parade their new trophies before the Americans, screaming, 'Look, chemical weapons—help us!' "

Standing upright, Nafissi readjusted his Sam Browne belt. "For your sake, and that of the revolution, pray to Allah that the Americans ignore the Egyptians and the Egyptians do not have time to destroy our remaining rocket units."

"Colonel Nafissi, even if the Egyptians know of the weapons, will that still not serve our purposes just as well?"

Nafissi, looking at Radin, did not understand.

Radin explained. "The shock of finding chemical weapons may be enough to slow or even stop the Egyptians. If they are not ready for chemical warfare, they may pull back sooner than they had planned rather than risk mass annihilation. To the rest of the world, it will seem that our army and the Revolutionary Guard turned back the Egyptians. We will have defended Libya—and you, you will be hailed as a hero, the defender of the True Faith and our people."

Though Nafissi knew that Radin was desperately trying to save his skin, what he said made sense. The mere threat of chemical weapons could be as effective as their actual use. After all, if the weapons were not used, it would be far easier to deny to the rest of the world that they even existed. Once they were used, there would be far too much evidence to hide. And if the Egyptians did parade those weapons already captured before the media of the world, Libya could deny that they were of Libyan origin. After all, to the rest of the world, Egyptian FROG-7 rockets could very easily be made to look just like Libyan FROG-7 rockets—an argument Nafissi intended to use.

Sitting down, Nafissi mulled over the possibilities that this accident presented him. But he rejected them. He wanted to inflict a crushing defeat on the Egyptians. He wanted smashed and depleted units streaming east in retreat out of Libya. In short, only a crushing victory would serve his purposes. If the Egyptians stopped on their own accord and withdrew intact and without pressure, they could easily claim that they had accomplished their objectives and won. Radin's stupidity put his plan in jeopardy.

For a moment Nafissi smiled. Radin felt a rush of relief—a feeling that was short-lived. Seeing Radin's relief, Nafissi forced the smile off his face. "You have betrayed the revolution, Colonel Radin, by disobeying my orders and endangering our operations." This sudden announcement shocked Radin. To the staff officer Nafissi barked, "Captain, Colonel Radin is under arrest, charged with treason. Have him confined under guard in his quarters until such time as he can be properly executed." As an afterthought, he added, "That is all," dismissing them both with a wave of his hand.

Kambut, Libya * 1725 Hours, 14 December

Swinging about into a shallow turn, the Egyptian MI-8 helicopter prepared to land. Dixon turned to look out the small round window, hoping to see the site before they landed. The scene that flashed by, however, was the same monotonous desert landscape that he had been watching for the last hour. Turning back, he looked at the Egyptian major who was their translator and guide. His arms were tightly folded onto his chest, his head bobbing up and down as the helicopter jolted and bucked. He was asleep. Next to Dixon, First Lieutenant Allen Masterson of the Chemical Corps was rearranging his equipment in preparation for landing. Assigned to the U.S. brigade that was still deployed in Egypt just west of Cairo, Masterson was there at Dixon's insistence. Not that anyone had to twist Masterson's arm to volunteer. The young lieutenant was delighted with the idea of getting away from the staging area where he and the rest of the brigade had been held since the beginning of the crisis. When Dixon briefed him on their mission, his excitement doubled.

At the request of the Egyptian army, Dixon and Masterson reported to the headquarters of the 1st Army in Matruh to verify the discovery of Libyan chemical weapons. Dixon had been brought in from the forward command post of the 2nd Brigade of the 14th Armored Division, then advancing on Al Adam from the south. Masterson was flown in from Cairo. In Matruh, the two Americans received a more detailed briefing on the circumstances concerning the discovery of a Libyan surface-to-surface rocket unit equipped with chemical weapons. Earlier that morning, a recon detachment of the 22nd Mechanized Division had overrun a Libyan unit equipped with FROG-7s (free rocket over ground) armed with warheads containing chemical weapons. Not realizing that the warheads of the rockets contained chemicals, the scout cars of the recon unit had fired indiscriminately. Several of the warheads, according to the Egyptian colonel that briefed them, were hit, releasing the persistent nerve agent. Twelve soldiers died before the commander of the unit realized what was happening and withdrew downwind of the site. The Egyptian high command wanted the American officers to verify their discovery. Dixon, working with the 1st Egyptian Army, was tagged to go.

As the helicopter landed, the Egyptian major woke up. Looking at Dixon, he smiled. "Ah, we are here." Checking that he had his protective mask, the major stood up and moved to the cabin door.

Turning to Masterson, Dixon said dryly, "Well, Lieutenant, it's time to earn your pay." Then, as an afterthought, he added glumly, "Let's get this over with."

Once out of the helicopter and on the ground, the major motioned Dixon and Masterson over to a BRDM armored car. In front of the BRDM an Egyptian lieutenant, covered with dust and grime, stood waiting for them. Even from a distance Dixon could see that the recon lieutenant was haggard and tired. His mouth was locked in a frown, his eyes cold and vacant. Dixon knew the look—the look of a man who had seen war up close and personal. Dixon also noticed that the recon lieutenant, like the rest of the BRDM's crew, was wearing a chemical-protective suit. About the lieutenant's waist his protective mask hung dangling at the end of the air hose attached to its filter container. Instinctively Dixon's left hand dropped to touch his own protective mask carrier, just to be sure.

Introductions were short and perfunctory. The recon lieutenant spoke to the major. While Dixon waited for the translation, he watched as the Egyptian crewmen, responding to something in the lieutenant's conversation with the major, removed their helmets and started putting on their protective masks. By the time the major began his translation, both Dixon and Masterson had already begun to pull out their own protective masks.

The well-rehearsed masking procedure was second-nature to Dixon. He removed his helmet and placed it between his knees. Though there was no fear of contaminants on the ground, force of habit kept him from putting his helmet down. He held his breath. With his left hand he pulled open the cover to the mask's carrying case while reaching around for the mask itself with his right hand. Grabbing the elasticized harness of the mask in both hands, Dixon brought the mask up to and over his chin. Once his chin was seated in the mask, he pulled the harness over and down the back of his head. The rubbery hood of the mask, meant to cover the head, was folded forward and obscured Dixon's vision. When he had the harness set, Dixon took both hands and reached up inside the hood. Cupping his hands over the air vents, Dixon exhaled, blowing out all the air between his face and his mask. If there were a contaminant in the air, the blowing would clear it from his mask. Next he tried to inhale. When he had sucked what little air remained trapped between his face and the mask into his lungs, and he couldn't draw any more, that meant his mask was sealed properly and there were no leaks. Satisfied, he removed his hands from the air vents and pulled the hood over and into place while he began to breathe again. Though he didn't hurry, total masking time took less than twelve seconds—only three more than the Army standard for masking allowed for. With the mask on and hood secured, Dixon put his helmet back on and checked all the zippers, snaps, and flaps on his own chemical-protective suit before pulling on his rubber gloves.

Masterson and the Egyptian major were both ready by the time Dixon finished. At the direction of the Egyptian lieutenant, the three visitors climbed into the BRDM for the ride to the site where the Libyan unit had been overrun. It did not take long. And no one had to tell Dixon that they were approaching the site, either. Despite the protective mask and the smell of the BRDM, the oily stench of burning rubber and the pungent smell of charred flesh, all too familiar to Dixon, announced their arrival at their destination.

The opening of the door of the BRDM revealed a desert transformed into a graveyard. Dixon didn't wait for the others. He climbed out, adjusted his gear, then surveyed the scene before him. In the gathering darkness, Scott Dixon looked at the wreckage of a unit. Rocket transporters and trucks, trailers and jeeps were scattered about at random. Some were burned, others simply stationary with no apparent damage to them. Dispersed amongst the trucks and rocket transporters were the bodies.

Despite the cold, the corpses of the dead Libyan soldiers left where they had fallen were already bloated and showing signs of decomposing. The odor, peculiar to a modern battlefield, brought back images of other battlefields and other times. As he had in Iran, Dixon fought back his revulsion and the urge to vomit. He forced himself to concentrate on the matter at hand, counting transporters, examining rockets and recording markings on the side of the rockets' warheads. He ignored the bodies. They were not his concern. They were not his doing. In his short career as a commander of combat troops in battle, he had buried enough of his own. Thank God, he thought to himself, these corpses belong to someone else's mistakes. Satisfied that he was mentally ready, Dixon began to move to the nearest rocket transporter.

From behind, Masterson came up to Dixon's side. Any joy Masterson felt about going forward with Dixon vanished as soon as he saw the bodies and inhaled their odor. Though he tried to hide it, the sight of the bodies was a shock to the lieutenant. His efforts to ignore them, like Dixon's, failed. A morbid fascination of the horror overcame him. He could not ignore the stench. Within seconds he broke out in a cold sweat as his stomach muscles began to twitch, pumping vile acid up his throat.

Trying to choke down his own fear and the feeling of sickness welling up inside, Masterson glued his eyes onto Dixon's back and moved forward behind him, blocking out the horrors about them as best he could. Before he walked five paces, however, he stepped into a gooey substance that caused him to slip and stumble. Fearing that he had accidentally stepped into a pool of chemical agents, Masterson looked down at his feet.

Through the plastic eyepieces of his protective mask, Masterson saw that he was standing in what had once been a man's intestines. Across the ground, a long line of bowels and intestines trailed away from where he stood to the lower half of the dead man, cut in half by an explosion. Masterson lost all control. In one violent contraction, his stomach forced its contents up and out of Masterson's mouth, filling his protective mask with vomit.

With nowhere to go, the vomit in Masterson's mask floated about his mouth, nose, face, and eyes, ready to rush back in as soon as he gasped for breath. Whatever control Masterson had left was lost as soon as he began to gag on his own vomit. Dropping to his knees and overcome by the sensation of choking to death, Masterson tore his protective mask off, spit the vomit from his mouth, and drew in a deep breath. As soon as he had done so, he knew that he had made a mistake.

The screaming of the Egyptian major, though muted by his protective mask, alerted Dixon that something was wrong. Turning around, he saw Masterson on the ground, bent over and on his knees. Masterson had his mask off, held little more than a foot from his face by two wobbly arms. His face was white, covered with vomit and contorted in a mask of agony. Even before Dixon could turn and begin to run back to him, Masterson dropped his mask, toppled over, rolled onto his back, and began wild and spasmodic convulsions. He was dying. Dixon had no doubt that his lieutenant had inhaled a fatal dose of nerve agent. Unless he received an immediate injection of antidote, mere seconds separated Masterson from death.

Covering the distance between himself and Masterson in three quick bounds, Dixon dropped to his knees, grabbed the lieutenant's mask, shook out whatever vomit remained in it, and began to put it back on him. This was no easy feat. Masterson's violent twisting and convulsions and Dixon's own clumsy rubber gloves made the task difficult. Only after the Egyptian major grabbed and steadied Masterson's head was Dixon able to slide Masterson's mask back on.

That accomplished, Dixon reached into his mask carrier and fumbled about, searching for one of his nerve-agent antidote injectors. Again, the thick and unfeeling rubber gloves handicapped his efforts. Frustrated, Dixon stopped the fumbling, unsnapped the carrier, and turned it upside down.

From inside the carrier two injectors, little bigger than marking pens, fell onto the ground, along with a booklet of chemical detector paper and two small Army manuals. Throwing the carrier aside, Dixon grabbed one of the injectors and flicked the safety cap off. With the injector in his right hand, Dixon grabbed a handful of Masterson's chemical-protective suit and rolled him over onto his side in order to expose a thigh. With a short but quick jab he rammed the injector into Masterson's thigh. The impact activated the spring-loaded injector needle, which shot into Masterson and released the antidote.

Satisfied that the injector had emptied itself, Dixon withdrew it, released his grasp on Masterson's protective suit, then straightened up to watch. For the first time Dixon realized that he really didn't know what he should be looking for. He hoped that Masterson's convulsions would stop and that they could transport him to a hospital. But he wasn't sure. It was like many other things in the Army, Dixon thought: the first time you face a situation or are expected to do what you're trained for is when you do it for real.

Dixon and the Egyptian major watched. Ten seconds and Masterson still convulsed. Twenty seconds and the convulsions began to subside. Forty seconds and Masterson stopped moving altogether. For a moment Dixon's heart sank: Masterson had died. But then Dixon saw Masterson's chest rise, ever so slightly. He was alive.

Looking up to the Egyptian major, Dixon yelled through his mask, "Okay, let's get him out of here." Standing up, the major signed for several of the men from the BRDM to come over and lend a hand. Dixon and three Egyptians gathered around Masterson, reached down and grabbed the first part of Masterson's body that was handy, and picked him up off the ground. Though not coordinated, they managed to carry him over to the BRDM and hoist him onto the back deck of the armored scout car. They made no effort to stuff Masterson into the BRDM. It would take too long to get him in and then out again once they reached the helicopter. Dixon also rode on the outside, hanging on to the small turret of the BRDM with one hand and Masterson with the other as the BRDM raced back to the waiting helicopter.

On the way back to the helicopter, with the immediate crisis over, Dixon began to consider his best course of action. His first thought was to send Masterson back while he remained on site and continued to check out the rockets. Dixon, however, rejected that. First, it was dark now. The last thing he wanted to do was stumble around in a contaminated area in the dark. Second, even if he did go back, what would he do? Other than find a puddle of chemical agent, test it, and verify that there was something there, nothing. Besides, as long as he had Masterson, dead or alive, Dixon had all the proof he needed that there was a chemical agent present. As cold as that thought was, it was fact.

With a decision made and nothing more to do but hang on and wait till they reached the helicopter, Dixon felt first a feeling of relief, then one of revulsion. Because he, Dixon, had insisted, Lieutenant Masterson had come on a trip that could very well cost him his life. Then, with the lieutenant hanging on to life by a thin thread, Dixon actually had debated his best course of action, weighing the advantages and disadvantages of each option as if he were doing a peacetime staff drill. Finally, he had opted to stay with Masterson only after he decided he could accomplish his mission by using the lieutenant, dead or alive, as evidence. Have I become that cold and cynical? Dixon thought. Or was it just force of habit, the result of years of training designed to overlook the gruesome aspects of war and consider the situation in cold, dispassionate terms?

A sudden stop jarred Dixon's thoughts back to the present.

But as Dixon watched the Egyptians load Masterson onto the MI-8 helicopter, another dark and cynical thought began to well up in his mind. What, he thought, if the Egyptians had staged this? What if the whole thing was a sham aimed at drawing the United States into the conflict on Egypt's side? Dixon had no proof that the chemical agent was Libyan or Egyptian. Even if he did carry a sample back, there was, he was sure, no way of proving anything. Dixon looked back toward the site from which they had come. How utterly horrible it would be, he thought, if the first American casualty of the war was the result of an elaborate deception plan by their "ally."

Cairo, Egypt * 1955 Hours, 14 December

Standing across from the Nile Sheraton, Jan Fields faced the camera. A red-and-black scarf draped over her left shoulder and knotted on the right dressed up her light tan "war" outfit. Behind her, the lights of the city on the far bank and those on the boats passing along the Nile provided a serene backdrop. As soon as the red light of the camera flicked on, she began.

"The second day of the war between Egypt and Libya ended with both sides making claims of victory that are impossible, at this point, to verify. For their part, an official Egyptian press release spoke of steady advances by all columns moving into Libya and the gaining of air superiority of the Cyrenaica, or eastern desert of Libya. From Libya, government radio spoke of the ejection of all Egyptian forces from Libya and the shooting down of twelve Egyptian aircraft during a raid over Tobruk this morning.

"As to future operations, no one is commenting on that

officially. That the Egyptian operation is of a limited nature is no longer questioned. Few reserve forces have been mobilized, and no major combat units have been withdrawn west of the Suez Canal. The atmosphere throughout Egypt is calm. Instead of war chants, there is the quiet air of confidence that all is going well, and will continue to do so, for the Egyptian military. What is certain from the capital here is that the war has not made any changes in the way of life. After yesterday's initial flurry of activity, it's business as usual here in Cairo. Even the American ambassador, in a late-afternoon press conference, hinted that there would be little disruption in his schedule.

"If the Egyptians stop their advance in the next forty-eight hours, as rumors say, then the need to maintain an American military presence will become questionable. Neither the American ambassador nor Egyptian officials would comment on the possible role those American ground forces here have played or could play. Nor is the date for their withdrawal mentioned. The original date when all U.S. ground forces should have departed came and went without comment. According to one unofficial source here, as long as there is the possibility that there are Soviet or Cuban troops in Libya, the American brigade will remain in place, despite calls from Congress to bring them home. Regardless, American military personnel have been kept clear of any involvement in the Egyptian raid into Libya. According to a spokesman for the Egyptian president, there is no need for the Americans to concern themselves with, as he calls the raid, an 'internal matter.'

"From Cairo, this is Jan Fields for World News Network."

As the crew packed up its gear and prepared to leave, Jan turned and slowly walked along the sidewalk next to the river. A sudden chill caused her to pull the collar of her jacket up a little higher. Like many Americans, she had never associated cold with the desert until she spent her first winter there freezing in her light cotton outfits. She had eventually flown to England for a long weekend in November of that first year in order to shop for proper winter clothes. Looking out over the dark river and cold night brought Scott Dixon to mind. Where, she wondered, is he staying tonight? She knew he was out of Cairo—someplace, according to the sergeant to whom she had talked, in the Western Desert.

She wanted so much to talk to Scott, to see him, to touch him. Since sleeping with him, Jan had thought of little else. Even the war, far-removed and unreachable, came in a poor second. What had started as a chance encounter at the French embassy had slowly evolved into a quiet conversation about anything and everything, including the trouble between Scott and Fay. Before that night Jan secretly had been dying to hear Scott's side of the story out of simple curiosity. There was no doubt in her mind that Scott had been a real shit to Fay, keeping her apron strings tied to the stove. That was a foregone conclusion. Jan just wanted to hear it from the horse's mouth. But when she finally had the chance to do so, she found herself wavering in her preconceived convictions. Instead of Attila the Hun, she found a man who was confused, hurting from scars no one could see, and alone in a world rushing insanely to war.

What had caused her to dance with Scott that night still bewildered her. His invitation was spontaneous and her response unhesitating. Had it been a mindless act? Had it been kindness on her part, to ease some of Scott's pain? Or had it been love? That she even considered the idea of being in love with Scott, the husband of her closest colleague and best friend, bothered Jan. The flow of events that carried the two of them from the dance floor in the embassy to Jan's bed had been a slow, easy, seamless blur that reminded Jan of a dream. Whatever had carried them, she wouldn't be able to find out for sure until she saw Scott again. So until that happened, she puttered about, going through the motions of covering the news and praying that nothing happened to Scott.

11

The soldier often regards the man of politics as unreliable, inconstant and greedy for the limelight. Bred on imperatives, the military temperament is astonished by the number of pretenses in which the statesman has to indulge. The terrible simplicities of war contrast strongly to the devious methods demanded by the art of government. The impassioned twists and turns, the dominant concern with the effects produced, the appearance of weighing others in terms not of their merit but their influence—all inevitable characteristics in the civilian whose authority rests upon the popular will—cannot but worry the professional soldier, habituated as he is to a life of hard duties, self-effacement, and respect for services rendered.

—CHARLES DE GAULLE

60 Miles South of Al Adam, Libya * 1510 Hours, 15 December

The sharp turn temporarily threw the gunner on Captain Saada's tank to the left and away from his sight. Even Saada, braced in anticipation of the sudden maneuver, momentarily lost his footing, causing him to teeter to the left. Both men had no sooner adjusted themselves to compensate for the left turn than the driver centered the steering T-bar, throwing Saada and his gunner in back to the right. Rather than being upset, however, Saada was more than satisfied with his driver's wild maneuvering. The last turn had brought the M-60A3 tank and its main gun to bear on a column of Libyan tanks, now moving perpendicular to Saada's deploying tank company.

"Enemy tank ahead!" The gunner's voice betrayed both excitement and surprise. If he was surprised at the sudden appearance of several Libyan tanks in his sight, the performance of his duties didn't suffer. While Saada glanced to his left, then quickly to his right, to watch the remainder of his company complete the action he had ordered, the gunner prepared to engage. Placing the aiming dot of his primary sight onto the center of mass of the nearest Libyan tank, he announced that he was lasing at the same instant that he depressed the laser range finder's thumb switch.

Even though his commander had not issued a proper fire command, the loader took his cue from the gunner. Standing back, out of the path of the main gun's recoil, the loader armed the gun by pushing the safety lever forward and announced that he was ready.

This announcement caused Saada to lean over to his left and look down into the loader's hatch. The loader had by now flattened himself against the left turret wall and was watching the breech of the main gun, waiting for it to fire and recoil. Straightening up, Saada looked down at his gunner. He too was ready, his eye glued to his sight, oblivious to anything but the enemy tank. Dropping down, Saada brought his eye up to his own sight, careful to avoid hitting his broken nose and swollen eye on the brow pad. In his sight a Libyan tank, unaware of the danger that it was in, continued to move off to the east.

The Libyan tanks Saada was preparing to engage were part of a counterattack force moving forward to seal off a penetration of the Libyan main defensive belt by the Egyptian 14th Armored Division. Saada's company, now the spearhead of that effort, had rushed forward through the breech in Libyan lines in search of the Libyan counterattack force. Saada had found that force, moving to the east along the spin of a ridge. Without hesitation, anxious to avenge his honor and his broken nose, Saada had turned his company into the attack.

Pulling his head away from the commander's sight, Saada looked at the range returns. Almost without thought he selected the button marked "last" in order to input the laser range return into the fire control system. Putting his uninjured eye back at the sight, he watched the gunner track the Libyan tank that would be their first target. Despite the bucking and bouncing of the tank over the rough surface, the tank's fire control stabilization system and the gunner were maintaining a steady sight picture on the Libyan tank. Satisfied that he and his crew were ready, Saada gave the order to fire.

The fifty-three-ton tank gave only a slight shudder when the gun fired and began to recoil. Saada and his crew did not feel the heat or shock wave of the muzzle blast created when the armor-piercing projectile left the gun tube. Nor did they hear the sharp report of the 105mm rifle cannon firing. The only noise perceivable above the roar of the engine was the clanking of the steel shell casing from the expended round as it was automatically spit out of the gun's breech, slammed against the turret guard, and dropped to the floor.

Though his vision was momentarily obscured by the muzzle blast and the sand it kicked up, the gunner maintained the gun's position and his own position at the sight. Saada's tank quickly moved out of the obscuring dust cloud. As soon as it did, the gunner's sight was filled with the bright flashes and explosions of a Libyan tank in its death throes. Their round had hit true.

For a moment Saada watched the sheets of flame leap from the stricken tank as onboard ammunition destroyed it and its crew. He had his revenge. The embarrassment he had suffered because of his accident on the first day of war could now be forgotten. His company had led the exploitation force through the break in the Libyans' line and had found the enemy counterattack force. In a matter of minutes it would all be over.

With the greatest of effort Saada pulled his eye away from the sight, stood upright and out of his hatch, and panned the field of battle. There was no need to worry about Libyan artillery. Even if the Libyan commander had the presence of mind at that moment to request artillery fire, the odds of hitting Saada's moving company were slim—very slim. So he exposed himself, standing waist high and upright in his open hatch. He scanned the scene from horizon to horizon. On his left and his right, other Egyptian tanks were firing. To his front, on the ridge, half a dozen Libyan tanks, victims of the first volley from Saada's tank company, were already burning. Of those that survived, half had stopped and were in the process of turning their turrets toward Saada's attacking company. Some of the Libyan tank commanders had turned their tanks and were charging head-on into Saada's formation. A few had turned and disappeared behind the far side of the ridge, a faint diesel-smoke plume marking where they had disappeared. It was obvious that the Libyan commander had lost all command and control, if ever he had had it. All that remained for Saada's company to do was to press home their attack with violence.

"Enemy tank ahead!" Saada's gunner had another target. Looking over to the loader to make sure he was ready, Saada dropped down. He didn't even look through the sight this time. He merely looked at the range, again pressed the last-return button, and ordered the gunner to fire. Saada was standing upright when the gun fired.

This time he was pelted with sand kicked up by the muzzle blast. He felt the wave of heat pass over him as the projectile cleared the main gun and released the expanding propellant gases. The gases, suddenly free of the confines of the gun tube, sped past the just-fired projectile, creating for an instant an orange ball of fire. In the twinkling of an eye the flash was gone.

And so was another Libyan tank. Saada watched as his round impacted on its target on the far ridge, creating a bright white flash. The Libyan tank shuddered and halted; black smoke began to pour from its engine compartment. But it did not explode, as the first tank had done. Not satisfied with a mobility kill, Saada ordered the gunner to reengage the tank. Without hesitation the gunner did so—to good effect: the second round ripped through the hull just below the turret ring, igniting fuel and ammo.

As their second victim began to burn, Saada all but bounced up and down with joy. All the fireworks displays he had ever seen as a boy paled in comparison to the spectacle before him. The sight of his tanks charging forth, throwing up great clouds of dust as they fired, the dazzling colors of red and orange created by burning and exploding tanks, and the resulting jet-black pillars of smoke from destroyed tanks against the brilliant blue sky produced a scene of beauty and destruction no artist could ever capture. In an instant Saada knew why veterans spoke of war in such reverent tones. It was the most awe-inspiring thing he had ever witnessed.

His tank, surrounded by the rest of his company, rushed forward and continued to fire. As it did, Saada kept hoping that this wouldn't end. He didn't want it to end. Without considering what it was he was asking, he prayed that the battle could continue.

Al Fasher, Sudan * 1645 Hours, 15 December

Finished with the last rank in the third platoon, Ilvanich turned away from the platoon leader without a word and stormed off, moving around the platoon to the front of the company. The three platoon leaders had brought their platoons to attention by the time Ilvanich reached his position in front of the company formation. Once there, he stopped, pivoted on his heels, faced his company, and stood there for several minutes, debating what to do. The results of his precombat inspection had been, to say the least, a disappointment. After almost two weeks of doing nothing but providing internal security for the airfield, both officers and enlisted men had become lax in their discipline and the maintenance of their weapons. Not a single platoon was ready to move out. Empty canteens, half-empty ammo pouches, and dirty rifles were just a few of the deficiencies he found. And the deficiencies were not limited to the enlisted soldiers. One of his platoon leaders had shown up with his map case but no map. Logic told him to go back to his battalion commander and report that his unit was not ready to deploy that night.

To do so, however, simply would not be acceptable. Another company would be assigned the duties, and Ilvanich and his men would be back to pulling guard and conducting roving patrols within the confines of the airfield fence. Besides, since arriving at Al Fasher, Ilvanich had made himself a nuisance, requesting permission every day to send out patrols at night to sweep the surrounding area and establish ambushes. Ilvanich was not alone in his desire to do something. The battalion commander also wanted to take a more active role than they were given, but he reminded Ilvanich, as well as himself, that external security was a matter for the Sudanese army. Ilvanich countered by reminding him that the Sudanese army that was responsible for providing external security for the Soviet-held airfield was the same one that was the host to U.S. Army Special Forces teams. His battalion commander reluctantly restated that although that might be true, they had little choice. The original agreement between the U.S.S.R. and the Sudanese government included a clause that restricted Soviet personnel to the airfield. In the second place, the battalion commander pointed out, he did not have enough personnel to provide internal security around the clock and run ambush patrols and sweeps outside the fence.

The situation changed dramatically after the Egyptians invaded Libya. Within twenty-four hours of the commencement of hostilities to the north, two additional parachute battalions had been flown out of Ethiopia to Al Fasher. One battalion was held on strip alert, with orders to be ready to depart in less than an hour. Rumors as to its destination were varied. One had it that the battalion was going to seize the dam at Aswan and threaten to destroy it unless the Egyptians withdrew from Libya. Equally popular was the rumor that the ready unit was standing by to go into Khartoum in case the Sudanese government needed an incentive to allow the Soviets continued use of the airfield. Whatever the truth was, that battalion was kept together and free from routine security tasks. Only in the unlikely event of an attack on the airfield itself would it be used at the airfield.

The second battalion was committed to beef up the security of the airfield. With the need for better security due to the outbreak of fighting in Libya and the additional units on hand, the decision was made to "supplement" the Sudanese patrols providing security in the surrounding area. Because he had been so keen on the idea, and because his company had had a great deal of success in similar operations while fighting guerrillas in Iran, Ilvanich's company was picked to conduct sweeps and establish ambushes.

Any joy he had felt over the change of mission for his

company was washed away by the precombat inspection, which revealed how poorly prepared his company was. But dismal as his company's showing was, he decided to go as they were. To return to the barracks and correct all their deficiencies before moving out would take too long. The sun was already low in the west, and the moon, even though it was at 50 percent, would set at 2130 hours that night. The last thing Ilvanich wanted to do was to stumble about blindly without any moon, looking for their positions. Against his better judgment he gave the order to mount the trucks lined up to the rear of the company formation. As he watched his men do so, he decided that upon their return in the morning, no one was going to be released from duty, even for breakfast, until all the deficiencies he had noted were corrected. He had no intention of allowing sloppy performance to go uncorrected, or unpunished.

From a covered position on the side of a hill east of the airfield, Sergeant Jackson put his binoculars down and turned to wake his team leader. Even though they were a safe distance from the airfield, Jackson whispered. "Pssst . . . Hey, Lieutenant—I mean Captain . . . those Russians are mounting up onto trucks. Looks like they're gettin' ready to move out."

Removing the camouflaged bush hat from his face and opening his eyes, Kinsly noted that the sun was already dropping to the horizon. He stretched, rolled over onto his stomach, and crawled forward until he was next to Jackson. Jackson had the binos back up to his eyes and was intently watching the troops complete their loading. "How big a force?" Kinsly asked.

Without taking the binos down, Jackson responded that there were at least three platoons, each with thirty men, three machine guns, and a few antitank grenade launchers, or RPGs. So far he hadn't seen any mortars. Then he quickly added that the mortars could already be on the trucks.

Kinsly considered this new development before he spoke. "Ambush patrols?"

Lowering the binos but still watching the airfield, Jackson thought about Kinsly's question for a moment. "A little big, but then Russians like to do things in a big way. Right weapons, right time of day, right sequence of events, like the combat inspection and all. Yes, sir, ambush patrols. Looks like easy days are over. The bear is gonna come out lookin' for us, sir.''

Kinsly reached over and motioned to Jackson to pass the binos over to him. Without a word Jackson took them from around his neck and handed them to Kinsly. Putting the binos up to his eyes, Kinsly looked at the line of trucks for a moment. The exhaust stack on the lead truck choked out a buff of dirty black smoke as he watched, signaling that the drivers were cranking up their vehicles. Sweeping to the left, Kinsly turned his gaze over to the line of attack helicopters located south of the trucks. Other than some mechanics working on one helicopter and a guard slowly shuffling around them, there was no sign of activity. ''Well, they don't know we're here. If they did, there'd be at least a pair of those helicopters up and sweeping the road for the trucks or working us over.'' Handing the binos back to Jackson, he ordered him to keep an eye on the trucks. If they started to move in their direction or helicopters began to crank, Jackson was to get back to the team's hidden position ASAP to warn them. After Jackson acknowledged the orders, Kinsly slithered down the hill backwards until he was sure he could stand without being seen over the crest of the hill.

On his way back to the patrol base his team was using, Kinsly pondered whether he needed or wanted to move that night or should wait. Assuming that the Russians were smart enough not to use the same ambush site and would sweep different areas each night, Kinsly decided to wait and attempt to find out where the Russians had swept and set up their ambush sites. That way he could move his force to that area the following day. With this being the first such patrol, odds were the Russians would sweep the more likely ambush sites along the roads.

While the location of their patrol base wasn't ideal, it had the virtue of being well away from the obvious, textbook sites. Altogether there were eight Americans and eight Sudanese operating out of the base camp. The Sudanese major, unable to accompany Kinsly and his team, had insisted on sending some of his best and most loyal troops. He and two members of

Kinsly's team stayed behind and covered for the rest of the Americans by parading the rest of the Sudanese garrison in public whenever possible. It was a dangerous game both men played. The major was in violation of orders from his government to restrict the movements of the Americans while the Soviets were in country. Kinsly and his group were just as likely to run into trouble with the local Sudanese army units as with the Soviets, since the Sudanese up to this point had been providing external security.

Even the trip to Al Fasher had been a covert operation. Using the excuse of conducting training in dismounted long-range patrols, Kinsly and his American-Sudanese team had left by night on foot and headed east. Just before dawn, they had been greeted by one of the major's uncles, a bus driver. The uncle had had an old, beat-up bus and civilian clothing waiting for Kinsly and his men. Traveling like that, they had crossed the country into Darfur Province. Throughout the trip Sergeant Jackson had kept complaining of how much he hated taking the bus to work. Every time he did so, Kinsly had reminded him that the alternative to the bus was walking. With the assistance of the major's uncle, the Sudanese soldiers, and a roundabout route, the trip had been quick and uneventful. Once they had reached a point ten kilometers from the airfield, the major's uncle had dropped them off. On their own, Kinsly's men had switched back into uniforms, then went about accomplishing their mission.

The sentry at the entrance of the camp did not challenge Kinsly. They were under orders not to challenge a man if they recognized him. Walking over to a clump of trees and bushes that he and Jackson used as a command post and sleeping area, Kinsly motioned to Staff Sergeant Eddie Lee Jefferson and Specialist Floyd Huey to join him.

When the three reached the tree, Kinsly began to issue orders. "Sergeant Jefferson, the Russians are moving a company out tonight. They're probably going to sweep the area east of the airfield and set up several patrols on the trails coming down onto that road."

Jefferson took notes, betraying no surprise as Kinsly talked. "I want you to double the guard. In addition, send two of our men and two Sudanese out to track the Russians. In the morning I want to know where the Russians patrolled and where their ambush sites had been.''

Jefferson responded with a short, businesslike "Roger," then turned and went about accomplishing his tasks.

Turning to Huey, Kinsly continued, "Huey, take this message and send it to 2nd Corps.'' Kinsly paused until Huey had whipped out a pad and pencil from his pocket and was ready to copy. '' 'Soviets commencing active patrolling outside airfield perimeter with company-sized unit this p.m. Expect Russians will establish ambush patrols. Ability to conduct successful or even meaningful raid on airfield with forces on hand not possible—repeat, not possible. Will continue to observe and report.' '' Kinsly stopped until Huey finished writing. "Along with that, send the usual data on aircraft that have been added to those since yesterday, number and type of inbound and outbound flights, etc. Any questions?''

Huey shook his head no. Kinsly, just to be sure, had the radio man repeat the message. Satisfied, he told him to get it out ASAP. With nothing more to do, Kinsly plopped down next to the small hooch made from his and Jackson's camouflaged ponchos, pulled an MRE ration out of his rucksack, and began to eat. While he tore at the plastic food pouches, he considered Jackson's remark. If the Russians were serious about the patrols and ambushes, the good days were indeed over. They'd all have to start being a little more careful and a lot more vigilant.

Washington, D.C. * 1035 Hours, 15 December

"Can I come in, Ed?''

The unexpected question startled Ed Lewis, who had been sitting at his desk, busily banging away on the keys of his laptop computer. Turning toward the door, he saw Congressman William Banes Bateman standing there. Bateman, nicknamed Wild Bill by both friends and opponents, was the House majority whip. "Sure, let me finish up this paragraph and I'll be right with you, Bill.''

While Lewis turned back to close the file on which he had

been working, Bateman walked over to a sofa facing him. Taking a seat in the corner of the sofa, Bateman leaned back, crossed his legs, and studied the young congressman as he worked on his computer. Like many freshman congressmen, Lewis had come to Washington wanting to change the world. Unlike many, his party loyalties were a matter of convenience; he had joined the party simply to get elected. His popularity with the people of his district and the attention the media showered on him made getting elected simple. That was good for the party. But it was also dangerous, because it gave Lewis a sense of invulnerability and independence; he believed that his future rested in the hands of the electorate and not of the party. On more than one occasion he had embarrassed party leaders by not only voting against them but publicly siding with the opposition. Bateman would just as soon be without the seat than have it filled by a mustang.

"You know, Ed, I never could get the hang of those things."

Without looking up, Lewis responded, all the while wondering why Bateman was there. "Neither can I. It's actually a crime what I do with these things. Except for the word processor and a few select entertainment disks, I hardly touch its potential."

"Don't you mean games, Ed?"

Finished, Lewis spun in his swivel seat to face Bateman. "I prefer to think of my computer games as a method of relaxation. Now, I doubt if you are here taking a poll on which party members in the House use PCs and which ones don't."

Bateman flashed a friendly smile that reminded Lewis of a barracuda. "Ed, Frank asked me to speak to you about the resolution you intend to introduce this afternoon and see if there is any way we can convince you to at least delay it for, say, two or three days."

The resolution Bateman was talking about, co-sponsored by Lewis in the House and Senator Patricia Stowell in the Senate, called for the immediate withdrawal of all U.S. ground and air units from Egypt. Like everyone in Congress, Lewis had a great deal of concern over the war in the Middle East. What to do about it was the question. Some, including Lewis, while expressing a sincere desire for a quick and just end to the war, wanted to ensure that whatever the final outcome, U.S. forces didn't become involved. All hope of effective U.N. intervention was scuttled by the inability of the Security Council to act. Resolutions in that body favorable to the Libyans were vetoed by the American representative on the Security Council, while resolutions favorable to Egypt were vetoed by the Soviet representative. Seeing no hope there, Lewis had decided to do whatever was in his power to prevent the President, or anyone else, from drawing Americans into another confrontation with the Soviets.

In a joint press conference the previous afternoon, Lewis and Stowell had announced their intention to submit to both houses of Congress a resolution that would require the immediate and unilateral withdrawal of American forces from Egypt. Overnight a storm of controversy erupted. Not only was the measure itself critical of the policy that put those forces in Egypt, its wording and timing were controversial, opening it to sharp criticism from both parties. Drafted by Lewis, it condemned Egypt as an aggressor, and accused Egyptians of staging the naval battle of 8 December. Though the resolution was intended to be bipartisan, the other party rapidly closed ranks behind the President, lashing out at Lewis, Stowell, and their party. By midmorning, the purpose of the resolution had been lost as both parties prepared for a hot and heavy debate. In order to avoid a major and potentially bloody fight on the floor of Congress, a last-minute behind-the-door effort by the leadership of Lewis's party to muzzle Lewis or scuttle the resolution was under way. If they could delay the proceedings and adjourn for the Christmas holidays, the crisis would resolve itself before anyone had to commit himself to any single course of action.

Lewis looked at the old man seated across from him and felt contempt for him and what he was trying to do. With a tone that barely hid his contempt, Lewis told Bateman that the answer was not only no but hell no.

The smile on Bateman's face disappeared. Uncrossing his legs and leaning forward toward Lewis, Bateman dropped any attempt to be subtle or friendly and went instead right into the attack. ''Now you look here, mister. Believe it or not, I really know where you're coming from, and in principle I agree with you." Bateman paused and sat back on the sofa, throwing his right hand up for emphasis as he continued. "Hell, Ed, if I thought that this mess could be resolved by simply pulling our troops out, I'd be running up and down the halls of this building promoting it myself. Unfortunately, there's more than just the protecting our people. There's the Russians. Or have you forgotten them?"

Angry, Lewis got up and began to pace behind his desk, fighting back the urge to choke the shit out of the old fart sitting across from him. "The Russians, the Russians! Every time this administration gets into trouble, they yell, 'The Russians are coming, the Russians are coming!' Christ, it reminds me of the Chicken Little story." Lewis stopped his pacing and pointed a finger at Bateman. "Well, my friend, I'm here to tell you I don't buy that line anymore. That same bullshit got us into Korea in '50, Vietnam in '64, and Iran two years ago. I for one believe that what the Soviet premier is doing is an honest and sincere effort to resolve our differences and make this world a safer place."

Bateman again leaned forward. "In the first place, young man, your grasp of world history and politics appears to be quite selective. The communist attack of South Korea was the result of a misunderstanding, a belief by the communists that the U.S. had no interest in Korea and would do nothing to aid that government. The Soviets crushed the Hungarian revolution in '56 with tanks and jets because they knew we would do nothing. Ditto the Prague spring in '68, Ethiopia in '77, Afghanistan in '79, and Iran. Before you buy a used car from the premier, I recommend you think hard about the consequences this resolution could have."

Despite the fact that he was upset at being lectured at like an undergrad, Lewis pulled his horns back in and settled himself before he continued. When he did, he spoke with a deep, steady tone that left no doubt of his resolve. "I have considered what the results will be if we don't act. If we do nothing, young Americans will be thrown into battle, again, in a foreign country. I cannot believe that you, or any other responsible official, could condone such a thought.''

Bateman felt the blood rushing to his cheeks. His patience was at an end. Still, he mustered the strength to keep himself in check and hold his voice down. ''And I, sir, cannot believe that a man of your background and education, as well as being a former soldier yourself, does not understand the implications of what the withdrawal of our troops will mean. The question is no longer whether they should have been there in the first place or not. Right now that's a moot point. The fact is that they *are* there, in Egypt, and the Russians are in Libya. To pull our troops out without some type of similar move by the other people can only be viewed as a retreat. The world, and the Russians, will believe that we are abandoning a friendly nation to her fate in her greatest time of need. Even more dangerous, such a move will give the Russians a free hand. Once our people are gone, the other people will be able to act freely, without any possibility of us responding in kind at the same level.''

''Congressman Bateman, I am going to do what I believe is right. I believe that the Russians will see our move for what it is, an effort to defuse the crisis. Furthermore, they will respond in kind. The Soviet premier has on many occasions shown that he is a man of peace, willing to do whatever is necessary to make the world a safer place. I, sir, am willing to bet my political career on that.''

Seeing there was no hope of stopping Lewis, Bateman turned and walked to the door. Just before he exited, he stopped and faced Lewis. ''You may be willing to gamble with your political career, but remember, if you're wrong, the soldiers who will have to sort out our mistakes are going to lose a lot more than a career.'' With that, he turned and left.

Al Gardabah, Libya ★ 2235 Hours, 15 December

In the operations center for the North African Front, a collapsible camp stool sat two meters from the situation map where Soviet staff officers posted the current situation. It was the general's stool, a relic that he had carried with him from his earliest days. It had once belonged to his father, a regimental commander of the 32nd Guards Tank Regiment, in the Great Patriotic War. According to the legend his father told him when he passed the stool on to his newly commissioned son, the stool had once been the property of a German division commander. The 32nd Guards, after crossing a river that was supposed to be unfordable and advancing all night, came upon the headquarters for a German division and promptly overran it. In the process of rounding up the prisoners, Uvarov's father walked into the operations center and found the division commander sitting on the stool, alone, his face in his hands, crying. When Uvarov's father came up to him, the German general looked up at him and, tears streaming down his cheeks, pointed to the map: "This is impossible! You can't be here. You're supposed to be on the other side of the river!" Uvarov relieved the German of the stool and kept it. Now it was his son's. His only words when he passed it to the young officer were, "You can use it when you're thinking, but don't ever think that you can command from it."

Uvarov had remembered those words and lived by them. Doing so, however, occasionally had dire consequences. More than once in Iran he had found himself in the middle of a fire fight, crawling around in the dirt with his soldiers. At one point in the Iranian war, when the situation was fluid, Uvarov and his small command group became lost as they were headed back to their division CP in the dark. Coming up to a road intersection manned by military police, Uvarov stopped and asked the soldier on duty where they were. Instead of answering, the soldier on the ground turned and ran, yelling in English as he went, "Jesus Christ! The Russians are here!"

Since being in Libya, Uvarov had already had two run-ins with death. Though he survived both, the one that afternoon had cost his aide his life. As he sat on his stool that evening, sipping tea and pondering the large map on the wall, he thought about how fickle luck was. Here he was, a man who had found himself in life-threatening situations, in peace as well as in war, and he had never had so much as a scratch. On the other hand, his young aide, exposed to war for the first time, was killed by a stray round. Though he knew that a good commander had to be technically and tactically proficient, he understood that the commander also needed a large measure of luck. His father had often told him, "A commander killed while bravely leading his men in battle may provide a good heroic story, but he wins fewer battles than a live commander."

Unfortunately for the Libyans, at that moment the man who was in charge of defending the Cyrenaica was neither brave nor equal to the task of commanding a large force. The proof of that was in front of him. Two large red arrows, one coming from the east along the coastal road, one coming from the south along the pipeline that ran from Sarir to Tobruk, were converging on Tobruk. Libyan units, marked in blue, were scattered about in an almost haphazard manner. Only along the coastal road itself, where units of the regular Libyan army had been posted, was the Egyptian advance slow. Already the Egyptian commander advancing along the coastal road had had to commit his second-echelon unit in order to maintain the pressure.

The real danger was in the south. The Libyan forces deployed to the southeast of Tobruk, equal to a division, had been destroyed. The Egyptian forces advancing from Al Haira had easily penetrated the thin defensive belt the Libyans had thrown up, then turned north for Tobruk. Not satisfied with bypassing the Libyan units that had survived the initial assault and letting them wither on the vine, the Egyptians had turned on those Libyan units isolated by the penetration and systematically annihilated them. This had taken them the better part of the day, giving the Libyans time to shift their reserve to Al Adam and prepare to face the new threat from the south. Earlier in the day Uvarov had considered that the destruction of Libyan units was the Egyptians' real objective. Since they were on a punitive raid, the destruction of a Libyan division would be more than enough to teach their neighbor a lesson. If that was their true purpose, once they were finished, the Egyptians would withdraw. That theory, however, fell through when it was reported that the Egyptians were repositioning units in preparation for continuation of their drive north.

So once again all focus turned to Tobruk, the last major

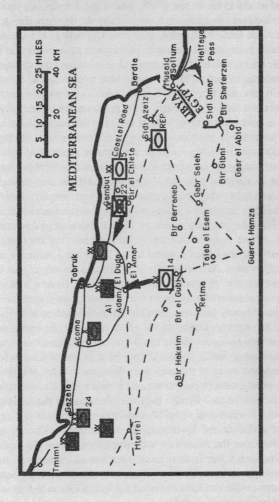

target in eastern Cyrenaica of any value left in Libyan hands. Jabal al Awaynat in the south, where the Libyan, Egyptian, and Sudanese borders met, had fallen on the first day to a motorized unit. Al Khofra, in central Cyrenaica, fell the second day to an airborne assault. Tobruk was next. Sitting on his stool, his eyes riveted to the map, Uvarov studied the situation, attempting to picture how it would look twelve hours, twenty-four hours, and forty-eight hours ahead. There was no need to go beyond forty-eight hours. If the performance of the Libyan forces held true to form, Tobruk would have long since been in Egyptian hands. By morning, Egyptian recon units would be as far north as Bir Hakeim and the escarpment south of Al Adam. An assault on the Libyan defenses along that escarpment could come as early as tomorrow afternoon, perhaps even tonight.

It was then, when the Egyptian forces were heavily involved with either penetrating or bypassing the Libyan forces defending Tobruk, that they would be most vulnerable to counterattack. A tank-heavy attack force, swinging south of Bir Hakeim into the flank of the Egyptian forces attacking Tobruk, would be devastating. Unfortunately, the Libyans no longer had the forces capable of making such a maneuver. Uvarov's Soviet tank corps was the only major tank formation not committed in battle. Uvarov, however, quickly dismissed that option. Even if he had the freedom to do so, which he didn't, he would not. There was no doubt in his mind that once his tank corps was committed to battle, it would only be a matter of time before American forces in the area were brought to bear. While the American ground forces to the east were a major consideration, one he did not take lightly, they were only part of the equation. Though it was out of sight, he could feel the presence of the 6th Fleet just over the horizon to the north. Attack aircraft and gunfire from the American battleships would have no trouble closing down the coastal road wherever and whenever they wanted to. It was his line of communication running south through Sudan and Ethiopia, over the Indian Ocean to Iran, and overland to the Soviet Union, however, that caused him his greatest concern. It was long, fragile, and easily broken at any point.

For a moment, he considered not even mentioning that possibility in his nightly report to STAVKA. To do so, he thought, might give some amateur strategist sitting in the basement of the Kremlin the idea that we could actually pull it off and win. Not to address it, however, would serve no purpose. A bright young staff officer at STAVKA, analyzing the information provided by the North African Front, would see the same possibility. If that happened, STAVKA would wonder why Uvarov hadn't seen such a maneuver and addressed it, bringing his abilities as a commander into question. No, he thought, better to discuss the matter, as pointless as it is, and explain, in clear and unemotional terms, why we shouldn't.

The decision made, Uvarov stood up and stretched. He looked at the clock, then turned to the operations duty officer. "How long before you are ready with the daily operations report?"

The young major stood up and came around his small field desk to where the general stood. When he reached Uvarov, he held out a clipboard to which the draft report was attached. "Sir, with the exception of your portion of the report, it is finished and ready for your review and approval."

Uvarov took the clipboard in his free hand and glanced at the first page. "Very good. Perhaps we shall get it in on time tonight." When he said that, he winked at the major. The major smiled. Uvarov always waited until the last possible minute to add his comments. This practice caused a great deal of distress for the poor duty officer, who had to scramble to submit the report on time. Uvarov's chief of staff, a stickler for punctuality, would tolerate no excuse for late reports.

Satisfied with what he saw, Uvarov handed the major his empty cup and asked if there was someone who could possibly find some hot tea. The major responded that there was a kettle of hot water ready and waiting. As he turned to leave, the major paused, then turned back to the general. "One more thing, Comrade General. Major Neboatov is here to see you."

Uvarov looked at the major quizzically. The major reminded him that he had requested to see the senior surviving advisor from the destroyed Libyan division. Neboatov was that man.

Remembering the request, Uvarov shook his head and asked the major to show Neboatov in. When the major left, Uvarov sat back down onto the camp stool, balanced the clipboard on his right leg, and began to write. He was still writing when he heard footsteps come pounding up behind, then around him. The man he had asked to see stopped midway between the map board on the wall and Uvarov, brought his heels together, and shouted, "Major Neboatov reporting *as ordered*, Comrade General."

The sudden disturbance and the harsh emphasis on the words "as ordered" surprised Uvarov. Prepared to jump up and bark at the impetuous major who had disturbed his train of thought, Uvarov looked up, then instantly changed his mind. Uvarov was shocked by the apparition before him. For a moment he studied the man who stood there at attention and saluting. Neboatov looked like hell. He had no hat. His hair was dirty and greasy, with clumps and strands sticking out in all directions. His face was covered with dirt and grime—the only clean parts were two white circles around his eyes where his desert goggles had been. His uniform was splotched with alternating patches of oil stains, dirt, and dried blood. What gear he had was arranged properly but just as dirty.

Regaining his thoughts, Uvarov signaled a soldier to bring Neboatov a chair and invited him to sit. Still stiff and formal, Neboatov thanked Uvarov and seated himself, using only the front three inches of the chair and maintaining a ramrod-straight posture. Inquiring about the bloodstains, Uvarov asked if Neboatov was wounded. Dryly, and making no effort to hide his sarcasm, Neboatov responded that no, he wasn't wounded, the blood belonged to his driver, adding that he was sorry he hadn't had the time to finish picking the man's brains off his tunic before reporting to the general.

The last comment made the general angry, but he contained himself. Neboatov, he reasoned, had just been through hell and was still not fully recovered from the trauma of combat. Instead, Uvarov offered Neboatov some hot tea, explaining that the reason Neboatov had been asked to come to the front headquarters was so that he could personally report his observations on the performance of the Libyans and shed some light on what had happened. While they waited for the tea, which came with a small stack of biscuits, Uvarov made some small talk in an attempt to put the major at ease and get his mind off the horrors he had just been party to. Slowly Neboatov relaxed and eased himself back into his seat. When Uvarov felt he was ready, they began to go over what had happened and why.

The story Neboatov told was no surprise. Poor staff work at all levels, erroneous reporting or no reporting at all, the inability to fight the subordinate brigades as part of a division battle, the inability to project with any degree of accuracy where the enemy was going and what he was up to, and the panic that paralyzed all levels of command when the Egyptians broke through—all this confirmed Uvarov's belief that the Libyans would be unable to stop the Egyptians. Without intervention by Soviet and Cuban forces—an option Uvarov violently opposed—the war was lost.

Uvarov asked a few questions, then called the duty officer over and instructed him to find a place where Neboatov could clean up and get some sleep. Neboatov, sensing that he was about to be dismissed, stood. When Uvarov thanked him and told him to get some sleep, Neboatov hesitated. Noting that he didn't move, Uvarov looked up and asked if there was something else he wanted to say.

"Comrade General, with the destruction of the last unit I was with, I have no duty assignment. To whom will I report in the morning?"

Uvarov grunted. "Oh, yes—I forgot." He thought about it for a moment, then looked up at Neboatov. "Report to my chief of staff."

Uvarov went back to work on the report, but Neboatov still didn't move. Slightly agitated, Uvarov again looked up. "Now what, Comrade Major?"

"Begging the general's pardon, what duty position should I tell the chief of staff I am filling?"

Again Uvarov grunted. "Oh, yes—quite right. I'm sorry. I forgot to tell you. Inform the chief of staff that you will be my new aide." Finished, he went back to writing, then paused just as Neboatov, dumbfounded, was turning to leave. "And Major Neboatov—when you report to me in the morning at 0630 hours for duty, make sure your driver's brains are off your uniform."

12

War is the realm of the unexpected.

—B. H. LIDDELL HART

Northwest of Cairo * 0945 Hours, 16 December

Flying at less than one hundred feet, the Blackhawk helicopter skimmed along effortlessly. From the helicopter, the wind-swept sands below, blowing this way, then that, looked like haze. Jan Fields, who enjoyed helicopter rides under any conditions, was glad that they were not traveling by road that day. Of all the curses of the desert, being pelted with sand for hours on end was the worst. Turning away from the small window, she looked at Johnny sitting with his head between his knees, busily filling his second barf bag. She smiled a wicked little smile. Serves him right, she thought. He wanted to come along for the ride—well, he's having one he won't soon forget.

The helicopter's crew chief tapped Jan on the shoulder. When he had her attention, he pointed out the door. Looking out, she saw the temporary airfield where the 1st of the 11th Heavy Attack Battalion was established. Although she had been there before, this would be the first time since the war had begun. And it would be the last.

The announcement that the President was ordering forces out of Egypt had taken everyone by surprise. Prompted into action by Congressman Ed Lewis's resolution, dubbed the "Home by Christmas" resolution, the leadership of both parties had gone to the President with the recommendation that he make the decision rather than let the resolution go before Congress. In the words of the House majority leader, the resulting fight on the floor of Congress would yield nothing but bad blood between the two parties. Though the President's order had not specified a date for the final withdrawal, everyone assumed it would be done quickly. Seeing the final curtain coming down on the drama, Fay thought it would be a good idea for Jan to go out to the American units. With luck, she would be able to get some good comments and reactions from the soldiers.

Making a wide sweep, the helicopter came in for a landing near the battalion command post. The bump of the wheels on the ground announced to the passengers that they had landed. The crew chief undid his seat belt, slid the door open, and hopped out. Jan followed without being told. As she stepped down and looked around, there was little doubt that the unit was preparing to move. Camouflage nets and the tents under them were already being pulled down. From behind a truck, a young captain came out and jogged over to where Jan and her camera crew were assembling. "Miss Fields, if you and your party would follow me . . . the battalion commander is with someone right now but is expecting you."

Leading them between the trucks and tents, the captain took them to a GP medium tent. The captain held the flaps of the tent open for Jan and followed her, leaving the camera crew behind to manage for themselves. Serving as the headquarters for the battalion, it was filled with a number of folding tables, large and small, chairs, phones, radios, computers, and maps hung along the walls. Across the tent was a group of officers, seated in front of one of the maps, their backs to her, listening to a briefing. No doubt, Jan thought, the information being put out was unclassified, the "good" information that meant something having already been covered before she was allowed in.

Behind her the cameraman and sound technician came in, lugging boxes and cases. The noise of their stumbling and bumping about caused several of the officers in the back row of the briefing to look, then turn back to listen to the briefer. Jan turned to the cameraman and technician and put her finger to her mouth, indicating that they needed to be quiet. They paused for a moment, looked around, then immediately began to carefully open up the camera and equipment cases as they prepared to check the equipment and set it up. Not seeing Johnny, Jan began to leave the tent to look for him. The captain who had escorted them stopped her, quietly whispering, "He's still outside. Probably something he ate."

With nothing to do until the battalion commander and the camera crew were ready, Jan moved to where she could hear the briefing. Perhaps she could pick something up to use in the report. A major was finishing a briefing on the sequence of their redeployment. From the questions asked and the major's responses, it seemed that the order to redeploy had already been issued. The major had difficulty answering some of the questions. When an officer in the back row asked him a question he could not answer, an officer in the front row, whom Jan suspected was the battalion commander, turned to the man to his right and spoke. "Scott, perhaps you can answer that one."

As Scott Dixon stood and turned to face the assembled officers, Jan felt her heart skip a beat. Like a reflex, her left hand went up and swept through her hair, making sure it was neat and presentable. Scott, caught in the crossed beams of two headlights bolted to a board hung from the ceiling of the tent, began to speak. He explained that because the Navy wanted to be ready for action at all times, the use of carriers as refuel points was out. He had begun to detail some of the restrictions the aircraft would be under while they were flying to Crete when he saw Jan. He paused in mid-sentence when their eyes met. Noting that Dixon was distracted by someone in the rear of the group, the battalion commander turned in his seat to see who it was. When he saw Jan standing there, he smiled. "Miss Fields, sorry for the inconvenience. We're about to wrap this up." Turning back, he nodded to Dixon, indicating that it was all right to continue.

Dixon, regaining his train of thought, continued, answering the question by referring to the map. For the moment he ignored Jan, intentionally averting his eyes from where she stood. Jan, however, could not take hers off him. As much as she had wanted to see him, to speak to him, since their night together, she was at a loss as to what she would say. Was she going to yell at him for leaving her without waking her and saying goodbye? Was she going to tell him that it had been great but he had a wife and family to go back to? Or was she going to tell him what she really felt, what she really wanted?

The briefing ended before she had resolved her dilemma. The officers stood up as a group and saluted the battalion commander. Some men grabbed their gear and filed out of the tent; others gathered around the map or broke into small two- and three-man groups to discuss some part of the plan. The battalion commander, a Lieutenant Colonel Tom Garrison, moved toward Jan. Immediately behind him was Scott. "Miss Fields, it's a pleasure to meet you again." When Dixon, his face set in an expressionless mask, moved up next to Garrison, the battalion commander held his hand up, pointing to Dixon. "Do you know Colonel Scott Dixon from Corps staff?"

A small smile flashed across Jan's face. "Yes, I've had the pleasure of the colonel's company."

Dixon's eyes widened for a second, and the tips of his ears became red. Clearing his throat, he asked if Garrison would mind if he had a word with Miss Fields. Garrison, still smiling, nodded his head. "Of course, take whatever time you need. The S-3 and I need to get a few things straight before the interview." Turning to Jan, he said, "Miss Fields, I'll be over there by the map, ready whenever you are."

Jan smiled and told him she wouldn't be a minute. As soon as he was gone, she turned to Scott. "Is there some place where we can talk?"

Dixon wrapped his hand around her upper arm and led her out of the tent. Once outside, he looked about, then took her between two trucks parked next to the tent.

They faced each other and simply looked at each other for a second. Both waited for the other to speak, neither knowing what to say. Finally Scott, looking down in hangdog fashion, began slowly. "Jan, I'm sorry for leaving you that night like I did. I was going to wake you but—"

Jan reached over with her right hand and placed the tips of her fingers under Scott's chin. Lifting his face toward hers, she smiled when their eyes met. "Scott, since that night I've often thought about what I was going to say to you when I finally caught up with you. Every conceivable thought and emotion came and went, from wanting to scratch your eyes out for leaving me like you did to . . ."

When she paused, Dixon reached up with both hands and clasped the hand she still had on his chin. "To what, Jan? Running up and grabbing me like the long-lost lover coming home?" He paused for a moment, looking up at the sky as he thought. He caught his breath and swallowed hard, as if the next sentence were lodged in his throat, all the while holding her hand. Ready, he lowered his head. "This is wrong. I know it's wrong. Everything about this is wrong." He paused, then chuckled. "You know, this whole affair wouldn't even make a decent class-B movie."

Jan withdrew her hand, stepped back, folded her arms across her chest, and turned away from Dixon. "There are a lot of people who would love seeing me go around like a moonstruck puppy." Looking over her shoulder, she added, "One of them being your wife. Of course, I doubt if she would find any humor if she knew that you were the man I was pining over."

Dixon walked up behind her and put his hands on her shoulders. She wanted to pull away again but didn't. "Jan, this is neither the time nor the place. Perhaps all we had was one good night. I hope that's not the case. But the last thing I'm going to do is screw up another person's life. I've already done quite a wonderful job with Fay's and mine."

Jan turned. "Well, Scotty boy, it's too late to spare me. Whether you want it or not, I think I'm in love with you."

"Like I said, I'm not doing anything until this small-scale disaster is over and Fay and I have a chance to square up."

Up to this point Jan had hesitated to mention Fay's name, reluctant to discuss her best friend with the woman's husband. Since Scott had opened the subject, however, she went ahead. "Scott, do you still love Fay?"

Dixon thought for a moment before answering. "Like I said, there's a lot that I need to get straight before I commit myself to anything. Right now, love, you're looking at a guy Sigmund Freud could write volumes on."

Scott's reference to her as "love" caused her heart to skip another beat. Whether he had meant it or it was just a handy term, Jan hung on it. She missed the next sentence or two, tuning back into Scott only when he mentioned Fay again.

"Perhaps I do love Fay. But the mere fact that I have to ask that question, along with the fact that I have no regrets about having slept with you, makes me wonder."

For a minute, maybe two, neither of them said anything. Neither wanted to leave the issue hanging. Dixon, however, knew that hang it would. Looking at his watch, then at Jan, he simply said it was time to leave, that he had another unit briefing to attend. Jan said nothing. Instead, she put her hands on his cheeks, leaned forward, and kissed him. It was a light kiss on the mouth which Scott didn't respond to. Nor did he resist.

Stepping back, she looked at him again. "Scott, take care." With that she turned and walked away.

As Johnny watched Jan walk around the front of the truck and into the tent, he wondered what he should do. He liked Ms. Fields a great deal. She had been a good boss and a great teacher. But he liked Mrs. Dixon too, probably more. She treated him with kindness and, almost more important, with respect. She was so much like his mom. And so beautiful. The last thing he wanted to see was Mrs. Dixon hurt, by anyone. The conversation he had overheard between Ms. Fields and Colonel Dixon bothered him. How could anyone do that, he thought, to a woman as beautiful and as kind as Mrs. Dixon? She was too nice.

Spitting out a few drops of vomit, he wiped his mouth with his handkerchief, waited a few more seconds, then went into the tent. Perhaps, he thought, he could ask one of the girls at the office what to do. They were always talking about such things and might have some good advice.

Al Gardabah, Libya * 1015 Hours, 16 December

From across the room Neboatov watched the general sitting on his stool in the middle of the operations center. As he did so, he wondered if the general always reacted so violently when he received an order from STAVKA. Perhaps, he thought, there was something about this order that he didn't understand. Maybe the general was just upset over this order in particular. That would also explain why everyone on the staff, who had been friendly and professional the night before, had turned inhospitable and rude that morning.

Standing up, Neboatov walked over to where the operations officer, the intelligence officer, and the chief of artillery were working with a group of officers. They paid him no attention as he reached over and picked up the folder containing a copy of the message that had everyone in the headquarters scrambling. Stepping over near the mapboard, Neboatov opened the folder and read the message for the first time. The first paragraph explained that a personal appeal from the Libyan leader to the Soviet premier for assistance, coupled with the imminent removal of U.S. forces from the theater of operation, had made the use of Soviet forces possible. The rest of the message directed the commander of the North African Front to commence offensive operations, in cooperation with Libyan forces, against the exposed flank of Egyptian units in the vicinity of Al Adam. The attack was to be conducted as soon as possible in order to prevent the fall of Tobruk. A follow-on mission for the Front, the restoration of the original Libyan-Egyptian border, would be initiated on order by STAVKA once the danger to Tobruk was removed.

Closing the folder, Neboatov walked over and returned it to the table from which he had gotten it. He looked around the room. Everyone was doing something; everyone was hustling or madly writing something on a pad or a map. Everyone, that was, except himself and the general, who still sat on his stool, looking at the map as if he were waiting for it to talk to him. With nothing to do, Neboatov walked over to the tea kettle and poured himself a cup. As he was doing so, he thought that perhaps the general would like a cup of tea. Such tasks, as far as he knew, were what aides did for their generals. After pouring a second cup, he took both over to a man who looked as if the weight of the whole world had just been dropped on his shoulders.

Tobruk, Libya * 1025 Hours, 16 December

The commander of artillery and rocket troops, Colonel Boahen, was about to enter Colonel Nafissi's private office when a loud bang from inside caused the artilleryman to stop. There was a moment of silence, then more loud banging from behind the closed door. Boahen looked at Nafissi's aide, seated at a desk to one side of the door leading into Nafissi's office.

The aide looked about first to see if anyone else was in the immediate area. Seeing no one, he stood up, leaned over the desk, and whispered to Boahen. "The Leader of the Revolution has requested that the Soviets attack in order to save Tobruk."

With a knowing look, Boahen shook his head, then backed away from the door to a seat where he could wait until Nafissi finished his tantrum.

Inside his office, Nafissi paced back and forth behind his desk. About the room, books, papers, and small pieces of furniture were strewn about where he had thrown them. He had been betrayed, stabbed in the back by the Leader of the Revolution. Without Nafissi's knowledge, the Leader of the Revolution had gone to the Russians and asked them to immediately intervene. With one division destroyed in four days and the Egyptians virtually at the gates, Nafissi would be seen as the man who almost lost the Cyrenaica, and the Russians as the saviors. The next step, stripping him of all power, and exile—or worse—wasn't difficult to predict. It would only be a matter of time.

That was, of course, unless he managed to save the city before the Russians became decisively engaged. He needed time. And he needed to act—now. Turning to the map on his wall, Nafissi looked at the disposition of his units, of the Egyptians and the Russians. He needed to engineer it so that the Russians were sent on a wild goose chase, away from the decisive point, for a few hours. With enough time, the FROG rocket units with the chemical weapons could be brought into play, hitting the Egyptian forces massing at Al Adam. A quick attack by the few mobile forces he had left while the Egyptians attempted to recover just might do the trick.

Excited at the prospect of salvation, Nafissi walked over to the door, opened it, and told his aide to have Colonel Ammed, the chief of staff, report to him immediately. As the aide picked up the phone, Nafissi turned to Boahen. "Are your units in place yet?"

Boahen jumped to his feet. "As of fifteen minutes ago, all but the 4th Battalion are in their assigned hide positions. That battalion will be in place within the next thirty minutes."

The smile on Nafissi's face surprised both the colonel of artillery and the aide. "Have someone fetch some tea," Nafissi said, turning back to the aide. "When Colonel Ammed arrives, have both him and Colonel Boahen come into my office. Also, inform the Russian liaison officer that I will need to see him in, say, two hours."

Gorky Park, Moscow * 1445 Hours, 16 December

Anna trudged along the trail, looking for her friend from the Ministry of Tourism. She was nowhere to be seen. Looking at her watch, she saw that it was five minutes past the time she had told her friend to meet her. Anna decided that she would wait another five minutes, then leave and try to contact her friend another way.

The two militia men strolling along their beat paused when they saw Anna pacing back and forth, looking at her watch, then around the park as if she was watching for someone. The first militia man looked at his watch, then commented that it was a little late for a noontime stroll in the park. The second militia man laughed, then commented that a good bargain and trade didn't follow established timetables.

The first militia man didn't respond. "There is something wrong, my friend. What possible reason could counterintelligence have for following the brown-haired girl."

The mention of counterintelligence took the second militia man by surprise. "What are you talking about? Where?"

The first officer pointed out a man, thirty meters behind Anna. "His name is Medvedev. I've met him before. He works foreign intelligence. What possible reason could he have for following the girl?"

The second militia man laughed. "Perhaps he is a dirty old man who enjoys tracking beautiful young girls in the park, like you do."

The first militia man was about to comment when the red-head ran up to the girl. Both militia men, and Medvedev, paused and watched, trying not to be obvious as they did so.

"Anna, are you crazy? What do you mean calling me like this? Do you know how risky this is?"

Anna didn't respond to the redhead's questions. "Listen, this is important. You must see that this gets sent immediately." As Anna said that, she shoved a piece of paper into the redhead's pocket.

Appalled, the redhead stepped back. "Anna, have you gone mad?"

Stepping up to the redhead, Anna looked into her eyes. "No, but those old fools in the Kremlin are. Do you know what they are doing? They have ordered the Red Army units in Africa to join the Libyans! They are starting another war! We must warn someone. Maybe the Americans can stop us."

The redhead again stepped back, trying gracefully to get away from Anna. But Anna wouldn't be put off. She kept closing up to the redhead, talking as she did so. Unseen by the two girls, the counterintelligence man reached up and lifted his hat. From behind a closed kiosk and a parked car, three more men, in a loose circle, came out and began to close in on the girls. The first militia man groaned. "Oh, shit—trouble."

He was about to move down to where the counterintelligence men were closing in when the second militia man grabbed his arm. "No, wait. Let them do their job. When they need us, they'll let us know."

South of Al Adam, Libya * 1345 Hours, 16 December

The refueling and rearming of Captain Saada's company was almost completed. In ten minutes they would be ready to go. Unfortunately, the attack was not scheduled to commence until 0800 hours the following morning. When his commander briefed the plan for the next day's operation, he explained that there was a big problem with resupply. The well-planned and -coordinated use of artillery had been very effective, resulting in great destruction at little cost to the maneuver units of the 14th Armored. That effort, however, had expended more ammunition than the planners of the operation had allocated to the artillery units. The stocks of ammunition needed to replenish the battalions were still in Egypt, at Mersa Matruh. To bring it forward was requiring a major effort, most of the division's transports, and time.

Saada feared that the time being lost was costing them any advantage that they had gained as a result of the victory in the south. He also reasoned that any advantage to be gained by waiting for the artillery to be resupplied before attacking would be offset by the time given to the Libyans to prepare to receive that attack. Like many of his fellow tank officers, he would have preferred to have continued north into Tobruk while the Libyans were still disorganized and Tobruk was uncovered in the south. Much better, he told his commander, to continue and risk a defeat than to stop and put a victory at risk.

The decision, however, had been made to halt the tanks before they reached Tobruk. The reasoning, according to the battalion commander, was to ensure that overwhelming combat power was available for the final, crushing attack. Saada, however, suspected that the decision by the American government to withdraw its forces had caused his government to reconsider its position. Without the presence of U.S. forces in Egypt to counterbalance the Soviet threat in Libya, it would be foolish to continue to drive deeper. The lead Soviet units, after all, were only fifty kilometers from Tobruk and little more than eighty kilometers from where his unit sat. Even traveling cross-country, the Soviets could cover that distance in less than four hours.

Saada walked out from the circle of tanks toward the north, then paused. Looking into the empty desert to the north for a moment, he felt a great sadness in his heart. This, he thought, was probably the closest he would ever be to Tobruk. Though the city was of little value, to say that he had been there after defeating all the Libyan forces in the Cyrenaica would have been wonderful. No, he thought, the order to withdraw back to Egypt would no doubt arrive soon. Perhaps another day they would finally be allowed to destroy the enemy that menaced them to the west.

Al Gardabah, Libya * 1345 Hours, 16 December

From a corner of the operations center that he had claimed as his own, Neboatov watched the proceedings. The primary staff was gathered around the map board in a tight circle. In the center was Uvarov, standing less than a meter from the board. To his right was the operations officer, to his left the intelligence officer. The chief of staff stood next to the board, completing the circle to the left, while the lieutenant colonel who was serving as liaison to Nafissi's headquarters completed the circle to the right. Immediately behind the operations officer, looking over his shoulder and that of Uvarov, was the chief of artillery and rocket troops. The logistics officer was in a similar position behind the intelligence office. They were silently studying the overlay the liaison officer had pinned to the map. Their expressions as they did so were grim, except for Uvarov's. His face was blank, betraying no emotion despite the disgust he felt.

Uvarov leaned forward to study the boundaries that Nafissi had given the Soviets for the forthcoming operation. He curled the three middle fingers into the palm of his right hand and stretched the thumb and pinky out to their fullest extent. Using his hand as a ruler, he measured the distance on the map from the center of mass of where his units were deployed to the line of departure designated for the attack in the morning. From there, he measured the distance to their first objective, then their follow-on objective. Grunting, he dropped his hand to his side and stood upright. He faced the liaison officer. "Go ahead, Colonel—please continue."

The colonel raised his notebook and began to read from where he had stopped. " 'At the direction of the commander-in-chief of Allied forces in the Cyrenaica, the Soviet North African Front will commence offensive operations commencing no sooner than 0700 hours 17 December. Soviet and Cuban forces will attack south from Ayn Al Ghazalah, south of Bir Hakeim, to the Al Jagbub–Tobruk road, and then to Al Burdi. The purpose of your maneuver is to cut off Egyptian forces now operating in our country and restore the international border.' "

The liaison officer paused while Uvarov considered the map. When he was ready to hear more, Uvarov looked the liaison officer in the eye and nodded for him to continue. " 'Under no circumstances are forces of the North African Front, including aircraft, to cross north of a line from Bir Hakeim to Bir el Gubi.' "

The liaison officer closed his notebook and looked at Uvarov. Uvarov, expecting more, looked at the colonel expectantly, then realized that he was finished. "That's all? That's the entire order?"

Understanding Uvarov's amazement, the liaison replied that yes, that was the entire order. All he had been given was the overlay that depicted the North African Front's area of operation and a quick verbal order. His questions concerning the intention and operations of Libyan forces, as well as known Egyptian locations, had been ignored. He hadn't even been allowed into the operations room where the Libyans had been working on their plan.

Uvarov was about to snap but managed to control himself. Instead he looked at the map and tried to understand what could be happening. Without looking away from the map, he ordered the liaison officer to get together with one of the assistant operations officers and draft a message to STAVKA. Uvarov paused while the liaison officer reopened his pad. "I want you to tell STAVKA what the order said, word for word. Then I want you to tell them that either they do not understand how to coordinate a major operation with an allied army, or . . ." Uvarov paused and considered his next remark carefully. ". . . Or there is something happening, or about to happen, that the Libyans are intentionally keeping from us. Regardless of the reason, I believe it is ill advised to commit Soviet or Cuban forces until the situation is clarified. I will continue to plan for the operation and commence necessary moves to comply with Libyan directives; but I will not—I repeat, *I will not*—cross the line of departure until STAVKA has reviewed the situation and orders me to do so."

For a moment there was silence as the officers gathered at the map stared at Uvarov. Uvarov, still looking at the map, waited for what he had said to sink in before he spoke again. Looking about the tight circle, he asked if everyone understood his position. All responded with a slight nod of their heads. "Good, now we must commence serious planning." Turning to the chief of staff, he said, "Assume that we will cross the line of departure at 0700 hours tomorrow morning and develop your options and plans accordingly. Make sure that you include a detailed deception plan aimed at the American AWACS and intelligence ships. I want you to be prepared to brief me with your initial concept by—" Uvarov looked at his watch—"by 1500 hours. Any questions?"

Having none, the staff remained in place while Uvarov walked away from the map toward Neboatov. Once the commander was gone, the chief of staff began to issue additional instructions to the planning staff.

Neboatov stood as the general approached. Upon reaching Neboatov, the general asked if he had had lunch yet. Neboatov replied that he had not. Uvarov smiled. "Good. Then come with me and we shall see if there is something around here worth eating." As they walked out, he added, "I've got to get out of this madhouse before I go insane."

Cairo * 1945 Hours, 16 December

After spending every waking hour for the last nine days working in the WNN offices, it felt strange to Fay to be walking around in the "real" world. It was almost as if she were visiting another planet, one that did not have phones and video recorders and wall-to-wall people screaming at each other. For the first time since the crisis had begun, Jan and Fay had left the office early. They and the rest of the staff were beginning to suffer the stress of short deadlines, long and irregular hours, missed meals, and being confined together in their cramped offices. With the tape of the interviews with homeward-bound American troops finished early, Fay recommended that she and Jan go out to dinner that night.

While they waited for their table at the Nile Hilton's Italian restaurant, Jan was struck by the crowd of people and the general lack of concern with the war that was raging less than five hundred miles away. Even more amazing were the lights. She asked the waiter to seat them next to the window overlooking the river. For the first ten minutes she did nothing but watch the boats and ferries moving up and down the Nile as she sipped her wine. With their lights blazing, it was easy to convince herself that there was no war, at least not that night. Perhaps, she thought, the American withdrawal would put an end to it.

When the waiter took their order, Jan asked for veal parmigiana with the largest plate of spaghetti they had. Fay laughed, reminding Jan that she would pay for every ounce of it for a month. Jan made a face, telling Fay that she was tired of living like a hermit and eating yogurt and salads, that the soul needed a good shot of Italian food every now and then.

When the waiter finished taking their order and left, Jan went back to looking out the window, thinking of what she would do once the U.S. forces were gone and Scott was back in town on a more stable basis. Fay sat across from her quietly sipping her wine, looking down at her glass between sips.

Several minutes passed before Fay spoke. "I heard you saw Scott today."

The mention of Scott's name by Fay caused Jan to jump.

"I'm sorry, Jan. I didn't mean to disturb you."

Jan, recovering her composure, wondered who had told Fay that Dixon was there. No matter—the damage was done. But was there more? Jan looked into Fay's eyes for some kind of sign. She didn't know what she expected to see; she never had been in a situation like this before. Seeing curiosity and not anger, Jan collected her thoughts for a second before responding. "Yes . . . he was there when we arrived, doing some kind of briefing."

Half in jest, half bitterly, Fay asked, "Did you manage to talk to him without scratching out his eyes?"

Cautiously, not knowing where Fay was going with the conversation, Jan answered yes, they had not even argued. It was the truth, but she was beginning to feel uncomfortable.

Fay paused, picked up her glass, and drank, emptying it in one long sip. Finished, she placed the glass on the table, filled it again, then played with the stem, slowly turning it, looking at the red wine, thinking. Jan watched her, not knowing what to expect. Finally Fay began to speak in a low tone, staring at the glass while she did so. "Jan, now that this thing is over, I'm going to ask Scott for a divorce." Pausing, she continued to fiddle with her glass.

Jan was fighting a dozen emotions, urges, and fears. The word "divorce" surprised her, then, in a flash, brought joy. In the next second the joy was replaced by fear—fear that someone had seen or, worse, heard Scott and her. So Jan sat there, outwardly as dispassionate as she could be, inwardly wanting to scream at Fay to continue instead of torturing her like that.

Lifting her glass, Fay took a long sip, then put it down. "I don't think I love Scott anymore." She paused, made a face, and shook her head, as if she were trying to erase her last sentence. "No—what I meant to say was that I don't think we love each other." Again she paused and thought about what she had said. Finally, with a questioning look on her face, she looked at Jan. "You know what I mean, don't you?"

With a straight face Jan simply nodded. "Jan, I thought that I could make Scott see . . . I mean, make Scott understand that I'm just not cut out for the Army anymore." Fay paused long enough to empty her glass and refill it before she continued. Her face was so serious, so intent, that it was streaked with hard, deep lines. She leaned over the table toward Jan, almost knocking over the half-empty wine bottle. "God, Jan, you don't know how horrible it is to go to another woman, a friend, and tell her that her husband is dead, that he's not coming home anymore."

Sitting up fast, Fay picked up her glass, took another drink, and put the glass down without looking, almost missing the table. "I did that. Sixteen times I did that. Ten of those visits were on one day . . . the third of August." Fay looked at Jan; her eyes were becoming glassy. "You see, Jan," Fay said cynically, "the boys had a hard day at the office." Pausing only long enough for another drink, she continued. "For weeks I lived in fear of the doorbell. Every time it rang I died a little, sure that it was another wife coming with the chaplain to tell me I was a widow." Fay put a mock smile on her face. "But do you know, that wasn't the worst of it. No. I thought that was hard. But I was wrong." She pointed a finger at Jan. "It's the funerals that get to you. They're so long. And so sad. And so . . ."

Fay stopped. For a second she fought back the tears. She looked away from Jan, out the window, taking deep breaths and clenching her jaw until she had regained her composure. When she continued, she didn't look at Jan, fearful that Jan would see the tears welling up in her eyes. Instead, Fay set her gaze on an object in the distance.

"The escort officer brings the widow and family to the cemetery in one of the limousines. A soldier opens the door for the widow and holds it until the escort officer comes around. He's the very image of the soldier: tall, straight, and proper, decked out in his dress blues, hair freshly trimmed, ribbons in place and brass gleaming. Next to him the widow—a woman in black—a broken woman. They slowly walk past the coffin. It's there already, with a clean, bright flag neatly draped over it. People on either side say nothing. They only bow their heads and avert their eyes when the widow passes.

"Once everyone is in place, the ceremony commences. A friend who knew the man, if any are left, says something.

Mostly they mumble a few words that are meant to cheer the widow and her children.'' Fay turned and looked at Jan, a forced smile on her face. ''They never do—the words, that is. They never make anyone feel good about what happened.''

Jan could feel herself fighting back her own tears. She so wanted to get up and wrap her arms around her friend, to ease her pain. But she didn't.

Looking back out the window, Fay continued. ''The chaplain follows. Like the friend, he tries hard to create meaning out of death, to provide a word that will put it all in perspective. At least they speak better. When he's finished, the officer in charge of the funeral detail takes over. From out of nowhere they come—the firing squad—eight of them. They advance at a slow pace, very deliberate, very precise. It's almost as if they want to prolong the agony, to remind everyone assembled that this is it, the last time the deceased will be with them. Once they're in place, the officer orders the firing squad to prepare. In quick, precise, mechanical moves the firing squad bring their rifles up and fire. I always jump. Three times the commander of the firing squad calls out his commands. Three times they fire. Then . . .''

Fay paused and took a long drink, emptying her glass again. ''Those who have managed to hold their tears up to that point lose it as soon as the bugle starts. God, I hate that bugle!'' Jan sat for the longest time and waited for Fay to continue, but she didn't. She just looked out the window, lost in her memories.

They remained silent, Fay looking out the window, Jan watching Fay. Only the arrival of dinner broke the silence. As the waiter put the plates down and arranged the meal, Fay looked back at Jan, forcing a smile. ''I swore that I would never, never do that again. Scott promised me he wouldn't let it happen. But he lied. So now he can go tromping around playing the world-class boy scout all he wants. But he'll have to do it without me.'' Fay picked up her fork, stabbed at the veal, then looked up at Jan again. As she spoke, her face grew serious, deadly serious. ''I refuse to wait patiently at the door like a good Army wife, waiting, waiting. I want a husband, not a folded flag and twenty-one shell casings.''

Jan sat there for a moment, watching Fay begin to eat. She had never felt so awkward, so uncomfortable in her life. And the reason she felt so uneasy was not Fay's story or her unsolicited outpouring of sorrow. Jan felt uncomfortable because in the depth of Fay's despair, she had seen a glimmer of hope for her and Scott.

Al Gardabah, Libya * 1955 Hours, 16 December

The plan that his staff had prepared for the next day's operation pleased Uvarov immensely. Frustrated after a pointless and totally nonproductive visit to the Libyans' Cyrenaica headquarters, Uvarov had stormed into his operations center and sat on his stool, speaking to no one, gazing only at the map board.

Unlike the map he had studied in the Libyan command post, the one before Uvarov sang to him like a well-composed piece of music. The neat, curved lines, arrows, circles, and symbols danced an eloquent ballet across the face of northern Libya. With the timing of a master choreographer, the operations officer had managed to bring together the various components of the army, synchronizing them, combining them, blending them into a composition that flowed from their assembly areas around Al Gardabah to the sea at Al Burdi. Though musicians would blast his comparison of the operations overlay before him with the work of Tchaikovsky, the work of his staff sang to him in a way only a professional soldier would understand and appreciate.

In a few hours the Soviet 24th Tank Corps and one Cuban motorized rifle division, the 8th Division, would begin to move along two separate routes. The other Cuban division would remain in place to play a role in the deception plan. More to the point, however, was the fact that there was insufficient motor transportation available to the front to keep more than the tank corps and one division supplied. Crossing the line of departure at exactly 0700 hours the next morning, the tank corps would move in a bell formation, one tank brigade in the lead and on each flank. The center of the bell would be occupied by the motorized rifle brigade, followed by the artillery battalion and supply column. Further to the south and a little behind, the Cuban division would do likewise.

By striking well to the south, Uvarov could bypass Egyptian units protecting the flank of the main Egyptian force while keeping his forces uncommitted. This, combined with a steady pace, would allow the Egyptians to see the danger and move. Uvarov hoped, and expected, they would move east, back across the border. If they did, he would pursue, but at a respectable distance and without pressure. What an accomplishment, he thought, to be able to achieve your objective without fighting. The epitome of the master stroke.

Uvarov's operations officer, however, was also a realist. The plan included contingency operations that would allow Uvarov to wheel the tank corps due north toward Tobruk and into the Egyptian rear if the Egyptians decided to stand fast. Another option would allow the tank corps to drive for the sea and cut off any Egyptian units that decided to stay in Libya. Though he had no intention of doing so if it could be helped, Uvarov's front was prepared to fight.

From behind him a hand came down, holding a cup of tea. Twisting his head and looking up, he saw Neboatov. Smiling, Uvarov took the tea. ''You are fast becoming an adept aide. Again I have been blessed with the right man at the right time.''

Neboatov smiled. ''Comrade General, I must confess. Your aide is a coward.''

Uvarov turned in his seat, then motioned for Neboatov to sit next to him in a chair where the chief of staff normally sat. When he was comfortable, Uvarov leaned forward. ''So what is so special about you? I am also a coward.''

Neboatov watched the general as he sipped his tea.

Uvarov let his thought hang for a moment, then continued. ''Look—look at that plan.'' Uvarov waved his right hand at the map without breaking eye contact with Neboatov. ''That, my good major, is the plan of a coward. I have no intention of fighting the Egyptians.''

Neboatov looked at the general, then the map, then back at the general.

Uvarov continued. ''If I can do my duty without fighting, I

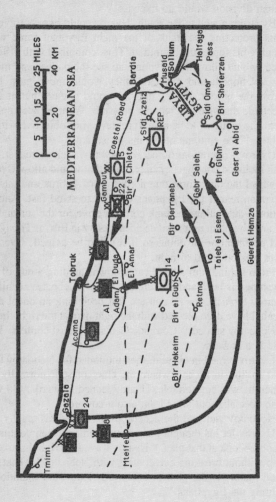

will do so. We all, in our hearts, pray that we can do that. Deep down in each of us is a coward striving to get out.''

Seeing that the general was really talking to him, Neboatov let go. ''Last night, when I came in, I was finished. I knew that if you told me to go out there again, with another unit, ours or a Libyan, I wouldn't be able to. Even now I don't think I could. I have been too lucky. Too many of my men and friends have died at my feet. I do not want to join them. If you had told me to go, I would have refused, consequences be damned.''

Uvarov smiled. It was an understanding smile, like one a father gave his son. ''No man is expected to be a hero every day. No soldier is expected to willingly march into every battle ready to die. We are not like that. The party and the state can demand that we close with and destroy the enemy, but they cannot take our hearts and minds out of our bodies. No, Major, you are not a coward. You are only a man who had been asked to do more than any man should. In time, your wounds will heal. They will leave scars, but in your own time you will heal and be ready to do what you know is right.'' Uvarov paused and straightened up in his seat. ''I make it a habit of picking only the best men to serve me. You are no exception.''

Uvarov stood up; Neboatov jumped up at his side. ''Now, if you would be so kind as to refill my cup. Then, tell the chief of staff that I want one last update on the enemy situation before we turn in for a few hours' sleep.'' Neboatov had turned to accomplish his tasks when Uvarov stopped him. ''And Major, see if you can find some cakes to go with our tea.''

13

Paradise is under the shadow of our swords. Forward.

—CALIPH OMAR IBN ALKHATTAB,
at the battle of Kadisya, A.D. 637

West of Tobruk * 0540 Hours, 17 December

Standing in the door of the communications van, the commander of the 2nd Rocket Battalion looked at his watch for the fifth time in as many minutes. Except for the soft glow of critical gauges and indicators, the van was as dark as the surrounding night. Looking up at the black, predawn darkness, the Libyan major couldn't even see the camouflage net that covered the van less than five meters from where he stood. Letting his arm slowly fall to his side, he was glad that it was almost over. Timing, this morning, was everything. The Soviet Cosmos reconnaissance satellite was just dropping over the horizon to the east. It would be thirty-five minutes before the American KH-14 surveillance began to move over the horizon from the west. Though the satellite wouldn't be able to stop the major from accomplishing his mission, the chief of artillery and rocket troops had stressed the importance of deploying, launching, and dispersing without being observed by anyone. Even if the major didn't understand the reasoning, he understood the order. And it was time to execute it.

Moving back into the van, the major closed and secured the door, then turned on the red light. To a young lieutenant sitting at the communications console, he gave the order to move the transporter-erector-launchers, or TELs, into position. Standing behind him, he watched and listened as the lieutenant picked up the phone and turned the hand crank. The lieutenant listened for the three firing battery commanders to respond. Each firing battery controlled four TELs, each TEL having one SS-21 surface-to-surface missile. When the commander of a firing battery came up on the line, the lieutenant in the van told him to stand by for orders. When all the commanders were on the line, the lieutenant issued the order to deploy and prepare to launch. He then held the line until the commanders, in sequence, had acknowledged. Finished, the lieutenant replaced the phone into its cradle, turned to the major, and reported that all missile sections had been notified of the order, had acknowledged, and were complying.

Satisfied, the major put his hand on the shoulder of another lieutenant, sitting next to the first, and instructed him to contact headquarters to confirm target locations and data. Then, with nothing to do for the next five minutes, the major stepped back to a chair near the wall across from the communications console. He didn't stay there long, however. No sooner had he sat down than he jumped back to his feet. He turned to pace, but there was nowhere to pace in the crowded van. There had to be something to do, but he couldn't think of anything. Looking at his watch, he was amazed at how the time crept along at a snail's pace.

Outside the van, in scattered sites, the crews of the TELs were not at a loss for something to do. The soldier receiving the order hadn't even placed the phone back in its cradle before half a dozen men began to roll back a canvas tarp covered with sand. While they did so, two other men, the TEL's crew, scrambled into the hole exposed by the rolled canvas. By the time the tarp was rolled back and secured, the sounds of a heavy diesel engine erupted from the black hole into which the TEL's crew had disappeared. Once the engine had reached normal operating range, there was a change in pitch as the driver of the TEL shifted gears and began to move it forward and up out of the huge hole in the ground. Preceding the TEL was one of the two men who had gone into the hole. He was walking backwards, holding a filtered flashlight and guiding the TEL driver.

For days the TELs sat in holes excavated around Tobruk before the invasion. To prevent observation from surveillance and reconnaissance satellites, a system of canvas tarps, supported by poles and spreaders and hidden by a layer of sand, covered the holes. To keep the sand on the tarps from being heated to a different temperature than the rest of the sand, the crews of the transporter-erector-launchers had been forbidden to run the TELs or even go near them unless absolutely necessary. Whether those measures would defeat the thermal detectors on the Soviet and American satellites was unknown. Even their friends the Soviets refused to provide the Libyan army with any details on the capabilities of Soviet intelligence.

Whether the measures taken to hide the SS-21 missiles and their TELs were actually successful or the Soviets and Americans had detected them and chosen to ignore them was unimportant. Such matters were not the concern of the crews preparing for launch. In a few minutes the missiles would be lifted into firing position and expended. Last-minute information provided by the firing battery's meteorological section and an update on target location was passed to the TEL crew. When the crews were ready, word was relayed back to the battalion command post.

The major in the command post van waited, impatiently tapping his watch. Each time a firing battery reported in that it was ready to fire, he nodded his head, then went back to nervously tapping his watch. When the final battery reported ready to fire, he ordered the lieutenant operating the net to Nafissi's headquarters to contact the chief of artillery and rocket troops and report their ready status. The lieutenant complied. The response was short and simple: execute as directed.

Walking over to the phone tied into the firing batteries, the major picked up the receiver and turned the hand crank. Every time a battery answered, he told it to stand by, as the lieutenant had done before. Once all the batteries had acknowledged, the major looked at his watch. The sweep hand raced around the face of the watch. As it approached the number 12, the major gave the order to launch.

In an arch that stretched to the west and southwest of Tobruk, the morning darkness was shattered by the launching of SS-21 and SCUD B missiles as well as ancient FROG-7 rockets. With few exceptions, the booster engines of the surface-to-surface missiles and rockets ignited and sent them aloft. Above the earth's surface, in the lower regions of space, satellites designed to detect the infrared energy created by the exhaust plume of launching missiles detected the sudden flurry of activity on the fringe of North Africa. The satellites duly relayed that information to duty officers in both the Soviet Union and the United States. The duty officers, in their appropriate air defense commands, automatically alerted the watch officers. They, in turn, initiated a sequence of steps in accordance with standard operating procedures. Chief among them was notification of the national command authorities, orders to bring more intelligence assets to bear on the threat and confirm its location and probable targets. When the watch officers had confirmation that the data was correct—that they were missile launches—each, in his own country, began to bring the nation's strategic strike forces to immediate readiness for a counterstrike, should that be necessary. Though the origin of the launches was suspect, all personnel involved took action, deciding to err on the safe side.

South of Al Adam * 0603 Hours, 17 December

With his naked eye Captain Saada could not see the lead tank of his company move out of the assembly area and begin the move north. The squeaking of its drive sprocket grinding on the steel end connectors of the track, however, told him that it was in motion. When the blackout markers of the tank to his immediate front jiggled, then began to move, Saada ordered his driver to follow.

Slowly the column began to creep forward. Saada, standing in the cupola of his tank, looked at his watch. They had twenty-seven minutes to cover the five kilometers to their designated line of departure. They would be able to do so with ease. Time was not a concern, provided there were no unexpected delays, or halts, or that the lead platoon did not miss the marked route, or, or. . . . Such concerns raced through Saada's mind every time his unit began an operation. Once involved in the attack itself, and once in contact, he was able to handle the situation. Then there was no time to worry; there was no time for his mind to wander freely and create problems and potential problems where none existed. In battle there was time only to act, to execute. It would be the same that day, Saada was sure of it.

Saada was wrestling with his problems, real and imagined, when the SS-21 missile reached booster cutoff, casting off the warhead from the booster section. Free of the expended booster, the warhead began its free-fall ballistic trajectory. There was no telltale streak rising over the horizon to warn Saada and his company. The noise of the engines covered the sound of the small detonation as the break-up charge of the warhead shattered it and freed the encased liquid. Blurred by the dust generated by the tanks, the sudden pinprick of light in the dark sky caused by that detonation also went unnoticed. Free of the now ruptured warhead but still propelled forward by momentum, the liquid began to spread, forming a huge cloud of millions of droplets arcing down as gravity pulled it back to earth.

The splattering of those droplets onto Saada and his tank broke his train of thought. He had not noticed a rain cloud or a change in weather—he had been too preoccupied with the unfolding operation. Instinctively he looked up while holding out his right hand, palm up, to catch a few of the drops. They pelted his face, almost as if he had been hit with a stream of water from a hose. Looking down, he brought his hand to his face to inspect the unexpected rain. It was a strange, thick rain, almost like oil. Reaching over for the flashlight hanging just inside the cupola with his free hand, he grabbed it but dropped it, unable to get a firm grasp.

Turning to look for the flashlight, Saada noticed his vision blurring. He was unable to focus. In addition, his eyelids began to flicker and twitch. Bringing his hands up to his face, Saada tried to rub his eyes. As he did so, he began to experience difficulty breathing; the muscles in his chest began to spasm. Dropping his arms, he tried to steady himself. His arms, however, no longer responded. They dropped limply to his side, resisting all efforts to move as he wanted. As his legs began to quiver and his knees to buckle, the realization of what was happening hit him. The liquid that had fallen on him was a chemical agent—nerve gas. He was dying.

As if an invisible hammer had struck him, Saada collapsed. The nerve agent spread rapidly throughout his body, destroying his central nervous system. Muscles, no longer controlled by the brain, involuntarily spasmed. As Saada fell to the floor, unable to do anything to break his fall, his bowels and kidneys discharged their contents. The gunner, surprised by Saada's fall and by the overpowering odor of loose bowels and urine, turned in his seat to see what had happened. For a moment he sat there, watching his commander's body twitch and jerk. In the eerie red glow of the tank's interior dome lights, the gunner looked into Saada's eyes. They were vacant, almost lifeless. When the loader, who had come down from his position to help Saada, keeled over on top of Saada and began to twitch, the reality of what was happening struck the gunner.

The gunner yelled "Gas!" at the top of his lungs so that the driver would hear as he tore at the cover of his protective-mask carrier. Pulling it out with one hand, he jerked his tank crewman's helmet off with the other. By the time he was ready to pull the mask over his head, however, he no longer had the ability to do so. Though he was not immediately exposed to the agent, as Saada and the loader had been, and not in direct contact, the vapors from the droplets on Saada and the loader had already permeated the tank. Struggle as he might, the gunner was unable to fit his mask to his face. Like his commander before him, he lost all control of his body, lapsing into a short coma before he died. The driver's death followed within seconds.

Southwest of Bir Hakeim, Libya * 0635 Hours, 17 December

Standing in an open hatch of the specially equipped eight-wheeled BTR-80 armored personnel carrier–command vehicle,

Uvarov watched the deployment of the lead Soviet tank battalion as it prepared to cross the line of departure. He knew that he was in all probability too far forward. Only the recon company and the tank battalion coming up alongside were between him and the Egyptians. But the Egyptians, if his intelligence officer was right, were still twenty kilometers to the east and northeast. So he paid little heed to the warnings of his chief of staff and went to where he could see something.

Besides, there was nothing for him to do at that particular moment. The deployment had gone well. Until something unexpected happened—something that required a command decision because it was not part of the plan and the commander in contact could not deal with it—there was nothing for Uvarov to do. Watching a tank battalion deploy in the early-morning twilight served to occupy his thoughts and time until he was needed.

Inside the BTR, Neboatov sat scrunched over in a corner, arms folded over his chest, dozing off. He wore an extra headset but used only one earphone as he listened to the command radio net. There had been no traffic on that net for the last ten minutes. Until contact, there wouldn't be. Opening one eye and glancing down at his watch, Neboatov noted the time. He gave a slight shiver from the early-morning cold, pulling his arms in tighter in an effort to warm himself. Looking around the interior of the BTR, he watched the assistant operations officer and assistant intelligence officer as they sat facing the radios. If a call came in, they would answer. The general, along with his chief of artillery and rocket troops, was standing with the upper part of his body out of the BTR. Neboatov could see only their legs. With nothing to do, he closed his eyes.

He had just begun to doze off again when the radio came to life. Neboatov recognized the voice of the front operations officer, Colonel Krasin, before he recognized the call sign. Krasin's voice was excited as he demanded to speak to General Uvarov immediately. Pushing himself into a seated position, Neboatov moved over to where Uvarov stood, and tapped the general on the leg. Uvarov looked down as Neboatov removed the headset and handed it up to Uvarov, telling the general that

Colonel Krasin needed to speak to him urgently. Uvarov, making a face, took the headset, put it on, and spoke into the microphone.

Neboatov moved over behind the assistant operations officer to listen in on the conversation over the radio's speaker. The operations officer turned to Neboatov and put his hand over his microphone. "Moscow—I'll bet you it's Moscow with new orders."

The intelligence officer leaned over. "No—the Americans. They've seen us and they're committing forces. It has to be."

They were both wrong. As they listened, the three majors made faces and stared at each other with alternating looks of shock and amazement. Krasin informed Uvarov that the Libyans had just completed a massive chemical strike against the Egyptian 14th Armored Division. There were few details. Radio intercepts from both Egyptian and Libyan radio nets and reports from the airborne early-warning radars were the only source of information at that time. Attempts to contact the Libyan headquarters in Tobruk had been unsuccessful. Not even the Soviet liaison officer could be reached. Krasin didn't know whether or not that was intentional. He didn't, however, rule out the possibility of foul play.

For a moment no one spoke. It was all suddenly very clear to Uvarov: the evasiveness of Nafissi and his staff; the restrictions on where the Soviet attack would go; and, worse, the timing of the Soviet commitment and the Libyan chemical attack. In a bind the Libyans would be free to disavow any knowledge of the attack, claiming that it was initiated by the Soviets as part of their preattack bombardment. In any case the Soviets would be viewed as being just as responsible. They, after all, had trained, equipped, and advised the Libyans. It would be guilt through association.

Recovering from his shock, Uvarov asked some quick questions, including whether or not Moscow had been informed. Krasin responded that STAVKA had just contacted them, asking what the purpose of the missile attack was. Uvarov instructed Krasin to immediately contact STAVKA and demand that their commitment be halted. Perhaps, Uvarov said, there was still the chance that they could extricate themselves from a situation that would only spell disaster.

Finished with the conversation, Uvarov removed the headset and handed it back down to Neboatov. Lowering himself into the BTR, Uvarov sat across from Neboatov and the two majors at the radio. The general took off his hat with his right hand and ran the fingers of his left hand through his hair. No one spoke. The seriousness of their situation was overwhelming.

Finally Neboatov broke the silence. "Comrade General, should I order the helicopter to come here to pick you up for your return to headquarters?"

Uvarov paused and looked at Neboatov, pondering where he should go to best respond to the new, developing crisis. After a brief rundown of his options, he nodded his head. "Yes, Major. We must go back to the command post. I need to talk to STAVKA myself."

Cairo * 0645 Hours, 17 December

As was his custom, General Horn met with key staff officers before receiving his morning briefings, affectionately known as "the Seven O'clock Follies." With him were his chief of staff, Brigadier General Billy Darruznak, known alternately as General D or THE Chief, and the operations officer, Colonel Alexander Benton. They were drinking coffee and munching on doughnuts, going over details of the redeployment, when Dixon walked in unannounced. Horn looked up, surprised, but said nothing. Darruznak was angry at Dixon's intrusion but didn't have a chance to say anything before Benton turned on Dixon. "Colonel, we're in the middle of a meeting."

Dixon, visibly shaken, didn't take offense at Benton's tone. Clutching the clipboard he carried in both hands, Dixon stood in the center of the room before he spoke. He didn't think to apologize. Nor could he think of any way to tell the commander other than blurting it out. "Sir, the Soviets have committed at least two divisions into an attack in the vicinity of Bir Hakeim against the flank of the Egyptian 14th Armored Division."

Dixon paused as the news sank in. Horn, looking at Dixon,

then at Darruznak and Benton in turn, said nothing. There was a look of surprise on his face, one of embarrassment on Darruznak's at being caught by surprise, and one of disbelief on Benton's. Again, it was Benton who spoke first. "When did they move from their assembly areas? How is it that the G-2 missed it?"

Still fidgeting, Dixon surprised everyone by announcing that that wasn't important.

Angry, Benton shot back, asking him what *was* important.

Again Dixon took no offense but simply blurted it out. "Sir, the Soviets preceded their attack with massive chemical attacks. Initial reports indicate persistent nerve agents were delivered by SCUD and SS-21 missiles at 0600 hours this morning. North American Air Defense Command confirmed the launch of sixty-plus missiles and rockets in the vicinity of Tobruk through Air Force channels. Full extent of the attacks and their effectiveness are unknown at this time."

There was a stunned silence. Horn considered Dixon's news for a minute, maybe two, before turning to Darruznak. "Billy, I want you to gather up the crisis action team ASAP. I want them to be prepared to discuss the following: one, cancellation of the redeployment; two, evacuation of American civilians from Egypt; three, the need to deploy the force to new assembly areas; and four, protective measures we need to take to protect our force, our evacuating civilians, and our equipment storage sites." Turning to Benton, he said, "Put everyone into MOPP level 2 and back into their assembly areas. Notify the commander of the 16th Armored Division to have the 2nd Brigade, 11th Air Assault prepare to execute the evacuation of dependents."

Darruznak was about to recommend that they should clear those steps with the chief of staff of the Army first, but then decided not to. They were sensible steps, to be expected. Besides, Horn had three stars, and three-star generals got paid to make hard decisions. Instead, Darruznak just nodded, jumped up, and was starting out of the room, followed by Benton, when Horn called, "Hold it!" Pausing, they turned back.

"Alex, do we still have that contingency plan for the attack on Al Fasher with the Apaches?"

Benton didn't answer but instead looked at Dixon. Dixon looked back at Benton, realizing that Benton was waiting for him to answer the question. Turning to Horn, Dixon replied that he had saved the plan.

Horn looked at Darruznak while pointing an index finger at Dixon. "Billy, as a separate issue, I want Dixon to pull that plan out and begin putting it together. I want a low-level, low-cost response in hand when I talk to Washington. No doubt the Navy and the Air Force will get the job. But who knows—someone might ask us." Turning to Dixon but still pointing his finger at him, he said, "When they do, I want to be ready. Clear?"

Dixon nodded his head. "Clear, sir."

Standing up, Horn looked down at his desk, closing the folder that contained the order that almost had gotten them out of Egypt before Christmas. Without looking up, he sighed. "Thank you, gentlemen—that's all."

Dixon prepared to follow but was stopped by Horn. "Colonel, have my aide patch me through to the chief of staff of the Army."

Dixon mumbled, "Yes, sir," turned, and began to leave when Horn stopped him again.

"Scott, you have family here, don't you?"

Dixon paused. "Yes, sir. They're here."

From behind his desk Horn walked over to Dixon. "Do me a favor, Scott. Forget about telling my aide about the call—I'll do it. Instead, I want you to gather the members of the staff who are permanent party and have family in Egypt. Tell them what's going on. Go ahead and have them notify their families immediately. You have my permission to pass whatever information you need to in order to convey the gravity of the situation to the wives. Do you understand?"

Dixon thought about that. The general was right. Inevitably, some of the wives would insist that things weren't really so bad and would insist on staying, invoking the "for better or worse" clause. By letting everyone know from the start how bad things were, many arguments would be avoided. "Yes, sir, I understand. Is there anything else?"

Horn hesitated. "Back to the raid on Al Fasher . . . how much lead time do we need?"

Dixon considered the question before answering. "By 'lead time,' I am assuming you want to know how long it will be from when you give the order before we have the Apaches on target."

"Exactly."

"Thirty-six hours to pull it together, sir. That includes staging at Abu Simbel near Aswan the night before."

Horn thought about it for a moment. "How much time do you need before you can give me a detailed briefing, including a time line?"

"I can be ready to brief you in three hours, maybe less, sir."

"Okay, Scott, thank you. Now go take care of that other matter first and then get cranking on the raid. Let the chief know if the Air Force gives you any static."

Dixon, convinced that he was finally released, saluted, and left Horn's office. Moving along the corridor back to the war room, he had to dodge half a dozen officers and NCOs traveling at high speed without paying attention to where they were going. Turning the corner into the war room brought no relief. Officers from both the day and the night shift were crammed in there, as well as personnel from other staff sections who normally worked elsewhere. In the center of the room, standing there like the eye of a storm, stood General Darruznak, Colonel Benton, and Colonel Linsum, the intelligence officer. They were being briefed in front of the intelligence map by one of Linsum's assistant intelligence officers and Lieutenant Colonel Pfiffer, the staff chemical officer. About them a ring of straphangers and second-echelon staff officers stood, listening in and cluttering the room.

Dixon looked around the room for his senior NCO. Spotting him in the corner, he waved. Sergeant Major London saw Dixon, finished giving one of his sergeants some instructions, and worked his way through the crowd. Dixon smiled when London reached him. "Looks like your plan for keeping nonessential personnel out of the war room has gone to hell, Sergeant Major.''

London grunted and made a face. ''If you don't mind me saying so, Colonel, we have too many staff officers. Someday, when we have the time, sir, could you explain what they all do for a living?''

Dixon chuckled. ''Someday, after I find out myself.''

London waited for Dixon to tell him what he needed. Dixon paused, looking around the room, before he spoke. He was collecting his thoughts. When he did speak, his voice was cold. There was no hint of humor, no emotion. ''Gather up all the permanent party members with families in Egypt in the conference room immediately.''

London waited for further information but got none. ''Why, sir?'' he finally asked. ''And does that mean people on duty?''

''Yes, everyone,'' Dixon told him, again with a voice that betrayed no emotion, no inflection. ''There aren't that many of us with families here. The people that came over as part of Bright Star can cover for us. You see, Sergeant Major, the dependents are going to be evacuated. We need to get that started before we get involved in serious planning.''

Understanding the gravity of the situation and the need to tend to the soldiers' needs as quickly as possible, London acknowledged the order and moved to comply. With that taken care of, Dixon worked his way over to his duty station at the long desk that ran down the center of the war room and picked up the phone. With luck he would be able to reach Fay before she went to work.

Try as hard as she could, Fay Dixon couldn't ignore the ringing in her ears. At first, she thought it was just part of her hangover, the first she'd had in two years. It took a moment for it to register that the ringing was the phone. Again she considered ignoring it, hoping that it would stop. It did, but only because her younger son picked it up. It wasn't until he squealed, at the top of his lungs, ''IT'S DADDY!'' that Fay bounced out of bed, grabbed a robe, and went into the living room.

By the time she had reached the phone, her older boy was

there too, trying to pry the phone out of his brother's hands. Fay ended the fight by taking the phone and sending them back to their room. They marched off, protesting, and closed the door behind them. Fay sat before she put the receiver to her ear and answered with a simple "Yes?"

Holding the receiver pressed against one ear, and with his free hand covering his other ear in an effort to block out the noise of the war room, Dixon answered. "Fay, listen. I don't have much time and I can't explain everything to you, but you need to get yourself and the boys over to the embassy immediately—"

Fay cut in, asking why.

"Fay, they're going to announce the evacuation of all Americans from Egypt, probably within the hour. Once they do, it'll be a madhouse there."

Again Fay interrupted, asking why now, when the threat to Americans was winding down.

Dixon was losing his temper. He managed, however, to control himself. He knew Fay would be one of the wives who would resist. As he collected his thoughts, he looked up. An intelligence major who worked across from Dixon was staring at him with a look of horror on his face. No doubt the major thought he was giving away state secrets. Ignoring him, Dixon told Fay about the Russian intervention and their chemical attacks that morning. Dixon looked back up at the major. His mouth hung open in shock. Dixon was pleased with himself. He enjoyed getting a rise out of the intel weenies.

On the other end of the line, Fay was silent. Dixon asked if she was still there. When she answered, he came on strong, telling her in no uncertain terms that she had to get herself and the children out of Egypt, now. Fay didn't respond. As he waited for her to do so, Sergeant Major London tapped him on his shoulder. Dixon pulled the receiver from his ear. "Colonel, the people are ready in the conference room."

Dixon told London that he'd be right there, then put the receiver back to his ear. "Fay, you still there?"

"Yes, Scott, I'm here."

"Listen, Fay, I have to go. And so do you. Leave everything. You know the drill. One blanket for each of you, enough food for three meals, and some warm clothes. That's it. Leave everything else. Do you understand?"

Fay sat there silently. It was really happening. She looked around the small apartment, lost in thought.

"Fay, did you hear me? Get going—now!"

She didn't answer. Slowly she put the receiver back on its cradle. Folding her arms tightly across her chest, she sat there for a moment, looking at the floor. Then it struck her: Jan might not know. Grabbing the phone, she dialed Jan's number, letting it ring until Jan, in a groggy voice, answered. Excited, Fay blurted out the news to her friend and boss. "Jan, the Russians have intervened!"

Disgusted, Dixon slammed the receiver down. The intelligence major was still staring at him, a stern look on his face. "Colonel, do you know what you have just done?"

Dixon, lost in his thoughts, looked at the major. "Excuse me?"

The major repeated the question. "Colonel, I said, do you know what you just did?"

Dixon didn't understand. He just stared at the major with a quizzical look.

Seeing that Dixon did not understand the gravity of his offense, the major explained. "Sir, you just passed classified information over an unsecured phone."

Dixon looked at the major, shook his head. "Huh? What classified information?"

In a self-righteous tone the major pointed out that Dixon had mentioned that the Soviets had intervened and used chemical weapons. The phone, he said, might be tapped.

Dixon's quizzical look turned to one of disgust. "For chrissakes, Major. Don't you think the Russians know what they're doing? Who the hell do you think gave the order to use chemical weapons?"

Al Gardabah, Libya * 0805 Hours, 17 December

Pushing his way through the crowd gathered about the map board, Neboatov tried to steady the cup of tea he was bringing to the general. He wasn't succeeding. Half of it already had spilled over his hand and down his tunic. The operations center was a madhouse, far worse than it had been the night before. It seemed to Neboatov that every Soviet officer in Africa was in the operations center, using a phone or carrying on a conversation. Only around the map, where General Uvarov stood, was there any semblance of calm. Finally reaching his general, Neboatov reached his hand with the cup of tea around in front of Uvarov.

Uvarov took the cup without looking or saying anything. His eyes and his mind were riveted to the map board. The front chemical officer, alternating with an intelligence officer, was bringing the general up to date on what he knew of the situation. It wasn't very much, or very good, for either the Egyptians or the Soviet forces. The only information the staff had at front headquarters had been obtained from its own intelligence sources. Most of that had been gleaned from monitoring both Egyptian and Libyan radio nets.

Nothing, to date, had been provided by the Libyan high command. There had been, in fact, no communications with Colonel Nafissi's headquarters all morning. Uvarov's chief of staff explained that when they could not reach their own liaison officer at Nafissi's headquarters outside of Tobruk, he had dispatched another officer in a helicopter. As the helicopter with the new liaison officer approached, it was warned to stay away. The voice on the radio claimed that the area around the headquarters was contaminated. As the liaison officer had no way of telling, and since there was no chemical detection kit on board, he turned back.

The chief of staff, hearing this, sent a second helicopter before the first had even returned. It had a chemical survey and monitoring team on board. As it approached Nafissi's headquarters, it too was warned to stay away. The officer in charge got on the radio and explained that he had a chemical team on board and was there to help. The Libyans responded that they did not need any help, that the situation was in hand. When the officer in charge ordered the helicopter to continue and insisted that he be allowed to land to evacuate Soviet personnel from the bunker, warning shots were fired at the helicopter. Not knowing what to do, the second helicopter returned without accomplishing its mission.

Uvarov was convinced that Nafissi's headquarters had not been attacked. He was equally convinced that the Soviet government had been duped into intervening. But neither STAVKA nor the Politburo understood that yet. Uvarov's personal appeal to halt further advances by Soviet units had been denied: no such order, STAVKA stated, could be given until the situation had been clarified. As they listened to the briefing, the only thing that Uvarov and his staff were sure of was that outside of the Soviet and Cuban units assigned to the North African Front, they had no idea what was going on.

For a moment Uvarov's mind wandered off. The situation he and his command faced was appalling. The allied army he was supposed to be supporting was refusing to communicate with him. In fact, there was the real possibility that the Russian personnel attached to that headquarters for that purpose were being held hostage, or worse. That same allied army had without any warning initiated chemical warfare, a decision that only the Politburo in the Soviet Union could make. Even worse, the chemical attacks had been timed and located in such a manner that the connection between them and the Soviet attack could not be helped. It seemed, to Uvarov, as if the Libyans were intentionally setting the Soviets up. But for what? And why? And if so, what next?

He had no answers to anything. Instead, he imagined himself to be a man tied to a railroad track, watching a locomotive thundering down on him. He could see it coming, and he knew what would happen when it reached him, but he was powerless to do anything about it. Sooner or later it would crash into him—and when it did, there would only be darkness.

Recovering from his dark thoughts, Uvarov looked at the map. He had to do something. He refused to be run over. Reaching out, he indicated a point east of the Al Jagbub–

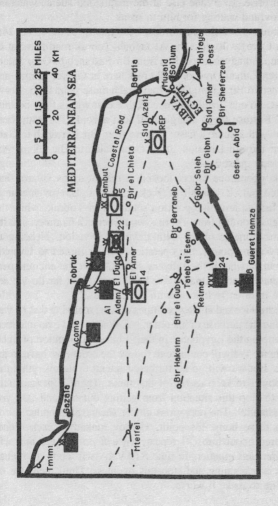

Tobruk road. His actions caught the officer who was briefing by surprise. Everyone else at the map stood silent, watching Uvarov and waiting for him to speak.

"Issue the following order," he finally said. "The 24th Tank Corps will cross the Al Jagbub–Tobruk road here, at El Cuasc, and advance to a line from Bir Berraneb to Gabr Saleh. The 8th Cuban Division will cross here at Gueret Hamza and advance to Bir Gibni. Once they reach those points, no one—I repeat, no one—will continue further east without my permission. I refuse to go charging off into a void. The 24th Tank Corps will assume a hasty defense from Bir Berraneb to Gabr Saleh; the 8th Division, from Gabr Saleh to Bir Gibni. Are there any questions?"

The operations officer looked at the locations Uvarov had pointed out. It was all very clear to him. Uvarov meant to establish an anvillike position southeast of Tobruk, while the Libyans, coming from Tobruk, would act as a hammer, smashing the remains of the 14th Egyptian Division. Needing to clarify some points, the operations officer turned to Uvarov. "General, what if the Libyans cannot finish the encirclement and the Egyptians manage to break out? How far do we advance in order to link up with the Libyans?"

Uvarov looked at the operations officer, realizing that he was missing the purpose of his order. "Colonel, I have no intention of trapping the Egyptians. In fact, I have no intention of fighting them. We will continue to follow the orders we have to the letter. But we will go no further. I intend to do everything in my power to keep us out of this mess. There is perhaps still time to stop this situation from getting out of hand. Do you understand?" The operations officer sheepishly nodded.

To drive home his point, Uvarov looked at each officer gathered about him. "I repeat, *we will do nothing that will broaden this conflict*. In time STAVKA will come to realize what is happening and stop this madness. Until then, we do nothing to make it worse."

14

When you are occupying a position which the enemy threatens to surround, collect all your forces immediately, and menace him with an offensive movement.

—NAPOLEON I

Sidi Azeiz, Libya * 1545 Hours, 17 December

From his position north of the road, Lieutenant Colonel Ahmed Hafez watched the remnants of the 22nd Mechanized Division as it moved back east. Less than twelve hours before, that same division had been preparing to begin the final assault on Tobruk. Soviet intervention, and the widespread use of chemical weapons, had changed all that. Now, instead of driving west to complete the campaign, Egyptian forces were retreating back to Egypt in an effort to avoid encirclement and destruction.

Hafez could hear the distant rumble of artillery to the west. The 5th Armored Division was heavily engaged with Libyan forces coming out of Tobruk. Shortly after the chemical attacks the 5th Armored, which had escaped those attacks, assumed a hasty defensive posture east of Tobruk from Abiar el Amar to the Mediterranean. It did not, however, escape the Libyans' attention. Throughout the day it had beaten back numerically superior Libyan forces. Still, the Libyan attacks, though piecemeal and poorly coordinated, were persistent; eventually they would succeed in grinding down the 5th Armored. Before that happened, the 22nd Division, and the 14th Armored coming up from the south, had to reach the coastal road and get back into

Egypt. Only then would the 5th Armored Division be allowed to begin its own withdrawal. Whether or not that would happen depended on the skill of the soldiers of the 5th Armored, the speed of the Russian attack, and how much of a threat the Republican Brigade could make itself.

Since early morning Hafez's tank battalion, part of the Republican Brigade, had been on alert. They were under orders to counterattack to the southwest to blunt the Soviet drive once the lead Soviet units crossed the Al Jagbub–Tobruk road. In the event the Libyans managed to break through the 5th Armored Division before the Russians reached the Al Jagbub–Tobruk road, the Republican Brigade would counterattack to the west and cover the withdrawal of the 5th Armored. The Brigade, consisting of three tank, one mechanized, and one artillery battalion, stood ready for either possibility.

Hafez's battalion would be the lead battalion for either option and was ready after six days of relative inactivity. Along with the rest of the Republican Brigade, it had followed the advance of the lead divisions along the coastal road. The Brigade had almost been committed on two occasions. The first was when the 22nd Division had difficulty destroying an enemy unit fighting a delaying action near Bir el Hariga on the second day. At the last minute the Libyans withdrew, allowing the 22nd to continue west. The second time was on the fourth day, when the same division failed to penetrate Libyan defense south of Gambut. Success in the south, however, by the 14th Armored Division, had caused the commander of the 1st Army to cancel the direct attack on Tobruk from the east. Instead, the focus of the attack, and hence the Republican Brigade, shifted to Al Adam.

The inactivity had been particularly hard on Hafez. Since the seventh of December he had been living in fear that his role in the assassination attempt would be discovered. Though he had not actually done anything to assist the assassins, he was guilty of treason. Simple association with the assassins and failure to inform his superiors was more than enough to earn him a death sentence and his family undying disgrace. The war had offered him an honorable means to purge himself of his guilt. Death in battle would bring an end to his life of fear and cleanse his soul. But his unit's relegation to reserve status almost robbed him of his chance. When the final attack on Tobruk was being prepared with no active role for his unit, Hafez had been gripped with a despondency that had almost paralyzed him.

The intervention by the Russians, therefore, as terrible as it was for his country, was greeted by Hafez as a salvation. Not only would he be afforded an opportunity to atone for his sins; he would be able to do so in a spectacular manner—in a manner befitting a soldier.

West of Cairo * 1545 Hours, 17 December

Slowly Captain Bob Mennzinger walked around his helicopter. His pilot followed him, calling off items from a check list for Mennzinger to inspect. Most of the items were routine—normal checks done before every flight. Even the two 230-gallon external fuel tanks were nothing big. They had, after all, flown the Atlantic using them.

The weapons load for that night, however, was not normal. On the outer-wing storage pylons were two rocket pods. Each rocket pod was uploaded with nineteen 2.75-inch M-261 Hydra multipurpose submunition rockets. The Hydra rocket was new to the inventory and had great potential. Each Hydra carried six small bomblets, called submunitions. The rockets, able to release the bomblets at any range designated by the copilot-gunner, could be fired singly, in groups, or in a continuous volley. Regardless of how the target was engaged, the effects of the Hydra on lightly armored vehicles, to say nothing of soft-skinned vehicles and exposed troops, would be devastating. Other Apaches preparing for lift-off carried a different mix of stores. Four were armed with Hellfire missiles, two with a mix of 2.75-inch M-261 Hydra MPSM rockets and Hellfire missiles, and four with M-255 2.75-inch fléchette rockets. All ten carried their combat load of twelve hundred 30mm cannon rounds.

The mission Mennzinger's unit had been assigned was going

to be long and most unusual. Ten of the battalion's eighteen aircraft would move south that night to Abu Simbel. Their departure was scheduled for after dark, at a time when there would be no Soviet reconnaissance satellite overhead or approaching. Immediately after their departure, their places would be taken by ten inflatable dummies that looked like Apaches from the distance and gave off similar heat signatures. The next day some of the eight remaining Apaches would fly about the area at designated times that coincided with Soviet satellite overflights. By mixing real Apaches with the dummies, the deception just might work.

The ten Apaches assigned to the mission, accompanied by eight UH-60 Blackhawk helicopters, would arrive at the airfield at Abu Simbel early the next morning. There the helicopters would be put into hangars during the daylight hours while the crews rested. Because there were only ten Apaches, the battalion had enough personnel rated to fly them to have two crews per helicopter. The assigned crew would fly to the target, execute the mission, and return to a forward refuel point. That feat would require only eight hours and forty minutes at the stick. The relief crew would take over at the refuel point and return the Apaches to Egypt when the raid was completed.

Beginning at twilight the following night, 18 December, six UH-60s with fuel handlers, some of the spare Apache crews, and equipment for a refuel point would depart south. Their destination was a point on the north slopes of the Meidob Hills, over six hundred miles inside Sudan. There they would establish a refuel point where the Apaches would be able to stop en route to and from the target. Two hours after the advance party left to establish the refuel point, the ten Apaches would follow, in two flights of five Apaches each. Moving along separate routes, each flight of Apaches would be trailed by a Blackhawk carrying the spare crews. As with the transatlantic flight, the Blackhawk would recover any crew whose Apache went down en route due to mechanical failure.

Shortly after the Apaches left Abu Simbel, three U.S. Air Force C-130 transport planes would depart Cairo. Aboard two of the aircraft would be nine 400-gallon fuel blivets. They would be air-dropped at the refueling point, which had been marked by members of an American Special Forces team operating in Sudan. Aboard the third C-130 would be an ad-hoc airborne infantry platoon that would secure the blivets until the Blackhawks arrived with the fuel handlers and their equipment. Once the fuel handlers were on the ground with the blivets, they would have two hours to set up the refuel point. Using the Blackhawks to gather up the scattered fuel blivets by sling-loading the blivets under them, the fuel handlers would arrange the blivets in the proper manner and hook up the fuel lines and pumping equipment.

The operation would not, and could not, be conducted in a vacuum. The Soviets had airborne early-warning aircraft operating out of Ethiopia, along their air corridor from Ethiopia to Libya. In order to draw off those aircraft and the fighters that would respond to their calls, a deception operation was needed. The U.S. Navy was assigned this task. In an operation similar to the deception operation used to support the Son Tay raid in Vietnam, the Navy would commence massive air and surface operations off the coast of Ethiopia and Sudan on the night of 18 December. These operations, feigning preparations for an attack on seaports and airfields, would coincide with the approach flight of the Apaches in western Sudan.

To further reduce the effectiveness of Soviet (as well as the sparse Sudanese) air defenses, electronic warfare aircraft would be used. Navy EA-6 Prowlers operating with the fleet would jam as many radar and communications frequencies as possible. This would cause Soviet airborne early-warning aircraft to fly closer to the coast in order to burn through the jamming and monitor the activities of the American fleet. Coming down from Egypt, a pair of EF-111s would also jam radar and communications frequencies. This would have the effect of throwing a wall of jamming between the Soviets moving to the coast to observe the U.S. Navy and the Apache strike in the west.

As a final insurance policy, if the naval demonstration off Ethiopia and the electronic warfare aircraft failed, a squadron of F-15 Eagles operating out of Abu Simbel would provide cover for the Apaches during their run-in and return.

The Apaches, upon reaching the refuel point, would refuel and regroup. Any last-minute information or instructions would be passed out at that time. One hour after arriving at the refuel point, the Apaches would take off and head south for the last leg of their run in to the target, the airfield at Al Fasher.

Their lift-off would coincide with the crossing of the Egypt-Sudan border by six F-111 bombers. Once on station at Al Fasher, the Apaches, in conjunction with Air Force F-111s, would attack the Soviet facilities. The F-111s would strike first. Six Apaches, using their laser designator–range finder, would spot targets for the F-111s. The other four Apaches would take out Soviet air defense systems and radars.

The F-111s would approach Al Fasher low and at high speed. Their fire control systems would detect the laser spots provided by the Apaches—the reflected laser energy bouncing off the targets—and lock onto where the laser spots were illuminating. Each plane's system then would automatically compute release time for the aircraft's bombs.

When the F-111s were thirty seconds out, the four Apaches targeting the air defense systems would open fire. Great care had to be taken during this phase. The Apaches' angle of attack and the air defense systems attacked had to be considered so as not to interfere with the laser designation of the F-111's targets. It would do no good to destroy an air defense system if the smoke and debris blocked a laser beam designating a target for an approaching F-111. Each F-111 would make only one pass. With the F-111s screaming in at five hundred miles an hour, there was no room for error, as there would be no second chance.

Targets for the F-111s would be fuel tanks, maintenance facilities, ammo dumps, and the runway itself. The F-111s would use Rockeye cluster bombs for the fuel tanks and munitions dumps, 750-pound general-purpose bombs for the maintenance facilities, and Durandal antirunway bombs to crater the runway. Inside of sixty seconds the main facilities at Al Fasher would be smashed.

With the bombers gone and the chaos created by the sudden

and massive destruction by the F-111s, the Apaches would move into their positions and commence their attack. They would use 2.75-inch rockets, Hellfire missiles, and 30mm guns. Where the F-111s had come in and hammered the airfield like a sledgehammer, the Apaches would move from firing position to firing position, carefully setting up their targets as a sharpshooter would. Transports, fighters and helicopters that happened to be on the ground, and surviving facilities such as the control tower, truck parks, and equipment would be systematically destroyed in a twenty-minute attack. When there was nothing worthwhile left to destroy, the Apaches would break off the attack and return north.

Mennzinger and his men were told that aside from the obvious one—the destruction of the facility—the objective of the raid was twofold. First, it would demonstrate to the Soviets how vulnerable their line of communications and supply was. More important, however, was the need to communicate to the Soviets, in a manner that left little doubt in the minds of their leadership, that the United States was not going to allow their use of chemical weapons to go unpunished.

So as Mennzinger and his men checked their Apaches, they took special care, especially when it came to the weapons. A lot, a hell of a lot, was riding on their ability to put steel on target. Everyone, from the youngest aviation warrant officer to Mennzinger himself, wanted to pull it off without a hitch.

Al Fasher, Sudan * 1605 Hours, 17 December

Captain Kinsly watched as Sergeant Jackson prepared his small pathfinder team for their move. Besides Jackson, two of the eight Americans at Al Fasher were going north to locate and mark a suitable refuel point. The Sudanese lieutenant, two of his soldiers, and a guide who knew the northern portion of Darfur Province would also be traveling with them. Kinsly would remain at Al Fasher with the balance of the force, keeping the airfield under observation. They would provide information to the strike force, from meteorological data, to the location and number of aircraft on the ground, to changes in location of air defense weapons.

His inspection finished, Jackson's team began to load its equipment and gear onto its newly "procured" truck. After receiving their warning order for the mission late that morning, the Sudanese lieutenant and Sergeant Jackson had gone foraging, looking for things that would be needed, transportation being the main item. In short order the lieutenant was able to "borrow" a truck by hot-wiring it. Sergeant Jackson also had a run of good fortune. Wandering through the market-place in the town, unarmed and dressed like a goat herder, he noticed two Russians at the entrance to an alley. Since they were unarmed, he watched them to see what they were up to. As he watched, Sudanese would come up to them with a bucket or container, hand the Russians money, and then disappear around the corner for a moment. It didn't take long to figure out that the Russians were selling things, running their own black market.

Being bold and curious rather than smart, Jackson walked up to them. All he wanted to do was to see what they were selling. To his surprise, they had several drums of gasoline along with other odds and ends in the alley. The bigger of the two Russians, a sergeant, stopped Jackson, putting out his palm for payment before letting him go further. Without saying a word, Jackson pulled a wad of money out of his pocket. Though it was the last of their operations funds, known as the captain's mad money, gasoline, from any source, was hard to pass up.

Seeing the money, the Russian sergeant's eyes lit up. He grabbed for it. Now it was Jackson's turn to have some fun with the Russians. Babbling in Arabic, Jackson made motions indicating that he would be back. When the Russian sergeant nodded that he understood, Jackson went looking for the Sudanese lieutenant and the truck. The lieutenant didn't want to bring the truck into the marketplace. He feared that someone would recognize it, but not the driver, and call the police. Jackson, however, prevailed. Returning, he bilked the Russians out of two drums of gasoline, the hand pump they had been using, six blankets, four pairs of boots, a box of rations, two water cans, a shovel, and both their belt buckles.

The negotiations, done by pointing and mumbling languages that neither side understood, were at times fierce. Whenever the Russian sergeant shouted "Nyet," Jackson would flap his arms, mumble in Arabic, turn his back, and begin to walk away. Inevitably the Russian would grab his arm and accept Jackson's lower offer. The Sudanese lieutenant didn't share Jackson's idea of fun. Every time Jackson pushed the Russian sergeant to the point of argument, the lieutenant all but passed out. Only time and the expenditure of all the Russians' commodities ended Jackson's wheeling and dealing. As he departed, both parties smiled and waved, the Russians calling out a phrase he recognized as the Russian equivalent of "Up yours." Smiling broadly and waving as he left, Jackson shouted in Arabic, "So long, shithead!"

The one thing that Jackson wouldn't have that concerned Kinsly was a radio, of any type. When ordered to Al Fasher, they had brought only a single tactical/satellite radio and a homing beacon. Kinsly had not foreseen the need to operate two independent teams over great distances. The decision had to be made who got the radio and who got the beacon. Since it was important to warn the strike force of any last-minute changes, both Kinsly and Jackson agreed that the radio needed to stay with Kinsly.

That solved one problem but created a new one. Jackson had the beacon to guide in the C-130s, the refuel team, and the strike force, but he didn't have a time for when those elements would arrive. When the order had come that morning to send the pathfinder team, no exact time was available for when the various elements would converge at the refuel point. Kinsly could have delayed Jackson's departure and waited for the exact time but opted to send him. He wanted to give Sergeant Jackson the maximum amount of time for travel to the refuel point and recon for a suitable site. Contacting 2nd Corps headquarters in Cairo just before Jackson's final inspection provided them with an approximate time, but nothing firm. Seeing no alternative, Kinsly instructed Jackson to establish the refuel point in the northern slopes of the Meidob Hills. Commencing at 2000 hours the night of 18 December, Jackson was to turn on the beacon to guide in the aircraft for ten seconds every thirty minutes. Only after Jackson heard the approach of aircraft would he switch it to the continuous mode. Kinsly relayed this information, along with the beacon's frequency, to Cairo.

Extraction of the two teams would be done in conjunction with the raid. Jackson and his team would leave with the fuel handlers after the Apaches had returned to the refuel stop and topped off. Kinsly's team would be picked up immediately after the raid by a UH-60 that would follow the Apaches to Al Fasher. Since it would be night and he had no beacon, the pickup point for Kinsly's team had to be near an easily identifiable terrain feature. Though he wasn't happy about that, a road junction five kilometers north of the airfield was selected. There was a deep ditch on one side of the junction and a stand of trees on the other. Either would provide cover for Kinsly and his men while they waited to be extracted.

Sergeant Jackson reported that all was ready. Kinsly went over his own checklist to make sure that Jackson had missed nothing. Included on the list was a detailed map that showed everything of tactical significance—in particular, the location of air defense weapons—on the airfield. That information had already been sent via radio to Cairo. Kinsly, however, felt that a map, in the hands of a man who had seen the actual airfield and sites, might help the Apache pilots during their last-minute briefings at the refuel site.

When both men were satisfied, Jackson smiled. "Well, sir, can't say I'm sorry to leave this garden spot. See you on the other side of hell, sir."

Kinsly smiled. "Sergeant Jackson, in case you haven't noticed, we *are* on the other side of hell. Take care, and good luck."

Cairo * 1615 Hours, 17 December

While no trip by car in Cairo was ever easy, today's seemed particularly gruesome. Fay had left the WNN offices with Johnny in a network van and returned to her apartment to pick up her two boys and their bags. That part of the trip was easy. Getting close to the American embassy was not. For an hour they slowly moved south along Corniche El Nile. Traffic, heading both ways, was appalling. Part of the reason was provided when they passed under the 6 October Overpass. Above them, on the overpass, columns of Egyptian military vehicles could be seen headed west. That road, the 6 October Bridge over the Nile, and several other bridges were closed to civilian traffic. There had been no warning, no plan what to do with the civilian traffic. Such trivial matters were of little concern to the Egyptian government at that moment.

As they sat stalled behind the Egyptian Museum, a flight of three helicopters in a line came zipping down the Nile from the north. Just before they reached the museum, they veered right and flew low between the Nile Hilton and the museum, right in front of the van. The helicopters were so low (and they were still descending) that Johnny and Fay could see the faces of the pilot and the door gunner. With their cargo doors open despite the cold, Fay could see combat troops sitting on the floor, their weapons at the ready. She knew things were going to be sticky, but she wasn't prepared to see armed troops.

"Those are ours, aren't they, Mrs. Dixon?" Johnny was leaning forward over the steering wheel, watching the first helicopter fly down the narrow street.

Fay watched the second roll in and disappear between the two buildings. "Yes, Johnny—they're UH-60s."

Johnny was wide-eyed and excited. "What are the troops for? Do you think they're going to have to fight to get you out?"

Fay, with a scowl on her face, turned to him. "You really know how to cheer someone up, don't you?"

Johnny suddenly realized what he had said. Sheepishly, he apologized. Fay, however, didn't hear him. She was lost in her own thoughts. What, she thought, if they had to fight their way out?

The wheels of the lead Blackhawk hadn't even touched down in Tahrir Square before Captain Harold Cerro and his men began to pile out. Crouching low, the men ran to the front of the helicopter, deploying into a semicircle. Once they reached the edge of the square, they knelt down, keeping their rifles at the ready. Cerro, followed by two radio/telephone operators—RTOs for short—each with a radio on his back, remained in the center of the semicircle. They also knelt, at least until the Blackhawk they had just exited took off, flying over the Mugamaa Government Building and back north over the Nile. The other two helicopters, having landed on either side and a little behind the first, did likewise after discharging their troops. When they were gone, Cerro and his two RTOs were the only ones standing in a complete circle of sixty American combat troops.

After a quick visual inspection of his troops from where he stood, he took the hand mike from one of the RTOs. Keying the mike, he waited a second before broadcasting. "EAGLE SIX—THIS IS BRAVO FIVE SEVEN—LEAD BRAVO ELEMENT HAS SECURED PADDOCK—OVER."

There was a delay of several seconds before Eagle Six, the commander of the Marine guard detachment at the American embassy, answered. As Cerro acknowledged the response, a second flight of three Blackhawks came thundering around the corner of the Nile Hilton toward Tahrir Square. As the first helicopters had done, they touched down in a wedge. The troops scampered out but did not go to the perimeter of the square as the first lift had. Instead, they formed up by squad in tight groups within the ring of troops. The company executive officer, First Lieutenant George Prentice, jumped out of the lead Blackhawk and trotted up to Cerro, followed by one RTO. A few seconds later First Sergeant Andy Duncan joined them.

As soon as the second lift departed, Prentice reported in, telling Cerro there were no mishaps, no problems. As before, Cerro radioed the embassy that all his troops were on the ground and he was ready to move to Eagle Base, the American embassy. As the Marine commander was giving Cerro permission, an Egyptian army colonel, escorted by one of Cerro's men from the perimeter, came up to Cerro, the XO, and their party. The soldier reported that the Egyptian colonel said that he was here to escort them to the embassy. Coming to attention, Cerro saluted the Egyptian. "Captain Harold Cerro, commander of B Company, 1st of the 506th, Airborne, Air Assault."

The Egyptian colonel didn't catch everything Cerro said but let it drop. Instead, he informed Cerro that he was ready to escort them to the embassy as soon as they were ready. Cerro thought about the situation for a moment. He and his company, there to escort the American evacuees from the embassy to Tahrir Square, were in turn going to be escorted by the Egyptian army. Cerro was sure it all made sense to someone.

He turned to Prentice and Duncan, "Okay—we all straight on what we do?"

Prentice spoke first. "I secure the PZ with 2nd and 3rd Platoons, receive the evacuees, position them for loading, and then load them into the slicks. I'll operate on three radio nets: Eagle net, company net for movement of evacuees, and battalion net for talking to the slicks. If something goes down while you have a group of evacuees between here and the embassy, I take 3rd Platoon and come get you."

Cerro nodded. "Check." He turned to Duncan.

As Prentice had done, Duncan recited his tasks. "I stay in the embassy with 1st Squad, 1st Platoon and organize the evacuees into caulks. I also maintain liaison with the Marine detachment commander. For commo, I use their radios to talk to you. If you get into trouble, 1st Squad and the Marines will come chargin' out after ya."

Cerro chuckled. "You know, First Sergeant, the reason I put you with the Marines is because you're the only guy in this outfit that can understand them."

Duncan made a face. "Sir, I resemble that remark."

The three laughed as the Egyptian colonel looked on. He was amazed that these professional soldiers, men who might be called on to help defend his country, were joking at such a time. Americans, he thought—were an odd and undisciplined race of people.

Cerro regained his posture. "And I, gentlemen, will escort the evacuees from the embassy to the square using the rest of 1st Platoon. Any questions?"

Prentice piped up. "Yes, sir. If you don't mind me saying so, and I'm sure you don't, isn't it kind of dumb to start doing this at nightfall?"

"Not at all," Cerro responded. "You see, it took all afternoon for some shit-for-brains in the embassy to figure out that maybe, just maybe, the Egyptian army might be shifting forces from the east to the west. Little did he realize that the normally abominable traffic was going to be impassable. The decision to switch from ground evac to air evac wasn't made until after 1500 hours."

Prentice looked at Cerro. "Thank you, sir, for providing that insight into the minds of our Foreign Service Corps."

Taking one last look around, Cerro called to the platoon leader of the 1st Platoon to saddle up, fix bayonets, and prepare to move.

Duncan made a face when Cerro ordered bayonets to be fixed. "Sir, do you think that's wise?"

"Don't worry, First Sergeant. I doubt if they're going to get into a serious run-in with any Egyptians. The bayonets may be just the thing that keeps a young lion from trying us."

Duncan shook his head. "It's not the Egyptians I'm worried about." He looked at Prentice. "It's our own people I'm worried about. You remember what happened the last time we had bayonet practice?"

Prentice rubbed his right hind cheek. "That's a cheap shot, First Sergeant. It was an accident."

Cerro suppressed the urge to laugh. "All right, sports fans, give me three cheers for Virginia Mil, and let's go."

Cerro and Prentice, both graduates of the Virginia Military Institute, yelled out an old school cheer while Duncan watched in amusement and the Egyptian colonel watched in horror.

Turning onto Kamal Eddin Salah, the WNN van ran into a police barrier. An Egyptian policeman, armed with an AK assault rifle, waved at them, indicating that they needed to turn around. Johnny shifted the van into reverse and started to back up. Fay stopped him. "Don't you dare back up," she yelled. "Tell them you're press. Here." She grabbed the sign from the window of the van, with the English and Arabic words for "press" on it. Thrusting it into Johnny's hand, she told him to wave it and drive forward.

Clenching the sign between his teeth, Johnny shifted the van back into a forward gear and began to move. As he did so, the Egyptian with the AK put his rifle up to his shoulder, aimed it at Johnny, and yelled something in Arabic. Johnny slammed on the brakes, throwing everyone in the van forward. "Mrs. Dixon, I don't think they want us to go through here."

Fay looked at the police. For the first time she looked beyond the barrier. Further down the street there was a mass of people blocking the road. Even if they had gotten past the barrier, they would never have been able to make it through the crowd. Opening the door, she yelled to the children to grab their stuff and get out. Johnny turned to her, a look of surprise on his face. "I don't think that's a good idea, Mrs. Dixon—I mean, just you and the kids fighting through that crowd. Besides, they might not let you in."

Fay looked at him, then at the crowd. The thought had never occurred to her that the gates might be barred or that there might be violence. The images of old news clips of the fall of Saigon and the evacuation at the American embassy flashed through her mind. "Johnny, you stay here for a half-hour—no, forty-five minutes. If I'm not back by then, go ahead and leave."

"Are you sure you want to take the chance on your own, Mrs. Dixon?"

"You want to come with me, Johnny?"

Johnny looked down the street and thought about Fay's challenge. "You're right. I better stay here."

That resolved, Fay gathered up their bags and the boys and walked around the barrier. The same policeman started to block her way but she shot him a cold, hard look that convinced him that she wasn't going to be stopped. Walking down the street at a brisk pace, the three of them reached the rear of the crowd. Telling the boys to hang on to her and not to let go no matter what, she began to plow her way through.

Though there was no frenzy yet, there was a great deal of tension in the crowd, and Fay sensed that things could go bad any second. As quickly as she thought that, she pushed it from her mind, concentrating instead on getting forward. They had just turned the corner and onto Ragheb Latin America, the street where the American embassy was located, when the crowd suddenly pushed back. There was much shouting as those in front tried to move back. The deafening noise of the crowd, the sudden turn of events, and the gathering darkness were frightening. Fay, however, resisted the push, standing her ground. Even though she had no idea why everyone was moving back, she was determined not to lose any forward gains they had made.

The crowd to her front suddenly parted, leaving her and the two boys alone in the center of the street. There was a moment of panic as she looked about to see what was happening. The noise of the crowd was now subsiding, replaced by the rhythmic tromping of rubber-soled boots on the pavement to her rear. Turning, she found herself face to face with a solid phalanx of American combat troops advancing on her. Their rifles, with fixed bayonets, were carried at the ready. In full combat gear and helmets, their faces lost in the shadows of the gathering night, they were without any vestige of human appearance. Instead, they presented the very image of a menacing machine, moving forward at a steady pace, irresistible in their advance, ready to strike if provoked.

For a moment she stood there transfixed.

The sudden appearance of a woman and two children standing in the middle of the street caught Cerro by surprise. All three were blond; they carried suitcases and clutched each other as if their very lives depended on it. Cerro had no doubt they were Americans who had decided to come to the embassy at the last minute. Instinctively, he threw his right hand up, signaling the company following him to halt before they ran the lady down.

"We're Americans—Americans."

For a moment Fay feared they were too late, that they might not be allowed in. That fear, however, was quickly dispelled as the captain leading the troops came forward. "Yes, ma'am, we know. Now, if you just get in between the first two ranks, we'll take you into the embassy."

Suddenly it was there, the moment of truth. Right up to that very second, Fay had had no doubt that she was going to leave with the boys. That was, after all, her duty as a mother. Scott had told her to do so. And all she had to do was walk a few steps, squeeze in between the soldiers, and she would be safe. She would be headed home—just like a good Army wife.

From the depths of her soul a voice screamed "No!" Fay hesitated. If she fell in with the soldiers and marched into the embassy with them, she would be just one more Army wife, another family member, a dependent, waiting to be whisked away to safety. That was, after all, what good Army wives did in times of crisis. And like all good Army wives, she would sit at home, alone, waiting—waiting for the knock at the door, the kind words meant to calm her, the funeral, the flag-draped coffin, the firing squad. And worst of all, the bugle, the goddamn bugle that announced it was all over, that her dreams, her hopes, and her future were at an end.

If she left now, all her talk of starting a new life, of creating her own person, able to stand up on her own two feet and make it on her own in the world, would end. There would be no second chance, no salvation from a life chained to a husband and family. In a single, irretrievable second she had to decide where her ultimate loyalty lay: to herself as a person or to her family.

Cerro stood there watching the woman as she stared at him with a blank look on her face. It occurred to him that he might have been wrong: perhaps she wasn't an American, just someone trying to bull her way into the embassy and get out with the

Americans. He was about to advance to check her papers when the woman suddenly rushed forward, pushing the children ahead of her. "Captain, here," she said, offering him the boys' hands; without thinking, he took them. "Please, take these children to the airport and get them out of here," she continued, talking fast as she dug into her pocketbook in search of something. "They're Americans. Their father's a colonel. Here—here are their passports."

In shock Cerro let go of the older boy's hand and reached out to take the two blue passports. Recovering, he started to explain that he couldn't accept responsibility for the children. The lady, however, cut him off. "You have to. I'm with World News here and can't leave." Reaching into her pocketbook again, she pulled out an envelope. "Here, this is the address of their grandparents in Virginia. They'll pick them up at Dover."

Not believing what this woman was doing, Cerro tried to protest. The woman ignored him. Instead, she knelt down to kiss the two boys goodbye. She told them to be good, that Grandma and Grandpa would come and get them, and to mind the captain. Before Cerro could react, the woman was up and gone, lost in the crowd that was beginning to close in on them. With no choice, and sensing that a dangerous situation was building up, he stuffed the passports in his pocket and grabbed the older boy's hand. Turning back to his company, he yelled to two soldiers in the front rank to come up and take the boys. The soldiers ran up to Cerro at the double, slung their rifles, and led the boys back, placing them securely in the center of the column. In the growing darkness and noise Cerro never saw the tears streaming down the boys' cheeks or heard their low, mournful goodbyes to a mother already gone.

Giza, Egypt * 1745 Hours, 17 December

In the shadows of the Great Pyramids, Jan Fields watched the long columns of vehicles inching their way west. For hours the traffic had all been one-way. Neither the Egyptian government nor the U.S. military command had released any details on the current situation. It didn't take a military genius, however, to figure out that there was a crisis at the front and that the situation was deteriorating. The war, though its end was in sight, had taken an unexpected and dangerous turn. Like the approach of night, Jan could see only darkness and uncertainty in the future.

From behind, a sudden gust of wind swept over her, causing her to shiver. Folding her arms, trying to get warm, she continued to watch the long columns snake their way west in silence. The camera crew, finished with its shooting, was busy packing its gear and had paid Jan no mind when she wandered away.

For the first time that day she was alone. The cold night air, the silence, broken only by the distant rumble of trucks, and the darkness crashing down about her only served to deepen the depression and foreboding she had felt all day. As hard as she tried, Jan was unable to whip up the enthusiasm and drive that the current situation dictated. Instead of applying all her energies and talents to the single most important opportunity in her life, Jan found her thoughts drifting away from the business at hand and to the one thing she could do nothing about—Scott Dixon.

The fact that she was so preoccupied with him was disturbing, but at the same time it was a source of great joy. In her life she had known many men. No matter where she went, Jan never lacked for company or a date. But she had never felt any particular attachment to any of them, never any desire to give more of herself than the occasion demanded. While she enjoyed sex as much as the next girl, she knew that a permanent relationship was built on more than foreplay and intercourse.

Without her knowing what it was or how it had manifested itself, Scott Dixon had provided that something more. For years she had viewed him as an enemy, the man who had taken her best friend and co-worker from her. In her search for answers she wondered if her infatuation with Scott was nothing more than a love-hate relationship. Or perhaps she was secretly harboring a deep-seated urge for revenge. But neither of those answers held up to the test Jan had faced when she saw Scott in the field. In a single instant all doubts and concerns about how she felt about him had been swept away as he held her hand. For the first time in her adult life Jan knew love.

But with that settled, new problems reared their ugly heads. Jan didn't know what to do about Fay. Though Fay had announced her intent to divorce Scott, and that decision was based on other, deep-seated reasons, Jan still felt uncomfortable in the presence of her friend-turned-rival. "Awkward" did little to describe how Jan felt every time Fay mentioned Scott. On one hand, Jan felt as if she were privy to a private conversation she shouldn't be hearing. On the other, she felt the urge to defend Scott.

She had come close to doing so on one occasion. When Fay was carrying on about how Scott had mishandled their reunion after returning from Iran, Jan became angry. Surprising Fay, she had shouted that she didn't want to hear that—that she didn't want to hear anything from Fay about Scott. For the longest time there was silence. Jan, realizing what she had said, thought Fay would put two and two together. Fay, however, passed it off as just a temper tantrum from a woman under tremendous pressure. Since that incident, no mention of Scott had been made. Though Jan was sorry she had said what she did, the end results were a blessing.

Jan saw in the distance the lights of a large aircraft as it began its climb for altitude. Perhaps, Jan thought, Fay was on board. With Fay gone, her life would be easier—no more awkward conversations, no more guilty feelings. And besides, that would only leave Jan and Scott in Egypt. As improbable as it was that the two of them would be able to get together, there was always the chance. Fay's departure increased that chance and raised Jan's spirits.

Tahrir Square, Cairo * 2035 Hours, 17 December

The crowds along Ragheb Latin America and surrounding the square had become bigger and noisier. Finishing his third trip,

Cerro decided that he would take the squad from the first sergeant to reinforce the escort platoon. Duncan and the Marines could make due with what they had. If trouble came, if the crowds went berserk while he was escorting civilians, Cerro would need every man he could get.

As Cerro entered the square, the soldiers defending the perimeter parted to let him and the next group of evacuees in. Prentice was waiting for him. "Captain, battalion wants you and the first sergeant to report to the airfield right away. Something about you being detached for a special mission."

Cerro looked at Prentice. "You kidding? Things are on the verge of going to shit and he wants me to leave?"

"The colonel said that the battalion XO, along with that other platoon you requested, will be coming in on the next lift. The battalion XO will take charge of the operation here. You're to turn the company over to me and report to battalion."

Cerro looked about for a moment. "Don't get me wrong—I know you can handle things here. It's just that I hate like hell leaving the company. Kind of like Custer riding off to find Benteen."

Prentice chuckled. "If you don't mind me saying so, sir, that's a shitty analogy to use at a time like this."

"Well, that's how I feel." Cerro paused. "Okay—I'll make one more run and get the first sergeant. You take the escort duty. Lieutenant Alliban will run things from the embassy, and the XO, the Iron Major himself, will run things here. Any questions?"

Prentice didn't have any. Though the situation was still sticky, and would be until the very end, Cerro doubted if there would be any serious problems. Things, in fact, had gone quite well. Except for the crazy lady and her two children, the whole operation had gone down like clockwork. Cerro hoped that he and the first sergeant would have as much luck in their next task, whatever that was.

El Esem, Libya * 2045 Hours, 17 December

Crossing the track that ran from El Esem to Bir Gibni, Hafez gave the order for his companies to deploy into a wedge for-

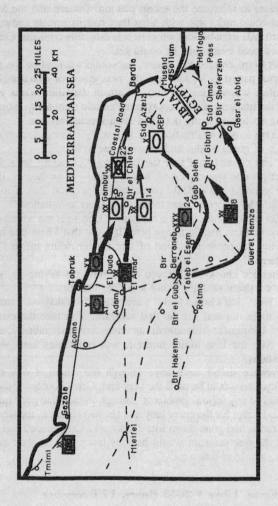

mation. In the darkness, which shrouded them from sight, the Republican Brigade crossed its line of departure and prepared to seek out the Soviets. Finally receiving orders, the brigade was ordered to avoid contact with the lead combat units of the Soviet tank units moving on Gabr Saleh. Instead, they were to move through a gap between the Russians, surging ahead with elements at Gabr Saleh, and the Cubans to their south, who were lagging behind.

The objective of the brigade was not a head-on confrontation with the Soviet forces. On the contrary, the battalion commanders of the Republican Brigade were ordered to avoid an open fight, if possible. The Egyptians, outnumbered three to one by the Soviets alone, were also outclassed by them. As the Soviets were equipped with T-72 tanks armed with 125mm guns and BMP-2 infantry fighting vehicles, the Republican Brigade was outclassed in weapons as well as numbers. Instead, its objective was the artillery and the supply trains of both the Soviet tank corps and the Cuban division. It was hoped that by destroying those elements and running about throughout the Soviets' rear areas, the Egyptians would stop the Soviets, or at least slow them down. Only as a last resort was the Republican Brigade to attack the Soviets' main battle forces. That decision, which rested with the commander of the 1st Army, would be made only if the Egyptian divisions retreating from Tobruk needed more time to escape the encirclement that threatened them.

Fanning out, the tank companies of Hafez's battalion opened up like a great net. Turning slightly to the west, they began their advance to a point south of Gueret Hamza. Once there, the Brigade would turn north. One tank battalion would travel up the east side of the road that ran to Tobruk; the other would deploy west of the road. The Brigade would advance from Gueret Hamza to Bir el Gubi. The Soviets' support elements, lacking good terrain feature to guide on or set up in, and wanting to stay near a road, would no doubt be found somewhere along that route.

Upon reaching Bir el Gubi, the Brigade would turn southeast and sweep the area from Bir el Gubi to Taieb el Esem, then to

Gasr el Abid, located on the Libyan-Egyptian border. Thus, any Soviet support units missed on the sweep of the road might be found. That route would also take the Brigade through the area where the Cubans were expected to be and, in the end, back into Egypt. Though part of the mission was to save the divisions to the northwest, the commander of the 1st Army pointed out to the commander of the Republican Brigade that he was not to lose the Brigade while doing so. Egyptian Army combat units of the 2nd Army in the Sinai needed time to deploy from the east to the west. If the Republican Brigade could not save the 1st Army, it would be needed to buy time for the deployment of the 2nd Army.

With the Brigade's recon company deployed to his front and his own security element to his flank, Hafez prepared to drive his unit into the night, seeking to rip out the heart of his enemy and avenge his honor.

15

When I am without orders, and unexpected occurrences arise, I shall always act as I think the honor and glory of my King and Country demand.

—LORD NELSON

On the Road North of Gueret Hamza, Libya *
0035 Hours, 18 December

Struggling with the heavy tow cables, the crew of the BTR managed to free them from General Uvarov's BTR-80 armored personnel carrier. In a ditch on one side of the road, the crew of an overturned BRDM-2 armored car waited. On the other side of the road a lieutenant from Uvarov's BTR was bandaging the driver of the armored car. The BRDM-2, escorting and providing security for General Uvarov's command group, had run off the road in the darkness and flipped over. Standing between the two vehicles, Neboatov watched. The crew of the armored car had been lucky: only the driver had been injured, and he, in Neboatov's mind, deserved it. That would be the last time, no doubt, that the man would fall asleep while driving.

Neboatov, of course, could not blame the driver for falling asleep. Unable to suppress it, he yawned. He considered curling up in the BTR and catching some sleep while the crews worked on recovering the armored car. Just as quickly as he thought of that, he dismissed the idea. The general, no doubt, would need something as soon as he fell asleep, and Neboatov would look like a lazy sod in his eyes. Instead, he stretched his arms over his head, then, bending at the waist, reached down to touch his toes in an effort to fight off the urge to sleep.

Straightening up, Neboatov looked around for the general. Stepping over to where the lieutenant was finishing his work on the driver, Neboatov asked if he had seen the general. The lieutenant pointed to a lone figure standing off in the desert. Neboatov watched for a moment, trying to decide whether to disturb the general. Everyone, generals included, needed time alone.

The clatter of the tow cable falling to the road followed by a stream of cursing caused Neboatov to turn. The commander of the overturned car had stumbled, tripped, and dropped the cable. He was tired; they were all tired. Rest was what they needed more than anything else. The lack of regular sleep and the need to execute endless tasks, coupled with the cold, the harshness of the desert, and the stress of participating in combat operations, were taking their toll. People were beginning to make mistakes, like the driver of the armored car, and the captain who had managed to get the general's BTR lost while they were looking for the 24th Tank Corps command post. Rest and a good night's sleep was what they needed. But that was the last thing that they were going to be able to get.

Cranking up the BTR, the commander of the overturned armored car prepared to guide the BTR to where it could turn the armored car over, then back onto the road. Since he was in the way where he was standing, Neboatov went over to where the general stood.

"Are they finished yet?" Uvarov asked, without turning to see who was approaching.

Neboatov stopped. "No, General. It will be another fifteen, twenty minutes, at least."

Uvarov took a deep breath. The cold night air filled his lungs and cooled his temper. Slowly he exhaled. "Time is one commodity we don't have much of. Did General Boldin acknowledge the order to stop his advance?"

"Yes, Comrade General. Lead element of the 24th has assumed hasty defenses northeast of Gabr Saleh."

Waiting for more, Uvarov turned toward Neboatov. "And his response, Major? What was his response to the order?"

Neboatov hesitated before he told Uvarov Boldin's response.

Turning away from Neboatov, Uvarov sighed. "Never mind. I can imagine what it was. At least he stopped."

Boldin, after Uvarov, the senior Soviet officer in Libya, commanded the 24th Tank Corps. Seeing the opportunity to reach the coast of the Mediterranean in a single thrust and not understanding the reasoning behind Uvarov's orders, Boldin had spurred his corps forward that afternoon. Uvarov, in turn, slowed, then stopped him. In a lively radio conversation Uvarov became convinced that Boldin couldn't be trusted to act appropriately unless he knew what the political situation was and what was at stake. He did not want to trust such a conversation to an open radio net, even though it was secured. Uvarov suspected that all nets were being monitored by the KGB. At the first opportunity Uvarov left front headquarters for Boldin's, to talk to him face to face. It was, in Uvarov's mind, critical that Boldin understood how things stood and the role Soviet forces would play.

It was not that Boldin was disloyal. Boldin was in fact an outstanding officer, perhaps the best tank general in the Red Army. His selection for command of the 24th Tank Corps ahead of several dozen generals with greater seniority spoke well of his abilities. Boldin, however, was politically naive. Dedicated to his profession, he had no time for political considerations. He saw all problems through the eyes of a professional soldier. In all things he applied the accepted formulas and doctrine, as he had been trained, to achieve the desired results. In a war in Europe, Uvarov knew, Boldin would excel. In Africa, where the political sands were shifting faster than the sands beneath his feet, Boldin's approach to war could be dangerous.

Believing that the general wanted to be alone, Neboatov backed up, turned, and prepared to leave. Uvarov stopped him. "Don't go, Major. I could use some company. This night is very lonely, and very long."

Neboatov trudged through the soft sand up to the general's right side. He stood there for several minutes before he spoke. "Are you going to relieve General Boldin?"

"No. There's no need to relieve him. I just have to do a better job explaining my intentions to him. General Boldin is a fine soldier, one of the best. He just needs to understand that this is not a purely military problem." Uvarov paused for a few moments. "I have no doubt he will try to convince me to let him push on. It makes sense, militarily, to encircle the Egyptian 1st Army."

Neboatov was both fascinated by the general's conversation and flattered that the general had taken him into his confidence.

"But politically, such a move would be dangerous. It would force the Egyptians to have to make one of two bad choices. They would either have to accept a military defeat or bring more forces to bear against us in order to save their surrounded army, and their honor. There is always the danger they might even convince the Americans to intervene. Even without direct military intervention by the Americans, however, we cannot win a long war in Africa." Uvarov turned to look at Neboatov. "You see, the Egyptians are a proud people. So long as they have the means, they will fight to save their surrounded forces. Politically, the president of Egypt cannot allow the 1st Army to be eradicated. So we keep him from having to make a bad choice by allowing the Egyptians to escape. We stop at the border and tell the Americans that politically, we are even. Their surrogates attacked one of our surrogates, and our surrogate defended itself. Common sense prevails, and peace breaks out."

They stood there for a few moments in silence. Neboatov, taking the liberty, spoke first. "I must admit, General, I do not fully understand the dynamics of the situation. But what you say makes sense. Do you believe the Egyptians will see it that way?"

Uvarov was about to answer but paused. In the distance he heard the squeaking and grinding of metal on metal. Tanks!

The commander of Hafez's lead company was surprised to see the small group of armored vehicles clustered on the road. The Republican Brigade's recon company, supposed to be well ahead, hadn't reported any contact. Therefore he reported to Hafez before he gave his company the order to engage. There was, after all, the possibility that the BTR, the BRDM, and the people he saw in his thermal sight were Egyptian.

Responding to the report forwarded to him, Hafez called the Brigade operations officer and asked if the recon company had any vehicles stopped on the road at the coordinates given by his lead company commander. There was a pause while the Brigade operations officer told the Brigade intelligence officer to contact the recon company commander and ask him to confirm the location of his recon elements. The recon company commander acknowledged the order from the intelligence officer and queried his platoon leaders. They, in turn, called each of their vehicles and accounted for all of them and confirmed their locations. Once that was done, the information on the location and activity of all the recon vehicles and elements was passed back up the chain to the intelligence officer. When he had plotted and checked all vehicle locations on his map, he informed the operations officer that there were no friendly recon vehicles at the location given by Hafez. The operations officer passed that information back to Hafez. Calmly and matter-of-factly Hafez reported that he was therefore going to consider the vehicles enemy and destroy them.

Switching his radio to the battalion command net, he ordered the lead company commander to destroy the vehicles. With unmasked glee in his voice, the company commander acknowledged Hafez's order and prepared to order his company to engage.

Uvarov cocked his head, listening to the noise of advancing tanks. "Ours?"

Trained as a motorized rifleman and with practical experience in Iran, Neboatov knew tanks. In Iran he had heard Soviet, American, and British tanks up close. A series of bright flashes, followed by the boom of tank cannons firing, confirmed what Neboatov already knew. "M-60 tanks—the Egyptians!" The same training and experience told Neboatov to seek cover. He dropped to his stomach and then looked for some place to crawl to.

Uvarov, transfixed by the sudden appearance of enemy forces so deep in their rear area, remained standing. Another volley of rounds from the approaching tanks found their mark. The night was lit up as the BTR blew up. Turning, Uvarov watched as the armored car that had been in the ditch, and was now halfway out, received two direct hits. Like the BTR, it blew up, throwing off a large ball of fire.

Disappointed that he had not been able to fire at the armored vehicles, the platoon leader of the left flank platoon began to search for targets further to the left. As his gunner traversed the turret, the image of a man standing alone in the desert appeared in the gunner's thermal sight. The gunner called out his newly acquired target to his tank commander. Dropping his head down, the platoon leader saw the target in his thermal viewer. Though not as good as a BTR, at least it was a target. He ordered the gunner to engage with the coaxially mounted machine gun.

Quickly, before the target dropped down or disappeared, the gunner laid his aiming dot onto the man's chest and depressed the button for the laser range finder. The invisible laser beam fired, hit the target, and reflected some of its energy back to the tank. The tank's fire control detected the reflected laser light, measured how long it took the light to return, and translated that information into range data for the ballistic computer. With input from other sensors, a ballistic solution was arrived at and automatically sent to the gun/turret drive system. By the time the commander gave the order to fire, the necessary information to allow a first-round hit was in the system and applied to the gun. Aided by the turret stabilization system, the gunner made a last, fine lay onto the center of the target and squeezed the trigger.

To his and the tank commander's surprise, instead of the rattling and chattering of the 7.62mm coax machine gun, they heard the main gun discharge, driving the breech back out of battery and spitting the spent shell casing of a 105mm main gun round onto the floor. In his haste, the gunner had forgotten to move the gun select switch from the main gun position to the machine-gun position.

*   *   *

Still undecided as to which direction to crawl in, Neboatov heard the crack of a tank cannon, followed by a gasp from the general. Looking up, he watched Uvarov fall over and hit the ground like a freshly chopped tree. Spinning on his stomach like a top, Neboatov crawled over to the general. In the light thrown off the burning BTR, he could see a look of surprise frozen on the general's face. Putting his hand on the general's chest to see if he was breathing, he felt a mass of goo. Carefully he ran his fingers about the wound to see how badly the general was hit.

The wound, however, didn't feel right. Propping himself up to visually inspect the wound, Neboatov was appalled by the sight that greeted him. The main gun round fired by accident had struck Uvarov square in the back. The armor piercing fin stabilized round had ripped through the general's chest as if it had been made of papier-mâché. The fins, undeterred by mere flesh and bone, had not fallen off the penetrator. Instead, they had stayed with the round, pulling bits and pieces of lung and heart muscle out the front as they passed through the general's chest.

Pulling his hand away, Neboatov lowered himself behind the general's body. There was nowhere to go, nowhere to hide. Unable to do anything but play dead, Neboatov began to wipe his bloody hand in the sand while he hid behind the general's body and prepared to wait for the Egyptians to pass.

The gunner of the platoon leader's tank braced himself just before the heel of his tank commander's boot slammed into the back of his head. As the tank continued to roll on into the night, the commander cursed his gunner, then cursed his luck for having such a stupid man as a gunner. "How can we win," he yelled, "with men who do not know the difference between a cannon and a machine gun!" He knew it was a mistake: the excitement of battle often fostered such errors. But the thought did little to calm his anger.

Off the Coast of Libya North of Al Gardabah * 0059 Hours, 18 December

With the exception of the noise generated by electrical systems and a few hushed conversations, the combat information center of the battleship USS *Kansas* was quiet. At general quarters since 0030 hours, the tactical action officer watched the clock on the wall of the strike warfare center. To one side the ship's captain watched but said nothing. He had no need to say anything: all was running as planned. In sixty seconds they would fire the first rounds by Americans in the latest Middle East war.

By order of the President, the commander of the 6th Fleet was directed to destroy all surface-to-surface missile units and their controlling headquarters. When announced publicly, the official communiqué would state that the attack was in response to the use of chemical weapons by the Soviet-Cuban-Libyan forces. Unofficially, the targeting would include headquarters and support elements, which would slow the Soviet advance and buy time for the Egyptian forces to withdraw into Egypt. The USS *Kansas* was part of that effort. Its target was the headquarters for the Soviet North African Front in Al Gardabah and the headquarters for the Cuban division still located near Gazala.

As the second sweep hand finally finished its climb to the number 12 on the clock, the tactical operations officer issued the order to fire to the plotting room officer. In the main battery plotting room, the plotting room officer pulled the trigger that fired the main battery. There was a momentary pause before the ship shuddered under the weight of nine 16-inch guns firing simultaneously. Topside, the entire port side of the *Kansas* was briefly illuminated by the muzzle blast.

Ashore, in scattered assembly areas, Cuban soldiers of the division that had remained behind at Gazala were woken by a distant rumble. Those on guard and close to the sea saw the sudden flash out to sea, just over the horizon. All heard the rumbling noise that resembled that made by a freight train that followed shortly thereafter. None knew that the noise passing overhead belonged to nine 16-inch rounds. Four of those rounds were Mark 144 Improved Conventional Munitions rounds, weighing close to nineteen hundred pounds apiece and carrying 666 shaped-charge bomblets. The other five were Mark 143 high-explosive rounds, also weighing nineteen hundred pounds but carrying 160 pounds of high explosive. Each

projectile, pushed out of its 16-inch gun by 660 pounds of
D-839 smokeless powder, was traveling at 2,500 feet per second, or just under a mile every two seconds. By the time any
of those who witnessed the strange occurrence thought to report it, the projectiles had found their target.

There was no warning, no time for the staff of the North
African Front to seek cover. In a single, terrible moment, the
building that housed the headquarters, and the very ground that
surrounded it, were heaved skyward as the rounds from the
Kansas impacted. Only a lone Pioneer remotely piloted drone
from the *Kansas* stood witness to the destruction of the Soviet
command post. Its infrared eye watched and recorded the incident dispassionately.

Aboard the *Kansas* the plotting room officer, the tactical
operations officer, and the ship's captain watched TV monitors. One second the thermal images of the building where the
North African Front was housed sat center of screen. For the
briefest moment several streaks appeared on the corner of the
screen and raced for the building. Then the screen glowed
white as the Mark 144 ICM projectiles broke up and scattered
their bomblets. When the bomblets and the HE rounds impacted, the screen went white. Before the sudden burst of heat
dissipated and allowed the image to clarify, the shock wave
created by the explosions of the HE rounds reached the tiny
Pioneer remotely piloted vehicle, or RPV. The image on the
monitor jiggled as the sailor controlling the RPV fought to
regain control of his remote airplane. Once he had it stabilized,
he reoriented its camera back to the building that had just been
hit. He had difficulty finding it. Panning the area and decreas-
ing the magnification so he could cover a larger area, he flew
past the remains of the building on his first try. The plotting
room officer called over the intercom to the RPV pilot and told
him to hold the view he had. Then he ordered the pilot to scan
back slowly. When the RPV's camera reached the spot the
plotting room officer wanted to view, he ordered the drone's
pilot to stop scanning, then to increase magnification.

As soon as the thermal image flipped on, showing the magnified scene, everyone saw what the intelligence officer had seen. There was no longer a building to find. Instead, there was a very hot spot, made by many tiny craters, surrounded by the warm spoil thrown out of them by the bomblets. Just to be sure, the plotting room officer instructed the pilot to confirm the grid they were observing. As the pilot called out the grid numbers, the tactical operations officer and plotting room officer both checked their target data.

The plotting room officer was overjoyed. "We got 'em. They be history! No one's going to make any calls to Moscow from that phone booth today."

In the strike warfare center, the tactical operations officer looked at the captain. The captain nodded his approval. "Okay—that was a lucky shot. Now let's see if you can take out their alternate command post. I want to nail that Cuban division CP before they realize what happened to the front CP."

Gabr Saleh, Libya * 0430 Hours, 18 December

"General Boldin, wake up. We have them."

Boldin rubbed his eyes before he opened them. When he did, they were greeted by a sky full of stars. Choking, the general threw off the blanket that someone had put over him and sat up on his cot. Awake now, he asked who it was that they finally had.

The duty officer realized the general's mind was still groggy from sleep. "The Egyptian armored unit. They passed through Taieb el Esem ten minutes ago headed southeast toward the Cuban sector. They have at least two tank battalions accompanied by artillery."

Reaching down for a canteen, Boldin thought for a moment. "Don't we know for sure? Have we received no intelligence from the front?"

The duty officer waited until the general was finished drinking before he responded. "Comrade General, we have had no contact with front headquarters, the alternate command post, or General Uvarov's forward CP since 0100 hours. We have tried all frequencies but have nothing."

Boldin looked at his watch. "General Uvarov has not arrived?"

The duty officer shook his head from side to side.

Boldin thought for a moment. Three and a half hours and no contact from any higher headquarters. On top of that, the front commander, who had been so anxious to see him and had been en route, was also off the net. It would be light in two hours—another day. He couldn't wait any longer for orders. With an enemy force moving through his rear areas, no intelligence coming from higher headquarters, and possibly no higher headquarters, he had to make decisions. "All right, Captain, I'll be along in a minute. Tell Colonel Pospelov that we are assuming control of the battle for the front headquarters until they, or General Uvarov, come up on the net. Have him pass that word on to the 8th Division and Colonel Nafissi at Libyan headquarters in Tobruk."

The captain saluted, turned, and had started back to the command post when Boldin yelled to him to wait. Spinning about in his tracks, the captain trotted back to the general. Now that he had assumed command, Boldin needed to put out warning orders so that his subordinates could begin their planning. The young captain stood before his general while the general reviewed options available to the 24th in a mind just woken from a sound sleep.

In the end only two made sense to Boldin. They, the 24th Tank Corps and the 8th Division, could remain where they were and do nothing. By doing so, they were allowing the Egyptian 1st Army to escape, since the Libyans could not complete the encirclement themselves. In addition, their current positions were indefensible. The Egyptian armored raid, still in progress, had demonstrated that.

The other option was far more attractive and militarily sound. The 24th Tank Corps and the 8th Division could continue to the coast, seizing Sollum and Halfaya Pass. Such a move would block the withdrawal of the Egyptians, put the Tank Corps and the Cuban division in more defensible terrain, and allow them to contact and coordinate operations with the Soviet Mediterranean Squadron of the Black Sea Fleet.

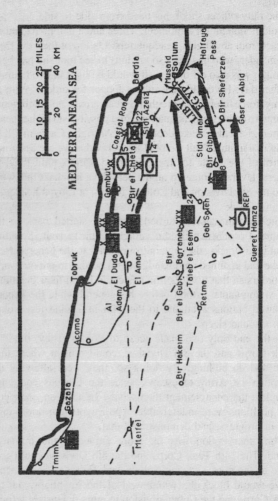

For a moment he considered both options, weighing and debating. The duty officer patiently waited for an order. He knew the general was hard at work, thinking, planning, debating with himself. Such matters, the captain knew, took time.

Unable to seek guidance from any higher authority, Boldin was left with his own thoughts. One thought that kept cropping up had no real tie to the current military situation. It occurred to him that for the first time in his life, he had a major decision to make, one that would influence real events. This was no theoretical exercise, no command-post training exercise. Finding himself faced with such a decision, he considered those who had gone before him, the great military men whom he had been forced to study. Like them, he was faced with the need to make a choice. Of all the generals in history he had ever studied and admired, those who had been bold and decisive stood out. The men of action, able to seize the initiative and act boldly, were inevitably the winners.

In the end his classic military training dictated the option he would select. It suddenly occurred to him that there really had never been a real choice. There was only one right answer. Boldin looked up at the young captain, standing at a relaxed parade rest. "Also tell Colonel Pospelov to issue a warning order to the Corps. All units are to be prepared to continue the attack to seize Sollum and Halfaya Pass. To hell with the Egyptians in our rear, Captain. Let's continue the attack to the Mediterranean and see who flinches first."

The general's fighting words brought a broad smile to the captain's face. "Yes, Comrade General. I will do so immediately." Without waiting for the general to return his salute, the captain ran back to the command post, literally bursting in and shouting the long-awaited word that the attack would continue.

Tobruk, Libya * 0945 Hours, 18 December

The arrival of General Boldin at Nafissi's headquarters and the conversations between Boldin and Nafissi that followed resulted in a change in the relationship between their respective forces. Nafissi, pleased with the sudden turn of events, found new opportunities. The attack by the Egyptian Republican Brigade had been a failure, nothing more than a ride in the desert. Lead elements of the 24th Tank Corps were in Musaid, Egypt, by 0900 hours and were preparing to attack Sollum, also in Egypt. Recon elements of the 8th Cuban Division had followed the withdrawal of the Republican Brigade to Sidi Omar and Bir Sheferzen, both in Egypt. With the coastal road severed, the bulk of three Egyptian divisions were encircled with their backs against the sea.

By any measure a great victory had been achieved. Though there were rumblings in the United Nations, Europe, and the United States about the reported use of chemical weapons, only the United States had done anything. Everyone else was waiting for independent verification of the reports. Even the allies of the United States, NATO in particular, were attempting to distance themselves from the action taken and proposed by the United States. One by one the countries of Europe were denying use of their facilities or air space to American forces en route to or operating in Egypt. Even the evacuation of American dependents was affected temporarily when one European government refused to allow military aircraft carrying the dependents to land and the dependents to transfer to civilian charter flights. With such tenuous support for Egypt and its ally, Nafissi felt he could press a little harder, a little farther.

While Boldin was there, Nafissi extracted several agreements from the new Soviet commander. One of them was for control of aircraft flown by Soviet and East German pilots. Nafissi wanted to use them, along with Libyan aircraft, to interdict the flow of Egyptian reinforcements into the Western desert. Boldin agreed to this readily, not knowing the scale of the operation or where Nafissi wanted to conduct the attacks. The second agreement was that Soviet and Cuban forces would contain and eliminate the encircled 1st Army while a Libyan corps of three divisions advanced into Egypt to Mersa Matruh. Again, Nafissi didn't tell Boldin that it was his intent to go further if the air raids he had planned were successful. Mersa Matruh was only an intermediate objective.

In fact, though Boldin left believing he understood his role, he knew only half the plan—the half Nafissi wanted him to know. Boldin concentrated only on the destruction of the 1st Egyptian Army and the restoration of the original border. Nafissi, however, was playing for higher stakes. His gaze was fixed on Cairo and a jihad that would topple the Egyptian government. The defeat of the 1st Army was the first step. Next, Nafissi needed to demonstrate to the people of Egypt that their government could not defend them. The third and final part would be the sweeping advance of Revolutionary Guard units out of the Western Desert, flying the green banner. Their irresistible advance would bring true believers to the forefront and the Egyptian government down—as Mohammed had done over a thousand years before.

Cairo * 1305 Hours, 18 December

"All right—one more time, guys. This time, let's see if we can make it to the door without tripping." Cerro's remarks brought a few nervous chuckles from the thirty soldiers sitting in the red nylon jump seat of the C-130 transport. They had been practicing procedures for making a combat jump, procedures that in less than seven hours they would use for real. Though all had jump training, and fully half of them had made combat jumps in Iran, none were current. The fact was, most of those who had jumped in Iran were in the 11th Airborne Division because it was air assault, not a jump-rated airborne unit.

As difficult as the jump would be—at night, with no backup and little prep time—the actual jump was the least of Cerro's concerns. He knew they would all make it, most of them uninjured. What they did on the ground was a different matter. As First Sergeant Duncan kept reminding Cerro, a collection of thirty soldiers does not a platoon make. The real challenge facing Cerro at that moment was creating an effective organization, with a chain of command and some basic drills that would allow this collection of soldiers to function as a unit. Cerro had therefore spent most of the morning getting to know the men he would lead that night and running some dismounted squad drills along the edge of the runway.

Fortunately their mission, the securing of a refuel point, was simple. Only mission-essential tasks were worked on in the little time they had. Cerro started with squad and platoon defensive operations. When they reached a level of competency in those drills, he ran a few squad attack drills, in case there was the need to conduct a counterattack. Finally, at noon, he ran everyone through some parachute refresher training.

Morale of the soldiers was surprisingly good. Most were glad to be doing something besides sitting in an assembly area waiting for God knew what to happen. One sergeant E-5 even commented to Cerro that his selection to go on the mission was a real stroke of luck: he was behind on some car payments and the jump pay they were promised would help out. Cerro wondered if the young sergeant even considered the possibility that he might not live long enough to make those payments, let alone drive the car.

Ready for the last drill, Cerro went through the jump commands. He watched their procedures. The copilot of the plane, ready for the simulated jump, hit the green light on Cerro's cue. Cerro went out the door, followed by the soldiers shuffling behind him. As they reached the door, each man exited onto bales of rags under the watchful eye of Duncan.

When Cerro had rolled to one side of the rag pile to clear the way for the man behind him, he noticed a lieutenant colonel standing next to Duncan, watching them. Standing up, Cerro took off his parachute and gear, set them down in a neat pile, and walked over to Duncan and the lieutenant colonel.

As he approached, he recognized the colonel as the one who had been in charge of the live fire demonstration on 7 December. Cerro also realized, for the first time, that the children the lady at the embassy had given him must be the colonel's. Coming up to Duncan, Cerro saluted Dixon. "Good afternoon, sir. What can we do for you, sir?"

"I was out here to see that everything was in order and on hand. Your first sergeant has already gone over your training for the day and your schedule from now till lift-off."

Cerro wondered if the colonel was in charge or just visiting as an excuse to get out of some office. "Is there anything in particular that the colonel wishes to see?"

Dixon shook his head no, telling Cerro to carry on with his training. Cerro responded that the practice exit, their third for the day, was the last training event they had planned. The rest of the time before takeoff was going to be used loading their gear, eating, getting some sleep, and making precombat inspections. Dixon noted his approval.

"In that case, Captain, I'll be leaving you to go about your business. No doubt the last thing you need is a Corps staff officer hanging around. Just give a yell if there's anything you need." Dixon was about to leave when Cerro stopped him.

"There is one thing, sir. It doesn't concern the jump. We're ready for that. It's in reference to your children."

Dixon looked at Cerro. The smile disappeared from Dixon's face in a flash. It was replaced by a blank stare. "What about my wife and children?"

Cerro didn't pick up on the change in Dixon's mood, the mention of his wife, or the blank stare. "The children should be in Britain by now. My company had the task of escorting the dependents out of the embassy to the pickup zone yesterday. When your wife gave me the children, I made sure they got on the transports. I sent one of my platoon sergeants with them to the airfield. He turned the boys over to the crew chief of one of the transports. The platoon sergeant stayed with them at the airfield till that plane left."

"And my wife? What about her?" While he may have missed the look in Dixon's eyes as he was telling him of the boys, Cerro couldn't miss the cold, barely controlled rage in Dixon's voice when he asked about the lady.

"Well, sir, I don't know. After she turned the boys over to me, she left. Ran back into the crowd. I assume she went back to her job."

Dixon said nothing. For a moment he stood there, rooted to the ground. His eyes were wide, bulging, and wild. His face went flush, then turned red. His hands, held close to his side, were knotted up so tight that the knuckles were turning white. Cerro was about to ask if there was a problem but then decided

that would be dumb. It was obvious that Dixon was as surprised to find out his wife had stayed as Cerro had been when
she gave her children to him.

Without a word Dixon pivoted about and stormed off. When
he was gone, Duncan turned to Cerro. "Something tells me
that the colonel is not happy with his wife."

Cerro looked at Duncan. "Ya know, First Sergeant, that's
what I like about you—you're so observant. And quick on the
uptake."

Duncan stared at Cerro. "You're lucky you're an officer,
sir. Otherwise I'd tell you to fuck yourself, sir. Now, if we
could get back to the platoon, with all due respect, sir."

Cerro chuckled. "Temper, temper, First Sergeant." Stepping off toward the platoon, Duncan followed. He signaled to
the platoon to form up by making a circling motion over his
head as they approached.

Cerro and Duncan had just about reached the assembled
platoon when air-raid sirens near the airfield control tower and
in the town just outside the airfield began to wail. Stopping,
both Cerro and Duncan looked up in the sky, then around the
airfield. "Do you think this is for real, First Sergeant?"

Duncan noted the haste with which the Egyptian personnel
scattered. "Well, sir, this sure ain't exactly a good time to be
messing with drills. We better—"

At the end of the runway, from a position neither man had
noticed, the rocket of a Hawk surface-to-air missile ignited,
cutting Duncan off in mid-sentence. By the time Cerro and
Duncan turned to where the launcher was, the first missile was
aloft and racing for its target. A few seconds later, another
Hawk missile followed.

Turning to the platoon, Cerro yelled to the men to grab their
weapons only and follow him. Duncan stood fast for a moment, making sure they were all going the right way. When the
last man had passed him, he fell in behind the group and began
to run with them, wondering if Captain Cerro knew where he
was going. In front, Cerro was wondering the same thing.

* * *

346

The sudden blare of the sirens caught everyone in the WNN offices by surprise. Looking up from her desk, Fay asked what was going on. Johnny rushed by, headed for the window. "It's an air raid, Mrs. Dixon. Hassan just heard it on the radio. Everyone's supposed to seek shelter."

Fay got up and followed Johnny to the window. He was already there, looking up at the sky. Fay came up beside him and also looked up, then down. On the street below there was a scramble as people ran into buildings, searching for cover. Cars weaved around other cars stopped in the center of the street, abandoned by their drivers, who were seeking shelter. Fay looked around the office behind her. The Egyptians were gone. The other Americans in the office were either standing back against the wall or moving to the window to watch the show.

Nervously Johnny looked at Fay. "Shouldn't we go to the shelter too?"

Fay continued to look. "Johnny, we're news people. Can't get good copy from a hole in the ground." She looked down at the street, then back to the sky. "Besides, Johnny dear, do you know where the nearest fallout shelter is?"

Standing at the 6 October Bridge with the camera crew, Jan was preparing to shoot a piece on the flow of military traffic through Cairo. Behind her, huge tractor trailers hauling tanks were slowly rumbling across the bridge. She, and all other reporters, had been denied permission to go to the front to film the action because of the threat of chemicals. They hadn't even been allowed near the airfields to film the evacuation process. "*Too* dangerous," they had been told. Jan, being the suspicious type, didn't believe that. No doubt there were things going on out there that neither the Egyptians nor the American government wanted the press to see. So, as in the first days of the crisis, they were back to filming tanks and trucks moving through Cairo. At least this time she and her camera crew had been allowed near the bridge.

Almost ready to start shooting, the cameraman asked Jan to hold up something white so he could color-balance his camera.

Taking pages from her script and waving them, she asked if that would do. "Great, love, just great. Now if you could quit jigglin' the bloody thing, we'll be ready in a moment."

She was standing there like that when an air-raid siren not twenty feet from them began blasting. The sound man ripped the earphones off his head, cursing and dancing about as he did so. The cameraman let the camera down to his side and looked up. He turned to Jan. "Looks like we're in luck, love. We're about to get some real action shots."

Jan looked around. "Oh, come on, Tim. You don't think the Libyans are going to bomb downtown Cairo, do you?"

Tim was busy preparing his camera. The sound man, regaining his composure, was resetting the volume to compensate for the screeching of the air-raid siren.

Jan stood where she was and asked the same question, this time in earnest. Tim looked up. "Come on, love. You don't hav' ta be a bleedin' Napoleon to figure out they're after the bloody bridges. Do you think old Nafissi in Tobruk wants to see that tank behind ya knockin' at his front door?" Tim pointed behind him to a tank sitting on the bed of a transporter.

The sound man pointed to something in the distance. "Look—they're firing SAMs!"

Jan turned in the direction where he was pointing. In the distance she saw a white trail of smoke racing skyward. SAM, she remembered, was short for surface-to-air missile. As she watched, a second, then a third missile raced up following the first. They really were under attack.

Racing along at less than one hundred feet, Major Hans Bruchmann, East German air force, struggled for control of his damaged MIG-23. By going low and maintaining an air speed far in excess of what would have been thought prudent in a peacetime exercise, he had survived longer than the rest of his flight of four. Bounced by a pair of Egyptian F-16s before they had even left Libyan air space, two of the MIG-23s had gone down without any loss to the interceptors. Bruchmann and his lone wingman had no sooner cleared that engagement than a pair of Egyptian MIG-21s hit them head on. As soon as both sides had acquired each other, they exchanged air-to-air missiles. In this engagement Bruchmann hit one of the attackers. But the exchange was even, as his wingman was brought down by an Egyptian missile.

As he closed on Cairo, Bruchmann's radar warning indicator began to squawk, telling him that his MIG had been detected by the acquisition radar of an American-built Hawk missile battery. He watched and waited, dropping as low as he dared go. Seconds later the radar warning tone changed, indicating that the Hawk battery illuminator radar was locked on his aircraft. He waited before he took any action to counter the lock-on. As he did, he could feel the sweat roll down his forehead and into his eyes. He fought the urge to react too soon. Nervously he waited for the missiles. Only after he saw the volley of surface-to-air missiles streaking toward him did he fire chaff and take his plane lower, accelerating as he went. For a split second he broke radar lock—but only for a moment. In quick order the illuminator radar locked back onto him. Hitting his chaff dispenser trigger, he let fly another stream of aluminum strips that puffed out of their canisters like ticker tape.

Unfortunately, he let up on the chaff too soon. The missile, momentarily confused by the clouds of chaff, had lost Bruchmann's plane, but then reacquired it when the clouds of chaff slowed and dispersed and Bruchmann's plane did not. Veering back onto an intercept course, Bruchmann discovered his error almost too late. Instead of firing more chaff, he cut his joystick hard and to the right just as the proximity fuse of the missile detonated the missile's warhead.

Most of the deadly fragments flew past Bruchmann's plane into empty space. A few, however, cut through his tail section. The impact almost caused Bruchmann to plow into the ground. Whether it was through instinct, training, or just incredible luck, Bruchmann was able to regain control of the aircraft. Bringing it back to level flight, he once again dove to an even lower altitude and accelerated. Though there was the possibility that he might crash at any second flying in this manner, there was no doubt in Bruchmann's mind that he would eventually be brought down by missiles or aircraft if he flew higher.

In an instant the ground under him fell away. To his immediate front the massive forms of the pyramids of Giza appeared. He was on course and thirty seconds out. Setting his bombing computer on, he slowed and prepared to make a right turn as soon as he hit the Nile. Once he was over the Nile, it would be a short run to the 6 October Bridge and the point where he would release the more than three metric tons of bombs he carried.

East of Cairo, on the high ground overlooking the city and the Nile valley, the acquisition radar of a Hawk battery acquired a new contact. It was a hostile aircraft coming in from the west over Giza, low and fast. Without hesitation, the automated system switched an illuminator onto the new threat and gave the controller a ready-to-fire indicator. Although the Hawk was meant to be a mid-to-high-altitude air defense weapon, the Hawk batteries on the high ground had been ordered to engage whenever possible. Therefore, after a quick check to confirm target and lock on, the controller launched a missile at the low-flying aircraft approaching the city.

When his radar warning receivers picked up the acquisition radar, then the illuminator painting his aircraft, Bruchmann jerked his plane to the right, barely missing a tall building he hadn't seen. As he started the turn, he began to pump the chaff dispenser trigger. He was too close to his target now to be brought down. Only five seconds, no more than ten, to target.

Deciding to check on the radio to see if Jan was all right, Fay walked over to the counter at the rear of the office. Her back was to the window when a jet came screaming around the corner in front of the window. Twisting where she stood, she saw only a blur race by, trailing white puffs right in front of the window. Johnny blinked as the jet went by. "Wow! Did you see that?"

Fay yelled from across the room. "Was there a camera on that?"

* * *

"Jesus Christ—here they come!"

Jan pivoted to see where Tim was pointing. There was a blur that appeared to swing in from behind a building. Finished with its turn, the blur turned into the image of a jet as it leveled out and began to dive toward them.

"Well, love, you wanted action shots. Here it comes!"

For a moment Jan didn't understand what Tim was saying. What did he mean? She was about to yell over to him when she saw black objects under the wings of the approaching aircraft fall away. In an instant she realized they were bombs—and she was standing on their target!

The sudden turn caused the illuminator to jerk left to reacquire the target. The radar locked onto the first moving target it found. Illuminating the reacquired target, the Hawk missile made a final course correction onto the cloud of chaff being illuminated just before impact.

The flash of the exploding Hawk missile blinded Fay. It was followed almost instantaneously by the heat of the explosion, sweeping over her like a wave. By the time the shock wave hit her and threw her against the wall, Johnny and half a dozen other people who had been at the window were already dead.

The first missile had no sooner failed to hit the enemy jet than the radar reacquired the correct target. It switched the illuminator away from the now-dispersed cloud of chaff and onto the real target. Ready to fire, the indicator light came on in the control center. The controller checked, then launched the second missile.

Throwing herself against the concrete embankment, Jan squeezed herself into the corner as best she could. Though she knew her life might well end in the next second, she couldn't resist the urge to look up. Rolling over onto her back, she caught the image of the attacking jet screaming across the bridge. The jet, barely clearing it, was suddenly engulfed by a fireball. The momentum of the shattered jet carried it and the fireball over the bridge and out of Jan's view. No sooner had that image cleared than the bombs hit the bridge. The overpressure from the jarring impact hit her like a hammer. In an instant the bridge and everything about her were obscured in a choking cloud of black smoke and dust.

From the edge of the airfield Cerro and Duncan watched the smoke rising over the city. The men of his platoon, unable to find a suitable shelter, were on their bellies in the sand and dispersed in a line on either side of Cerro and Duncan. Expecting an attack on the field, each man had his weapon ready to fire. When his men had dispersed, Cerro noted that the initial attacks were being made on the town. He therefore decided to give a quick, impromptu class on how to mass small-arms fire against aircraft.

To do so, he had to stand out alone, on the edge of the runway, and shout to his dispersed soldiers. At first he felt ridiculous, standing in the open, giving a class while there was an air raid in progress. But as soon as he got into his instruction, he noticed that he had never before seen such attentive students. By the time he was finished, he was really getting into it. At the end of his class, he turned to view the smoke rising over Cairo for a second. Turning back to his platoon, he put his hands on his hips. "Now, gentlemen, if you are patient, our training aids will be along presently and we can go into the practical application phase of this class. Until then, First Sergeant Duncan is going to conduct some on-the-job training on how to dig a hasty foxhole."

The men laughed. Though nervous and fearful, each man in his own way, they felt confidence in the company of the captain and the first sergeant standing before them. Though they never had seen either of them before that morning, the men were ready to follow them anywhere.

Cairo * 1950 Hours, 18 December

Their first attempt to shoot the report failed miserably. Midway through the first paragraph of handwritten script, Jan's voice trailed away as she fought back the urge to cry. Though tired like everyone else, Tim, the cameraman, was patient. Cutting the camera and handing it to the sound man, he walked over to Jan and wrapped his arm about her. He didn't say anything; he just touched her and comforted her for a moment. Jan was just a little shaken. They all were. In less than thirty-six hours the war that was winding down had blown up out of all proportions, reaching out to touch each of them. A brush with death at the bridge had been only the beginning. As harrowing as that had been, none of them were prepared for the news that they were the only members of the WNN news staff to survive the attack unscathed.

Returning to the office, they found emergency rescue crews removing bodies. As the only permanent member of the WNN news staff in Cairo, Jan had to identify each of them. Though Jan, like Tim and the sound man, had seen death, the victims had always been strangers, the subjects of stories. The corpses lined up on the sidewalk outside the building were friends and coworkers, real people Jan had known and lived with for two years. The process was made worse by the condition of some of the bodies. Young Johnny, just learning the trade, could only be identified by the few clumps of red hair that had not been burned away. The bodies of two women had nothing that allowed immediate identification. Never had Jan been so touched by the horror that she had so fervently chased around the world. By the time she finished looking at all the remains, she knew that she would never again be able to look at a news story as nothing but a product to be packaged and marketed. She couldn't.

Only the word that survivors had in fact been found kept Jan going that afternoon. They had been evacuated to the Kasr el Aini Hospital on the north end of Roda Island and to the Anglo-American Hospital on Gezira, and Jan and Tim spent the afternoon looking for survivors from the office. Jan found that task was no easier than identifying the dead. Still, the hope that there was someone left was enough to allow them to continue.

Andy, the sound man, was a veteran of the Royal Marines and the '82 Falklands campaign. While Jan and Tim went about their grim task, he worked on getting the story together. Contacting a friend on the staff of another news agency, he arranged for the use of its facilities to process WNN's story and beam it back to the U.S. With the equipment they had at the bridge and some borrowed tapes, Jan's crew agreed to finish the story for the day with a follow-up. The question of whether they would try to continue to report from Cairo or accept evacuation the next day was left open.

Looking up, Jan inhaled deeply. "I'm okay now, Tim. Please, let's try it again."

Tim looked into her eyes and smiled. "We don't have to carry through with this if you're not up to it, love. Red eyes don't show well on the TV, you know."

Jan gave him a weak smile. "Really, I'm ready. Let's do it before I lose my nerve."

Retrieving his camera from Andy, Tim set up the shot. Ready, he gave Jan the signal to start.

Taking in another deep breath, Jan began. "Tonight, the city of Cairo and communities along the Nile continue to recover from the massive air raids launched by Soviet and Libyan forces this afternoon. Though their targets were military—the bridges over the Nile—the bombs they dropped didn't discriminate between soldiers and civilians. Initial reports of the casualties inflicted continue to grow. By one account, well over three hundred civilians were killed and several times that number wounded in the raids that ranged along the Nile from Cairo to the Mediterranean. In our own news offices here in Cairo, six members of the WNN news staff are dead and four others are hospitalized."

For a moment Jan paused. Taking a couple of deep breaths, she continued. "As terrible as this bombing has been, the news from the Western Desert becomes more distressing by the hour. Confirmation that the 1st Egyptian Army has been encircled at Bardia, Libya, came this afternoon. Soviet forces, in a lightning thrust from the Cyrenaica Desert early this morning, seized the Egyptian town of Sollum and the critical Halfaya Pass just inside of Egypt. Supported by at least one Cuban division, the Soviet tank corps that spearheaded the attack pinned the Egyptian 1st Army against the Mediterranean, clearing the way for the advance of Libyan forces into Egypt.

"Destruction of the Nile River bridges has effectively halted the flow of forces from the Sinai to the Western Desert for now. This and the movement of Libyan forces through the Halfaya Pass leave little chance that the Egyptian army will be able to muster the forces necessary to launch a counteroffensive in time to save the 1st Army. Of more immediate concern is the defense of Matruh, the provincial capital of the Western Desert. If the Egyptian forces are unable to halt the Libyan advance before Matruh, few natural obstacles will lie in the path of the now victorious Libyans toward Alexandria, less than one hundred and seventy miles away.

"To date, U.S. forces have remained aloof and uncommitted to the growing conflict. Except for their role in the evacuation, Bright Star units and elements of the 6th Fleet have yet to take an active role in the war. Whether they will be able to do so, now that Soviet forces have set foot on Egyptian soil, remains to be seen. Rumors that the president of Egypt has sent a personal letter to the President of the United States appear to be true. The contents of that letter, and the American President's response, when made public, cannot but influence the course of this war. Until that time, American forces remain postured and ready for any eventuality.

"From Cairo, this is Jan Fields for World News Network."

16

Air power is a thunderbolt launched from an egg shell invisibly tethered to a base.

—HOFFMAN NICKERSON

Meidob Hills, Sudan * 2140 Hours, 18 December

In the distance the faint drone of turboprop engines cut through the cold night air. Squatting next to the beacon, Sergeant Jackson cocked his head. "Willy, do you hear that?"

Sergeant E-5 Willy Hall stood up. Like Jackson, he cocked his head and listened. For a second the noise faded. None of the pathfinder team moved. Most were hardly breathing. All were listening, waiting.

When they heard the drone again, it was stronger, steady. "C-130s. At least two of 'em."

Jackson listened for a few more seconds, then concurred with Willy's call. "Okay. That's got to be them. Switch the beacon to continuous mode. Lou, get ready to hit the light. Those airborne paratroopers 'bout to make their big jump might need a little help findin' us."

The C-130s approached the Meidob Hills in line, the pilot of the lead aircraft homing in on the beacon's steady signal. In the rear of his aircraft and the one following, the load masters were lowering the ramp to where it was even with the aircraft's deck. Other crewmen prepared the pallets with the fuel blivets for the drop. In the third C-130 Cerro stood postured in the open door, hands gripping the side of the aircraft as the cold wind whipped his face. His eyes were glued to the red light next to the door. In a second it would turn green, and once again he would be expected to throw his body into the black abyss below. As he waited, every reason he hated jumping raced through his mind.

He looked down at the dark, featureless terrain passing beneath the toes of his boots, now hanging out over the lip of the open door. He didn't know the wind direction or speed. Ground cover and composition were unknown. He, and his ad hoc platoon, would literally be jumping in the dark.

"God, this is dumb! This is fucking dumb!" He knew what would happen. He knew every sensation, every pain he was about to experience. Once he was out the door, the prop blast of the C-130's engines would push him back and catch the deploying parachute. By the time the chute was stretched out, he would be almost horizontal. Then the opening shock came. The stiff nylon risers on either side of his neck would suddenly be jerked taut. If a man didn't have his chin firmly planted into his chest, the risers would cut his neck cleaner than a straight razor. When the canopy was open, there was little time for joy. A quick check of the canopy had to be followed immediately by the unlocking of equipment bags and untying of the rifle bag. Without doing either, it was hell landing. Just as embarrassing was accidentally unhooking the wrong thing. As soon as the jumper felt the equipment bag tug at the end of its rope, there was only enough time to put feet and knees together, bend the knees, and prepare for the landing.

In theory, the paratrooper hit with the balls of his feet and twisted. That set him up for a proper parachute landing fall, or PLF. After the feet, his calves, followed by his buttocks, shoulder blades, and finally his head, made contact with the ground in a controlled, orderly manner. That, at least, was the theory—a theory that even in combat Cerro had never been able to make work.

The planes carrying the fuel blivets started their drop. From the rear of the C-130s, large pallets with the fuel blivets and parachutes strapped to them rolled out into the darkness. On the ground, Jackson could see only faint, black forms above him. That was enough, though, to tell him that he and his crew were in the wrong place. Just as a good transport pilot was trained to do, the pallets were being dropped right over the beacon—which was where Jackson and his men were. Hall looked up and yelled to Jackson. "Are those mothers makin' a heavy drop or a bombin' run?"

As if to underscore his comment, the parachutes on one pallet failed. Instead of a slow, controlled descent, the pallet tumbled down, gaining momentum. "Jesus! That one's comin' through! Heads up, it's comin' through!" Jackson began to run at first, then stopped. There was no way to predict where the tumbling mass of wooden pallet, rubber blivet, yards of worthless nylon parachute, and four hundred gallons of fuel would hit.

Jackson's heart, like everyone else's in the drop zone, skipped a beat just before the pallet impacted. The blivet, the heaviest part, hit first, splitting open like a water balloon dropped from a second-story window. And like a water balloon, it spewed fuel all over the place. They were still recovering from the near miss when the paratroopers began to exit.

Like a shock to his system, the flashing green light caused a momentary tension, then an automatic response. Cerro jumped up as best he could and pushed away from the side of the aircraft with all his might. In quick succession he experienced deployment, opening, and stabilization. Still swinging, he checked the canopy as he fumbled with his gear, dropping his equipment bag, untying the rifle bag, and bringing his feet together. Impact, like the good airborne sergeant at Benning used to tell them, should come almost as a surprise. If that was a measure of a good jump, Cerro's jump that night was a howling success.

Jackson watched as the first man came in. Instead of a PLF, the man hit the ground like a rock, right in the middle of a newly created pond of fuel left by the impact of the blivet. Running over to see if the paratrooper needed help, Jackson heard the sounds of splashing and cursing. Jackson stopped at the edge of the pool of fuel. "Hey, you—you need help?"

The figure rose to his knees, shaking his outstretched arms. "What the fuck makes you think I need help, whoever you are?"

"Staff Sergeant Jackson, Special Forces. I figured you might need some. It's just that I've never seen a man hit the ground so hard and live."

The figure rose to his feet, his arms still held out to his side. "Well, Staff Sergeant Jackson, the first thing you need to do is pass the word that the smoking lamp is definitely out." Slowly the figure started to shed his parachute and retrieve his gear, mumbling and cursing as he did so. Jackson stood and watched until the figure was done and advanced toward him. Sticking out his right hand to shake Jackson's, he introduced himself as Captain Harold Cerro, B Company, 1st of the 506th Airborne, Air Assault.

Surprised, Jackson started to salute but stopped and grabbed the captain's hand instead. "Glad to see you made it, sir. Captain Kinsly sends his compliments."

Cerro stopped shaking. "Kinsly? Jesse Kinsly? Big black guy with muscles from ear to ear?"

"Yes, sir, that's him. You know him?"

"Know him? We were in Iran together. He was my XO when I took over our company. Where is he?"

Jackson pointed south. "Still at the airfield."

As if there were some chance of seeing him, Cerro looked south, over the dark rim of the Meidob Hills. Cerro couldn't believe his incredible luck. After almost two years they were going to be back together again.

Five Kilometers North of Al Fasher, Sudan *
2205 Hours, 18 December

Moving down the ditch that ran along the road, Senior Lieutenant Shegayev led the squad of men into position. Despite the cold breeze that was beginning to whip at their backs, Shegayev was happy and excited. After weeks of doing nothing but the administrative work of the company, his commander,

Captain Ilvanich, agreed to allow him to lead an ambush patrol. Ilvanich, involved in assisting the battalion operations officer plan for a new operation, was unable to lead the patrol himself. Rumor had it that the new operation would be somewhere in southern Egypt against the airfield at Abu Simbel.

Besides, to date there had been no contacts during any of the nightly patrols. Ilvanich saw this as a good opportunity to give Shegayev some practical experience in independent command and small-unit operations. For the most part the ambush patrols had become nothing more than training exercises. The platoon leaders, in fact, had been complaining to Ilvanich that it was becoming difficult keeping the men alert and awake. Without the element of danger or even the hint of contact, the men were getting careless. Ilvanich's answer to that problem was unique. He formed a special squad of those soldiers who had been reported for neglect of their duties. He then personally led them out on foot patrol for two consecutive nights. After that, simply the threat of another such training session was able to motivate even the most slovenly soldier in the company.

Reaching the road junction, Shegayev paused. He could make out a stand of trees across the road. He gave the signal to the men behind him to halt and drop down. Shegayev crouched, surveying the terrain around him as he pulled his map out. With the aid of a small pen light, he checked the map. If he got lost leading his first patrol and set up in the wrong place, there'd be no second chance—not with Captain Ilvanich.

Satisfied they were in the right place, Shegayev put away his map and began to deploy his men. As in any peacetime training exercise, one man inevitably was slow and had to be told everything twice. But he was the exception. In less than five minutes the squad was settled into position and set. Security was out, and the road junction was covered. Now came the waiting.

East of Bir Milani Oasis, Sudan * 2247 Hours, 18 December

On the screen of his heads-out display, or HOD, Mennzinger could see a cluster of hot spots on the horizon to their west.

Looking at his watch, he noted the time, then checked his map: they would be the dwellings in and about the oasis called Bir Milani. Their route, the westernmost of the two, was marked in black on his flight map. At selected points along the line were tick marks and times. The number next to the tick mark at Bir Milani read 2047Z, the "Z" standing for ZULU time. The actual time in Sudan was 2247 hours, but they were on time. Although the operation was taking place in Sudan and Egypt, which are in the BRAVO time zone, the planners and units participating in the operation were spread throughout different time zones. The F-111 bombers were coming out of Britain, which is in the ZULU time zone, or two hours behind Egypt and Sudan. The naval demonstration off Ethiopia and the coast of Sudan was taking place in the CHARLIE time zone, one hour ahead of Egypt and Sudan. Surveillance and communications satellites being used to support the operation were being controlled from Virginia in the United States, which is in the ROMEO time zone, seven hours behind Egypt and Sudan. In order to avoid confusion and ensure complete synchronization of the operation, ZULU time, popularly known as Greenwich mean time, was used by all participants.

The plan, as laid out in the operations order and its time schedule, was the only controlling element for the operation. All participants were expected to follow both, without exception. Any margin of error was already factored into the plan. Because of tight planning, there was no need to use the radio or to coordinate the various elements of the operation until just before the actual attack. Since their departure from Abu Simbel, there had been no radio transmissions from either group of Apaches. Even the C-130s that had dropped the fuel blivets and paratroopers under Cerro had not reported that event.

That night, participants in the actual raid on Al Fasher were ordered to report by exception only. In English, that meant that only someone who missed a scheduled check point or event would report. Silence meant all was going well. It was a simple concept and very effective. But to the participants in the operation, it had the tendency to be unnerving at times. Reporting— positive confirmation that something has actually happened—

was far preferable. Despite training and incessant drilling, there was always the nagging fear that perhaps something had gone wrong and the reports hadn't gotten sent or couldn't be sent. Perhaps the other guy's radio was out and he couldn't transmit. Or maybe his battery power was low and he didn't know that his transmission wasn't reaching anyone. And what if he walked into an ambush and everyone was taken out before anyone could report. There could even be a problem with the station intended to receive the message. The receiver could be out, or he could be in dead space when the message was sent. Chatter on the radio, though frivolous at times, is a useful means of relieving tension and building confidence. Like the lonely truck driver using his CB on the highway at night, soldiers sometimes talk on the radio to relieve fears, real and imagined.

Radios, however, are dangerous. The enemy operates on the same wavelengths. That leaves the sender open to accidental detection through the sheer bad luck commonly referred to as "mutual interference": it would not take a genius to figure something was wrong when radio broadcasts in English started to bleed over onto Soviet radio nets in Sudan. Additionally, electronic warfare units, operating with sophisticated scanning and detection equipment, sweep the electronic spectrum, looking for radio, radar, and other electronic signals, locking onto whatever source they find. They then can locate it, study it to determine who or what is generating the signal, and block or jam it. If the resources such as artillery or aircraft are available, the source of the signal can also be attacked.

Though the pilot and the copilot-gunner in Apaches were hooked in by intercom, conversations between Mennzinger and his pilot were short, often confined to functional necessity. They were within feet of each other and operating within the same environment. Both were deprived of any news from the outside world other than what their instruments and sights provided to them. The copilot-gunner had the same displays as the pilot, so there was no need for the exchange of even basic information. And, like most copilot-gunners and pilots, Mennzinger and his pilot had little new and exciting to discuss: after all, they had been together for three weeks, living under the same conditions, in the same tent, eating in the same mess hall for the past twenty days. Idle chatter just to make noise can also have the effect of heightening loneliness and the sense of isolation.

So the crews of most of the Apaches flew on in silence. The crews could control their aircraft but, at that point, nothing else. Inside their cockpits they had the soft glow of instruments and the green images of the world as seen through the eye of a thermal imaging device to provide security and relief from their fears. Outside, there was only darkness and the unknown. In that darkness outside the canopy, the enemy sat at Al Fasher, perhaps alerted and ready, waiting for their arrival. Refuel crews were on the ground, busily gathering up the fuel blivets and setting up their refuel points, maybe. F-111s would be landing at Cairo to refuel, if they had made it from Britain. It was conceivable that the Navy's demonstration was drawing Soviet surveillance aircraft and fighters off to the east. And the Special Forces team at Al Fasher was watching, preparing to send their final report on the situation there, provided the team could still do so.

These things, and many more, Mennzinger could only guess at. What he did know was that his Apache was moving due south along its prescribed course at a rate of 120 knots and at an altitude of 100 feet. Everything else rested in the hands of others, who, like him and his pilot, were speeding forward in time toward the same point.

Headquarters, 2nd U.S. Corps, Cairo * 2305 Hours, 18 December

From his desk in the center of the war room, Dixon looked up at the cluster of clocks. There were four of them hanging over the operations map on the wall opposite him. He scanned them, from left to right, looking at the times they showed. Each one told Dixon something different. On the far left the clock, set on ROMEO time, showed 1605 hours. Under it hung a sign that read "Washington, D.C." The masses of office workers in that city would be preparing to leave their offices to brave the commute home. Paramount in their minds would be what was for dinner and getting that last-minute Christmas shopping done. The next clock, showing 2105 hours, was labeled "ZULU," representing the base time used for the operation and the actual time in Britain. The wives of the F-111 pilots now landing on a military airfield outside Cairo would be putting their children to bed in Britain. As far as they knew, their husbands were on another training flight, buzzing about in the darkness wherever pilots go to do such things.

The third clock was passing 2305 hours. Labeled "BRAVO/ LOCAL," it showed the time for Egypt and Sudan, the eye of the storm. And like the eye of a storm, things were, for the moment, deceptively quiet. Forces, however, were in motion. The 3rd Brigade of the 16th Armored Division had just begun its move from assembly areas it had occupied for the last eleven days. It was headed west down the coastal road to a new assembly area on the high ground south of El Imayid. The three infantry and one artillery battalion of the 2nd Brigade, 11th Airborne Division (Air Assault) were already there, flown in by their own aircraft earlier that evening. A nice, clean one-by-two-inch blue symbol on the operations map showed where the 3,500 soldiers and 1,500 vehicles of the 3rd Brigade were at that moment.

A thousand miles south of the symbol for the 2nd Air Assault and 3rd Armored brigades was a blue circle north of the Meidob Hills with the letters FARP written in it. There, the fuel handlers of the 1st of the 11th Attack Helicopter Battalion would be finishing setup of the refuel point within the next twenty-five minutes. The Apache strike force, represented by a blue box with a symbol that looked like a bow tie with a nail driven up through the center of it, was eighty-five minutes out from the refuel point. Further south, another symbol just east of Al Fasher, a blue box with "SF" in the center, showed where the Special Forces team was. They would be preparing their final report on the situation at the airfield.

The last clock showed five minutes past midnight. In Moscow and Addis Ababa, it was now December 19. Passing from the Gulf of Aden into the Red Sea just after dusk, ships of the 6th Fleet's Mid-East Squadron were increasing the tempo of their operations. The ships, carrying a Marine amphibious expeditionary unit, had just turned west and began their run in toward Port Sudan on the Red Sea. Aircraft launches from the carrier USS *Hornet* were increasing. Radio traffic, all part of the deception plan, was beginning to crowd the airwaves over the Red Sea as well as the coastal regions of Sudan and Ethiopia. Within thirty minutes, Dixon had no doubt, phones would be ringing throughout Moscow.

That was, Dixon thought, provided everyone was hitting their marks. Lifting his right arm with an exaggerated motion, he checked his own watch. As usual, it was two minutes ahead. To those who had known him as a second lieutenant, the two-minute difference was a joke. Always worried about being late for a meeting, Dixon maintained his watch ahead of the official time. Not that it ever made a difference. Knowing he had two extra minutes, Dixon normally procrastinated them away, arriving at his appointed meetings and duties just in time. With nothing better to do than wait, he wondered how many people out there were using his own personal time zone.

Swiveling about in his chair, Dixon looked at a small enclosed area on a raised platform behind him. Nicknamed "the bridge," it was where the generals and primary staff officers watched and conferred. At that moment General Horn, General Darruznak, and Colonel Benton were sitting on the bridge, drinking coffee and discussing some matter or another. Odds were, Dixon thought, it had nothing to do with either the deployment of the 16th Armored Division or the raid on Al Fasher. There were operations under way, being executed by the commanders on the ground. Though the monitoring of their progress was important, the 2nd Corps could no longer reach out and effectively influence what was happening out there. Instead, the proper focus of the commander and the staff of the 2nd Corps was what would happen in the next forty-eight to ninety-six hours.

Like a chess player, the corps commander had to look where

his pieces and those of the enemy sat on the board. With the assistance of his staff, he had to plan not only his next move but a whole series of moves in advance. These moves became a campaign, a series of battles and operations designed to achieve a defined goal or objective. At 1425 hours eastern standard time, the President of the United States invoked the War Powers Act. Subsequent orders from the Joint Chiefs of Staff authorized General Horn to use the 2nd Corps, in cooperation with Egyptian forces, to defend the Nile delta. Campaign planning could begin in earnest while those forces were deployed forward.

Swinging back toward the map board, Dixon watched as a sergeant moved the symbol for the Apache strike groups further south. That move was based on a time hack, not a report. Dixon was wondering to himself how accurate their tracking of the raid was when Sergeant Major London caught his attention. Standing in the doorway leading into the war room, London motioned to Dixon to come over to the door. Nodding to London, Dixon stood up, turned to a captain seated next to him, and told the captain to hold the fort until he got back.

Making his way to the door through the crowded room, Dixon walked up to London. "Vee gates, Sergeant Major?"

London leaned toward Dixon and whispered. "There's a Ms. Jan Fields here to see you."

Dixon made a funny face. He thought for a moment. "Does she want me or the public affairs pukes?"

"She insists on seeing you."

Dixon thought for a moment. He turned to look at the bridge for a moment. The generals and Benton hadn't moved. They were still deep in heavy discussion. He turned back to London. "Okay, Sergeant Major. Captain Kronauer has the helm. I'll be back in a few minutes. If someone starts looking for me, cover me."

Outside the guard room at the entrance to the command post, Dixon saw Jan leaning against the frame of the guard shack doorway. Looking out into the night, she didn't notice him. Even from a distance he could see she was exhausted and troubled. Her clothes were dirty and stained. Dixon walked up to within a few feet of her and waited till she saw him. When she did, he could see her eyes were red and puffy. Their soft warmth was missing. He had considered jumping all over her about Fay's staying, but decided against it. In an instant he knew not only that this wasn't the time or the place but that something was wrong.

"Are you all right, Jan?" There was true concern in his voice. That made it harder for Jan.

Reaching out with both of her hands, she grasped his right hand and pulled it to her chest. "Scott, it's Fay."

He waited, but Jan did not finish. He looked into her eyes. There were tears beginning to well up in their corners. She couldn't finish. She didn't have to. Her eyes told him everything. For a moment Dixon felt nothing—neither remorse nor regret. Perhaps the numbness he felt was the result of too many hours without sleep. There should have been something. But what? A twinge . . . an empty feeling . . . *something*.

They stood there, both at a loss as to what to say or do. Jan's warm, soft hands on his were the only sensation he was aware of, the only conscious feeling he allowed. He was spent, physically, mentally, and emotionally. He had no more tears to give, no more feelings. Finally, reluctantly, Dixon pulled his hand free. As he did, he averted his eyes from Jan's. "I have to go." He pivoted and began to walk away.

Jan took a step toward him. "Scott, I love you."

Jan's soft plea struck at Dixon's very soul. He stopped, but he didn't turn back. Instead, he looked at the sand between his feet and took a deep breath. He fought back an urge to cry, a desire to turn around and go back to Jan. Once he had regained his composure, he continued without a word back into the command post.

Meidob Hills * 0035 Hours, 19 December

Activity at the refuel point came in spurts that night. The pathfinders, alone in their vigil for so long, had watched the blivets and paratroops come. Then another hour of waiting.

Next, the Blackhawks with the equipment and men to man the refuel point came thundering in. For better than an hour there was frenzied activity as everyone on the ground pitched in and laid out the refuel site. The scattered blivets, already marked by the pathfinders and Cerro's men, were hauled in and set in place under the direction of the sergeant in charge of the refuel team. As soon as a blivet was set, crews began to lay yards of connecting lines from blivet to blivet and to the pumps. Once these were set, the sergeant in charge had his fuel handlers crank up the system and test it by refueling the Blackhawks already on site.

When he was satisfied that all was ready, the Blackhawks moved off, away from the refuel point and the incoming Apaches. Lights were set out to guide the Apaches. Then there was another lull as everyone waited. Each man settled into place, resting and listening for the approaching Apaches. The only break came when the final intelligence weather report from the Special Forces team at Al Fasher came in. Cerro and Jackson put the information together for the commander of the attack force.

At 0015 hours Jackson turned the beacon on. Shortly thereafter, at 0028, the sound of helicopter rotor blades beating the cold night air could be heard over the blowing wind and sand. There was again a flurry of activity as the fuel handlers scrambled into place. Some of Cerro's men turned on the lights, then scurried out of the way. Soldiers stood by the generators for the fuel pumps, prepared to crank them up. Within minutes, the black outline of the approaching Apaches could be seen against the dark sky. A man at the farthest fuel point flicked on a pair of flashlights with red filters. Though the pilot could clearly see the man through his thermal viewer, the lights served to guide the Apache to its proper refuel point. A soldier at the next refuel point did likewise as soon as the first Apache had passed his location. At each of the five points the same procedures were followed, with the lights on only when necessary to reduce confusion.

On the ground, as the pilot of the aircraft shut down the right engine, the fuel handlers moved forward to the aircraft's right side. While one soldier held the nozzle, another opened the fuel serving port, then opened the refueling panel and switched the fuel indicator and refuel valve switches to the "on" position. In the meantime, the soldier with the nozzle hooked it onto the refuel port, locked it down, and waited. When all indicator lights on the panel were lit, the soldier at the panel gave the word to crank up the generator and begin passing fuel. Under fifteen-pounds-per-square-inch pressure, fifty-six gallons of fuel a minute were shot into the internal fuel tanks of the Apaches. The external fuel cells, emptied during the flight south, would not be refueled. It had been decided that it was better to go into combat with them empty. They would be topped off only after the attack, on the return trip.

As their aircraft were being refueled, the copilot-gunners gathered off to the left of their aircraft. A few, stopping to relieve themselves first, were slow in rallying. While they waited for everyone to gather, there was the customary stretching and yawning of men confined in a tight space for a long time. There was little talk. The battalion commander conferred with Jackson and Cerro while Mennzinger and the C Company commander counted their people as they closed up on the group. When all were ready, Mennzinger, designated second in command for the operation, gave the battalion commander the high sign.

The briefing was short. The battalion commander informed them that as of 2300 hours local, there had been no changes in the composition or location of the airfield's air defense weapons. Therefore, there was no need to change the plan. The four aircraft from C Company had kept the mission of taking out the air defense positions. Pausing for a moment, the battalion commander introduced the C Company commander to Sergeant Jackson. He told them to get together after the briefing to make sure C Company understood everything there was to know about the enemy. After that there was a weather update. With the winds coming from the southwest, the battalion commander decided to take the Apaches that would designate for the F-111s to a position southeast of the airfield. From there, they would mark the targets with their lasers, hitting those to the north and northeast first, then working south and southeast, so that smoke and debris from the first load of bombs dropped from the F-111s would not interfere with those following.

The briefing was over in fifteen minutes, and each crew went to its own aircraft. Those who had not done so earlier stopped on their way to relieve themselves. By the time they reached their Apaches, the fuel handlers were disconnecting the nozzles and preparing the aircraft for departure.

From one side Cerro watched with Duncan. "Well, First Sergeant, so far so good. Ten Apaches planned for and ten in."

Duncan grunted. "If you don't mind me saying so, sir, I'll be a damned sight happier when there's ten sitting here at 0430 pointed the other way. I'm not exactly keen on being this far out in bad-guy country."

Cerro didn't respond. He only watched. As the aircraft began to crank up, he prepared to leave. "Well, First Sergeant, I'm off."

"You sure you want to do this? I mean, you're already six hundred miles inside somebody else's country. I really don't see the need to go any further just to be there when the Blackhawks pick up your buddy."

Cerro put a hand on Duncan's shoulder. "First Sergeant, not only do I feel honor-bound to do so, I'm bored shitless sitting here listening to the wind blow and smelling fumes from aviation fuel. Besides, you know I never pass up a helicopter ride."

Duncan shook his head. "You're lucky you're an officer, sir. Otherwise I'd tell you how stupid that kind of thinking is."

"That's what I like about you, First Sergeant—you have tact. Well, adios." Cerro turned and walked over to where the two Blackhawks designated to follow the strike were cranking up. The Blackhawks would recover both the Special Forces team, under Kinsly, and any Apache crews that went down before, during, or after the raid.

At 0130 hours, without any signals or radio calls, the lead Apache lifted off and started to head south. In a staggered line the other nine rose up and followed. Two minutes behind them, the Blackhawks followed. By 0135 hours the refuel point was quiet again. There'd be a slight readjustment of blivets, a relaying of fuel lines, and then three hours of waiting.

17

I am your king. You are Frenchmen. There is the enemy. Charge!

—HENRY IV OF FRANCE,
At the battle of Ivry, 14 March 1590

East of Atbara, Sudan * 0200 Hours, 19 December

The Soviet Ilyushin 76 airborne warning aircraft continued to inch its way to the coast. Ordered to monitor the activities of the American warships and their aircraft in the Red Sea, the Ilyushin 76 left its normal patrol pattern. As it began its surveillance, the Ilyushin became the target of several American electronic warfare aircraft. Determined to blind the Ilyushin with jamming and interference, one of the American EW aircraft was operating to the north, coming out of Egypt. The other apparently was operating from the American carrier in the Red Sea. Unable to maintain his cover in western Sudan and accomplish its new mission, the commander of the Ilyushin found himself moving eastward. Dutifully he reported that he could no longer cover the area around Al Fasher and Port Sudan simultaneously. He asked for clarification as to which area had priority. There was a pause on the radio; he then was told to wait for further orders. It took twenty minutes before someone on the ground in Africa, or Moscow, made a decision. The orders—to monitor the American fleet—were relayed through the Soviet embassy in Khartoum, Sudan.

Even before he received those orders, the senior officer on board the Ilyushin had initiated steps to work through the jamming. The operators sitting at their consoles in the body of the Ilyushin 76 waged a silent war with American electronic warfare aircraft to the north and east. Using frequency hopping, increases in power, multiple assets aimed at a single source, and other techniques, the crew of the Ilyushin worked to gather intelligence on the Americans. The shifting of the aircraft to the east made their task easier.

A quick analysis by the senior officer on board the Ilyushin showed moves and deployments that normally preceded an amphibious assault. He and his crew had seen it all before. They had studied it and had had an opportunity to observe it during NATO and 6th Fleet exercises in the Mediterranean. Therefore, determining what was happening was easy. It was the why and where that puzzled everyone. In Moscow, intelligence officers searched for an answer. To put troops ashore in Sudan, ostensibly a friendly country, made no sense. There was no way that U.S. possession of that port would be able to interfere with the airlift further west. Perhaps, one naval officer suggested, the Americans were trying to secure the southern flank of Egypt. Perhaps, another suggested, they were conducting a feint against Port Sudan, that the real target was in Ethiopia.

There was little time to pinpoint intended point of attack. There was even less time to devote to the why. With so few assets in the area, orders had to be given soon. What forces they had needed to be massed in order to counteract, and perhaps even prevent, the Americans' operation. Until the decision was made as to what to do, the Ilyushin operating east of Atbara, Sudan, and another over the Red Sea flying out of Gondar, Ethiopia, would continue to watch and report.

East of Al Fasher * 0250 Hours, 19 December

Anticipation began to build, gradually replacing the dull monotony of the approach flight. Mennzinger could feel his heart rate slowly increase as they began to close on the target. The checkpoints were more numerous now, their turns more fre-

quent and their altitude lower. They were well within range
of the Soviet SA-9 surface-to-air defense missiles. So far
they had been lucky. Their radar warning receivers hadn't
picked up any Soviet radar signals bouncing off them.
Mennzinger hoped their luck would hold for another ten minutes. Even if it didn't, however, they were committed. There
would be no backing out. At this point the only thing staying
undetected by the Soviets for as long as possible did was to
increase their chances of surprise and, equally important,
their chances of survival.

Mennzinger looked at the map in his lap, checking their
progress, and looking at what lay ahead. As he did so, he
pressed down with the toe of his right foot on the intercom
transmit switch. "Next checkpoint is forty-three. It'll be a road
junction with a wide ditch to the south of it and a stand of trees
to the north. We'll be able to see them as soon as you clear that
next rise. When we get there, hover to the north of the trees.
We need to allow the rest of the company to close up before we
move into battle position COBRA."

Mennzinger's pilot acknowledged with a simple "Check."
Flying mere feet above the ground at 100 knots plus required
his undivided attention. Putting his map back into its stowage
box, Mennzinger began to prepare the Apache's fire control
system. Starting with the fire control panel, he checked each
switch setting and each laser code input, arming the laser as he
went along. Satisfied, he checked the controls and display on
his optical relay tube, starting with the heads-out view screen,
then the heads-down display. He fine-tuned the images until
they were as sharp and clear as possible. He was still fiddling
with his fire controls when they reached checkpoint 43.

Shegayev felt, more than heard, the beating of helicopter
blades out in the darkness. He sat up and looked down the
ditch. The men on either side had heard the same thing. With
his hand and a whispered command, he instructed them to pass
the word to stay down and be quiet. Moving to the edge of the
ditch, he slowly raised his head just as a dark shadow zipped
overhead. The sudden burst of noise and the pressure of air

forced down by powerful rotor blades caused Shegayev to pull his head down and seek safety at the bottom of the ditch.

Mennzinger was still busy when the Apaches suddenly made a violent banking maneuver to the right. Without bothering to key the intercom, he yelled out. "Jesus, Andy! Next time you want to stand this helicopter on its side, at least give me a warning."

Over the intercom the pilot replied, a little sheepishly, "Sorry, boss—I almost missed the checkpoint. Didn't want to overshoot the trees."

Looking out into the night, Mennzinger could make out the image of the trees they were now slowly approaching. "Okay. Almost time to go to work. Maintain a position on the north side of the trees, Andy, while I gather in the flock." Moving his left foot to the radio transmit switch, Mennzinger pressed his toe down, keying the radio net for the first time since leaving Cairo.

Using the company's "Bandit" call sign instead of the official call signs of letters and numbers randomly generated by a computer, Mennzinger put out a net call. "Bandits, Bandits. This is Bandit 6. Rally at checkpoint 43 and report. Bandit 6 out."

As he waited for his company to close up on him, Mennzinger continued with the check of the fire control system that the pilot's turn had so suddenly disrupted.

Recovering his composure, Shegayev crawled back to the wall of the ditch and slowly, carefully began to raise his head. There was a ringing in his right ear, which probably accounted for his not hearing the slow approach of the next helicopter. When he finally became aware of its presence, it was practically on top of him.

Shegayev froze in place. To his immediate front, less than twenty meters from where he sat, a large, black apparition appeared before him. It hung there as if suspended by an invisible string. Then it began to rotate toward him. Common sense told him to pull his head down and seek the safety of the ditch. Curiosity kept him watching. When the apparition reached a point in its turn where they were facing each other, it paused for a second. Shegayev found himself looking at the black, sinister form of the Apache attack helicopter head on, silhouetted against the dark sky, with most of its features and details obscured. He imagined he was facing a huge black insect. Its low, swept-back wings were heavily ladened with ordnance. The whirling rotors beat the night air, holding it in place like an insect preparing to strike. Like a poisonous stinger, a single large-caliber gun protruded from its chin. And its one large, shiny eye twisted and turned, probing the darkness for prey.

Just before they came eye to eye, Shegayev dropped down. Turning and placing his back against the wall, he fought to regain his composure. Despite the cold, sweat was running down his face in rivulets. He was hyperventilating, gasping for his breath. The only external sensation he felt was the beating of the blades over him. All other senses were paralyzed, unable to deal with the image burned in his mind of the huge black bug about to attack him.

The last Apache to report into Mennzinger was Bandit 5, George Katzenberg, the Cat. When he did, he informed Mennzinger that Bandit 3, crewed by First Lieutenant Tommy Hightower and Warrant Officer One Ed Franks, had made an emergency landing. Cat reported that he had circled and recorded the grid where Bandit 3 had set down. There was silence on the radio net for a moment as Mennzinger recalled what task Hightower had been given and who could best take it. Based on Cat's location, Mennzinger ordered Cat to take Hightower's tasks as well as his own. When Katzenberg acknowledged, Mennzinger ordered the company to follow him and occupy battle position COBRA.

"Comrade Lieutenant, they're leaving."
Shegayev heard his sergeant but didn't make any immediate effort to move. He was still struggling to pull himself together. For an instant he considered himself lucky. They were going.

Good! They would soon be someone else's problem. But his duty wasn't finished. He had to do something. Even if it was only counting and reporting the helicopters, he had to do something.

Turning back to the front of the ditch, Shegayev carefully stuck his head over the lip of the ditch. He was in time to see the last of the Apaches leave the cover of the trees and head off to the west, toward the airfield. When he was sure they were gone, Shegayev asked the sergeant how many there had been. Four was the answer. Only four.

Shegayev was able to think rationally for the first time since seeing the helicopters. He called to the radioman, who came scampering down the ditch, bouncing from wall to wall. He found Shegayev and reported. "Aliyev—contact battalion—quickly," Shegayev said. "We must warn them."

Aliyev was a good radioman, the son of a coal miner, but at times a little slow. "What is it that you want me to report?"

When he heard the helicopters passing overhead, Kinsly paused and looked up. Seeing them thundering in toward the target gave him both satisfaction and relief—satisfaction that he and his men had been able to play a part in setting up the attack that was about to go down, relief that his role was finished. The fight belonged to the chopper jockeys and zoomies. He and his men were out of there.

Looking back down the ditch, he could see the rest of his team had also paused to look. With a low "Pssst" he got the attention of the man behind him, signaling to him to start moving again and pass the word to the rest.

Turning back to the east, Kinsly began to move along the ditch. The road junction and clump of trees where they would wait for pickup was only another two hundred meters down the ditch.

As the rest of his company moved into place, Mennzinger ordered Andy to hang back. To his far right Cat moved up, hovered, then found a position from which he could spot the maintenance sheds and then the runway. Between Cat and

Mennzinger Bandit 4 moved into a position from where he would spot the ammo dump for the incoming F-111s. Set on the right, Mennzinger traversed the target acquisition and designation sight, TADS for short. Through its green thermal eye he could see Bandit 1 was already in position and waiting to designate the far fuel tanks with his laser.

Satisfied that all was ready, he laid his TADS onto his target. To his front, at a range of eleven hundred meters, was a field full of fuel blivets. Unlike the ones back at their own refuel point, these blivets held five thousand gallons of fuel each. Between them a maze of pipes connected them into a system that allowed the Soviets to feed the steady stream of aircraft coming in and out of Libya. Satisfied that he had the target, Mennzinger ordered Andy to move forward slowly to a point behind a slight rise in the ground. As Andy eased the Apache forward, Mennzinger continued to watch the point he had selected for a spot. The idea was to get into the best-covered and -concealed position possible and still be able to designate the target.

They were still easing into that position when the UHF radio cracked to life. "Bandit Six, Bandit Six. This is Lone Star One. Daytona now." "Lone Star" was the call sign of the F-111s; Lone Star 1 was the flight leader—from his nickname and his drawl, it wasn't hard to tell where that zoomie came from. "Daytona" was the name given the initiation point, or IP. It was at that point that the F-111s would begin their bomb run.

Mennzinger switched his radio to the HF band to acknowledge the call. "Lone Star One, this is Bandit Six. Set and ready to spot."

The response was quick from the F-111s. "Lone Star One copies."

Switching to the battalion net, Mennzinger contacted the battalion commander. "Eagle Six, this is Bandit Six—Lone Star in contact and passed Daytona. Bandit set—we have not been picked up by search or acquisition radar—over."

"Roger, Bandit. Corsair Six, commence your attack—over."

Corsair 6—the call sign for the C company commander—acknowledged. That acknowledgment was followed by a volley of rockets from the battle position where C Company had been set and waiting. Mennzinger looked at his watch. It was 0300 hours local.

In the 2nd Corps operations center there was silence. All eyes were on the clock with local time as the sweep hand raced up to the 12. When it hit, it was as if everyone's heart skipped a beat. General Horn turned to his chief of staff. "Well, they're in. Now it's all theirs."

General Darruznak picked up his fourth cup of coffee, then turned to Horn. "A bullet or a brevet?"

Horn chuckled. "Yeah, something like that. Only we're not the ones who'll get the bullet."

In his frustration, Shegayev pounded the radio with his fist. "Can't you get this damned thing to work?"

Aliyev bent over to look at the radio and check the settings and connections. Finished, he looked up at Shegayev. "Comrade Lieutenant, the radio is functioning properly. It must be the other station, or perhaps jamming."

Shegayev, totally frustrated, was about to yell when the sky to the west was lit up by a series of flashes. Standing upright in the ditch, Shegayev looked in the direction of the flashes. The sound of the rockets firing, then impacting took several seconds to reach him. He had been too late. He had failed to warn his commander of the impending danger. He stood there for a second as the horror of his failure began to sink in. As he did, the rest of his patrol began to pop their heads up and look to the west at the wild light show that was beginning to grow in intensity.

Kinsly paused and turned to look back at the airfield. Satisfied that they had done their job, he turned and was about to duck down and continue through the ditch when he saw something. Dropping until his eyes were level with the rim of the ditch, Kinsly could clearly make out the image of a man stand-

ing waist high in the same ditch not thirty meters to his front.
The flashes also betrayed the round forms of helmets that
seemed to keep popping up around him.

Dropping down, he gave the signal to hold up. Quickly he
evaluated his options. He had twelve men against an ambush
patrol. On past nights the Russian ambush patrols consisted of
no more than ten men. He therefore didn't have any real superiority in manpower. The Russians would have at least one
PK machine gun. Kinsly had none, only rifles. But he did have
one advantage: surprise. He knew the Russians were there, and
they didn't know he had seen them. Guessing that the Russians
would be making a beeline to the airfield, Kinsly prepared to
ambush the ambush patrol.

"Lone Star One—thirty seconds."

The lead F-111 was thirty seconds out. Ignoring the flashes
and explosions rocking the airfield as C Company continued to
smash air defense emplacements, Mennzinger prepared to spot
for the F-111. With his head down on his sight, he laid the cued
line of sight reticle on a point in the center of the fuel blivets.
Satisfied, he hit the laser button with the middle finger of his
right hand and the radio transmit switch with his left toe.
"Bandit Six—laser on."

There was a pause. The F-111 was already climbing slightly,
ready to lob its bombs. Then it came back. "Lone Star One—
spot." Another pause. The PAVE TACK laser acquisition system had found the reflected laser light from Mennzinger's laser
beam. Automatically the F-111's PAVE TACK target designator locked onto the spot and began to provide the F-111's
navigation/attack computer with the data it would need for
bomb release. The F-111 pilot acknowledged that the spot had
been detected. "Lone Star One—lock—bombs away."

Watching, Mennzinger thought that he saw the cluster bombs
break up and the shower of bomblets that followed. There was
no doubt when they began to land on and between the blivets.
His sight turned from images of black and green to pure black
as the bomblets exploded, splitting the blivets and igniting the
fuel. Pulling his head back, Mennzinger watched the spectacle

as the entire fuel dump appeared to rise up in the sky in a huge fireball. In his ear he heard the attack sequence being repeated as Lone Star 2 contacted Bandit 1. Mennzinger watched and listened as, like clockwork, each F-111 in its turn hit the IP and began its run in.

After releasing his finger from the laser button, Mennzinger depressed the radio transmit switch with his left toe. "Bandit Six—laser off."

The fireball rising in the sky caught Shegayev by surprise. He stopped running and looked up. As he did so, the soldier behind him plowed into him. Shegayev didn't even notice the collision. The spectacle to his front was, all at once, mesmerizing and appalling. Neither did Shegayev, or any of the men behind him, notice half a dozen grenades come rolling into the ditch.

As soon as the grenades began to explode, Kinsly and Sergeant Lou Washington were up and running forward in the ditch, side by side, to where the Russians were. With their weapons at their hips, they fired as they went. Right behind them two more men from his team followed, lobbing grenades further down the ditch. Like a World War I trench raid, Kinsly took on the Russians. Outside the ditch, to their flank, Kinsly's Sudanese soldiers lay waiting, rifles leveled at the rim of the ditch. If the Russians realized what was happening and tried to get out of the ditch, they would be picked off by Sudanese.

They didn't have long to wait. Two Russians in the rear had survived the first grenade attack. Quickly realizing that the enemy was coming from the front, they stood and prepared to run back. The Sudanese sergeant told his men to hold fire for a moment. The Russians, not making fast enough progress, climbed out of the ditch and began to run for the clump of trees across the road. When they were in the center of the road, the Sudanese sergeant told his men to fire. In a hail of bullets, the two survivors were cut down.

Kinsly and his raiding party didn't stop until they had passed the last dead Russian and had gone twenty meters further down the trench. He yelled to his men to hold up. The four men dropped down and caught their breath. They were all sweating despite a cold breeze that was beginning to pick up. Turning to Washington, Kinsly asked if he thought they had gotten all the Russians. Washington was about to stick his head up and look but stopped when he remembered that the Sudanese were still out there, waiting. "Captain, we'd better call off our people before we check out the commies. Hate to end the night gettin' nailed by our own."

As spectacular and complete as their surprise was, the Russians at the airfield weren't totally paralyzed. As Lone Star 6, the last F-111, rolled in, a Russian paratrooper let go an SA-7 surface-to-air missile. Lone Star 6 had just released his load of bombs when the SA-7 exploded, damaging the right engine. In a single, terrible moment Mennzinger watched as the F-111 dipped to the right slightly and made a sharp descent. As it did so, its right wing tip scraped the runway, trailing a shower of sparks. Then the plane nosed down and flipped to the right, standing on its nose in the process. It had almost finished a full cartwheel when it exploded in the center of the runway. As if the crash of the F-111 were the grand finale at the end of an act, the runway cratering bombs began to explode around the remains of the stricken F-111.

There was a moment of silence before Mennzinger switched his radio back to the UHF frequency that the F-111s were on. He hit the transmit switch. "Lone Star One—this is Bandit Six—Lone Star Six went in—over."

There was a pause. "This is Lone Star One—anyone eject—over."

"Bandit Six—negative—SA-Seven up the tail—too low—too fast—over."

"Bandit Six—this is Lone One—thanks, good buddy—good luck and good hunting—over." The voice of Lone Star 1 was no longer that of the cocky Texan, ready to conquer the world. For a moment Mennzinger pitied him. In a few hours he would be knocking on a door in Britain. A woman who didn't know that she was a widow would answer it. She'd probably still be in a bathrobe. On her doorstep would be an Air Force colonel who went by the call sign Lone Star 1. He'd still be in his flight suit. With him there would be a major in class-A uniform and a chaplain. She would know them all. And they wouldn't have to say a word.

"Good luck and safe journey to you, Lone Star—this is Bandit Six out."

Switching back to the frequency his company was on, Mennzinger gave the order to move to battle position COTTON MOUTH and to begin to engage enemy aircraft parked in their revetments. He and his men still had a long fight ahead of them.

The attack on the airfield was clearly visible to the crew and the lone passenger of the Blackhawk headed into the pickup zone at the road junction. From where he sat, facing out the open door, Cerro could see everything—the rocket fire and Hellfire missiles launched from the Apaches and the resulting explosions on the airfield. It was spectacular. Over his headphones Cerro listened to the reports and orders of the attacking Apaches. Their radio traffic was minimal but informative. The Apaches that had spotted for the F-111s had shifted to their next battle position and were in the process of engaging Soviet transports and helicopters on the south side of the field. The company that had taken out the air defense at the beginning of the attack was finishing up the destruction of the fighters on the ground and was shifting its attention to a vehicle park. All seemed in order and going well. Even the loss of one F-111 and one Apache on the run in didn't seem to bother anyone or spoil the success of the attack.

"There they are." With that as his only warning, the pilot jerked the helicopter to the left and began to descend. Cerro looked to see what the pilot had seen, but was unable to. In a minute they'd be on the ground.

The pain shot through Shegayev's body like an electric shock. Though he had no idea what had happened, he knew he was hurt bad, perhaps even dying. Slowly he began to sort out his sensations and his pains in order to determine just where he was hurt and what, if anything, he could do.

As the first wave of pain subsided, he determined that he was lying face down in a pool of liquid. His efforts to lift his head brought a surge of crippling pain. He let out an involuntary groan as his head dropped back into the pool. Some of the liquid splashed into his mouth: the taste was salty and somewhat bitter. And it was warm. The liquid was blood, probably his own. For a second he rested, attempting to catch his breath. Even that was difficult and painful. When he was ready for his second attempt to lift himself, he tried to move his arms and push himself up. It was then that he discovered that he had no feeling in or response from his left arm.

Frustrated, he moved his right hand under his chest and pushed up. Though burning pain racked his body, almost causing him to pass out, Shegayev held on to consciousness and pushed. Like a drunk, he found that movements in one direction were not automatically compensated for by his body. Instead of bringing him up to his knees, the final effort to right himself almost caused him to topple over backwards. That in itself caused a new wave of pain. Still conscious, Shegayev struggled to gain his balance, his right arm flapping and his head gyrating wildly.

It worked. After a moment he settled into his new position. He was now on his knees, buttocks resting on his calves. With his good arm, he felt his left arm to determine how badly it was damaged. At first he thought he was running his fingers through the tattered remains of his blood-soaked field jacket. Still numb from the grenade attack, he froze in horror when the fingers of his right hand came in contact with the upper bone of his left arm. Slowly looking down, Shegayev watched as he withdrew his hand from the mass of loose skin and muscle that hung from his shredded left arm.

The sudden scream of a low-flying helicopter passing overhead drew his attention away from his arm. Looking up, he saw the black whalelike body of a helicopter slow, then settle down. They were back. The raid was over and they were returning. He had to do something. Though he didn't know what he could do, he couldn't simply lie down and die without doing something. He was a soldier, an officer. He had to avenge himself and his dead comrades. Wildly Shegayev began to look about the ditch, not knowing what he was looking for until his eyes fell upon the PK machine gun.

The wheels hadn't even touched down before Cerro had unbuckled his seat belt and crouched at the door. A figure ran from the ditch and began to move toward him. Even in the dark Cerro knew who owned the large frame that was lumbering toward him. Over the roar of the Blackhawk's engines Cerro yelled. "HEY! DID SOMEONE HERE ORDER A PIZZA?"

Kinsly picked up his pace. "Hal, is that you?"

"Yeah, who the hell else would make a delivery in a neighborhood like this?" With that, Cerro was out and running to embrace a man who was more than a brother to him.

Twice Shegayev collapsed from the pain as he dragged himself and the machine gun over to the wall of the ditch. Breathing was getting harder. He had to make an effort to draw in each breath, and each time he did there was a flash of pain. Once he reached the wall, Shegayev set the machine gun up against it, then pulled himself up until his head and chest were over the lip. Leaning his chest against the wall, he reached down with his right arm and pulled the machine gun up and over the lip of the ditch. Carefully he steadied the gun and put himself behind it, pulling the stock up to his right shoulder.

As he sighted down the barrel, he noticed his field of vision was narrowing. For a moment he thought his eyes were playing a trick on him. It seemed to him that he was looking down a long, dark tunnel. Only a small circular vision in the center of the tunnel was clear, visible. As he looked at the figure exiting the lead helicopter, he realized that he was dying. Slowly he was bleeding to death. The dark fringe that narrowed his field of vision was death's shroud closing over him.

In a last, desperate effort, driven by a determination to die fighting, Shegayev put his cheek to the stock of the machine gun. He made one final adjustment of his aim. The figure that had left the helicopter was stopped. It stood, arms held open in the PK's sight as Shegayev began to squeeze the trigger.

The figure racing toward the stationary one wasn't in Shegayev's field of vision.

Arms out, ready to embrace his long-lost friend, Cerro watched Kinsly's face suddenly contort and change. Instead of a wide smile, his eyes bulged out, his mouth gaping as if to let out a yelp of surprise. The chatter of machine-gun fire reached Cerro's ears as Kinsly stumbled forward one last step and collapsed into Cerro's arms. The weight of the big man pulled them both to their knees. As they went down, Kinsly's head came down onto Cerro's shoulder, allowing Cerro to see the flashes of a machine gun firing from the ditch.

"EVERYONE HIT IT! WE'RE UNDER FIRE! HIT IT!" Cerro's warning couldn't be heard by the door gunner in the Blackhawk. But that wasn't necessary: seeing the flashes, the door gunner laid his weapon onto them and let go a burst. The first was overline. With a slight move of his wrists, he moved the gun down and began to lean on the trigger, walking the tracers into the target.

Shegayev didn't understand what had happened. Just before he fired, the figure appeared to split in two. He paused for a moment to resight his weapon. His field of vision was narrower. His breathing was becoming harder, more painful. Little time. He knew he had little time. He was almost gone, dead.

There was no time for small targets—too hard to find and aim at. Turning the gun to the helicopter, he didn't notice the first wild burst fired by the door gunner. The second burst landed short initially, throwing up rock fragments and sand in front of Shegayev. The shower of fragments surprised Shegayev, causing him to jerk the machine gun's trigger. He was firing wildly when the stream of bullets coming from the helicopter found their mark. Hit square in the face, Shegayev was knocked over backwards into the ditch. His finger remained frozen on the trigger as he pulled the gun down with him.

"HE'S HIT! MEDIC! MEDIC! I'VE GOT A WOUNDED MAN HERE!" Cerro held on to Kinsly, holding him against his chest. He was afraid to let go, as if his holding him were the only thing that was keeping him alive. The helicopter's crew chief and Sergeant Washington reached the two captains at the same time. Washington took his captain and gently laid him face down onto the ground. The crew chief held Cerro by his shoulders for a moment to steady him, then went around to assist Washington.

Cerro remained sitting there on his knees, watching the two NCOs frantically working on his friend. As the rest of Kinsly's men closed up on the group, the crew chief yelled to them to lend a hand and get the body into the helicopter. Half a dozen pairs of hands surrounded Kinsly and lifted him before Cerro's eyes. Then they were gone.

For a moment Cerro remained there, still on his knees, looking where Kinsly had been. The crew chief put his hand on Cerro's shoulder again. Putting his mouth next to Cerro's ear, he told him that it was time to go.

Scanning to his right, Mennzinger looked for more targets. Acquisition was becoming difficult. The shattered remains of aircraft, large and small, were burning brightly. Here and there rivers of burning fuel ran down the runway and along drainage ditches. Checking his stores, he saw that they still had four rockets and nine hundred rounds of 30mm left. But there was nothing to fire it at. He was about to order Andy to slide over to the left, into another position, when Eagle 6 gave the order to break off and move back to their company rally points.

Mennzinger looked at his watch. It was 0320 hours local, right on time. "Okay, Andy. The boss man has decided we've had too much fun for one night. Let's ease on out of here and go back to checkpoint forty-three." Letting up on the intercom toe switch and depressing the radio toe switch, Mennzinger gave the order to his company to break off and move back to the rally point. He ordered Cat in Bandit 5 to bring up the rear.

By the time he had finished the order, Andy already had backed off of the battle position, swung the Apache about, and was zooming back to the rally point. With a conflagration consuming the airfield behind them and the attack complete, Mennzinger eased back into his seat. He felt drained. With the tension and pressure momentarily removed, there was a feeling of letdown, as if he were going through withdrawal. Looking out of the canopy, he let his mind go blank. In another hour it would be all over. Someone else would fly their Apaches back to Egypt.

Andy keyed the intercom and brought Mennzinger back from his wandering thoughts. ''Looks like the Blackhawks are late getting the Special Forces guys out.''

Reaching out and grasping the grips on either side of the optical relay tube, Mennzinger pulled himself forward and looked into the sight to see what Andy was talking about. Two hundred meters to their front, at checkpoint 43, two Blackhawks were just lifting off. Mennzinger considered the problem for a moment, then decided it wasn't a problem. Though they should have been gone five minutes ago, they were going now. Whatever it was that delayed them wouldn't interfere with his company. Keying the intercom, he told Andy not to worry about the Blackhawks. They were going. Instead, he wanted Andy to go back to where they had been before the attack and wait for everyone to join them.

Washington and the crew chief worked desperately, fighting a battle both knew they couldn't win. The captain lying on the floor before them had been hit five, maybe six times. At least one lung was punctured, probably both. There was the possibility that his spine was severed. And there was internal bleeding. Blood flowed from his nose and came up in clumps every time he coughed. He needed blood, which they didn't have. He needed surgery, which they, or the people at the refuel point, couldn't do. In the end, what he needed in order to live was a miracle—something that just wasn't going to happen.

Cerro sat on the floor beside Kinsly, holding Kinsly's big black hand in his lap. Cerro's eyes were blurred by tears that would not fall. He kept his thoughts to himself as Washington and the crew chief continued to work.

It was cold. For a moment Kinsly couldn't imagine why it was so cold in the house. He knew he had turned the heat up before he went to bed. He wanted it to be warm when they went down to unwrap the presents. He considered getting up and checking the thermostat but decided against it. He was tired, so terribly tired. He always got that way whenever he stayed up and put his daughter's toys together. Like his father before him, he always waited until the night before Christmas to put the toys together—and like his father, he cursed and vowed never to do it again. But he never changed. Every year was the same. And somehow the smile on his daughter's face when she saw the tree and the presents under it made it all worthwhile. Tomorrow would be no different.

It would be morning soon. He needed to get some rest. Christmas day was always a long one in the Kinsly house. Squeezing his wife's hand, he let himself drift off to sleep.

Washington paused and looked at the crew chief. Picking up Kinsly's free hand, Washington felt for a pulse. There was none. Putting the hand down, Washington felt for a pulse under Kinsly's chin. None. Cerro silently watched as he did so. Sitting up on his knees, Washington leaned over Kinsly's body toward Cerro. Washington wanted to whisper, to tell Cerro as gently as possible; but he had to shout in order to be heard over the noise of the helicopter's engine. "I'm sorry, sir, but he's dead. There's nothing we could do for him."

Cerro looked up, tears running down his cheeks, his chest heaving. "I know. I know."

18

Death is lighter than a feather; duty, heavy as a mountain.

—EMPEROR MEIJI OF JAPAN

South of El Imayid * 0530 Hours, 19 December

Hours of monotonous driving in the dark were about to come
to an end for the men of the 3rd Brigade. The distance from
their staging areas west of Cairo to their forward tactical assembly area was less than 150 miles. By car, any one of the
drivers in the column could have made the trip in a little under
three hours. Moving thirty-five hundred men and over fifteen
hundred vehicles in an orderly fashion, however, required that
some concessions be made.

For example, each march unit of fifteen to twenty-five vehicles required road space. An M-1 tank—thirty-two feet long,
or just under ten meters—requires at least that much road
space. Because there was a threat of air attack, the vehicles had
to be spread out lest a single air attack destroy many vehicles
traveling bumper to bumper. On this road march the distance
between tanks was fifty meters, or 164 feet. Thus, an M-1 tank
did not take ten meters of road; it took sixty meters. Multiply
that times fourteen for a single tank company with fourteen
M-1 tanks and that company will occupy eight-tenths of a
kilometer, or half a mile, worth of road. The fifteen hundred
vehicles of the 3rd Brigade, in column, without breaks, required 90 kilometers, or 55.8 miles, of road space. Every inch
of that column had to move down a single two-lane road, a

road the Egyptian 2nd Army was also trying to move west on.

Added to the above was the need to travel no faster than the slowest vehicle. It would do no good to arrive in battle with M-1 tanks cruising along at forty-five miles an hour, leaving their ancient M-88 recovery vehicles to the rear chugging along at a breathtaking twenty miles an hour. Finally, throw in a refuel stop—near the end of the road march, lest the tanks move into battle on empty—and you have a snail instead of a jaguar moving toward the Libyan frontier.

Road marches, even under the best of conditions, are hard on men and machines. At night, in the desert, after hours without sleep, and with an increasing threat of combat at the end, they are hell. Even for Lieutenant Colonel Vince Vennelli, commander of Task Force 3-5 Armor, the road march was tiring. He was traveling with A Company, an M-1 unit, that night. When they came to the right turn that led to the tactical assembly area where A Company would stop, Vennelli ordered the driver of his hummvee to pull over to the left and stop. The driver, groggy from the long, slow march, didn't hear him. Leaning over, Vennelli yelled in his ear. "TURN LEFT AND STOP—NOW!"

The driver jerked the wheel to the left, causing the hummvee to throw up a cloud of dust as it spun off the road, then back on. When the driver brought the vehicle to an abrupt halt, the cloud of dust continued forward and shrouded the vehicle. Angered by his driver's ineptness, Vennelli decided to wait until he tended to his personal needs before chewing him out. Stepping out of the hummvee, Vennelli walked around to the right side of the vehicle. Standing next to the right rear wheel, he undid the buttons of his fly and prepared to relieve himself.

On tank A-33 the driver lost sight of the vehicle to his front. Keying his intercom, he called to his tank commander for help. "Hey, Sarge. Where'd the hummvee go?"

Staff Sergeant Jonathan Maxwell looked to his front, then from side to side. To his right he saw a cloud of dust. "Right, Billy. Go right."

Confused, and seeing nothing but a cloud of dust and no road, Billy hesitated. "Where? I don't see a road."

Though he was a good driver, Billy Magee could be dense sometimes. Maxwell keyed the intercom again. "Now, Billy! Turn right—now!"

Jerking the steering T to the right, Billy brought the M-1 around to the right and into the cloud of dust. "Okay, Sarge, I hear ya. Ya don't hav'ta yell all the time."

The sudden grinding of tank tracks running through sprockets to his immediate left surprised Vennelli, causing him to urinate on his hands. Stepping back from the hummvee, Vennelli began to stuff himself back in while he looked for the tank that was approaching. From out of the darkness and dust, the fender of a tank emerged and smacked him on the shoulder, sending him sprawling to the ground. Looking up, Vennelli saw the dark gray sky obscured by total blackness as the track of A-33 came crushing down on him. Even his screams were smothered by the tank's sixty-three tons.

"Hey, Sarge—did you hear something?"

"Like what, Billy?"

There was a pause before Billy answered. "I don't know. Sounded like a scream."

Maxwell pulled his crewman's helmet away from his ear. The cold desert wind howled between his ear and his helmet. He eased the helmet down. "It's only the wind, Billy. Now, pay attention and see if you can catch up to the colonel's hummvee."

Startled by the tank that nearly hit his hummvee, Vennelli's driver picked his head up off the steering wheel and listened for a moment. After the tank passed, there was silence. Though he wanted to move, he decided against doing so until the colonel got back. Vicious Vinnie could be a real asshole when people did things without his permission. So the driver put his head back down on the steering wheel and went back to sleep as the column of tanks continued to grind past his hummvee.

Sidi Haneish, Egypt * 0630 Hours, 19 December

Positioning himself with a platoon of three tanks, Lieutenant Colonel Hafez stood high in the turret of his own M-60A3 tank and watched to the west. There was another platoon of tanks to his right, positioned between the railroad tracks and the coastal road. The bulk of his battalion, what was left of it, was deployed on the high ground two kilometers to his rear. In two days of fighting his battalion had been reduced to seventeen operational tanks. They had more than taken their fair share of the enemy, with a tank-to-tank kill ratio of better than three to one. But it seemed to make no difference. The Libyans kept coming, while relief for Hafez's unit or replacements for his losses didn't.

All day the eighteenth, the Republican Brigade had fought a series of delaying actions. The tank battalions of the brigade took turns setting up tank ambushes on the coastal road. Each battalion in turn set up in hasty defensive positions. When the Libyans came, the tank battalion in ambush would engage them for as long as possible. When the Libyans recovered from the initial contact and began to deploy, the tank battalion broke contact. Once free of the fight, it pulled back to its next position to set up again. In moving back, it would bypass its sister tank battalions, waiting in their ambush sites for their turns to pounce.

The idea of a delay is to force the enemy to stop and deploy, slowing its advance as much as possible without becoming decisively engaged. While the enemy is preparing to conduct a hasty attack, the force conducting the delay slips away. The advancing enemy, left with the battlefield, has to regroup, take stock of the situation, and begin its advance again. The problem for the unit conducting a delay is to get away after the enemy begins to deploy and before it is able to bring its weight to bear on the delay force or outmaneuver it. To prevent a flanking attack, the mechanized battalion of the Republican Brigade was screening to the south, making sure the Libyans didn't slip in behind the tank battalions on the coastal road.

There is a gruesome side to a delay, at least for the force

conducting it. Because a delaying unit is always firing, then rapidly moving back, there is little or no time for it to pick up its own wounded or men who have dismounted when their vehicles are damaged. Loss of one's vehicle, for any reason, in most cases means eventual death or capture. The wounded are at the mercy of the enemy, which not only has its own wounded to tend to but, after seeing its own men burned to death or blown apart, may be in a less than charitable mood. There is a natural desire on everyone's part to want to leave a delay position as soon as possible. Thus a commander is faced with the need to inflict maximum delay on the enemy while preserving his own force so it can fight again. That was why Hafez chose to place himself with the element farthest forward. From there he could judge for himself when to commence engaging the enemy and, more importantly, when it was time to leave.

Hafez's plan for this action was to fight the battle in two phases. He had reformed the remains of his battalion into two companies around his remaining officers. The company on the coastal road, the two platoons, would begin the fight. They would handle with ease the combat reconnaissance patrol and the forward security element, if the Libyans had one. When the enemy's main body began to close, Hafez would give the order for the two platoons to make a high-speed run to the east, past the rest of his battalion. The Libyans, seeing the Egyptians run, just might be induced into charging after the fleeing enemy in the hope of destroying them. If the Libyans did so, the second company of Hafez's battalion on the high ground would give the pursuing force another bloody nose.

Though he knew he would make the Libyans pay a stiff price for their advance, Hafez also knew they would not win the war by retreating. The loss of Matruh to the Libyans without a struggle angered him. It was an insult to him as a soldier and an Egyptian. The mere idea of having to flee before the Libyans was repugnant. But retreat he did. To stand and fight outnumbered and die would do nothing to save Egypt. The Republican Brigade had to buy time for the 2nd Egyptian Army to complete its redeployment from the Sinai and stage west of Alexandria. Only when the 2nd Army had completed regrouping would a counteroffensive and relief of the 1st Army, surrounded at Bardia, be possible.

The report that the Libyans were approaching didn't surprise Hafez. Though reconnaissance vehicles from the Brigade's recon company were deployed well to the front of Hafez's position, the dust clouds created by the advancing Libyans could be seen by Hafez himself. It would be another ten, maybe fifteen, minutes before the enemy was within range. In the meantime Hafez passed word to his unit to prepare to engage.

To Hafez the Libyan tanks seemed to take an inordinate amount of time to close the distance between them. Being able to see the enemy at a great distance did nothing to change the range at which the battle could be joined. As the Libyans closed to within two thousand meters of the Brigade's recon elements, the recon leader reported the type and number of vehicles in the lead Libyan formation: four Soviet-built T-55 tanks. Introduced in 1958, and based upon the T-54 tank, the T-55 was obsolete by Western standards. As the T-55 was armed with a rifled 100mm main gun and a simple mechanical fire control system, Hafez's M-60A3 tanks were more than a match. The lack of special armor on the T-55s would allow Hafez to open the engagement starting at fifteen hundred meters or less and take shots at any angle, including head-on. Had the approaching Libyans been equipped with more modern T-72 tanks, the initial engagement range would have been much shorter and Hafez would have needed to maneuver the two tank platoons to where they could get flank shots.

Putting his binoculars up, Hafez watched the Libyans continue to move toward him on either side of the coastal road for several moments. Letting the binoculars down, he looked at his watch, then turned to look at the rising sun to his rear. In a few more minutes the sun would be clear of the horizon. So long as it was low on the horizon, the Libyans, advancing to the east, would have it in their eyes. That would make it difficult for them to see Hafez's tanks both before and after the battle began. He hated to lose that advantage.

Over the battalion radio net the commander of the two platoons reported that the Libyans were within two thousand meters. Keying the radio, Hafez instructed him to hold his fire until the Libyans were within twelve hundred meters. At that range the seven Egyptian tanks would be able to destroy all four Libyan tanks with one volley, two at the most. Quick destruction of the combat recon patrol would prevent the Libyans from reporting with any degree of accuracy. That would leave the follow-on forward security element ignorant as to the exact composition and location of the Egyptian forces blocking the Libyan advance.

The commander of the Libyan forward security element would then be faced with a decision. He could halt and wait until the main body of the following force closed before continuing. That would give the Libyans a fighting chance against any Egyptians they encountered. Another option would be to deploy and conduct a hasty attack with little information on the location and size of the Egyptian unit he was attacking. Finally, he could maneuver his force inland, looking for the flank of the Egyptian force. Of course, he still would not have any information on the location or size of the Egyptian unit he was facing. Not until the Egyptians chose to fire would that be established.

Any way he looked at it, Hafez would achieve his goal. The Libyans would have to slow or stop their advance. His mission—delaying the enemy—would be well on its way to being accomplished. Whether or not his efforts, and the sacrifices of his men, would buy enough time for the 2nd Army, however, would not be known for days. Perhaps it never would.

Military Airfield at Tobruk, Libya * 0810 Hours, 19 December

Standing to one side, Major Neboatov watched dispassionately as the Soviet air force personnel removed the metal casket from the rear of the truck. General Uvarov's body, by order of the Politburo, was going home. The air force personnel were in a hurry to finish loading the transport and return to the safety of their bunker. In the last twenty-four hours, the airfield had been hit twice by carrier-based aircraft and once by naval gunfire.

Neboatov, too, was anxious to get the casket onto the air-craft. As the general's aide, he would escort the casket. Though he was doing so under circumstances that were not the best, any reason to leave Africa at this point was acceptable to Neboatov.

A man could cheat death only so often before his luck ran out. The night the general died should have been Neboatov's last. Had Uvarov stayed at front headquarters until dawn before going to find General Boldin, as the chief of staff advised, naval gunfire would have gotten them. Instead, the attack of the Egyptian Republican Brigade had taken only the general. Neboatov and the surviving members of the command group were left stranded in the desert for twelve hours as the battle swirled around them. That they survived at all was pure luck. The supply column from the 24th Tank Corps that found them initially mistook them for Egyptians and fired on them.

They were brought to General Boldin's headquarters in To-bruk, located five kilometers from Colonel Nafissi's. News of the deteriorating political situation and staff discussions there did nothing to cheer Neboatov. While arranging for transport of General Uvarov's body, he was able to determine that the political and military situation in the Soviet Union and Libya was at best confused. The sad story started with the ill-advised decision to actively assist the Libyans. It was a decision based on the misreading of the political situation in America and the perceived need to demonstrate the Soviet Union's ability to assist its client states in their time of need. The unexpected use of chemical weapons by the Libyans, coinciding with the in-troduction of Soviet and Cuban forces, resulted in the loss of valuable support from nonaligned nations and the world media as a whole. The crossing of the Egyptian border by Soviet forces, and the unrestrained advance of Libyan forces toward Alexandria, destroyed the claim that the conflict would be limited to the restoration of Libya's borders.

Finally, complicating this comedy of errors, the Politburo realized—too late—that there was a power struggle between Nafissi and the nominal head of the Libyan government in

Tripoli. This placed Soviet forces, as well as the Politburo, in a quandary. Militarily, Soviet forces had to cooperate with Nafissi, if for no other reason than mutual protection from growing American air and naval attacks and, of course, logistics. On the national level, the realization that they were being used, and had no control over the political or military situation, angered the men in Moscow, who had once seen the exercise in Libya as nothing more than a show of national resolve.

Efforts to extract the Soviet Union gracefully from this bottomless pit were being frustrated by increasingly brutal and direct American actions against Soviet forces in Africa. Public opinion, and conclusions drawn from the obvious, drove the Americans deeper into the conflict. Neboatov listened with sinking heart to two senior officers on General Boldin's staff discuss the raid on Al Fasher and the naval bombardment of Soviet positions around Bardia. Casualties to Soviet personnel were high and could not be ignored. On one hand, the Soviet Union could not withdraw its forces from Africa under pressure from the United States: diplomatically, it would spell the end of any Soviet influence in the African continent and jeopardize relations with other allies and client states. Events in the field, however, were outrunning efforts to mediate the crisis. So long as Soviet forces surrounded an Egyptian force in Libya and a Libyan force threatened Egyptian national, and internal, security, Egypt and the United States would not negotiate.

Though there had not yet been a direct military response to American actions by Soviet forces, it was only a matter of time before something had to be done. Nothing had been, or could be, done about the Al Fasher raid. It was over. Actions needed to be taken, however, to protect Soviet forces from air and naval attacks. Use of the Black Sea's Mediterranean Squadron to drive off the ships of the U.S. 6th Fleet was being planned. Neboatov saw little hope for moderation. He listened to the staff officers discuss the timing of those operations and the various options—options that would further complicate efforts to moderate the crisis.

As he prepared to leave, Neboatov knew the worst was yet to come. Once American and Soviet forces began to hack away at each other in a deliberate and methodical manner, the voices of reason would be drowned out by the din of battle. Watching the air force personnel secure the casket inside the transport, he was reminded of an ancient Spartan saying. It was said that when a Spartan mother gave her son his shield, she implored him to return with it or upon it. General Uvarov was coming home on his shield. Would the Politburo tell the Red Army units in Africa the same thing—return home with it or upon it? If so, Uvarov's body would be only the first of many.

Headquarters, 2nd Corps (U.S.) * 1115 Hours, 19 December

No sooner had Scott Dixon walked into the operations room than Sergeant Major London grabbed him and asked if he had been to see the chief of staff yet. With only four hours' sleep and a shower since leaving the command post, Dixon was slow in reacting. Drawing a cup of coffee from a well-used pot in the corner of the room, Dixon looked over to the situation map. He decided it might be a good idea to familiarize himself with the current situation before he saw the chief.

Walking over to the map, he stopped several feet from it. For several minutes he studied the map and sipped his coffee. Even as he stood there, NCOs from the operations and intelligence sections went up to the map and moved red and blue symbols representing units or changed some data written next to a unit symbol. The blue symbols, representing the Egyptian units, were farther to the east than they had been when he had walked out at 0730 that morning. Some red symbols, representing the Libyans, were closed up right next to the blue ones. The delaying action by the Republican Brigade continued. How neat the clean, two-dimensional map sheet and the well-defined symbols made war look, Dixon thought. One could almost believe by looking at the map and listening to briefings given by the staff that people actually were able to control and understand what was happening out there.

Dixon stepped closer to the map to study the terrain where the front line now stood. The fight continued to move east along the coastal road. Little effort had been made by the Libyans to sweep inland to outflank the Egyptians. Speed, and maintaining the solid line of communications back to Libya, seemed to be important to the Libyans. Along the line on the map where blue symbols met red symbols, there was a sliver of space separating the two. That sliver of space, representing the front line trace of friendly and enemy units, looked so inconsequential on the map. Dixon knew, however, that men were fighting and dying in the tiny sliver. In that minute space the neat, straight edges of the opposing map symbols blurred and merged as men and equipment crawled and stumbled about in the desert. The war that the blue and red symbols, neatly taped to the map, represented bore no resemblance to the war being fought by the soldiers who made up those units.

Stepping back, Dixon looked at the location of Libyan units posted on the map. Several units were spread out along the coastal road. Next to each unit symbol was a date and time written in the margin of the symbol, indicating the last time information on that unit had been updated. Seeing that the time on several Libyan units was more than twelve hours old, Dixon called an intel analyst over and asked what those Libyan units were up to. The analyst looked at the unit symbols in question, then at a clipboard where a sheet was maintained for each enemy unit. As she found each, she gave Dixon the reason it had not moved or was moving slowly. In most cases there appeared to be logistical problems. The Libyans, she said, were having difficulty getting fuel forward. In two cases the unit had been caught by naval gunfire. Chewed up and scattered, they had been forced to stop and reorganize. In a few cases there was no reason. The unit had simply stopped moving forward, and the cause was as yet undetermined. Not surprisingly, Soviet forces had not moved. They continued to besiege the Egyptian 1st Army in Bardia and hold Sollum and Halfaya Pass.

Satisfied that he had a handle on the situation, both friendly and enemy, Dixon told Sergeant Major London he was off to see the chief. Fortified with information and a cup of coffee, he was ready to deal with anything the chief could give him—or so he thought as he walked down the busy corridor to General Darruznak's office.

The door to General Darruznak's office was open. Seated at his desk, Darruznak was casually reviewing reports and intelligence summaries when Dixon knocked. Looking up over the rim of his reading glasses, Darruznak paused before motioning to Dixon to enter and take a seat. Standing up as Dixon sat, he walked over to a side table where a small coffee pot sat. There was silence as he poured coffee into two cups. He offered one to Dixon, who naturally took it, and carried his own back to his desk. Dixon could tell that Darruznak was stalling, working himself up to something. He thought he knew, but decided to wait until the general, in his own time, told him why he was there.

"Scott, I'd like to start by congratulating you and your people on a job well done. The raid on Al Fasher not only went without a hitch—its success far exceeded our expectations."

Dixon thought it strange that he should be getting any kind of recognition for the raid. Of all the people involved, he was the least active. As the concept man, he didn't have to fly deep into hostile territory. He didn't have to jump out of a C-130 into a strange drop zone. He didn't have to go eye to eye with Soviet air defense missiles and small-arms fire. It was the trigger pullers that had made it work.

Dixon let those thoughts pass as Darruznak continued. The chief was slow in doing so. He looked at his coffee as he began speaking. "Part of the reason I called you in here was to extend General Horn's and my condolences on the loss of your wife." Darruznak paused. He looked up at Dixon. "I know that there is nothing we can say or do that can possibly compensate for such a loss. In normal times I would insist that you tend to the needs of your surviving family."

Dixon didn't hear what the general said. His words faded as Dixon found himself searching for his feelings—his feelings for Fay. Until that moment he had denied himself any time to consider what Fay's death meant to him. How should he feel? Should he allow himself to be overcome with regret and grief? After all, he had just lost the woman to whom he had pledged eternal fidelity. Should he feel guilt for having so casually violated that trust when he slept with Jan? Or would despair over the thought of losing the mother of his children be in order? Perhaps righteous indignation was more appropriate for a woman who had so callously abandoned her children in a time of crisis, when they needed her the most? And why should he bother pitying a woman who had denied him comfort and understanding when he so badly needed it after returning from Iran?

Slowly Dixon began to wonder if he had become a little less human. Was it that he felt *all* these things? Or perhaps he wasn't touched by any of them? Possibly it was a little of both. Had exposure to death, both up close and personal and by remote control through the plans he developed, destroyed his ability to deal with feelings? Had he become so callous to suffering that nothing could touch him? Was he treating the death of his wife the way he did any other military problem— identify the problem, analyze all courses of action available, and select the best for the given situation? Was that what he was doing?

As if emerging from a daze, Dixon drifted from his own thoughts back to the present. Darruznak was still sitting at his desk, staring at his coffee and waiting while Dixon absorbed the blow. "I'm sorry, sir. I . . ."

Darruznak lifted his hand, indicating there was no need to apologize. "Scott, like I said, under normal circumstances I would insist that you go to your family and tend to their needs. But these are far from normal circumstances."

Dixon tried to recall the general saying that, but couldn't. No doubt he had been lost in his own thoughts, allowing that comment to pass over him. Now, however, Dixon gave the general his full attention. There was obviously more to this meeting than the obligatory regrets.

"Scott, this morning the commander of Task Force 3-5 Armor was killed in an accident. As you know, that task force, as part of the 16th Armored Division, is preparing to participate in the counteroffensive." Darruznak paused, sipping at his coffee, before he let the other shoe drop. "In a conversation with General Horn this morning, the commander of the 16th expressed his concern over sending that 3rd of the 5th Armor into battle without a capable commander. Neither he nor the 3rd Brigade commander feel comfortable with the abilities of the XO of that unit. Both feel that it would be unwise to commit 3rd of the 5th unless a suitable replacement for the commander can be found."

In an instant Dixon understood where Darruznak was going. His cautious introduction and slow approach toward the bottom line was unnecessary. Somehow, someone had suggested or recommended that Dixon be that replacement. That was why Darruznak had emphasized his point about these not being normal circumstances. He was setting Dixon up. Without being conscious that he was doing it, Dixon began to shake his head from side to side.

Seeing Dixon's reaction, Darruznak realized that he didn't need to continue, that Dixon had made the connection. "Scott, before you say anything, hear me out. In the first place, we know how you feel. Everyone involved in the decision knows that you turned down command of a task force. They know what happened in Iran and your belief that you cannot lead men into combat again. Finally, everyone knows about your personal tragedy. I—we—can appreciate the former and understand the latter. But for one moment you have to forget your own personal feelings and problems, as hard as that might be, and look at this the way we see it."

Dixon stopped shaking his head and eased back into the chair. Darruznak leaned forward, folding his hands in front of him on the desk. "Scott, in a few hours we are going to issue an order to 3rd Brigade telling them to commence the counteroffensive. That plan includes use of 3rd of the 5th. General Horn understands the concerns of the commanders in the 16th Armored Division. He also knows that we cannot afford to delay the operation until a new commander is found for 3rd of the 5th. Nor can we conduct the operation without that unit. Bottom line, Scott, is that 3rd of the 5th goes, with or without you. With you, their chances of coming out of this fight increase."

And what, Dixon thought, brought them to that conclusion? The last task force he commanded in combat didn't come out. Losses were so high that it never again was able to participate in combat operations in Iran. He wondered what perverse logic brought them to the conclusion that he could make a difference at a time when he was unable to sort out his own life. He couldn't. He wouldn't. Sitting up, Dixon looked Darruznak in the eye. "Sir, I cannot, and will not, accept command."

Returning the stare, Darruznak responded, any hint of reasonableness absent from his voice, "And you, Colonel, must understand that we are not asking you. You *will* assume command of that task force. When that unit crosses its line of departure, you are going to be with it. Is that clear?"

Dixon sat there looking at Darruznak. The general returned his stare. The silence was heavy, oppressive, and unbearable for Dixon. Darruznak broke it. "My aide will arrange for my chopper to take you to the 3rd Brigade headquarters. How much time do you need to get your affairs in order, Scott?"

Though the general was using his first name, his tone had changed; it left no doubt that the conversation was over. There was no room for discussion, no hint of an alternative. Dixon had his orders and was expected to carry them out.

Dixon slowly stood up and brought himself to attention. "Sir, I'll need two hours, maybe less. I need to go into Cairo first."

Darruznak nodded his approval. As Dixon turned to leave, Darruznak called out to him, wishing him luck.

Cairo * 1205 Hours, 19 December

The tan and brown camouflaged Chevy Blazer, called a CUCV by the Army and pronounced "cut-vee," swerved in and out of the traffic. The CUCV was waved through roadblocks and police barricades. Neither Dixon nor the driver, fully armed and in combat gear, had to show any ID or orders. Dixon had figured they wouldn't need to, which is why he opted for the CUCV instead of chancing a taxi. The driver, aware of the prohibition against taking military vehicles into Cairo, had protested. Dixon, however, easily overcame any argument, using his rank and bluff. Though he hated to do either, he was in no mood to mess around and didn't have the time. He really didn't care about the consequences. After all, he thought, what was the worst they could do? Send him to the front?

Dixon ordered the driver to park in front of the building to which the 2nd Corps public affairs officer said WNN had moved. Not finding a place to park, the driver made himself one on the sidewalk. Climbing out, Dixon paused, holding on to the door as he stared at the building. He knew why he had come. What he didn't know was what he was going to do. Telling the driver to wait where he was, Dixon closed the door and entered the building in search of Jan Fields.

His task was not easy. Because its own staff and facilities had yet to be reconstituted, WNN was sharing facilities with another American news agency. Most of the people in the building, and some in the other news agency, weren't aware of the arrangement. One girl finally volunteered to take Dixon to the office the WNN people were working out of.

When they arrived there, Dixon looked about. "Office" was a charitable term for the overly large closet where a handwritten WNN sign hung. In the office there were two desks, three chairs, and some camera equipment. None of the WNN staff, however, was there. The girl told Dixon that someone would be along in a minute. Looking at his watch, he decided to give himself fifteen minutes. After that he would have to leave. Sitting down in one of the chairs, Dixon leaned back and closed his eyes. He was still tired, though not nearly as tired, he thought, as he soon would be.

Dixon was sitting there, back to the wall and eyes closed, when a tall man with long, stringy blond hair walked in. He paused when he saw Dixon. "I'm Tim Masterson, cameraman for WNN. Can I help you?"

Dixon slowly opened his eyes and looked at the man. He seemed familiar. He had seen him somewhere before. Standing up, Dixon extended his right hand toward the cameraman. "Scott Dixon, U.S. Army. I'm looking for Jan Fields."

Taking Dixon's hand and shaking it, Tim remembered where

he had seen Dixon. "You're that chap that popped those assassins back on December seventh, aren't you?"

Dixon shook his head. "Yeah, I'm that chap. Is Jan available?"

Tim's friendly look turned into a frown. "I'm sorry. You just missed her. She's already left."

Reaching down and picking up his helmet, Dixon got ready to leave. "Can you tell me where she went? Perhaps I can catch her."

"I sort of doubt that. You see, she's left Egypt. Plane took off not more than a hour ago. Headed for London, then Brussels to cover the NATO meeting. That's where I just came from—the airport, that is. Dropped her off myself."

Dixon stopped and looked at Tim for a moment. In a way he was relieved. He could postpone his problem. For a while, perhaps forever, he could avoid facing something that he wasn't ready to face. Perhaps in time he could face it, but not now. Dixon started out the door past Tim.

Tim grabbed Dixon's arm as he went by. Surprised, Dixon looked at Tim's hand on his arm, then into Tim's eyes. They were serious yet gentle. "For what it's worth, gov'nor, Jan told me she loves you."

Dixon continued to stare into Tim's eyes. They were neither condemning him nor sympathetic. Tim let go, allowing Dixon to continue.

Pausing, Dixon turned back to Tim. "Thanks for telling me. And yes, that is worth something to me. It's worth a great deal." With that he walked out.

19

Nothing remains static in war or in military weapons, and it is consequently often dangerous to rely on courses suggested by apparent similarities in the past.

—ADMIRAL E. J. KING

South of El Imayid * 1930 Hours, 19 December

The trip from the 3rd Brigade command post to Task Force 3-5 Armor was done in total silence. The driver of Headquarters 6, the bumper number assigned to the task force commander's hummvee, kept his eyes glued to the trail and his instrument panel. Dixon hoped the lad was always that quiet. Though a casual conversation was good every now and then, there was nothing worse than having a driver whose mouth ran at a higher RPM rate than the transmission. Dixon liked to think when he was being driven from place to place. On this particular night he had much to think about.

His meeting with the commander of the 3rd Brigade had been long and quite informative. It started with a mission briefing by the brigade staff. Other than showing how the brigade viewed the enemy situation, the intelligence portion added very little to what Dixon already knew. With no organic recon elements deployed, all information the intel officer had came from the 2nd Corps intelligence summary, a copy of which was in Dixon's map case. The briefings by the brigade operations officer and fire support officer were more informative. Though Dixon knew what the 16th Division's mission was, he hadn't seen anything on how the 3rd Brigade intended to execute its assigned mission. Succeeding briefings by the brigade's personnel officer and logistics officer and commanders of combat support units attached to the brigade added little.

With the formal briefings over and a copy of the brigade operations order in hand, the brigade commander, Colonel Clyde Joy, accompanied by the brigade executive officer, had taken Dixon into his tent to discuss several matters with him. Joy went over again how he believed the operation would unfold and how he intended to fight it. Dixon learned a great deal from Joy in a very short period of time. It was critical that he be able to understand what was going on inside of Joy's head and how Joy viewed warfare. Even the words Joy used— "kill" instead of "engage," "attack" instead of "advance," "smash" instead of "destroy"—conveyed his personality and philosophy on waging war. Though some would argue that use of such colorful words was unnecessary, Dixon believed differently. The old adage "If he looks like a soldier, walks like a soldier, and talks like a soldier, by God, he's probably a soldier" was a fairly good gauge to go by when judging men. Until otherwise proven, Colonel Joy was a soldier in Dixon's eyes.

The major reason Joy wanted to talk to Dixon in private was to review how he, as the brigade commander, viewed Task Force 3-5 and its men. Joy prefaced that portion of the conversation by telling Dixon that under normal circumstances he would have allowed Dixon to discover who was good and who wasn't on his own. Given the timing and the nature of the operation, however, Dixon wouldn't have the chance. Starting with the task force's executive officer and operations officer, Joy went down the list, name by name, of the primary players in the task force. The story Joy told was not very encouraging. Under Lieutenant Colonel Vennelli, control and operation of the task force had been extremely centralized. And in a zero-defect environment, neither the staff nor the company commanders showed initiative.

Joy told Dixon that, given the prevailing conditions, the questionable ability of the officers, and the lack of time, he had a free hand in dealing with the unit's officers and NCOs. If Dixon thought that he needed to relieve a man, he was to do so. Joy would attempt to buy as much time as he could for Dixon to get a handle on things, but he didn't know how much time they had. Dixon, having listened to the 2nd Corps plans briefings, did. Whatever he had to do to make Task Force 3-5 Armor combat ready had to be accomplished within the next thirty-four hours.

Now, as the hummvee bumped and jerked along the desert track, Dixon mulled over how best to approach his assumption of command. He could go in like a lion, kicking ass and taking names. Though that might be effective in yielding some short-term results, the side effects might well spell disaster down the road. Or he could go in and let things ride as they were, dealing with each and every problem only as it came up. While he didn't know exactly how he would act, he knew how he *wouldn't*. Dixon had no intention of going into the unit like a lamb, the poor lost soul, the new boy on the block. Whether or not the soldiers of Task Force 3-5 Armor—officers, NCOs, and enlisted—liked him didn't matter to Dixon. Only two things mattered to him. One was that the task force made it to the Egyptian-Libyan border. The second was to ensure that most of the soldiers in that task force were still with it when they got there.

Dixon hadn't made up his mind when they pulled up near the tactical operations center, or TOC, of 3-5 Armor. Shutting off the engine, the driver pointed to the entrance of the TOC. Dixon got out and looked around. There were a number of other hummvees parked about the TOC in a haphazard fashion. None of them had camouflage nets up or even the hood raised to prevent glare from the windshield. As best he could see, there was no guard and no security about the command-post area or the TOC in particular. The TOC itself was poorly camouflaged. Its camouflage nets were dropping down and lying on the four command-post carriers and their canvas extensions. As a result, the camouflage nets did nothing, leaving the command post carriers and extensions clearly visible in the light of the three-quarter moon. Even worse, the noise of the vehicles running and the loud talking and laughing from the crowd gathered in the TOC could be heard all over the area. Dixon began to wonder if he had discounted the lion approach too soon.

Moving over to the TOC, Dixon found the entrance—three over-lapping canvas flaps arranged to prevent light from escaping when someone entered or exited. It was like moving through a maze: first, you went between the first and second flaps to find the end; then you changed direction and went between the second and third flap; finally, you found the end of the third flap, then changed direction again before entering the interior. Often soldiers burdened with pistol belts, holsters, canteens, ammo pouches, protective masks, or other gear had difficulty moving through them. When frustration overcame good light discipline practices, soldiers stuck their arms through all three flaps, forced them apart, and entered straight in. With the skill of an officer who had spent many months in the field, Dixon began to tangle with the flaps.

Emerging on the interior, Dixon bumped into someone blocking the door. Whoever it was didn't move. Instead a voice asked, in a rather put-out manner, what he wanted. Dixon simply said, "I'm coming in," and pushed. Free of the flaps and blockage, Dixon stood upright in the TOC and was momentarily blinded by the bright lights: all he could make out was wall-to-wall people. Sensing that no one noticed him, Dixon called out, "Who's in charge here?"

From somewhere on the other side of the TOC, a voice responded above the babble of conversation. "Who wants to know?"

Something inside Dixon, probably his self-restraint, snapped. In as deep a voice as he could muster, Dixon responded, "Lieutenant Colonel Scott A. Dixon, commander of Task Force 3-5 Armor, that's who."

Silence descended upon the TOC as if someone had flipped a switch. All heads turned to the entrance as everyone tried to get a look at the new commander. Dixon returned the stare. The first man to move was a major, who plowed through the crowd to Dixon. Reaching him, he stuck his right hand out to shake Dixon's as he introduced himself. "Sir, I'm Larry Pettit, task force S-3."

Dixon raised his right hand to his forehead, saluting Pettit and catching him by surprise. As Pettit pulled his hand back and raised it to return the salute, the smile that had been on his face disappeared. "Sir, I apologize for not meeting you. I'm in charge here."

Dixon was about to ask where the task force's executive officer was when a soldier attempting to get into the TOC through the entrance flaps rammed his helmet into Dixon's back. Yelling through the flaps, the intruder warned everyone that Headquarters 6 was back and the new old man was in the area. Stepping aside, Dixon opened the third flap to allow the soldier in. When the intruder, a young sergeant E-5, came face to face with Dixon, Dixon looked him in the eyes. "Don't worry, son. They already know."

For several minutes there was a scramble as people who didn't need to be at the initial briefing left the TOC. The operations sergeant—a tall, blond, heavy-set sergeant first class—grabbed Dixon and took him to a seat, shoving a cup of coffee in his hand as he did so. The S-3, in the meantime, got all the primary staff officers, company commanders, and combat service support unit leaders seated. Dixon overheard Pettit tell the soldier manning the radios in the command post carrier to contact the XO and have him report to the TOC ASAP.

As everyone settled, Dixon, seated three feet from the task force map, began to study the graphics that represented the task force's plan for the upcoming operation. Sipping his coffee, he tried hard to make sense of the lines and circles drawn on the plastic overlay that covered the map. He did not like what he saw. The map of the area was attached cockeyed to a sheet of unpainted plywood. The plastic overlay was taped to the plywood map board with many short, torn-off strips of tape. There was no other information, friendly or enemy, posted on the map board. Even the plan itself bothered him. Try as hard as he could, Dixon could not see how the task force plan coincided with the brigade plan. Even worse, all the map sheets needed to show the operation were not put together and posted.

The result was a series of lines (representing unit boundaries) and circles (representing objectives) sitting over blank plywood where the map had run out but the brigade plan hadn't.

Still, Dixon held his tongue. Perhaps, he thought, these people really do have their stuff together. Perhaps they have a good plan and just haven't been able to put together all the graphics and supporting data yet. Sitting back, Dixon cleared his mind and allowed the staff, orchestrated by the S-3, to brief their new commander. As they did so, Dixon's theory about them having a better plan than their map showed soon collapsed. Officer after officer stood up, mumbled, hemmed and hawed, danced this way and that before the map, then sat down without adding to Dixon's knowledge. Even when Dixon took into account that they were nervous, briefing their new commander for the first time, and preparing to go into combat, there was still no plan—at least not one that would support what the brigade commander intended to do. If there ever had been a plan, it died with the former task-force commander.

Just when Dixon had reached the conclusion that he had seen enough, the TOC entrance flaps flew open, allowing Major Jerry Grissins to enter. Without pausing, Grissins approached Dixon and reported, apologizing for not being there for Dixon's arrival: he had been, he explained, in the throes of securing two new engines and a transmission for three nonoperational tanks. Dixon nodded, telling Grissins that his arrival was timely, that he was about to end the briefings and issue some new guidance.

Dixon remained standing while he allowed the XO and the commanders and staff of the task force to settle. Once he had their undivided attention, he started. "First off, I want each and every one of you here to understand one thing. We are about to go to war. There is no 'maybe,' no 'possibly.' In less than thirty-two hours, this task force, and the rest of the 16th Armored Division, is going to cross the line of departure. When we do so, our sole task will be to close with and destroy the enemy by use of fire, maneuver, and shock effect." Dixon paused. Looking at them, he could tell that he had their undivided attention.

"You have all heard those words before. That happens to be the mission statement for the armored force. But I have no doubt that few of you have given serious thought to what that means. I'm going to tell you, right now. As a unit, we are going to leave here and attack. Right now, where that is doesn't matter. Even 2nd Corps doesn't know where we'll eventually smash into the enemy. But it will happen. Forget about rumors that there is a negotiated settlement in the offing. Forget about being held in reserve. Forget about making a policy statement with a simple show of force. In fact, forget about going home, 'cause you ain't!''

Easing back a bit and moderating his tone, Dixon let his last statement sit for a second before he continued. "I have been told that most of the men in this task force are not veterans. Well, in forty-eight hours, we will either all be veterans, or we will be dead. Do you know what will make the difference?'' Dixon waited, then answered his own question. "*We* will, gentlemen—you and me. The commanders, the staff, and the noncommissioned officers of this task force are going to be the deciding factor in who wins and who loses, who lives and who dies.

"It's too damned late for us to retrain everyone in their job. Right now, either the tank and Bradley crews of this task force can put steel on target, or they can't. What we can do, the officers and NCOs, is give them a plan that's worth a shit—come up with the best possible scheme of maneuver that will allow them to place their weapons systems where they can do the most damage and then execute it.

"Company commanders, prepare to copy a new warning order.'' Pausing, Dixon folded his arms across his chest while he waited. When all four line company commanders were ready and looking at him, he issued his first order to the task force. "I want you to go back to your units and get some sleep. The staff and I are going to develop a new operations order tonight. That order will be ready and briefed at 0600 hours tomorrow morning here. At 1100 hours, we're going to have a full brief back from each of you as well as the engineer company commander, scout platoon leader, mortar platoon leader, and air defense platoon leader. That will be followed by a mounted rehearsal at 1400 hours. Some time between those, you're to conduct precombat inspections. Commanders, you're to coordinate those inspections with the S-3 so that I can be there when you do them. Use your time wisely, and do not forget a sleep plan for your men, your leaders, and especially yourself. Once we go into the attack, we are going to be moving fast, and we ain't stopping till we hit the Libyan border.''

Dixon stopped, pondering whether he wanted to say more or hold it at that. There was so much to cover, so much to say, to discuss. But time would not permit him to cover it all. There was only so much he could do. He hoped that those things he chose to do were the best and wisest, the ones that would better their chances for success and survival. Deciding that he had said enough, Dixon dismissed the company commanders and told the XO to gather up the staff. There was a plan that needed to be developed and an order to write.

El Daba, Egypt * 2140 Hours, 19 December

On the side of the road, Colonel Hafez stood counting his vehicles as the remains of the Republican Brigade passed through the forward outpost line of the 3rd Armored Division, Egyptian 2nd Army. Next to him at the passage point were the commanders of both the 2nd Army and the 3rd Armored Division. They had both come forward to see Hafez, now the commander of the Republican Brigade, and receive his report and observations. Of ninety-four tanks that had been with the Brigade on 16 December, Hafez counted only thirty-seven returning to friendly lines that night. From the Libyan border to where they stood, the Brigade had fought the Libyans in a dozen minor fights, mauling its lead division. In their wake they had left hundreds of burning vehicles and thousands dead and dying.

As terrible as the cost had been to Hafez's Brigade, the sacrifice had not been in vain. Two complete divisions of the 2nd Army, the 3rd Armored and the 10th Mechanized, had

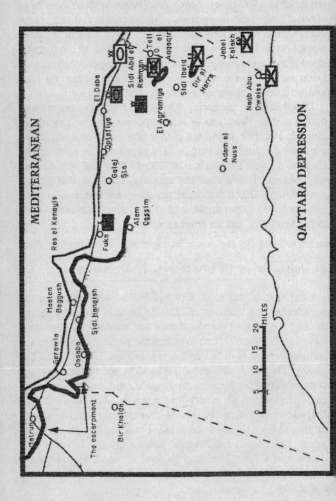

been able to deploy and assume hasty defensive positions from El Daba to Sidi Ibeid in the south. South of Sidi Ibeid, the American air assault brigade prepared to conduct a covering force operation between Sidi Ibeid and the Qattara Depression.

While they waited, a staff officer from the 2nd Army briefed Hafez on his next mission. When he told Hafez that he would become part of the army's reserve force, Hafez protested. Not letting the staff officer continue, he went over to the commander of the 2nd Army to protest. In a tone that bordered on insubordination, Hafez said that he and his soldiers had retreated too far and been in reserve too long. He demanded that they be allowed to participate in the counteroffensive. Though surprised, the general was pleased at Hafez's fighting spirit. When he asked how soon Hafez could be ready to attack, Hafez thought for a moment before he responded: given fuel, ammunition, and some rest, twenty-four hours.

Without hesitation the 2nd Army commander turned to the commander of the 3rd Armored Division, informing him that the Republican Brigade was attached to his command under the provision that it would be the lead unit when the counteroffensive began. The commander of the 3rd Armored looked at Hafez, then at the commander of the 2nd Army. Saluting, he announced that it would be an honor to have such a unit under his command.

Though he was tired—more tired than he had ever been in his life—Hafez was satisfied. They would be able to go back, to inflict upon the Libyans a humiliating defeat that would not be forgotten and save the 1st Army. There was nothing, not even life itself, that was more important to Hafez at that moment than going back. Only when he was finished with his duty, only when he had done all that he could to right his terrible wrong, would he worry about atonement for his sins.

Tobruk, Libya * 0730 Hours, 20 December

Colonel Nafissi watched as General Boldin, accompanied by his operations and political officers, climbed aboard their helicopter. Though he resented their meddling, the Russians were still a necessary evil. Nothing would please him more than to see the helicopter they were boarding shot down. If he had thought he could get away with it, he would have done it himself. As it was, with Russians all over, such an order would be hard to cover. Instead, he had to pray that the cursed Egyptians would do so.

In a meeting called by Boldin, Nafissi had listened politely as the Russians explained the situation as they saw it. The Soviet Union, Boldin pointed out, was willing to support the defense of Libya. The attack of the 24th Tank Corps and the 8th Division had, as Boldin pointed out, amply demonstrated that. Nafissi's operations east of Mersa Matruh, however, exceeded Libya's claim of self-defense by a wide margin. To continue east would cost them what little support they, the Soviet Union and Libya, had in the United Nations and the world community in general. Even the use of chemical weapons, stringently denied by both parties, could be ignored if a solution could be found before full commitment of American forces.

When Nafissi asked what difference the pitiful number of American forces in Africa would make, Boldin deferred to the political officer. The political officer, a colonel, answered carefully. "You must understand our position. We cannot afford even the appearance of a defeat. What we stand to lose in prestige around the world far outweighs any short-term advantages we might gain in Africa, even if we win. For years our premier has been working to build an image of trust and peace without giving up what our fathers gained with their blood and sweat. To survive and maintain our global interests, the Soviet Union needs peace and the cooperation of the West. When Russians start killing Americans, that peace and cooperation will cease."

Nafissi was confused. Interrupting, he asked about the raid on Al Fasher and the incessant naval bombardment.

"Those were small, isolated affairs," the political officer responded, carefully picking his words. "They can, through mutual agreement, be officially forgotten, if both sides so agree. A major ground battle between our units and American combat troops is another matter. We would have little choice but to respond in some way, somewhere. If that weren't possible in Africa, we would be forced to exert pressure elsewhere—Europe, or perhaps Central America. You see, what happens here could have worldwide repercussions. We, the Soviet Union, are a world power, with global responsibilities.''

Without realizing it, the political officer had captured Nafissi's imagination. That was exactly what *he* wanted for Libya; that was exactly *his* goal. From the very beginning Nafissi had been looking for change, a change that would sweep the Arab world. To topple Egypt and replace her as the head of the Islamic world and the leading power in Africa was his ambition. What happened in Europe, the Soviet Union, and America was of little concern to him. If they fell into war among themselves, it did not matter to him. They were, after all, infidels, nonbelievers. Both the Russians and the Americans could be used as he saw fit. But to do so he needed time, just a little more.

Incessant delaying actions by small Egyptian units had cost the force that had invaded Egypt heavy losses, not to mention expenditure of munitions and other supplies—losses that it could ill afford. Nafissi's dream of reaching Alexandria and Cairo seemed to diminish with every kilometer they advanced and every battle they fought. The blocking of supply columns by the Soviets at Halfaya Pass threatened to stop his divisions entirely. Searching for a solution, Nafissi agreed that he would halt the eastward movement of his forces only after they reached defensible terrain. Citing the North African campaign in World War II as his defense, he claimed that he would be able to hold only after he reached a line running from Sidi Abd el Rahman to Jebel Kalakh. Only there, where the Mediterranean and the Qattara Depression restricted maneuver space, would his two divisions be able to hold until a cease-fire was arranged.

For several minutes Boldin and the political officer discussed the matter in Russian. Though the political officer was uneasy about doing so, Boldin and Nafissi agreed to suspend offensive operations after reaching the line specified by Nafissi. For his part Boldin knew that there were only two Egyptian divisions deployed along the coastal road. Those two divisions were insufficient for a counteroffensive. According to his operations officer, at least six divisions would be needed. It would be ten to fourteen days before the Egyptians could muster that force in the Western Desert. The deliberate buildup of combat power and stockpiling of supplies, necessary for a prolonged offensive much like that of the British in 1942, would take weeks. The weak American division, covering the entire area from Sidi Ibeid to the depression, would be hard pressed to secure the southern flank. Spread as it was, it would be useless in any offensive operations.

Since it was nothing more than a simple adjustment of the front line, Boldin insisted that he had the authority to make that decision. Militarily it was a sound decision. It would be foolish to leave the Libyans hanging out in the desert in positions that could not be defended. The political officer disagreed but, in this case, deferred to Boldin's judgment. The line Nafissi proposed was, after all, nearly the same one at which Rommel had held the 8th Army for months. So Boldin agreed to let Nafissi press on a little further. If he got out of hand, Soviet forces in Halfaya could always turn off his supplies again.

Now, with the Russian helicopter safely away, Nafissi returned to his bunker. He had to finish his final orders to his commanders in Egypt. In sealed orders Nafissi instructed his two division commanders to mass their forces and break through the new Egyptian line. Once they were through, Alexandria was only sixty miles away. Another battlefield defeat, followed by the appearance of Libyan forces in Alexandria, would be more than enough to bring down the Egyptian government. It had to be. It was Nafissi's last hope.

Jebel Kalakh, Egypt * 0830 Hours, 20 December

To a casual observer, the mounds of dirt, strips of cloth, and lengths of string spread across the sand were meaningless. To

Captain Harold Cerro, his XO, his first sergeant, and the platoon leaders, platoon sergeants, and squad leaders of his company, they represented North Africa. Gathered around the
captain's sand table, the leadership of B Company listened as
Cerro reviewed the main points of the operation. Once he was
done, each platoon leader would brief Cerro on how their
platoons would perform their assigned tasks.

Using a section of antenna, Cerro pointed to each part of the
sand table, identifying the terrain feature it represented. "Here,
we have the coast of the Mediterranean in the north, and here,
in the south, the Qattara Depression. Jebel Kalakh is here, Ras
el Kenayis here." Cerro stopped and looked around the group.
Everyone was listening and paying close attention. Their taut
faces masked the wide spectrum of emotions, fears, and apprehensions that soldiers carry with them into battle. In the
past, at times like this, Cerro would always attempt to relieve
the strain with humor. Since his return from Sudan, however,
he found little amusement in the growing war. Even if he had
been so inclined, there was little in their upcoming operation
that lent itself to humor.

"Our mission is to establish a blocking position here, where
the coastal road and the railroad climb the high ground just
south of Ras el Kenayis. We are to hold there, blocking traffic
going back to Libya, until relieved by the 3rd Brigade, 16th
Armored Division."

Cerro drew a line in the dirt west of the rock that represented
Jebel Kalakh. "That brigade will cross a line of departure here,
at 0600 hours, 21 December. That coincides with our insertion
here." Cerro moved his pointer to the coastal road south of Ras
el Kenayis. He then traced the route the 3rd Brigade would
follow. "We expect that maneuver to take, at a minimum,
twelve hours. Link-up between our airhead and the armored
brigade will come no sooner than 1800 hours 20 December.
Should the Libyans turn to block or attack the 3rd Brigade in
the flank, one or both of the Egyptian divisions will attack the
Libyans on or south of the coastal road. Any way you look at
it, the Libyans will be between a rock and a hard place. In this

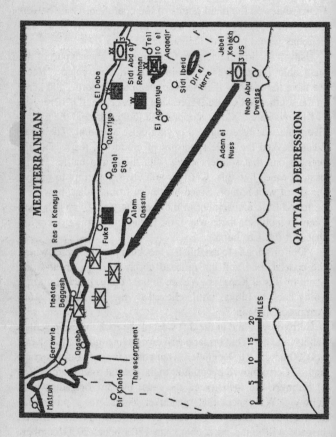

operation, we have to be the hard place fighting any- and everyone that comes our way."

Pointing to blocks of wood with the numerals 1, 2, and 3 painted on them, Cerro showed where each of the platoons would go. The company would deploy between the railroad and the road near and on top of the escarpment that rose up from the coastal plain south of Ras el Kenayis. The other companies of the battalion were deployed on either side of Cerro's on the escarpment. A Company would be on the left, C Company to the right. The five platoons of the antitank company were divided between the three line companies, with Cerro's company getting two of them. These two platoons, each with four TOW antitank guided-missile launchers per platoon, would provide his companies long-range antitank capability. Six organic Dragon antitank guided-missile launchers and over two hundred single-shot AT-4 light antitank rocket launchers would provide medium- and short-range antitank firepower.

The other two infantry battalions of the brigade were deployed to the south, bent back to the west and almost to the coast west of Cerro's position. A Marine battalion, attached to the brigade for this operation and landed by the 6th Fleet twelve miles west of Cerro's position, completed the perimeter. They, like Cerro's battalion, would establish blocking positions on the coastal road where it descended off of the escarpment down to the coastal plain. One Marine infantry company, reinforced with a Marine tank platoon and traveling in LAV armored personnel carriers, constituted the brigade reserve. Located in the center on the coastal road, this reserve force would go wherever the Libyans threatened a breakthrough.

In addition to the weapons organic and attached to Cerro's company, fire support would be available from several outside sources. The brigade's eighteen-gun 155mm howitzer battalion, reinforced with a six-gun Marine battery, would eventually provide the bulk of the artillery support. The brigade, however, lacked sufficient helicopters to move itself in one lift. Four lifts, each taking over two hours, would be needed to move the entire brigade's combat power into the airhead. The artillery battalion was slated for the third lift. As a result, its guns would not be in place, ready to fire, until 1000 hours, four hours after Cerro's unit was on the ground. During that initial period, naval gunfire would provide artillery support. The USS *Clancy*, a Butterworth class destroyer, would be in direct support of Cerro's battalion. The battleship USS *Kansas* would also be on call to provide additional support as needed.

Attack helicopters, U.S. Army Apaches and Marine Corps Cobras, were also available as needed, should Cerro's unit be the target of a major Libyan counterattack. They would operate from a forward rearm and refuel point established in the center of the brigade's airhead or defensive perimeter. Finally, aircraft from the carrier *Hornet* provided both close air support and MIG cap, or air superiority.

Finished with his initial briefing, Cerro signaled the 1st Platoon leader to commence his brief back. Squatting down and balancing himself on the heels of his boots, Cerro listened as each principal leader in his company briefed him. He was interested in more than a simple regurgitation of the information he put out. Each platoon leader was expected to explain in detail how he would prepare and organize his platoon and position to accomplish its mission. Cerro mentally checked off each item as the platoon leader discussed the execution of his tasks. Whenever it was appropriate, Cerro made corrections or asked a question if the platoon leader said something that didn't make sense. In this way he made sure that all of his leaders understood their mission, had a plan for executing it, and understood what the other platoons in the company were doing. Only when he was satisfied that everyone understood his role and the roles of the other units in the company did Cerro release them.

The next step, precombat inspections, would take place that afternoon. While Cerro was checking the soldiers and their combat loads, First Sergeant Duncan and the executive officer had to check the loads that would be carried under the helicopters. Those loads included antitank mines, barbed wire, sandbags, five-gallon cans of water, extra rations, antitank guided missiles, small-arms ammunition, and, to assist in hauling these items around, two hummvees.

When everyone had dispersed, Cerro looked at his watch. He considered the timetable he had set up for preparation and inspection. There was more than enough time to do what was necessary, get some sleep, and make the 0545-hour liftoff the following morning. Getting ready and getting there were easy. It was after they got there that things would get interesting.

His first concern was having enough time to prepare his position before the Libyans attacked. His second was holding, once they were attacked, until relieved. Provided the intelligence officer was correct and his planning and the company's preparation were sound, they would have just enough time to prepare their positions. Holding on, however, was as much a matter of luck as it was of preparation. Success would come if he guessed right and the enemy cooperated, hitting Cerro's unit where he expected them. If, however, the enemy did not cooperate and did something unexpected, or showed up in greater strength than expected or earlier than anticipated, things would be rough.

For now, however, there was nothing for him to do. Looking about, Cerro saw his officers and NCOs going about their jobs. Rather than become a nuisance, he decided to find himself a quiet spot and have his breakfast. Walking over to where his rucksack was, Cerro reached down, stuck his hand inside, and rummaged about until he found an MRE. Pulling it out, he looked at the brown plastic bag. When he saw it was chicken à la king, Cerro made a face. It ranked next to the notorious pork pattie. The main course of micro chicken chunks and unidentified green, brown, and red particles were suspended in a tan gravy that had the consistency of vomit. As a joke, First Sergeant Duncan started the rumor that feeding chicken à la king to prisoners of war constituted a war crime. At least, Cerro thought, the crackers and candy would be edible.

Reykjavik, Iceland * 1345 Hours, 20 December

Sitting in a hotel room, surrounded by equipment, suitcases, and clothing that still had store tags hanging from it, Jan Fields prepared for her next story. Originally brought out of Egypt to cover the meeting of the NATO ministers scheduled for 21 December, she was supposed to have a full day to recover and prepare herself. Her arrival in London, however, coincided with the surprise announcement that the President of the United States and the Soviet premier would meet in Reykjavik on the twenty-first. Instead of twenty-four hours, she was given less than four to pick up whatever winter clothing she needed before being rushed off to Iceland.

Caught in the eye of the storm, Jan had not kept up with all of the developments emanating from the conflict in Africa. Though appalled by the alleged use of chemical weapons and condemning Soviet intervention, most European nations had so far remained aloof and uncommitted. Active and increasing participation in the conflict by U.S. naval and ground forces, however, was forcing a decision upon those nations.

Italy, home base of the 6th Fleet, was the first to be drawn in. That government's decision to allow continued use of bases and facilities drew violent criticism from the Italian Communist party and an exchange of angry notes with the Soviet Union. Next came Britain, the home base for the F-111s that had hit Al Fasher. A letter of concern over the use of British bases for American aircraft involved in the war was sent from the premier of the Soviet Union to the British prime minister. The Soviet note was greeted with the announcement that ships of the Royal Navy would join the American 6th Fleet to ensure Egypt's sovereignty and free navigation of the Suez Canal. The Soviet response to the British announcement drew Turkey into the growing conflict. Transfer of ships from the Soviet Black Sea Squadron required traversing the Dardanelles. Turkey, a loyal NATO member, technically could not restrict the movement, as the conflict in Egypt was not a NATO matter. The issue was therefore officially ignored.

The next Soviet move, however, prompted out of necessity by the Al Fasher raid, could not be ignored by Turkey. A Soviet request to the Turkish government for permission for Soviet military aircraft to overfly Turkish air space was denied. In their response the Turkish government reminded the Soviet

Union of preconflict agreements concerning overflights and the number of Aeroflot aircraft that were permitted into Turkish air space. The reaction by the Soviet Union was a harsh response and moves by the Black Sea Squadron that could only be interpreted as threatening.

Unable to maintain total neutrality, NATO called an emergency meeting of its ministers. This act alone, meant to be a low-key affair to discuss the position NATO should take in an open forum, caused concern in the Soviet Union. Within twelve hours of the announcement of the NATO meeting, Warsaw Pact units were placed in a higher state of vigilance. The Soviet move was nothing more than a gesture. As NATO is a military alliance, a military response was used to demonstrate Soviet concerns. Within six hours of the Soviet increase in vigilance, NATO units were ordered to an increased state of vigilance.

Seeing the situation deteriorating, on the nineteenth of December the President of the United States called for a meeting between the principals involved in the conflict. Egypt rejected this proposal out of hand, claiming that it would not negotiate while its 1st Army was being held hostage by Soviet forces. Libya followed suit in rejecting such talks, though its reasoning was questionable and unclear. The American President did not give up. He was determined to take positive action in order to avoid a full-fledged confrontation between the two great powers. In a message to the Soviet premier he insisted that a meeting take place immediately, even if it was just the two of them. That message, carefully leaked to the press corps, was greeted with great enthusiasm worldwide. Lost in that enthusiasm, however, was the President's warning that no agreement would be possible without Egypt's participation or agreement.

Reviewing the draft script and the background information provided by the WNN crew's field producer, Jan was appalled by its lack of depth. There were many words but no complete thoughts, lots of sweeping statements and clichés but no focus. It was as if the field producer were trying to cram the history of the Western world since World War II into a ninety-second news spot. Fay, Jan thought, would never have handed her garbage like that.

The sudden thought of Fay brought Jan's preparation to an abrupt halt. Fay, of course, couldn't help. She was dead. The last time Jan had seen her friend was in a hospital in Cairo, lying on a tile floor in a pool of her own blood, covered by a bloodstained sheet. Fay's death bothered Jan like nothing else she had ever experienced. The revulsion and despair were natural, human reactions. Given the circumstances, they were expected. But what really bothered Jan was her sudden feeling of relief. Fay's death left Jan's life less complicated. Scott Dixon was now unencumbered by a wife, even a divorced one.

That line of logic—so cold, so selfish, so spontaneous—appalled Jan more than anything else. Had she, in her years as a correspondent, become so cynical, so hardened to the horrors and woes of the world around her, that she no longer felt them? Had her training to look at the facts only and treat the human side of tragedy only as an adjunct to a story diminished her own ability to feel?

In the wake of that incident Jan seized the opportunity to go to Britain when it was offered. To stay in Egypt would be too much. Though she had no doubt that she truly loved Scott, she wanted some distance, both temporal and physical, in order to sort out her feelings. When, in calmer times, the opportunity to see Scott again arose, she wanted it to be on her terms, unencumbered by guilt, no longer haunted by the memory of Fay, as a friend or a rival.

20

North of Jebel Kalakh, Egypt * 0330 Hours, 21 December

The massing of helicopters to the south of Task Force 3-5 Armor's forward assembly area woke Dixon. The drone of their engines and the beating of their blades carried for miles through the cold night air. Looking at his watch, Dixon decided to wait a few minutes before rising. Snug and secure in his arctic sleeping bag like a bug in its cocoon and perched on top of his tank's turret, Dixon felt like he was alone.

Through an opening no bigger than his face, he looked up at the stars. He had been born and raised in a city, so the dazzling display of stars that filled the desert sky always fascinated him. This morning was no different. For a few minutes Dixon allowed himself to be entertained by the spectacle created by suns and universes that were beyond his reach and comprehension. Other worlds, so different from his, lived and died in the cluster of lights that spanned from horizon to horizon. Gazing into infinity and having it look back at him eye to eye struck Dixon with awe. Though it all had a purpose, a beginning and an end, the universe that looked down on him betrayed no secrets. There was no reason why, no explanation. There was only the immense and overpowering presence of a universe that touched everyone and defied being touched by something so mortal as man.

In a few short hours he would be leading an armor heavy task force into battle. He would again, after a two-year void command men in battle. Those efforts would block his idle thoughts from his mind as effectively as the earth's sun would soon hide the stars. But in the end, at night, the stars would be back. And anything he and his men did was temporary, transient. Neither he nor any of his men had a claim to immortality. Neither he nor his men could ever hope to fully understand why they were there, or even why they were so willing to risk their lives. Though all of them asked the question and were given reasons, Dixon knew the responses were reasons, not explanations. In the end, he knew, nothing could explain, with any degree of satisfaction, why his wife had been taken from him. He knew that regardless of what he did, men in his command would die that day. And despite his best efforts, he himself would someday be called by his maker to atone for his deeds, good and evil. Until then he was on his own, left wandering through a maze of time and events that had no clear course, no discernible end.

With a tug at the end of Dixon's sleeping bag, the gunner of his tank indicated it was time to rise. There would be little time for himself over the next few days. Command in war, like no other occupation, touches and draws on every fiber and nerve of the man who wears its cloak. For some the experience is draining, literally drawing the life force from the man. For others it is not only invigorating, it is life itself. In his heart, despite his best efforts to deny it, Dixon knew he was born to command. Without it he was nothing, just another man existing in the eyes of the stars. With it he was alive. He had purpose. When his day of atonement came, he would stand alone before his God. He would need no explanations, no reasons. His life and his deeds, open to all, would justify his existence.

Pulling down the long, wide zipper of the sleeping bag, Dixon sat up and began to dress. Two hours and it would begin. He was ready.

**East of Sidi Abd el Rahman ★ 0730 Hours,
21 December**

In unison the guns of a 155mm artillery battery commenced
firing at targets to the west. Awakened by them, Colonel Hafez
sat up and looked around. He was as surprised by the fact that
it was day as he was by the presence and firing of the guns.
Throwing off a blanket that someone had covered him with,
Hafez stood on the back deck of his tank and looked around.
All about his position were the tanks, personnel carriers, and
howitzers of the Republican Brigade. They were scattered in a
loose and ill-defined circle, guns pointing out. Inside the circle
were trucks, jeeps, and other support vehicles.

For a moment he collected his thoughts. He had a headache
that was due as much to sleeping on the steel deck of the tank
as to lack of sleep. Still, it was the best night's sleep he had
managed to get in the last five days. About him he could see his
soldiers going about their tasks, preparing for their next operation. While there was not a great deal of haste, nor could the
level of activity be called a buzz, at least they were working.
Several fuel trucks were pumping fuel into tanks or moving to
their next customer. Soldiers lined up like chains of ants passed
ammunition from cargo trucks onto their vehicles. On board and
around those vehicles that had completed their rearming and refueling or were waiting to do so, soldiers adjusted the tension of
their tank's tracks, cleaned machine guns, or went on with some
check or service. With great satisfaction Hafez knew that his
forty-two tanks, company-and-a-half of infantry, and two batteries of artillery would soon be ready for combat again.

What concerned him were the guns near his position. The
battery of 155mm guns continued to unleash volley after volley
of shells to the southwest. When he had gone to sleep, the
nearest Libyan unit had been thirty kilometers from the spot
where the Republican Brigade sat. The fact that the 155mm
guns, with a range of eighteen kilometers, were firing meant
that the Libyans were closer. Obviously, some time in the night
or early morning, the Libyans had attacked and broken through
somewhere.

Hafez was about to climb down from the deck of the tank and go over to the personnel carrier that served as his command post when a captain came running from that carrier toward him. Seeing Hafez awake and watching him, the captain waved a piece of paper and yelled that they had orders from Division. Kneeling down, Hafez retrieved the paper from the captain and read it.

As he had expected, there was a major attack in progress. Though the commander of the 3rd Armored Division expected to be able to halt the Libyan thrust with organic units, he was issuing a warning order to Hafez just in case. The order instructed Hafez to move his brigade, when he was ready, to a position south of Sidi Abd el Rahman. From there he was to be prepared to attack either to the south, toward Tell el Aqqaqir, or to the west, to El Kharash. The attack south would be launched if the 10th Mechanized Division required assistance in sealing off a penetration that threatened them. The attack to the west—the one Hafez hoped for—was the opening move of the counteroffensive. It was the intent of the commander of the 2nd Army to attack as soon as the Libyan forces committed had expended all their offensive power and before they had the opportunity to switch over to the defense. Timed properly, the Egyptian blow would hit the Libyans when they were still disorganized and not yet recovered from the shock of their defeat.

Handing the message back to the captain, Hafez told him to have all commanders meet him at the command post track in thirty minutes. When the captain was gone, Hafez stood up and looked around. He made note of the activity in his unit's perimeter and tried to estimate how long it would be before they could move. As he did so, he listened to the guns, not only those near his position but those in the distance. He made a mental note of how loud they were. In thirty minutes, if they were no louder, he would tell his commanders to stop all preparation and begin to move. If, on the other hand, the noise of the distant battle had not changed, he would have them continue their work. He hoped he would be able to tell them the latter. He was ready to attack, to hit the Libyans back. The sooner they struck, the sooner the 1st Army would be freed.

Ras el Kenayis, Egypt * 0845 Hours, 21 December

Regardless of where Cerro went along the edge of the escarpment, he could hear First Sergeant Duncan's voice. "Come on! Come on, sweethearts! Let's see some hustlin' over there. It ain't the bleedin' Salvation Army that's comin' up the road after you. Let's go—let's get motivated here and do some serious mine laying." Given the task of emplacing the hasty protective mine fields, Duncan was everywhere, directing and supervising. In some cases he had to show the soldiers on the detail the proper techniques for arming the mines. It wasn't that they weren't trained; the men on the detail had all had refresher training the day before. Fear, anticipation of battle, and haste, however, can crowd a man's head, multiplying the number of thumbs he has to work with. At these times it is the mission of the NCO and officer to ensure that their soldiers are held to task and doing those things for which they were trained and that will allow them to succeed—and survive.

In front of the position Duncan was doing just that. By example, encouragement, and direction, he was ensuring that the antitank mines were sited, emplaced, and armed properly. On the escarpment First Lieutenant George Prentice, the company XO, was busy moving ammunition and supplies around to the proper locations with one of the two hummvees. Cerro himself was walking from position to position with the platoon leader responsible for the positions. This was his third tour of the morning.

On the first tour Cerro simply had reconfirmed his initial platoon and antitank positions. He wanted to make sure that the planned positions, plotted on a map, conformed to the realities of the actual ground. On the second trip Cerro took his time and looked at each position, now being dug, to make sure that the positions were mutually supporting. He also looked for dead space to his front and flanks. When he saw such a spot, where direct-fire weapons couldn't engage an approaching enemy due to a fold in the earth or a small wadi, Cerro took action to cover it. In most cases he turned to his fire support officer, or FIST chief, and directed that an artillery target be plotted on the dead spot. In some cases Cerro directed the platoon leader responsible for that sector to shift one or more positions or weapons to cover the dead spot. Without fail the soldiers, often nearly done digging their first position, moaned and groaned when told they had to dig a new one. And without fail they did so, knowing that if they didn't, they'd lose their asses, if not to the Libyans, then to Cerro.

By 0830 Cerro had begun to make his third tour. Most positions were finished. Those soldiers not on other details were busy improving their positions. These inspections and checks were to the accompaniment of explosions in the distance. Naval gunfire and an occasional screech of a high-performance jet screaming overhead reminded Cerro and his men that this was not a simple training exercise. In Fuka, less than ten miles to the east, a Libyan armored brigade sat. Everyone had expected that brigade, a unit recovering from earlier battles, to attack quickly in order to eliminate the airhead. Since landing, however, the only contact Cerro's unit had had been when a pair of BRDM armored recon vehicles came thundering down the coastal road. Both had been chased off by scout helicopters, which destroyed one of them in the process. Other than that, Cerro's men had seen nothing of the enemy. Looking to the east, Cerro studied the pillars of smoke rising in the distance. The Libyans had not been so fortunate. The Navy and the 1st of the 11th Attack Helicopter Battalion had been working the Libyans over without letup. If they never saw a Libyan tank, that would be all right in Cerro's book. Though he was confident that they would be able to hold, Cerro felt no burning desire to put that theory to test.

Turning away from the east, Cerro began to go back to his inspection, only to be interrupted by an overflight of Apaches. He paused and looked up. Two OH-58C Scout helicopters, with four AH-64 Apaches on their heels, thundered overhead, headed to the east. The pylons of Apaches were heavily ladened with Hellfire missiles. They were after tanks. Cerro watched, waving as the helicopters went by in a symbolic send-off. *"Give 'em hell!"*

*   *   *

Mennzinger watched the infantryman below them wave. He returned the wave before turning his full attention back to the east. Over the radio the tactical air controller called the leader of a flight of Navy A-6 Intruders. He notified them that the USS *Clancy* had ceased firing, allowing the A-6s to roll in and commence their attack. They were going after an armor formation forming southwest of Fuka, the same one Mennzinger and his company were after.

It wasn't even nine o'clock and they were on their third mission of the day. Already the company was down two aircraft. One had been left in Egypt due to an engine failure. The second one was back at the rearm/refuel point. Hit by small-arms fire on its last mission, every other warning light was flashing. It would be a while before it was up and ready. At least, Mennzinger thought, they hadn't lost any of the crews yet. That was something. Question was, however, who would give out first, the remaining crews or the aircraft. Sooner or later they would have to stand down to rest the crews and let the mechanics pull some maintenance on the aircraft. One could only run a surge operation for so long before both men and machines burned out. A sixteen-million-dollar helicopter that went in because the pilot was tired and made an error in judgment was just as dead as a helicopter shot down by a surface-to-air missile. Mennzinger knew that at some point they would have to hand the battle off to the men on the ground.

The deciding factor would be time. So long as the Libyans weren't given the time to mass and stage a deliberate attack, the soldiers of the 2nd Brigade, 11th Air Assault Division would hold. So long as the airhead held, the tanks of the 16th Armored Division could make it. It was Mennzinger's job, as well as the Navy's, to make sure the Libyans didn't have time to mount a full-scale attack and the 16th Armored Division had time to cover the distance from Jebel Kalakh to Ras el Kenayis. In the end, it was the units of the 16th Armored Division that would determine whether the operation was a success or failure. The heavy forces, going toe to toe with the Libyans, would be the final arbitrator. Until then Mennzinger had to make time.

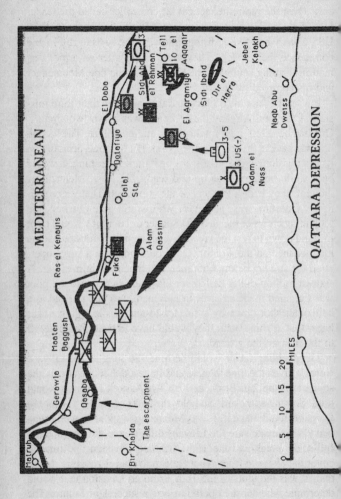

MEDITERRANEAN

Matruh

Gerawla

Maaten Baggush

Ras el Kenays

El Daba

Sidi Abd
el Rahman

Tell
el Aqqaqir

El Agramiya

Sidi Ibeid

Dir el
Harra

Jebel
Kalakh

Qasaba

Bir Khalda

The escarpment

Fuka

Alam
Qassim

Qotafiya

Galal
Sta.

Adam el
Nuss

Naqb Abu
Dweiss

QATTARA DEPRESSION

MILES
0   5   10   15   20

3
10

3-5

3 US(-)

Southwest of El Agramiya, Egypt * 0905 Hours, 21 December

The order to swing his task force north and engage a Libyan armored force coming south was greeted by Dixon with little fanfare, little emotion. He had been expecting it. The trail element of the brigade, Dixon's task force had the mission of attacking or blocking any Libyan forces that threatened the brigade's flank.

The Libyan force, fifteen miles to the northeast, had been found by a scout helicopter screening the brigade's flank. Operating in relays so as not to expose themselves for too long, other scout helicopters of the division's air cav troop began to shadow the Libyan force. Given information about the Libyan brigade, including its approximate size, location, direction of travel, and speed, Dixon decided to remain in diamond formation. That formation provided him the best all-round security and the most flexibility. Regardless of how they ran into the Libyans, only one unit would make initial contact. That would leave Dixon the freedom to maneuver the rest of the task force as he saw fit.

Traveling with B Company, Dixon issued a short frag order to the task force. In effect, all he did was change the direction of their movement from the west to the north. Along with that shift, a battery of 155mm self-propelled guns from the 5th of the 8th Field Artillery Battalion also dropped off and followed the task force.

From his tank Dixon watched the task force pivot to the north. Operating from a tank in the middle of the formation had several disadvantages that made themselves quite evident as the turning movement progressed. In a position no higher than that of any other tank commander in the task force, Dixon could see no more from his tank than the most junior tank commander could. His view obscured by dust, distance, and the flatness of the terrain, Dixon could see at best half a dozen other vehicles. Most of those belonged to B Company, to his front, and the engineer platoon, to his rear. C Company, to his right, and A Company, to the left, were great clouds of dust.

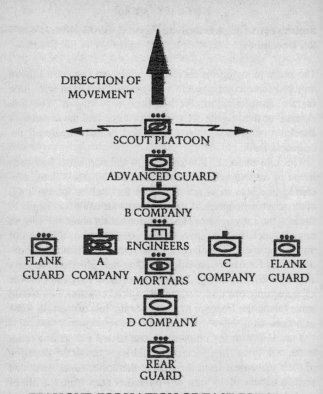

DIRECTION OF
MOVEMENT

SCOUT PLATOON

ADVANCED GUARD

B COMPANY

ENGINEERS

FLANK
GUARD

A
COMPANY

MORTARS

C
COMPANY

FLANK
GUARD

D COMPANY

REAR
GUARD

**DIAMOND FORMATION OF TASK FORCE 3-5
ARMOR, 0900 HOURS, 21 DECEMBER**

Only occasionally was a tank or Bradley from those units visible to Dixon. D Company, the mortars, the scout platoon, and all the flank guards were beyond Dixon's field of vision.

To see the battlefield, therefore, Dixon depended upon his company commanders and their platoon leaders. He would base his decisions and orders on their reports. If they were accurate and timely, Dixon would have time to maneuver the uncommitted companies into position to engage the enemy. If the reports were bad, erroneous, or, worse, nonexistent, the task force would blunder forward like a blind man, bumping into whatever lay in its path. Of all Dixon's concerns, this was the greatest. His experiences with such matters ran the gamut from very good to pitiful. With less than two days to work with the company commanders of 3-5 Armor, he had little time to assess their abilities and virtually none to train them in his way of making war. Whatever strengths and weaknesses they had when Dixon walked in were the ones that would make or break the unit once contact was gained.

Standing high in the open hatch of his tank, higher than was prudent, Dixon looked to his left and right. All appeared in order. B Company was now headed north. A Company was coming up fast to complete its wide turn. C Company was resuming normal speed after holding back while the rest of the task force pivoted on them. Behind him, the engineer platoon came trundling forward in their ancient M-113 armored personnel carriers. Outside of that Dixon knew nothing. He assumed that the rest of the task force was following suit. For a moment he considered checking with them on the radio, but he opted against that. Radio listening silence, except for extreme emergencies or contact, was still in effect. So Dixon let it go. After all, he had to show some confidence in the leadership of the task force.

Easing down into the open hatch, Dixon settled himself for the march north. The ground they were traversing was stony and flat, making the ride relatively smooth. The driver, hatch closed and buttoned up, did his best to avoid the occasional big rock or gully but he couldn't avoid them all. When he hit one, the tank would rock or lurch forward, throwing the unwary crewmen about. Like a modern version of the medieval knight, Dixon stood upright in the hatch, swaying with the occasional gentle rock of the tank as he went forth in search of his enemy. His crewman's helmet was pulled down to the midpoint of his forehead, its strap snugly buttoned under his chin. Goggles covered his eyes, while a yellow bandanna, usually wrapped about his neck, was pulled up over his nose and mouth, and the hood of his Goretex jacket was pulled up and over his helmet. Except for a small opening for the cord that connected Dixon's helmet to the radio and intercom, the jacket's collar was zipped

up, and fastened under his chin. With all this, and a pair of
black Goretex gloves, he was protected from the sand thrown
up by the tracks of his own tank and the others around him as
well as from the cold.

The caliber .50 machine gun sitting in front of Dixon,
slightly off center and to the right, was, by itself, an impressive
weapon. On an M-1A1 Abrams tank, however, it is only the
secondary weapon. The smooth-bore 120mm main gun pro-
truding from the front of the turret like a great heavy lance was
the true voice of the M-1A1. Its design was based on that of the
German Rhein Metal gun used in the West German Leopard II.
When engaging enemy tanks, it launched an armor piercing fin
stabilize discarding sabot round at over five thousand feet, or
roughly one mile, per second. This gun was coupled to a fire
control system that took into account such factors as wind
velocity at the tank's location, air temperature, ammunition
temperature, cant of the tank, gun tube wear, tank-to-target
range, and speed and motion of the M-1A1 and the target. To
move the gun and its sixty-three tons the tank was powered
by a turbine engine that put out fifteen hundred horsepower
and delivered a governed top speed of forty-five miles an hour.

Anyone who ever had the opportunity to command such a
weapons platform could understand the sheer childlike joy that
tankers took when moving out smartly in *their* tanks. And
because he took great pleasure from this seemingly unnatural
act, Scott Dixon was immediately part of the task force, one of
them. He didn't yet know the men by name, and hardly by
sight. But they had a common bond, Dixon and all the other
tank commanders of the task force. Their love of their tanks
and their pride in being able to put steel on target with the first
round while moving at thirty miles an hour transcended all
ranks and ages. Whether he was a company commander, or the
newly commissioned platoon leader, or one of the hard-core
E-7 platoon sergeants, a tank commander was a tank commander. Riding with the other commanders into combat, following the lead company and standing tall in the turret, Dixon
displayed his willingness to lead, his confidence as a tanker; he
wore his spurs proudly.

Fifteen minutes after the brigade order sent Dixon's task force racing to the north, the scout helicopter reported that the Libyan force and Dixon's task force were closing. Coming over the auxiliary radio in his tank, Dixon prepared to respond but was beaten to it by the task force XO, Major Grissins, moving with the TOC. Grissins then put out a call over the task force command net, repeating the information for the company commanders. Each of them in turn responded by acknowledging the information.

Grissins, traveling to the rear of the formation, handled routine reporting from the TOC. Designated the second in command, or 2IC, he did everything to coordinate the staff and combat support elements so that Dixon, up front with the main force, could fight the battle. The task force S-3, in his tank and traveling with D Company, was prepared to assume command of the battle should Dixon lose communications or become combat ineffective. In armored combat that happened frequently. When in contact, the task force commander was often faced with the need to fight his tank or die. Control of the task force therefore passed back and forth according to who was most capable of directing the battle. There would be times when the task force S-3 had control, until he, like the commander, reverted to the role of tank commander. During the same period, the actual task force commander would come up on the net and resume control. The task force XO, sitting back out of the fight, kept track of the battle. When neither the commander nor the S-3 could, the XO commanded. If the commander, after a long absence on the command net, came back up on the net, the XO would give him a quick update and pass command and control back to him. Flexibility, an agile mind, and the ability to understand what was happening in a fight that could involve over a hundred armored vehicles fighting and moving in a ten-square-mile area were the keys to controlling a modern tank battle.

With contact imminent, Dixon could feel himself getting

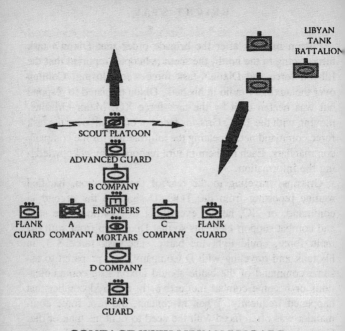

LIBYAN
TANK
BATTALION

SCOUT PLATOON

ADVANCED GUARD

B COMPANY

ENGINEERS

FLANK
GUARD

A
COMPANY

MORTARS

C
COMPANY

FLANK
GUARD

D COMPANY

REAR
GUARD

CONTACT WITH LIBYAN BRIGADE

pumped up. Turning to his left, then his right, then all the way around to the rear, he checked to ensure that the formation, at least where he was, was ready. Feeling the need to say something to his commanders before battle, Dixon reached up and pushed the switch on the side of his crewman's helmet forward, activating the radio transmitter. His message was short and all business. He reminded all units that the first unit in contact was to be the base of fire, regardless who it was. The rest of the task force would maneuver on that company. Reports, Dixon reminded them, had to be quick, accurate, and complete.

Satisfied that all was in order, Dixon moved the switch to the rear position, activating the intercom on his tank. He was in the process of going over prepare-to-fire checks with his gunner and loader when the C Company commander reported contact with a Libyan tank platoon.

Though his voice betrayed excitement and some confusion, the C Company executive officer provided all the information that Dixon needed to begin wheeling the task force into action. The Libyan force, coming out of the northeast, had hit C Company's flank guard platoon. That platoon was already deploying and preparing to return fire. The rest of C Company was doing likewise, forming up on either side of the flank guard platoon. Over the roar of his own tank's engine and through the earphones of his crewman's helmet, Dixon could hear the muffled crack of tank guns firing. They were in contact. The battle was joined.

From his position Dixon could see the tanks of C Company that had been to his right begin to veer off to the east. They were deploying. The tanks of B Company, to his front, were

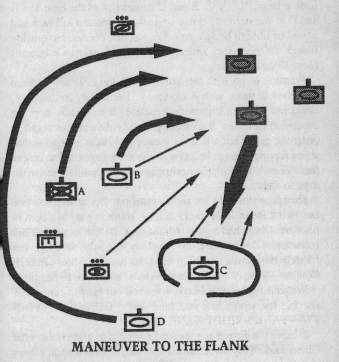

MANEUVER TO THE FLANK

continuing forward, to the north. Without giving the problem much thought, Dixon contacted the B Company commander and ordered him to swing his company to the right, maintaining contact with C Company. Dixon stressed the need to maintain contact: the last thing he wanted was to have his own companies disappear into clouds of dust, get lost, and then pop out and be engaged by another American unit.

With two companies deploying almost head-on, Dixon decided to swing wide with the other two. Both B and C companies, twenty-eight tanks total, should be more than a match for the three Libyan companies with no more than thirty tanks total. It was the second and third Libyan battalions that Dixon was after with his remaining two companies. His idea was to form a large "L" with B and C companies as the base and A and D as the stem. By doing so he would create a kill sack and would be able to bring a crossfire onto the enemy. He quickly issued the necessary orders and received acknowledgments from all commanders.

Wanting to go with the maneuvering force, Dixon ordered his driver to move with A Company. The driver, buttoned up, could not see A Company's Bradleys. Rather than stop, he continued to follow B Company's tanks. Dixon was about to order the driver left when the gunner yelled out a target acquisition report. Though he knew it was more important to ensure that the task force deploy properly, Dixon couldn't resist the urge to fight.

Dropping down to his sight extension, Dixon saw not one but two Libyan T-62 tanks rolling south. From his current position, Dixon had a good oblique shot. Before issuing his fire command, Dixon stuck his head up to make sure another friendly tank wasn't about to mask his fire. Two tanks from B Company were close. To get two shots, he'd have to be quick.

Without further ado Dixon screamed out his fire command, slurring the words into one long one. "GUNNER-SABOT-TWO-TANKS-RIGHT-TANK-FIRST!"

Neither the gunner nor the loader needed to understand what Dixon said. They were drilled and ready. Dixon hadn't even said the word "tank" before the gunner screeched "IDENTI-FIED!" and the loader yelled "UP!"

With the word "up" still ringing in his ear, Dixon yelled "FIRE!" and immediately stuck his head out of the hatch.

There was a pause while the gunner made a final lay on the target and relased. Ready, he screamed, "ON-THE-WAAAY!"

When the gunner hit the *y* of "way," he squeezed the trigger. The 120mm gun discharged the round in the chamber, sending a quick jolt through the tank. Upon leaving the gun tube, the projectile released the propellant gases which created a muzzle blast that blew up a great cloud of dust and dirt, obscuring Dixon's tank and the tanks they were firing at. In the driver's compartment, the driver's vision was momentarily obscured, forcing him to drive blind. He was ready for that, however. As the gunner announced "On the way," the driver had made a mental image of the next fifty meters of ground and drove across it, in the dust cloud, on faith alone.

The momentum of the tank, and a wind blowing from north to south, quickly cleared the dust and dirt. The gun, held on the first target by the gunner and the tank's stabilization system, was pointing at a burning hulk. Without another thought Dixon issued his subsequent fire command, again slurring his words. "TARGET-FIRST-TANK-LEFT-TANK-FIRE!"

Again the gunner and loader stumbled over each other on the intercom as the gunner announced "Identified!" and the loader "Up!" As before, the gunner paused, relaid his sight's aiming dot onto the new target, lased, yelled "On the way!" and fired. As soon as Dixon's tank emerged from its own dust cloud, the picture of a burning tank filled the gunner's sight. "WE GOT HIM! WE GOT HIM!"

Masking his own joy, Dixon responded with a simple, matter-of-fact "Target, cease fire." That was, for Dixon, the extent of the celebration. He had had his fun as a tank commander. Now he had to get back to being the task force commander. Looking to his left and right in order to get his bearings, he was surprised to find himself out in front of B Company. The three tanks he saw to his left and right, marked with three white bands on their gun tubes, told him he was with the 3rd Platoon of B Company. All three were straining to catch up with their task force commander. Further to the left, more B Company tanks were moving to catch up with the 3rd Platoon tanks. In his haste to kill Libyans, Dixon had unwittingly dragged the whole B Company line forward with him.

Keying the radio, Dixon contacted the B Company commander, ordering him to halt his forward movement and form a base of fire. Conforming with Dixon's last order and following Dixon's tank, the B Company commander had pivoted on C Company instead of pulling abreast of it. In effect, that move took B Company out of the base of the "L" and put it in the stem. Dixon considered this, then decided to go with the situation as it was. It would serve no good purpose to have B Company back up. They were in good firing positions where they were. Best to leave them there.

Ordering his driver to hold, Dixon let the rest of B Company sweep by before turning his tank to the left and in search of A Company. As Dixon's tank moved north, behind the line of B Company tanks, Dixon watched them engage the Libyans. From the reports from both B and C companies' XOs, there was not much left of the Libyan tank battalion. Those tanks that were left were thrashing about in a kill sack swept by the crossfires of B and C companies.

Dixon saw in the distance a pair of Bradleys from A Company racing to join B Company. He had no sooner ordered his driver to head for the two Bradleys than the scout platoon leader reported that a mix of Libyan BMP infantry fighting vehicles and tanks was coming up on the right of the remains of the Libyan tank battalion. Sheer luck, Dixon thought— nothing but sheer luck was bringing the rest of his task force into position just as a Libyan mechanized unit was coming into action. And the fact that his Bradleys were going head to head with BMPs was icing on the cake. The 25mm Chain Gun of A Company's Bradleys would make short work of the Soviet-built BMPs while D Company took on the tanks.

Dixon joined the Bradleys just as the commander of A Company reported that he saw the approaching BMPs and was pre-

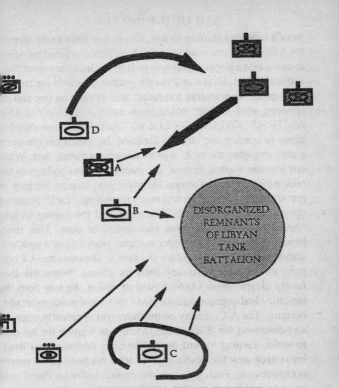

**FOLLOW-ON ATTACK BY LIBYAN
MECHANIZED BATTALION**

paring to engage. Wanting maximum effort, Dixon ordered the
D Company commander to continue his swing to the left, ensuring that he maintained contact with C Company. When the D
Company commander gave Dixon a wilco, Dixon contacted the
B Company commander, ordering him to shift the fires of at
least one platoon to the northeast onto the approaching BMPs.
Dixon finished his latest frag order by instructing B Company
and C Company to finish the Libyan tank battalion and be prepared to move once the third Libyan battalion was found.

With the task force completing its maneuvers and A Com-

445

pany's Bradleys starting to fire, Dixon had little to do. Seeing the A Company commander's Bradley, Dixon ordered his driver to move into a slight depression next to it. Once they were there and had halted, Dixon ordered his gunner to search for targets. His gunner, anticipating the order, was already on one and responded with a sharp acquisition report. "ENEMY TANK AND BMP! TWELVE O'CLOCK!" As before, Dixon dropped down to confirm the targets. Satisfied, he issued his fire command, engaging the tank, a more dangerous threat, first. Without a single wasted motion, the gunner laid his sight onto the tank while the loader armed the main gun, cleared the path of recoil, and announced he was ready by yelling "UP!" Standing upright in the open hatch, Dixon ordered the gunner to fire.

As before, the tank was enshrouded in dust. This time however, the dust took longer to clear, since Dixon's tank was stationary. As they waited for the dust to disperse, the A Company commander's Bradley fired its 25mm. When the dust finally cleared from Dixon's field of vision, he saw both the tank they had engaged and the BMP they were going to hit next burning. The A Company commander had apparently engaged and destroyed the BMP while Dixon was waiting for his dust to settle. Turning toward the A Company commander's Bradley, Dixon saw the young captain stick his head up to survey his handiwork. Facing Dixon, the captain had what could only be described as a shit-eating grin from ear to ear. Dixon smiled, nodded his head, and gave the captain a thumbs-up. The A Company commander returned the thumbs-up, then dropped down to search out more targets.

Boosting himself up onto the seat of his stand, Dixon stood as high as he could in order to survey the situation. To his left, or the north, he could see D Company coming on line, engaging the Libyan mechanized battalion as it did so. A Company's Bradleys were pumping round after round at the Libyan BMPs with telling effect. Here and there a Bradley let loose a TOW antitank guided missile at a distant Libyan tank. From behind them artillery rounds from the direct-support 155mm artillery battery screamed overhead. The artillery rounds—mostly improved conventional munitions and similar to the Air Force cluster bombs—scattered hundreds of tiny armor-piercing bomblets into the midst of the shattered Libyan formations.

As Dixon watched and assessed the situation, from C Company, then B Company, came the report that the Libyan tank battalion had been destroyed. Dixon considered moving both of those companies forward to join the fight but decided not to. The Libyan mechanized battalion had only a few minutes left. The only thing Dixon did do was to order the B Company commander to reposition the rest of his company to join in the engagement of the mechanized battalion. That order, however, was really unnecessary. Looking to his right, Dixon could see B Company tanks moving and swinging to the right, pivoting on A Company. Though that maneuver would mask C Company, Dixon did not stop it. He could now use C Company as his reserve force, maneuvering it as soon as the third Libyan battalion was identified.

Reminding himself that the fight wasn't over, Dixon contacted Grissins at the task force TOC, instructing him to get with the task force intel officer and the air scouts to find out where the third battalion was. No sooner had Grissins acknowledged Dixon's message than the task force forward air controller provided the answer. An Air Force captain who was the forward air controller followed the task force commander in an M-113 armored personnel carrier equipped with special radios, or FAC. Coming up on the net, he reported that two flights of A-16 ground attack aircraft had bounced the third battalion, a tank battalion, accompanied by an artillery battalion, before they had deployed. What was left of those two battalions was last seen by the A-16 pilots headed back north.

For a moment Dixon thought about pursuing the Libyans. He quickly dismissed that option, however. He had been ordered only to find and block the Libyan brigade. With two battalions wiped out and the third decimated and in retreat, the Libyan brigade posed no threat to the 3rd U.S. Brigade. Besides, if he pursued, Dixon would be moving into the sector belonging to the Egyptian 10th Mechanized Infantry Division. Since they weren't expecting him and he had no way of contacting them, such a move could lead to a fire fight with friendly forces.

Instead, he waited until all firing stopped. When all the companies reported that there was nothing left to engage, Dixon issued a new set of frag orders. The scout platoon was to screen to the north, watching in case the third battalion had a change of heart or more Libyan forces came down from the north. D Company was ordered to make a quick sweep of the battlefield, ensuring that there were no live tanks or BMPs mixed in with the dead ones. The other companies were ordered to stand fast where they were, reconsolidate, evacuate the wounded, and recover damaged vehicles.

The battle was over. The grim task of caring for the wounded and counting the dead now began.

Ras el Kenayis, Egypt * 1745 Hours, 21 December

Word that the 3rd Armored Brigade had made contact with the 2nd Brigade's airhead south of Cerro's position was greeted with mixed emotions. The young soldiers who had never seen combat were disappointed. First Lieutenant Prentice, noting that they had not had any contact all day, was bitter. "What was the point," he lamented, "in expending all this effort if we don't get to kill anything?" Cerro thought about talking to him about his attitude but decided not to. Later, when they were well rested, he would point out the grim realities of life, trying to impress upon Prentice that an operation such as this one, which achieved its goal without a major fight, was a double success: the enemy had been beaten with a maneuver, not a blood bath.

Neither officer, however, appreciated the fact that the link-up of the two American brigades did not mean the battle was over. Less than an hour before, the Egyptian commander, sensing that the Libyan attacks had run their course, ordered the 3rd Armored and the 10th Mechanized to commence the counter-offensive. Forty miles to the east, in the gathering darkness, a massive artillery barrage announced the beginning of that attack.

The Libyan forces were finished. After a day of attacking, they had been unable to penetrate the Egyptian line at Sidi Abd el Rahman. The air assault at Ras el Kenayis had severed their main line of communications with Libya and consumed their last reserve brigade at Fuka. With American forces operating at will on their exposed southern flank, pounding from the air and the sea without letup, the Libyans' collapse was inevitable and swift. Exhaustion, coupled with irregular rations, little water, and a loss of confidence, added to the general panic that ran through the ranks. Singly or in small groups, the Libyans abandoned their equipment and began to stream back to the west. Efforts by their officers—those who weren't fleeing themselves—to stem the westward tide were futile. The preparatory bombardment only served to hasten the slow and convince the few who had remained loyal up to that point to flee.

Leading the advance of the Republican Brigade from the vanguard, Colonel Hafez found the fleeing Libyans and the scores of vehicles they abandoned a great hindrance. At first his units engaged every Libyan they saw on sight. Soon, however, they discovered that doing so only slowed them down and wasted ammunition. Many of the Libyans tried to surrender. Hafez, however, didn't have the time for delays or surrender. His orders were to move fast, by passing resistance when and where necessary.

He therefore ordered his commanders to ignore any group of Libyans that offered no resistance and didn't appear to be a threat. He reminded them that their objective was not an impressive body count but the relief of the 1st Army. Ammunition was not to be squandered on defeated Libyans. It would be needed later, he told them, when they came into contact with the Russians sitting at Halfaya Pass and Sollum.

21

Policy is the intelligent faculty, war is only the instrument, not the reverse. The subordination of the military view to the political is, therefore, the only thing possible.

—KARL VON CLAUSEWITZ, *On War*

Reykjavik, Iceland * 1805 Hours, 20 December

Jan's mood was as dark and as cold as the Icelandic night. Even in the warm and friendly hotel an oppressive pall hung over her, tainting her conversation and clouding her face with a permanent frown. During dinner, in a room better than half-full with correspondents and other members of news teams, the only sounds she heard were the voices in her head telling her that she didn't belong there. Jan's move to the bar after dinner did nothing to shake her gloom or drive her thoughts for long from the one person she wanted so badly to be with, to touch, to hold. The idea that she might never see Scott Dixon again hadn't struck home until she was out of Egypt. Rather than providing an escape, her departure from Cairo only served to drive home to her, and everyone who knew her, how much she was in love.

As she sipped a screwdriver, Jan gave little thought to the short and almost secretive meeting between the American President and the Soviet premier. Though there had been no accord or agreement announced, the feeling was that some type of political solution was in the making. The two world leaders had left, trailing in their wakes rumors and hopes. All official statements and news reports that night were tempered with a cautionary note that much work remained to be done behind closed doors before the world would know if it was to be peace or war.

From the lobby, a tall blond man in his mid-forties entered the bar and looked around. A correspondent for the French National News Agency, he and Jan had once had an affair while she was assigned to WNN's Paris news bureau. Seeing Jan, he walked over and took a seat opposite her. Jan looked up. "I ordered you a scotch on the rocks," she said, indicating a drink on the table.

The man took the drink and downed it clean in one gulp. For a moment he held the glass and stared at it. "You should have ordered me a double." There was only a hint of a French accent in his voice.

Jan hesitated, waiting for him to continue. He didn't. He only sat in his chair, slouched down, looking at the empty glass as he slowly twisted it about in one hand. His silence was unbearable. "Well?" she finally asked.

Moving only his head, he looked up at Jan. "Yes, and no. While I was on the phone to our office in Paris, they were announcing that all crossing points, air corridors, and rail service into and out of West Berlin were still open, but"—he looked down at his glass—"Soviet forces are still very much in presence along the roads and at selected crossing points. Maneuvers, according to the Soviet embassy."

Turning to the bar, he lifted his glass and ordered a double. He waited for the cocktail waitress to bring him his second drink before he spoke again. "What do you suppose your President is up to?"

Jan thought for a moment, then shook her head before answering. "I don't really know, Paul. He's already ordered American ground forces to hold east of Matruh in order to avoid a clash with the Russians at Halfaya. Air and naval operations—at least American air and naval operations—against Soviet and Cuban forces are suspended. There is little more that he can do unless he can convince the Egyptian president to also stand down."

"And what, dear Jan, is the likelihood of that?"

Jan took a sip of her screwdriver before answering. "That depends on how reasonable the Soviets are willing to be. They, after all, have an entire Egyptian army surrounded in Libya. You don't think the Egyptians are going to agree to anything so long as the Russians have them by the—" Remembering how Paul became flustered when women cursed, Jan paused just short of saying "balls." "Well, you know."

Paul smirked. "Yes, I know. And I see your vocabulary has changed very little since Paris. . . . So you think it is up to the premier? As usual, I disagree. For a start, your President could lift the blockade on Libya. That, after all, is the pretext of the premier's threat to blockade American forces in Berlin and the continued encirclement of the 1st Egyptian Army. No, there is still much room for each side to give."

Jan became defensive, almost hostile. "You know as well as I do, that excuse is only a pretext. What the premier wants is to frighten NATO and the rest of Europe into forcing us to abandon Egypt."

Paul let out a chuckle. "Well, it seems the premier has succeeded. I doubt if there's a politician in Europe that isn't *very* concerned. After all, our friend from Moscow, in a single, bold move, has told Europe, 'You have a choice—America or glasnost.' If you were a European, how would you vote?"

Her voice rose higher. "Well, I'm not a European, and Egypt is a sovereign nation, not a client state. We cannot simply order them to stop. We can no more control them, ordering them to do whatever pleases us, than the Soviets can control the Libyans."

Paul sat back in his chair, raising his hands in mock surrender. "Janet, don't shoot me. I'm an ally. I understand." He let her simmer down before he asked her again. "What will your President do if their efforts here, whatever they were, come to nothing?"

Jan had calmed down; her response was less hostile. "We will do just as we did in 1948 and 1962 if the Russians really do close Berlin."

Grunting, Paul shook his head in disagreement. "Do you

suppose anyone is willing to risk a confrontation with the Soviets over a border dispute in Africa? Do you believe we will casually throw away a decade of economic and political progress between east and west for Egypt? No. We are not crazy."

Jan again changed her tone. She was sure of herself, almost defiant. "If access to Berlin is closed, it will no longer be a simple border skirmish in Africa. The premier, by his own hand, will see to that. Berlin has been a symbol of Western democracy for decades. From the blockade of 1948 to the tearing down of the Wall in 1989, Berlin has been the eye of the storm every time the super powers get nervous. How could you, or anyone, suppose that we would simply roll over? In Europe, we never have and never will. In a single stroke, he'll do what Stalin and every communist dictator after him couldn't." Jan lifted her glass in a mock toast. "Here's to Pax Russia."

Stung by Jan's tone, Paul became agitated. Leaning across the table, he looked into her eyes. "Yes, America has always been willing to face off with the Russians in Europe. After all, if someone makes a mistake, it will be Bavaria, not Connecticut, that suffers."

There was a moment of silence. Both knew they were getting nowhere fast. Finally Jan spoke, her voice soft, conciliatory. "Paul, I'm really not up to this. What does or doesn't happen won't be decided in this bar, not tonight. Besides, we're friends, fellow correspondents. We only look, listen, and report. Remember?"

Letting his expression soften, Paul again sat back in his chair, and finished his drink. He could not, however, resist one last cynical comment. "Yes, you are right. Fortunately, we will not have to spend the entire night trying to save the world. We can go to bed safe in the knowledge that our leaders will steer clear the shoals, just as they always have—*n'est-ce pas?*"

Jan did not answer. No longer interested in discussing geopolitics, she quietly stared at her drink while Paul ordered a refill for his. Slowly her mind drifted back to Egypt and Scott. Though she knew it had been cruel to leave him like she did, without a word, it was for the best. He had other things on his mind. He, unlike Paul and her, was doing something. Scott was part of the equation, a player in the world drama that Paul and she only watched and reported. For a moment she felt admiration for Scott. At least he did something.

Like a thunderbolt, the idea struck Jan: *she* could do something too. Rather than sitting in a bar on a rock island in the middle of the Atlantic and getting drunk with an ex-lover, Jan could do something for herself and Scott. When the crisis in Egypt had begun, Fay had complained that Scott was gone for the duration. Fay went on to explain that as far as she and the children were concerned, Scott had seemed to fall off the face of the earth. Once he was in the field, it took an act of Congress, according to Fay, to reach Scott. If that was true, Jan reasoned, Scott had had little opportunity to check on his children.

Looking at her watch, Jan figured that it was still early afternoon on the East Coast. She could call the WNN main office in Washington and have them track down the phone number of Fay's mother. While they were working on that, she could contact the London office and see about getting back to Cairo. Though it wasn't much, finding out how Scott's children were, then finding Scott and letting him know, was better than sitting in Iceland pining away.

Jan pushed herself away from the table and stood up. Paul was caught off guard. "Where are you going, Janet?"

"Egypt."

Paul also stood up, blocking Jan's exit. "But I thought you and I, later . . ."

Jan paused in front of him and looked into his eyes. "No, Paul, it's no longer 'you and I.' That's over. It was fun, but that ended years ago."

For a moment there was a hurt expression on Paul's face. He cast his eyes down as he took Jan's hands into his and brought them up to his chest. Holding her hands gently, he looked back up into her eyes. There was a small, mischievous smile on his face now. "No, Jan, it didn't end. We'll always have Paris."

Jan tilted her head to the side and also smiled. As she did so, she looked into his eyes, searching her own soul for some kind of emotion, some stirring of a love long past. But there was none. Perhaps, long ago, Jan had been truly in love with the tall Frenchman standing before her. Whatever it had been, it was gone. Without her realizing it, the smile slowly vanished from her face. When she responded, it was with a quiet, firm finality. "Yes, Paul, we'll always have Paris."

Slowly Paul pulled her hands up to his lips and kissed them. He let them fall away as he continued to stare into her eyes. "Now I am supposed to say, 'Here's looking at you, kid,' and let you walk away to your plane."

"Yes, Paul, I must go." They looked at each other for another second. Then, like a broken spell in a fairy tale, the moment was over. Paul stepped to one side and Jan hustled off in search of the nearest phone.

Southwest of El Agramiya, Egypt * 2305 Hours, 21 December

Dixon sat before the charred remains of the Libyan tank for the longest time. In the bright moon he could clearly make out every detail of a body half hanging out of the driver's hatch on the tank. The man, caught between the half-open hatch and the gun tube positioned over it, had been unable to escape. He had died in the fire that had consumed the tank. The dead driver's teeth and exposed jawbone glistened white in the light of the bright winter moon. The cold desert wind that cut through Dixon's jacket like a knife didn't bother the corpse. Nothing would ever bother it again.

Dixon's tired mind wandered ponderously from one thought to the next. Though he had tried to avoid it, he was at war again. As with the last war, he had not asked for it. And, again like in the last war, circumstances had thrust him into the forefront. Again he had commanded a task force in battle and won. Though losses had been light this time—less than two dozen total, according to Grissins's count—they were still losses. When, with relief and pride written all over his face,

Grissins had reported the figures to Dixon, Dixon's only response was curt, cryptic, and cold. Facing Grissins, Dixon told him to add one more. Then, without an explanation or another word, Dixon turned and walked out into the desert.

With Grissins and the task force sergeant major firmly in charge of the recovery operations, and orders to maintain current positions, there was nothing for Dixon to do. Still too keyed up from the day's fight, he wandered about, trying hard to push everything from his mind, but failing. When he came upon the Libyan tank with the dead driver hanging from it, he paused. At first he wondered if he had done that, if it had been his tank that had killed the Libyan driver. His answer bothered him. Yes, he had killed that man. Perhaps not his tank, but his orders, his soldiers, one of them, had.

Sitting down, Dixon studied the corpse. If that was true, he thought, if his decisions could kill, then was he responsible for Fay's death? Was his decision to stay in the Army the root cause of Fay's death? Where would he be right now if he had done as Fay had wanted and left the service? At home, sitting in front of the TV with his children and Fay? That was, Dixon knew, what Fay had wanted: a family, a home, and a husband who came home every night and made love to her once or twice a week. Nothing grand, nothing beyond the grasp of every normal American.

He, however, had chosen a different path. He had marched down it, blind to Fay's needs and desires for years. Submerging himself in a military career, he had dedicated himself to God and country, not always in that order. The cost had been high. In the cold desert night Dixon could feel the cost. Instead of being home, growing old in an obscure suburban home with his wife and children, he was in a desert, six thousand miles from where he had been born. His wife was dead, his children God knows where. Only the corpse of a man he did not know, one of many that lay in the wake of his life, kept him company.

In his despair Dixon began to wonder where that corpse would have been had he not been there. Would the dead Libyan still be at home, with his family? Or would he be in Alexandria, or maybe even Cairo? And if he had made it to Cairo with the rest of his crew, so what? Dixon didn't live in Cairo. The only people Dixon knew in Cairo were other Americans sent away from their homes, just like himself, to defend American interests.

It was not hard to make the mental leap to the next logical step. Even as tired as he was, the standard argument "They have to be stopped somewhere, so why not here?" ran through his mind. In his head Dixon knew that to be true. He knew that if he hadn't stayed in the Army, if he hadn't commanded the task force that morning, then perhaps, just perhaps, the battle would have been different. Maybe, just maybe, Dixon thought, he had made the decisive difference. It was possible. Anything was possible.

Yet there was more than defending freedom and the American way that motivated him. He had seen it that morning on the A Company commander's face. After Ken Armstrong and his crew had destroyed their first BMP, there had been joy, a real feeling of satisfaction, a perverse pleasure in having fought and won. In the heat of battle even Dixon himself had felt it. When they had acquired their first two victims, Dixon could have turned away, hiding behind his cloak of command in order to keep from killing. But he had not. Instinctively he had turned to fight. Should he have? Probably not. He was the task force commander. He had responsibilities that transcended a simple tank-to-tank duel. Dixon could easily have left the killing to others. But he hadn't. And when it was over, he, like Armstrong, had savored the kills, *his* kills.

Still, those thoughts brought little relief or comfort to him. They were not reasons, only explanations. In the end, they changed nothing. Dixon was still sitting alone in the desert, alone with a corpse. And Fay, his only true love, a woman who had given her best years to him and followed him, was dead. No logic, no explanation, no success, regardless of how great it was, could ever change that.

Tired of thinking and staring at ghosts, both new and old, Dixon got up and headed back to his hummvee. He needed to get some sleep while he could. The next morning would bring new missions, new battles—battles that he would have to see through.

Sollum, Libya * 0230 Hours, 22 December

Standing at the west end of Sollum, General Boldin, along with his chief of staff and aide, stood on the side of the road watching the flood of men and equipment streaming west. The vehicles of Boldin's forward command post were parked a hundred meters to their rear in a wadi. For two hours Boldin and his two subordinates had watched a beaten army retreat past them, blocking the road and preventing him from moving down to the coast. Though they could have gone around, Boldin decided not to. There was no need, he told his aide, to hurry forward to find the front. The front, he said, would no doubt find them in due course.

As he watched, Boldin could feel his sense of foreboding and depression deepening. Defeat and collapse of the Libyan forces eradicated all hope for a quick and favorable solution. It also meant that his Soviet and Cuban units would have to carry the brunt of the next battle. That there would be another battle was a given. Boldin could see no way out of one. It was only a matter of where, when, and how. The where and how should have been matters left to Boldin and his staff. That, however, was not the case. To Boldin's disgust, men in Moscow would make those decisions. How they, over three thousand kilometers away, would be able to do that was beyond Boldin. That they could imagine that they could added to his feeling of depression and to a growing sense of hopelessness. Instead of being a front commander, Boldin pictured himself reduced to a simple messenger boy, passing information, what little he had, back to Moscow and waiting for his orders.

For hours information concerning the exact whereabouts and activities of Libyan and Egyptian forces had been scant and confusing. What information came into General Boldin's headquarters came from satellite photos hours old, from confused and wild stories from Libyan soldiers fleeing to the west, and from their Soviet advisors. While the satellite photos provided great details and identified a large Egyptian armored force moving down the coastal road, they did not tell Boldin what was happening on the ground. Other than the fact that the Libyan forces in Egypt had collapsed, Boldin knew little. Needing information, he ordered reconnaissance units from the 24th Tank Corps further into Egypt, establishing an outpost line from Sidi Barrani on the coast to Bir al Khamsa eighty-two kilometers inland. They would at least give Boldin warning of an Egyptian or American advance.

Though communications with Moscow were better, the news from the outside world was also confusing. One message announced, rather matter-of-factly, an increase of tension in Europe along the inner zonal border between East and West Germany. At first Boldin took this to be an escalation, but to what end he did not know. Following that message Boldin received his first warning orders. STAVKA wanted all Soviet and Cuban forces to prepare for withdrawal from Egypt to a line east of Tobruk. Not believing them, Boldin immediately asked for a confirmation of that order. To carry out that order meant that the Egyptian 1st Army, still encircled in Bardia, would be uncovered and free to join the advancing units of the Egyptian 2nd Army.

With only two understrength Cuban divisions, the four brigades of the 24th Tank Corps, and three weak Libyan battalions, Boldin would be faced by almost five Egyptian divisions. Even worse, the line he was supposed to occupy could not be defended. In short order Boldin's force would be outflanked and pinned against the sea, in much the same way he had trapped the Egyptian 1st Army. Believing he saw the situation better than STAVKA did in Moscow, Boldin waited to issue any withdrawal orders. Instead, he submitted two alternate plans to Moscow. The first called for a total withdrawal from Cyrenaica all the way back to Agedabia, where he could establish a viable defense. The distance would also stretch the Egyptian supply lines beyond their limit and wear out the combat units in the process. In effect, Boldin's recommendation was to retreat faster and further than the Egyptians could follow.

The second option was to stay in place and fight it out. One Cuban division, reinforced with the Libyan battalions, would be left to maintain the encirclement at Bardia. The second Cuban division would hold a line from the coast to Bir Sheferzen. The 24th Tank Corps, held back as a mobile reserve, would be used to counterattack any Egyptian penetration of the Cuban divisions or a flanking movement south of Bir Sheferzen. This plan meant, of course, keeping Soviet forces in Egypt.

While they waited for the response, Boldin did order the withdrawal of Soviet air defense, electronic warfare, and service support units from Sidi Barrani. Advisors still with Libyan units retreating from Egypt were also recalled. Those tasks, however, were easier said than done. Although the retreating forces were no longer plagued by brutal shellings from the American fleet, Egyptian destroyers and frigates had moved in to take their place. Requests to have the Soviet Mediterranean Squadron intervene and cover the withdrawal were denied. That left movement along the coastal road slow and still dangerous. With no control over the panicked mob of refugees that had once been three Libyan divisions, complete evacuation of Soviet personnel even to Halfaya was doubtful. In a follow-on message, Boldin informed Moscow that regardless of what decision was made, a large number of Soviet personnel would fall into the hands of the advancing Egyptians.

From out of the darkness a young staff officer came scurrying up to Boldin's small party. Instinctively he reached out to hand the chief of staff a message. Upon seeing Boldin, however, the staff officer paused, pulled the message back, and turned to Boldin. Then, pausing again, the officer looked back to the chief of staff while he prepared to offer the message directly to Boldin. Tired and depressed, Boldin simply reached out and grabbed the message from the staff officer's hand, crumbling the paper as he did so. As Boldin pulled at the edges of the message to straighten it out, his aide came up behind him, flicked on a flashlight, and pointed its beam over Boldin's shoulder onto the paper.

Boldin read, then reread the message. Everyone in the small circle stood motionless, almost not daring to breathe as they watched him and waited for his reaction. That response was not long in coming. Letting out a grunt, Boldin lowered the hand holding the message to his side and looked up at the sky. Boldin's aide extinguished his flashlight and quietly backed away. It was several minutes before Boldin moved, looking at the chief of staff as he offered the message to him. "Well, instead of reinforcements, spare parts, ammunition, and fuel, Moscow is sending us a new political commissar to make sure we retreat in accordance with STAVKA's orders."

The chief of staff took the message. Lighting it with his own flashlight, he read it. The first part of the message confirmed STAVKA's earlier message requiring the North African Front to establish a line of defense east of Tobruk. The next portion of the message set a time for when that deployment was to be completed. The final portion of the message announced that a representative from STAVKA, equal in rank to Boldin and with direct contact with STAVKA, would be arriving in Tobruk at 0800 hours that morning. Boldin, the message went on to say, was to give copies of all his orders to the STAVKA representative, provide him with transportation and communications facilities, and consult with him before issuing any orders. In effect, Boldin would no longer be in command.

By the time the chief of staff finished reading the message and looked up, Boldin had walked away from the group. Turning to the aide, the chief of staff asked where Boldin had gone. The aide only shrugged his shoulders. The chief of staff ordered the aide to find Boldin and stay with him, then turned to the staff officer who had come with the message. "Well, there is much to do."

As they began to head to the command-post vehicles, the staff officer asked if the message meant that General Boldin had been relieved of command. Unsure of what the future would bring, the chief told the officer that such things were not his concern. Stung by the chief of staff's response, the staff officer

slowed his pace slightly and followed the chief of staff back t
the vehicles.

Checkpoint Alpha, Helmstedt, Germany *
0810 Hours, 22 December

Steadying his arms on the fender of one of his tanks, Lieuten
ant Colonel Anatol Vorishnov studied the British Challenge
tank with his binoculars. With him was his deputy battalio
commander and the company commander who commanded th
T-80 tank they were standing next to. The T-80, like the Chal
lenger, was sitting off to the side of the autobahn. It didn'
block the traffic moving through the checkpoint, but it wa
situated so that it was very visible to everyone. Both tanks ha
their gun tubes leveled and aimed at each other. Neither wa
meant to stop any serious intrusion. Instead, they were show
pieces for the Western media gathering around the British tank
By that evening, the image of a British tank confronting
Soviet tank in central Germany would be seen on the televisio
in every living room and public gathering place in Wester
Europe. The message to the viewers would be clear: support (
America and Egypt would mean the resurrection of the Iro
Curtain.

Vorishnov had been with his battalion less than a month
The deployment from their garrison to positions on the Eas
German side of the checkpoint was the first opportunity he ha
to move the entire battalion at once. Though he had hoped fc
better, the performance of his officers and soldiers had not bee
all bad. All but three of his tanks reached their assigned pos
tions under their own power. Of the three that had broken dow
en route, two were already repaired and with the unit. Time
tables had been met, and positions had been occupied in th
darkness even though there had been no recon beforehand
This, in spite of the fact that the sector they were in belonge
to another unit, more than made up for some of the sloppy loa
plans on several of the tanks.

Vorishnov and his deputy commander had been up we

before daylight, walking the positions to check on camouflage. Once it became light, they went back through the positions, checking to ensure that there were no blind spots or dead spaces in their fields of fire. It was wrong to call the transition from night to day "sunrise." Although the sun no doubt was shining above the leaden gray clouds, no warming rays penetrated. With the temperature hovering just below zero degrees centigrade, the clouds prepared to yield snow upon the positions Vorishnov was inspecting.

They were halfway through, inspecting the company that straddled the autobahn, when the British camera crews arrived. Stopping, Vorishnov decided to watch for a while. They were still watching when a lieutenant came trotting up behind him and announced that General Korchan was en route to their position. Putting his binoculars down, Vorishnov prepared to go and meet the general. Turning, he was surprised to find himself face to face with Korchan, commander of the 3rd Combined Arms Army. Automatically Vorishnov came to attention, saluted, and reported. "Lieutenant Colonel Vorishnov of the 2nd Battalion, 79th Tank Regiment, Comrade General."

Korchan's salute was casual and accompanied by a broad smile. "Well, I am glad to see that you took my little speech to heart." Upon his arrival in Germany to command his battalion, Vorishnov had been required to visit Korchan and receive the standard briefing he gave all new unit commanders. Rather than being a cold and formal briefing, filled with a standard party pitch or an appeal to patriotism, Vorishnov's meeting with Korchan had been enjoyable. The general's easy, quiet manner had immediately put Vorishnov at ease. The talk, more a discussion, was also easy and informal. For his part Korchan stressed the need to set the example in everything, leading his men instead of driving them. The Red Army, he had said, was changing. To make the new professional army work, a leader not only had to be proficient in tactics and technical matters; he had to lead from up front, pulling, not pushing. This appealed to Vorishnov.

As he had at their first meeting, Korchan put Vorishnov at

ease. "After your lecture to me, Comrade General, I would not dare be anywhere else."

Korchan laughed. "Yes, I suppose so. Come, show me what our British colleagues are up to."

Vorishnov took the general to the vantage point he had just left. The battalion deputy commander and company commander hung back, letting Vorishnov deal with the general. From the position next to the T-80 tank, Vorishnov explained what he knew of the British dispositions, pointing them out whenever possible. He followed that with a summary of his unit's actions from when it was notified to move out and how he had deployed his companies. Korchan only nodded his head every now and then as acknowledgment while he continued to survey the British across the barriers and barbed wire.

When Vorishnov had finished, Korchan turned away from the British and faced Vorishnov. Korchan's face was serious now, his voice all business. "You and your unit are in a highly visible spot. This deployment, this whole exercise, is for show. You must remember this. I do not expect anything major to happen. All the confrontations will take place across the conference tables. That is not our business. What *is* our business is to show the rest of Europe that glasnost has not weakened our resolve or our willingness to act appropriately when necessary." Korchan paused, allowing that to sink in before he continued. When he did, he eased his tone slightly. "This will all be over in four, maybe five, days. Unfortunately, I doubt that what we do here will help our forces in Libya. There is nothing we can do to improve that mess. At worst, when it's over, we will tear up some road, crush a few curbs, and churn up some farm fields. The politicians will get serious for a while. The African matter will be resolved, while the merchants can resume their trade. Do you understand, Comrade Colonel?"

Vorishnov nodded. Turning back to the British, Korchan and Vorishnov watched them through their binoculars while the British, in turn, watched Korchan and Vorishnov. Satisfied with what he saw of Vorishnov's unit, Korchan took his leave, moving on to the next unit to be inspected.

As soon as the general left, Vorishnov's deputy commander came up and asked what the general had said. Vorishnov, with a blank expression on his face and a stern voice, replied, "The general wants you to look sharp and smile when the British news crews film you." With that he turned and walked over to the customs building to get some hot tea and warm up.

Matruh, Egypt * 1235 Hours, 24 December

After crawling out of his pup tent, Cerro stood erect and stretched. On one hand he was disturbed that his first sergeant had let him sleep in, but at the same time he was glad: a person could deprive himself of sleep for only so long before it caught up with him. Last night Cerro had discovered his sleep debt was overdrawn and was demanding payment in full. He went down like a ton of bricks at 2030 hours and didn't stir until the rumble of tanks woke him at 1230 hours the next day.

Scratching himself as he looked about, Cerro pondered what he should do next. As his right hand made its way up to take care of an itch on his cheek, he felt the stubble of a well-developed beard. It was time for some personal hygiene. Turning around and dropping down to his knees, Cerro crawled halfway back into his tent and began to rummage through the gear strewn haphazardly about in his tent. As he found his shaving kit, his two-quart canteen, a washcloth and a small towel, and an empty .50-caliber ammo tin he used for washing, he threw them out of the tent. Finished, Cerro backed up and out of his tent, turned around, and sat on the ground, gathering up and organizing the items he had thrown out. Setting the ammo can firmly on the ground, he poured the better part of a quart of cold water into it. Opening the shaving kit, he pulled out his soap, shaving cream, metal mirror, and razor. Ready to start, Cerro stripped down to his waist, carefully hanging his Goretex field jacket, BDU shirt, and thermal underwear shirt on the front pole of his tent. Though he was cold, the need to clean up overrode the natural desire to stay warm. Besides, there was nothing like a good, cold bath and shave to shake off the cobwebs after a long night's sleep.

Cerro had just lathered up and was preparing to start shaving when First Sergeant Duncan came up to him and shouted out a cheerful "Good morning, sir."

Cerro's response was less than enthusiastic. "First Sergeant, someday you're going to get a commander who doesn't understand your slightly perverted sense of what is right and wrong," he said, without looking up from the small mirror he held in his left hand.

Duncan chuckled. "Now come on, Captain, tell me that you didn't need the extra sleep. Besides, what makes you think you're the only guy in this unit that can make it work?"

Waving his razor at Duncan, Cerro repeated his warning. "Someday, First Sergeant, someday."

With their small talk out of the way, Duncan began to give Cerro a quick rundown on what the company had done that morning and what he had planned for the afternoon. He had just gotten to discussing the rumors about redeployment when another company of tanks came rumbling into the assembly area of the desert. Turning around, Cerro looked at them for a moment. "What are the treadheads up to, First Sergeant?"

"That's the 3rd of the 5th Armor, the tank unit that tore that Libyan armored brigade a new asshole the other day. They're just coming in."

Grunting, Cerro turned around and continued to shave. "Well, there goes the neighborhood."

As the column began to slow, Dixon surveyed the sprawling assembly area from the cupola of his tank. There were tents, trucks, tracked vehicles and equipment all over. In a way the sight was disturbing. Dixon always expected organization and order. Whenever he came across confusion and disorganization, his gut would tighten and his blood pressure rise. On the other hand, the sight was reassuring. The closeness of the camp indicated that no one seriously expected a continuation of hostilities. The setup before him was that of a unit preparing for a peaceful redeployment.

That arrangement suited Dixon just fine. After a week in the desert he was ready to stand down. During the long road march to Matruh, one Dixon had opted to make on his tank, he had continued to ponder his future. There was much to consider, but he had little to go on. Whatever happened to him rested in the hands of people he barely knew or had never met. Dixon had begun to list the possibilities but soon gave that up as futile. Perhaps he would be asked to retain command of 3rd of the 5th and redeploy back with them to Fort Carson. An equally possible scenario was his reassignment back to Cairo as the assistant operations officer with the 2nd Corps (Forward). Then there were wild cards galore that the Department of the Army could play, such as reassignment to a training command slot. On top of this there were family considerations. Dixon needed to get back to his children, wherever they were, as soon as possible. The loss of their mother and readjustment to a single-parent family were going to be tough for them regardless of what the Army did.

And then there was Jan. The mere thought of her overwhelmed Dixon with feelings and thoughts that were contradictory and, at the same time, arousing. In his mind's eye he could still see her naked body lying in her bed. He could almost feel the warmth and softness of her skin under his hand. Perhaps it was nothing more than sheer animal attraction. But it was something that he could not easily pass off or forget. Eventually, Dixon would have to face Jan, like everything else, and decide.

The sudden halt caught Dixon off guard, throwing him forward. Grabbing the machine gun, he steadied himself and began to look about in order to discover why they had stopped. Up ahead was Major Grissins, the task force XO, directing tanks to the left and into a line. Sent ahead as an advance party, Grissins was greeting each column as it came in and directing it to its own motor park and assembly area. Deciding that there was nothing more to be gained from playing tank commander, Dixon called to his gunner to come up and take over while he dismounted and became task force commander again.

Two Miles North of Mussaid, Libya * 1735 Hours, 24 December

Slowly, carefully, six Egyptian infantrymen made their way forward in two lines, removing mines from their path as they did so. Fifty meters behind them, their M-113 armored personnel carrier followed. In the open hatch, a soldier manning the caliber .50 machine gun surveyed the horizon, watching for any sign of enemy activity. Two hundred meters further back half a dozen M-60A3 tanks of the Republican Brigade sat in shallow fighting positions. They, too, were watching for the enemy.

Standing on the top of his tank's turret, Colonel Hafez watched the progress of the infantrymen through his binoculars. They were being too careless in their clearing of the abandoned Soviet mine field. Though it was a hasty, surface laid mine field, the Soviets always managed to booby-trap some of the mines. At the rate his infantry was going, they would eventually stumble across such a booby trap.

He knew their slow and laborious progress was due mostly to exhaustion. Hafez's entire unit, like the infantrymen in the mine field, was exhausted, near collapse, and becoming careless. Even he felt the effects. His ability to think, reason clearly, and react were definitely impaired. The fact that he had not yet taken action but was merely watching his men stumble about in the mine field, taking no precautions to guard against booby traps, was ample evidence that Hafez was losing his ability to continue.

In the last seventy-two hours they had advanced over two hundred miles, mounted an attack, and repulsed a counterattack. In the process they had expended all but a handful of tank main-gun rounds and run their tanks and personnel carriers dry of fuel. Even if his men could muster the courage and determination to repulse another attack and Hafez, somehow, managed to sort out the situation and issue appropriate orders, they really didn't have the means to do so.

As if his very thoughts brought his worst nightmare to life an excited message reported the approach of a column of tanks from the west. Shifting his gaze from the infantrymen to the horizon, Hafez began to sweep it until he saw the clouds of dust. Dropping his binoculars for a moment, he looked around in order to get his bearings. The distant column was approaching from the north, not from the south as a Soviet attack would come. Since the report had not identified the tanks by type, Hafez bent over and grabbed his tank crewman's helmet. Keying the radio and speaking into the boom mike attached to the helmet, he warned all units to hold fire. No one was to engage the approaching tanks until they had positively identified them as enemy. They could just as easily be tanks of the 1st Army coming out to greet them.

When all commanders acknowledged his warning, Hafez put the helmet down. Calling to his loader, Hafez told him to pass the two green star clusters up from the storage rack in the turret. Used for signaling, two green star clusters fired by one force would be answered by a green and red if the approaching tanks were Egyptian. Deciding that it was better to establish now if the tanks were friendly rather than wait until they were on top of them, Hafez fired the star clusters in quick succession.

Once he had let the last star cluster go, he stood up and lifted the binoculars to his eyes. The immediate response of the approaching tanks was a sudden change of direction. They were now headed straight for him. Then the lead tanks slowed, almost stopping. This caused Hafez's heart to sink. Not only had he been wrong, he had helped the enemy locate his force. Letting his binoculars fall down around his neck, Hafez was about to jump down into his open hatch and prepare to fight when a green star cluster erupted from the third tank in the approaching column. He paused, looked, and waited to see what color star cluster, if any, followed. The wait was unnerving. Though it was only a matter of seconds, it seemed like an eternity to Hafez.

In the early-evening darkness, a second star cluster erupted from the same tank that had fired the green star cluster. When the rising pyrotechnic exploded into a brilliant red shower of sparks, there was a moment of silence. Then, from everyone in the Republican Brigade who saw the two star clusters, a spontaneous cheer went up. It was over. They had finally accomplished what they had failed to bring about seven days before—the salvation of the 1st Army. That the war might continue was unimportant to him. Perhaps his unit would have other battles to fight. Perhaps they would lose in the end. Hafez knew that anything was possible. But even if they did fight, and he died, he would die secure in the knowledge that the shame of his treason had been expunged. His success as a soldier would be remembered, not his failings as a man.

Cairo * 2005 Hours, 24 December

While she waited for the red record light on the camera to come on, Jan prepared herself. She was anxious to finish shooting the piece tonight. As soon as they did, Jan and her camera crew were slated to catch a military helicopter flying to Matruh. With the conflict winding down and the dangers diminished, the public affairs officer for the 2nd U.S. Corps had granted permission for correspondents to go forward as far as Matruh. There, on Christmas Day, while other correspondents were touring the battlefields, Jan and her crew were scheduled to interview the soldiers of the 16th Armored Division and 11th Air Assault Division as they prepared to leave Egypt. When offered the choice of the tour or the interviews, Jan surprised everyone by taking the interviews. Only Tim, her cameraman, understood why she had done so.

Knowing that Scott didn't expect her, she intended to surprise him by going to his unit first. No doubt Scott would be glad to hear that his children were safe with Fay's mother. And if one thing should lead to another, as Jan hoped it would, she could count on Tim and the sound man to make themselves scarce. Though she considered the possibility that Scott might not feel the same for her as she did for him, Jan had to go. She had to find out if her love was a one-sided affair. If it was, things could be embarrassing. But Jan was ready for that. At least she had convinced herself that she was ready.

"Ten seconds, love." Tim was ready and so was Jan. Counting down from ten, Tim began to roll as soon as he hit "one." The red light was on and so was Jan.

"Tonight, on Christmas Eve, it appears that the world will be given the gift that the birth of a poor boy in Bethlehem two thousand years ago promised—peace. Less than an hour ago the Egyptian minister of defense announced that elements of the famed Republican Brigade made contact with units of the 1st Egyptian Army surrounded since December 18th. The minister went on to say that with the destruction of the Libyan field force in Egypt and Cyrenaica and the relief of the 1st Army, all military goals and objectives had been achieved. When asked by this reporter when we could expect to see Egyptian forces withdrawn from Libya, the minister responded by saying that units of the 1st Army would begin moving back into assembly areas in Egypt tonight. He further stated that all forces would be back on Egyptian soil within forty-eight hours.

"Despite the fact that some type of compromise was expected due to the pressure applied by the American government on the Egyptian, the mood here is one of victory and great joy. Though the Egyptian forces did not seize Tobruk, military experts have rated the performance of the Egyptian military, at all levels, as good. Some foreign experts are now saying, in light of Egyptian performance, that intervention by U.S. forces was unnecessary. Even if that is so, the Egyptian government is not downplaying the role American forces played. Every Egyptian official I've talked to today has had nothing but praise for the performance and assistance the Americans gave in, as they say, 'their time of greatest need.'

"That sentiment has resulted, according to one official in the American embassy here, in a win-win-win situation that has made the compromised end of this conflict possible. For the Egyptians, victory on the battlefield, the destruction of four Libyan divisions, and finishing their operations on Libyan soil gives them a clear tactical victory. This allows them to end their punitive operations in a manner that fits their stated pre-war goals.

"For America, though the intervention of U.S. forces was of

short duration, it came at a critical time. Operations involving American troops appear to have been a key element in turning back the Libyan threat to Alexandria and allowing the Egyptians to mass for and launch their counteroffensive so quickly. If that is so, then the Department of Defense will also be able to claim tactical victory of its own, using this conflict to prove that it is able to rapidly project combat power anywhere, anytime. In addition to the military aspect, both the administration and the State Department will, in the future, be able to use this operation to demonstrate that the United States is ready and willing to stand by its friends and allies when needed.

"On the other side, the Soviets can do likewise. Though the Libyan forces were defeated, once in the opening Egyptian attack and again during the Egyptian counteroffensive, the Soviets can point to their allies and claim victory. The speed with which the Soviets massed forces in Libya, and their willingness to use them to support a third-world country, came as a surprise to most Western military analysts. Like the American intervention, though limited, it too had a decisive influence on the shape and outcome of this conflict. As the British military attaché in Cairo said earlier this evening, it is safe to say that had the Russians not been in Libya, the Egyptian 1st Army would have been washing the dust of Cyrenaica off their tanks with water from the Gulf of Sidra.

"Of the major players, on the surface the Libyans seem to have lost. That, however, is only a matter of one's perspective. According to news broadcasts from Tripoli, the capital of Libya, the announcement by Egypt that its forces were withdrawing was hailed as a decisive victory for Libya. In a speech to his people, the Leader of the Revolution has claimed that had it not been for the treasonous acts of Colonel Nafissi, Libyan minister of defense and commander of all forces in Cyrenaica, total victory would have been realized. Charged with the illegal use of chemical weapons and mismanagement of the defense of Cyrenaica, Nafissi has been arrested. In order to absolve the government of Libya of blame for their army's poor performance, Nafissi will be used as a scapegoat, receiving a quick public trial before he is found guilty and executed.

"Tonight it is too early to determine what effects this conflict will have on Middle Eastern and world politics. It will be weeks before the dust settles and the causes and results can be carefully studied, measured, and weighed in the capitals of the world. All that, however, is of little concern here and in Matruh, where Americans who fought this war await their return to the United States. Though separated from their home and family, most, if not all, have been given a Christmas gift that only a soldier who has seen battle can appreciate—peace.

"From Cairo, this is Jan Fields for World News Network. Goodnight, and merry Christmas."

EPILOGUE

Eternal peace lasts only until the next war.

RUSSIAN PROVERB

Matruh, Egypt * 2015 Hours, 24 December

Deciding that he had sat enough all day, Dixon set the retch green paper tray holding his meal on the hood of his hummvee and prepared to eat standing up. As he opened the plastic package of flatware, Dixon looked down at his tray of food. For a moment he watched the steam rise off the food into the cold night air. There was little point, he thought, of trying to figure out what the assorted piles of food were supposed to be. He didn't have much of a choice—eat that, eat another cold MRE, or starve. The meal on the tray was at least hot, his first hot meal in over three days. Whether or not he would enjoy it was immaterial.

Digging into his food with a tiny plastic fork, Dixon began to mechanically shovel it into his mouth, slowly chewing it without much thought. The last thing Dixon wanted to do right now was think. His only concern at that moment was the warm meal before him. Its main course was some type of meat covered by a heavy gravy that had the consistency of paste. Still, it was warm. That in itself was something to be thankful about. He was also thankful that the war was over. In addition, their arrival in the assembly area had been greeted by rumors that redeployment would commence on 25 December, Christmas Day. Those rumors had been confirmed in the middle of the afternoon when word arrived that Division had published its order for that operation. Though the Egyptian 1st Army still had to withdraw from Libya, and stray Libyan units in Egypt needed to be rounded up, the war was over.

Dixon was no more than half finished when Captain Armstrong, the A Company commander, came up to him. Still unsure of the quiet lieutenant colonel who said little, thought a great deal, but seemed to be everywhere, watching everything, Armstrong stopped and saluted. Dixon returned the captain's salute by touching the tip of his tiny plastic fork to the rim of his helmet. "What can I do for you on this fine night, Armstrong?"

Armstrong was brash, his speech strong, sure, as he began to talk to Dixon. "I've been wanting to talk to you, sir. But if you're busy, it can wait."

Swallowing a clump of meat, Dixon paused before he answered. "Not a problem. What's on your mind?"

"Well, sir, some of the other officers in the task force and I were talking about this last operation. We understand what we did, but none of us can quite figure out why we quit just when we had the chance to do some serious ass-kicking."

For a moment Dixon could feel himself becoming upset. What a dumb fucking question, Dixon thought. He couldn't imagine a commissioned officer being so naive. But he checked his anger. Instead, he considered how best to answer the captain's question. "We did what we were sent here to do," he said at last. "Our mission was to assist the Egyptian government reestablish its national borders. You can understand that, can't you?"

There was no pause as Armstrong continued. "That, sir, doesn't make any sense. I mean, Libya has been a pain in the ass for years. How many terrorist attacks have they sponsored? How many Americans have died because of the assholes they've trained and armed? Here we finally get a chance to smash them and we get stopped short by a bunch of wimp politicians."

The urge to choke the shit out of the obnoxious captain was threatening to overwhelm Dixon's self-control. Who the hell did this guy think he was? One quick, cheap battle and sudenly he's ready to take on the world. Instead of lashing out, owever, Dixon tried to figure out how he could gain the upper and in this exchange and make Armstrong understand. Needng time, Dixon decided to put the captain on the defensive. "Do you remember your oath of commission, Captain?"

Thrown by Dixon's question, Armstrong paused and thought or a moment before he answered. "I don't understand, sir."

"The oath that you swore to when you were commissioned— he one you obligate yourself to."

Dixon had Armstrong going. The young captain thought for moment. When he answered, he was hesitant. "To defend he United States and its people."

"Wrong. When you were commissioned, you pledged yourelf to support and defend the Constitution of the United States gainst all enemies, foreign and domestic. Furthermore, you ledged your true faith and allegiance to the same." Dixon aused and allowed Armstrong to consider his statement.

Puzzled, Armstrong, with a quizzical look on his face, stared t Dixon. "I'm sorry, sir, I don't make the connection."

Having put Armstrong into the listening mode, Dixon began o explain. "You see, the people who framed the Constitution et things up so that the people elected to the presidency and Congress by the American voters were the ones who determined policy and implemented it. Under the Constitution, the President establishes and pursues policy. He also appoints other civilians to head the Department of Defense and the various armed service departments. Congress, according to the Constitution, has the responsibility for raising and supporting armies and navies, approving the civilians appointed by the President to lead the military departments, and, most importantly, the responsibility of declaring war. When our national policy so demands it, and Congress approves, we, the soldiers, are used. Even then it is the President, through his civilian military chiefs, that determines what our missions and goals are and issues the appropriate directives. For over two hundred years that system has worked, and worked well."

For several seconds neither man said anything as Dixon waited for Armstrong's response. When Armstrong spoke, he was less hostile. "Okay, sir. I understand that. I don't question that. What I do question is the wisdom of their—our civilian leaders'—decision. I mean, wouldn't it be in our best interests to take out Libya?"

Dixon changed his approach. "All right, let's look at this from a military standpoint. Do you think the Russians are going to let us stroll into Libya and occupy it while there are some eighteen thousand Soviet and twenty-five thousand Cubans in there? No. We would have to fight them. And what do you think the response of the Soviet government and people would be to that? What do you think the American public would do if the Soviets cut off Berlin and slaughtered the American brigade there? And even if that didn't happen, consider what it would take to occupy Libya. Five divisions? Maybe six? After all, we would be invaders, foreigners. And even worse, Christians. Their leaders will paint us as infidels trying to subvert Islam and make them a colony again. When the Italians tried to suppress one and a half million Libyans in 1922, it took them ten years and the killing of over seven hundred fifty thousand Libyans to do so. Do you think the American public would condone a ten-year war and the killing of hundreds of thousands of Libyans?"

Armstrong didn't answer. He realized that Dixon was probably right. "So all we did was keep the status quo. We've changed nothing."

"It's not that easy. Things do change. They change all the time. But we aren't the people who should be making those changes. That's what the politicians are for. We're like the fire department. When things get out of hand, we're called out to put out the fire before it consumes that which we hold dear—freedom. Sometimes, like in Korea or Grenada, we get there in the nick of time. Sometimes, like in World War II, we get called in too late to save everything and everyone. Still, even in a world war, it is the politicians that determine what is and isn't policy. Does any of this make sense?"

There was a slight sigh before Armstrong answered. "Yes, sir. I still find it difficult to believe that there isn't a better way of doing business."

Dixon chuckled. "Well, don't feel alone. A lot of very smart people have tried to figure that one out. Don't worry. Perhaps someday you'll be able to get a handle on it. Maybe you never will. Doing so, if you remain in the Army, isn't really important. What is important is that you, and the men charged to your responsibility, are ready to go fight a fire, anywhere, anytime, when the President calls for you."

For several minutes both Armstrong and Dixon stood there. In the darkness they could only see each other's form, Armstrong standing at a loose parade rest, Dixon leaning forward on the hood of his hummvee. Coming to attention, Armstrong saluted. "I appreciate the time, sir. I hope I didn't ruin your meal."

Again Dixon let out another chuckle. "Don't worry about that either. This meal was ruined before they boxed it and shipped it to us."

"Goodnight, sir."

As he watched Armstrong walk back to his company area, Dixon thought about what he had just told his young company commander. Did he, Dixon, really believe everything he had said? Was their job all that simple? Perhaps it was. Maybe Dixon and his men were nothing more than firemen, charged with risking their lives to protect civilians against dangers the civilians couldn't handle or deal with.

Picking up his tray, Dixon slowly began to make his way to the trash point to throw it away. Since the trash point was set up where the field kitchen was, he passed a number of soldiers who had also just finished their meals and were headed to the same place. Some recognized Dixon and saluted. He did not, however, return their salutes. He was deep in thought, considering his own analogy and how he fit into it. Dixon decided that there was much to his comparing his soldiers to firemen. His grandfather and father had been volunteer firemen. Both had always been ready and willing, at a moment's notice, to drop everything and rush forward to risk their lives to protect others when the alarm was sounded. In doing so they had experienced life more than any normal man could ever hope. It hadn't been easy for either one. They saw things that neither could ever forget. Dead friends and broken dreams. But they had served. They had served well and willingly. Dixon doubted if either man would have, or could have, done otherwise.

Besides the idea of service, there was more. There had to be more. The warm fuzzes firemen and soldiers receive as payment from grateful citizens for serving the public need wear thin when it is night, the temperature is below zero, and duty calls. And the motivation that allows men to rush into a burning building or face a well-armed enemy in open battle didn't come from high principles and moral concepts that are at best mere abstractions. Like his father and grandfather before him, he enjoyed what he did for a living. The fear, the danger, the challenge, the risk—he enjoyed it all. Only through pushing himself to the limit was he able to exceed that limit, to see what he was truly made of. The fight just completed only served to confirm what he already suspected.

After dropping his tray on top of other discarded trays sitting precariously in a pile in an overfull trash can, Dixon turned away and wandered back to the small tent his driver had set up for him. Like a top, his mind continued to spin about the issue of who he was and where he was going. Though he used weapons instead of a hose, Dixon knew that what he did was no different than what his father and grandfather had done. And he also knew, at that moment, that he could do no differently. He was a soldier, a fireman who fought international brush fires. He might abhor what he did—every sane man who had seen battle did. The legacy of those battles was memories of the horrors he had seen and had helped create. Those memories, as vivid now as they had been at the moment, would never go away. Yet he knew in his heart that when the alarm sounded, he would drop everything and rush out to answer the call. For he was a soldier, clear and simple.

UNIT SYMBOLS

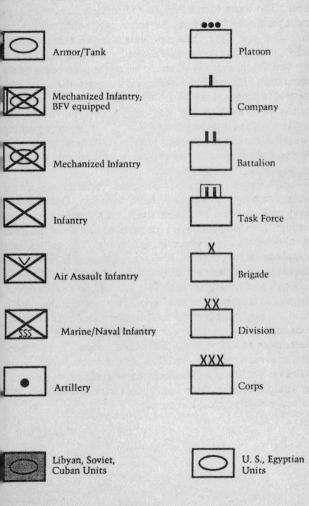

Armor/Tank

Mechanized Infantry;
BFV equipped

Mechanized Infantry

Infantry

Air Assault Infantry

Marine/Naval Infantry

Artillery

Libyan, Soviet,
Cuban Units

Platoon

Company

Battalion

Task Force

Brigade

Division

Corps

U. S., Egyptian
Units

GLOSSARY
OF MILITARY TERMS

-16 A ground-attack version of the F-16 fighter. This conversion of ⸱e F-16 has been discussed but not executed as of the writing of this ⸱ook.

K The Avtomat-Kalashnikov assault rifle, the standard rifle of the ⸱ed Army, its allies, and client states. The original AK, the famous ⸱K-47, was an air-cooled, 7.62mm rifle capable of either semiauto-⸱atic or full automatic firing with a cyclic rate of 600 rounds per ⸱inute. Maximum effective range of the AK-47 is 400 meters, while ⸱tual rate of fire is close to 90 rounds per minute due to the limit of ⸱ 30- or 40-round magazine. The successor to the AK-47, the AK-74, ⸱res a 5.45mm round with a maximum effective range of 500 meters.

pache (AH-64) A medium-speed, high-performance, single-rotor, ⸱win-turbine attack helicopter, the agile Apache is equipped with an ⸱xceptional suite of sights and night-vision devices, which, coupled ⸱ith a sophisticated fire-control system and the Hellfire missile, makes ⸱ capable and very lethal. Armament includes a 30mm chain gun ⸱naximum combat load of 1,200 rounds), the Hellfire laser guided ⸱issile (maximum of 16), and 2.75-inch rockets (maximum of 76). ⸱ruising speed is 175 knots (approx. 190 mph), and has an endurance ⸱f 105 minutes without external fuel tanks.

Team A 12-man Special Forces team that consists entirely of officers ⸱d NCOs, each a highly trained specialist in either light/heavy weap-⸱ns, communications, demolitions/engineering, or medicine.

AWACS Short for airborne warning and control system. The U.S. has two primary versions. The E-3A Sentry system, carried by a modified Boeing 707, is manned by a crew of seventeen and has an endurance of six hours on station. The E-2 Hawkeye, built by Grumman, is a smaller, carrier-based, prop-driven AWACS used by the U.S. Navy and by several other nations. Manned by a crew of five, the E-2 has an endurance of six hours. The Soviet version, NATO codename Candid, is mounted in an Ilyushin 76 jet.

Battalion A military organization consisting of three to five companies with personnel strength of 350 to 800 men.

Battle-Dress Uniform (BDUs) Camouflage fatigues worn by U.S. ground forces.

Blackhawk (UH-60) A high-performance, single-rotor, twin-engine tactical assault helicopter. This helicopter is replacing the venerable UH-1 "Huey" helicopter of Vietnam fame. The Blackhawk, manufactured by Sikorsky Aircraft, has a cruising speed of 145 knots, an endurance of two hours without external fuel tanks, a range of 290 nautical miles, and a service ceiling of 5,000 feet. Though it is rated to carry a crew of three and eleven fully armed and loaded combat troops, reliable sources claim that the Blackhawk can carry twenty-two passengers in a crunch.

BMP The primary infantry fighting vehicle of the Red Army, its allies, and its client states, the BMP-1 is equipped with a 73mm smooth-bore cannon, a 7.62 machine gun coaxially mounted with the cannon, and the SAGER AT-3 antitank guided missile. The BMP-2 has replaced the 73mm cannon with a 30mm cannon and the AT-3 with an AT-4 SPIGOT antitank guided missile. Both versions have a crew of three and carry eight infantrymen. The 11.3-ton BMP is amphibious, has a range of 310 miles, has an active chemical protection system for crew and infantry and a top speed of 34 mph. There are several variations of the BMP, including recon and command and control versions.

Bradley (M-2 or M-3) Fighting Vehicle A fully tracked, lightly armored infantry fighting vehicle that is replacing the M-113 armored personnel carrier in mechanized infantry and armored cavalry units. The Bradley, BFV for short, is armed with a two-tube TOW antitank guided missile launcher, a 25mm cannon, and a 7.62mm machine gun coaxially mounted with the 25mm cannon. The BFV has a crew of three (commander, gunner, driver), and can carry six infantrymen for dismounted operations.

BRDM The standard Soviet reconnaissance vehicle. Equipped with a 14.5mm gun and a 7.62mm machine gun, the BRDM-2 weighs 6.9 tons, is fully amphibious, and has a top speed of 62 mph and a range of 400 miles.

Brigade A flexible organization that consists of two to five combat maneuver battalions and various combat support and combat service support units, such as engineers, air defense artillery, military intelligence, supply, medical, and maintenance.

BTR-60/BTR-80 A Soviet eight-wheeled armored personnel carrier capable of carrying up to fourteen personnel. It weighs approximately ten tons, is amphibious, and is fielded in several versions, some of which include a small turret armed with a 14.5mm gun and a 7.62mm machine gun.

CENTCOM Short for Central Command. A unified command (i.e., all services, Army, Navy, Air Force, and USMC, are under a single commander, normally a four-star general or admiral), CENTCOM is responsible for American forces and military operations in Southwest Asia and Africa.

CO Short for commanding officer.

Combined Arms Army The Soviet equivalent to a U.S. Army corps in size and purpose, the combined arms has three or four motorized rifle divisions and one or two tank divisions. In addition, combat support units, such as artillery, rocket troops, air defense, attack helicopter, and engineers, as well as supply and transportation units, are attached to the combined arms army to support the combat divisions.

The combined arms army is the main weapon of the Red Army at the operational level.

Combined Arms Maneuver Task Force A battalion that has been permanently tasked, organized with a mix of tank and infantry companies.

Company A military organization that numbers from 50 to 180 personnel and is normally divided into platoons and/or sections.

Corps An organization that is comprised of several combat divisions, independent combat brigades, armored cavalry regiments, combat support units, such as artillery, rocket troops, air defense, attack helicopter, and engineers, as well as supply and transportation units. In the West, the corps is a flexible organization that can be added to or subtracted from depending on the corps' missions. The corps is commanded by a lieutenant general, three stars, and can number from 50,000 to over 100,000 men.

CP (Command Post) The center where commanders and their operations and intelligence staff, along with special staff officers, plan, monitor, and control the battle.

CQ Short for charge of quarters. This is a noncommissioned officer who is put on duty at company level during nonduty hours. He is responsible for the maintenance of unit rules and regulations and is the point of contact for receiving and passing important information at the company.

Division A major military organization that consists of brigades and/or regiments and can have a personnel strength as low as 6,500 men or as high as 20,000, depending on the type.

Hummer (also Hummvee and HMMWV) Popular name applied to the high-mobility multipurpose wheeled vehicle (hence HMMWV). The hummer has replaced the old jeep as the Army's four-wheel-drive all-purpose utility truck.

M-1/M-1A1 Abrams Tank The Army's primary ground weapon system for closing with and destroying enemy forces using fire power, mobility, and shock effect. The tank weighs 61 tons for the basic M-1 and 63 for the M-1A1 fully combat-loaded. The M-1 is equipped with a 105mm rifled cannon of British origin, while the M-1A1 has a 120mm smooth bore of German origin. The tank also has a secondary armament of one caliber-.50 M-2 heavy-barreled machine gun (the commander's weapon), a 7.62mm machine gun coaxially mounted with the main gun controlled by the gunner, and a 7.62 machine gun mounted at the loader's position. The crew consists of a commander, a gunner, a loader, and a driver. Equipped with a 1,500-horsepower turbine engine, the M-1 is capable of 45 mph when the engine is governed. Earlier models that did not have governors on their engines reportedly reached speeds of 70 mph and were duly ticketed by the authorities. Not only does the M-1/M-1A1 have special armor that increases survivability, but fuel and ammunition are stored in special armored compartments away from the crew, further increasing the chances of survival in the event an enemy round penetrates into the tank's interior.

M-16 The standard rifle of U.S. ground combat forces, the M-16 fires a 5.56mm round either semiautomatically or fully automatically and is gas operated, magazine fed, and air cooled. The M-16A2, now being fielded, eliminates the automatic mode and fires a three-round burst instead and has several other improvements, including a heavier barrel that allows greater accuracy at longer ranges.

M-60A3 Last of the M-60 series Patton tanks which were initially introduced into active service in 1960, the M-60A3 is a highly modified version that includes a sophisticated fire-control system, onboard stabilization for the main gun, and either thermal or passive night sights. The tank weighs 53 tons fully combat-loaded. The M-60A3 is equipped with the same 105mm rifled cannon as the basic M-1, a secondary armament of one caliber-.50 M-85 machine gun (the commander's weapon), and a 7.62mm machine gun coaxially mounted with the main gun. The crew consists of a commander, a gunner, a loader, and a driver. Equipped with a 750 horsepower diesel engine, the M-60A3 is capable of a breathtaking 20 mph. Armor consists of rolled homogeneous armor up to four inches thick, but no special armor. Most active Army units have had the M-60A3 tanks replaced by the M-1 or the M-1A1, with National Guard and Army Reserve units receiving the M-60A3 to replace both the M-48A5 and the M-60/M-60A1. A number of foreign nations, including Egypt, have purchased the M-60A3.

M-113 A fully tracked armored personnel carrier that resembles a metal shoebox. Introduced in the late 1950s, the M-113 was the primary personnel carrier for American infantry units until the introduction of the M-2 Bradley. Weighing 12.1 tons, the M-113 has a top speed of 40 mph, a cruising range of 300 miles, a crew of one (the driver), and can carry eleven passengers. Still the workhorse, the M-113 is used for a variety of tasks and has been modified to carry mortars and antitank guided missiles, as a battlefield ambulance, for command and control (the M-577 is nothing more than a built-up M-113), and for general cargo hauling to and from the battlefield.

M-577 A fully armored and tracked command post carrier. Used in tactical units, battalion/task-force level and above, by the unit staff for planning and command and control. One or more of these used in a command post configuration by the unit's operations staff compose the tactical operations center, TOC for short.

Mechanized Term used in the U.S. Army to refer to infantry units equipped with armored personnel carriers or infantry fighting vehicles. In the Red Army, these units are referred to as motorized rifle units.

MIG Short for Mikoyan, the company that has been producing first-rate fighters for the Red Air Force since before World War II.

Motorized Rifle Term used in the Red Army to refer to infantry units equipped with armored personnel carriers or infantry fighting vehicles. In the U.S. Army, these units are referred to as mechanized units.

NATO Acronym for the North Atlantic Treaty Organization, which includes Norway, Denmark, the Federal Republic of Germany, the

Netherlands, Belgium, Luxembourg, France, Italy, Great Britain, Spain, Portugal, Canada, and the United States.

NCO Short for noncommissioned officer or sergeant.

OPFOR Short for opposing force, a term used to describe the enemy used during maneuver training exercises.

Orders Group Selected commanders and staff officers who receive the mission/operations order from their higher headquarters. These people, in turn, with assistance from the rest of the unit's staff, will produce the necessary orders at their level to accomplish the mission assigned to them.

Overwatch A term applied to a tactical method of movement in which part of a unit remains stationary, watching for enemy activity, while another part of the unit moves forward. It is the task of the overwatch element to engage any enemy forces that threaten the element in motion.

PERSCOM Short for Personnel Support Command, the agency at the Department of the Army responsible for the management of all Army personnel, including assignments and career management.

Platoon A military organization that consists of as few as nine men and three tanks, in the case of a Soviet tank platoon, or as many as fifty men, in some U.S. platoons.

Regiment A military organization similar to a brigade but more rigid in its organization. It usually consists of one type of unit, such as an infantry regiment or an armor regiment. All battalions within a regiment carry the same regimental number.

S-3 The "S" stands for "staff" in battalion- and brigade-sized units in the U.S. Army. The S-1 is responsible for personnel matters; the S-2 is the intelligence officer; the S-3 is operations, plans, and training; and the S-4 is supply and maintenance. At division and Corps level, the "S" is replaced by a "G," which stands for "general staff." When more than one service is involved, as in a joint Army and Navy operation, staffs use ''J'' for joint staff.

SAM See Surface-to-Air Missile.

Special Forces (SF) Popularly known as the Green Berets, these special operations forces have missions that include assisting foreign nations with internal defense through training, unconventional warfare, strategic reconnaissance, and strike operations (or raids).

Squad The smallest military organization, normally commanded by a sergeant and consisting of nine to twelve men.

Surface-to-Air Missile (SAM) An antiaircraft guided missile that is launched from a ground platform against aircraft. SAMs come in a wide variety, running from the man-portable Stinger missile, with a range of 4 kilometers and fired by a single man, to the Hawk, whose range exceeds 40 kilometers.

T-54/55 An outdated tank of Soviet design and manufacture, the tank weighs 35.9 tons fully combat-loaded. Both the T-54 and the T-55 are equipped with a 100mm main gun and a secondary armament of one 12.7mm machine gun (the commander's weapon) and one 7.62mm machine gun coaxially mounted with the main gun. The crew consists of a commander, a gunner, a loader, and a driver. Equipped with either a 520 (T-54) or a 580 (T-55) horsepower or a vee-12 water-cooled diesel engine, either is capable of 30 mph.

T-62 An outdated tank of Soviet design and manufacture, the tank weighs 36.93 tons fully combat-loaded. The T-62 is equipped with a 115mm main gun and has a secondary armament of one 12.7mm machine gun (the commander's weapon) and one 7.62mm machine gun coaxially mounted with the main gun. The crew consists of a commander, a gunner, a loader, and a driver. Equipped with either a 700 horsepower or a vee-12 water-cooled diesel engine, either is capable of 34 mph. The T-62 tank is protected with steel armor up to 100mm thick on the front slope of the hull and 170mm on the gun mantlet.

T-80 The Soviet army's primary tank, the T-80 weighs 39.3 tons fully combat-loaded. It is equipped with a 125mm main gun and has a secondary armament of one 12.7mm machine gun (the commander's weapon) and one 7.62mm machine gun coaxially mounted with the main gun. The crew consists of a commander, a gunner, and a driver. Since the T-80 has an automatic loader, there is no need (or room) for a human loader. Equipped with a 700-horsepower water-cooled diesel engine, the tank is capable of 50 mph. Like the M-1/M-1A1, the T-80 has special armor that increases survivability. Unlike the M-1, the T-80 has been equipped with reactive armor.

Tank-Heavy A maneuver unit, company, battalion/task force, or brigade that has a preponderance of tank units assigned to it. For example, a battalion/task force that has three tank companies and one mechanized infantry company would be tank heavy. A battalion that has two tank and two mechanized infantry companies would be a balanced task force. A battalion with three mechanized infantry and one tank company would be mech heavy.

Task Force A grouping of units, under one commander, formed for the purpose of carrying out a specific operation or mission. In the past, this term was applied only to Army battalions that had additional units assigned to it, in particular units of a different type. For example, a tank battalion that normally has four tank companies might give up one tank company to a mechanized infantry battalion and receive a mechanized infantry company as well as one or more engineer platoons and an air defense platoon. That tank battalion would then become a tank-heavy task force.

XO Short for executive officer, the officer second in command of a unit. Sometimes the XO is referred to as a deputy commander, as in the Red Army.

ACKNOWLEDGMENTS

No effort of this magnitude can be accomplished in isolation. I owe a great deal to a cast of wonderful people who have given freely of themselves and their time in an effort to make *Bright Star* a reality. Some of the primary contributors and helpers in this effort follow.

Major General Allen and the soldiers of the 101st Airborne, Air Assault Division, for their friendship, hospitality and cooperation during my June '89 visit to Fort Campbell, Kentucky. Bill Butterworth, a Dutch Uncle of the best kind, who has his hands full keeping me on the straight-and-narrow. Dr. C. H. Burgess, Professor of English (Emeritus), for his review and comments on a very sick and disjointed first try at *Bright Star*. Yours is an influence that transcends time and distance. Chet Burgess of CNN News for his comments and assistance in making the media side of *Bright Star* credible. Your kind words helped too. Janet Ciganick, who, through her review and comments, brought Jan Fields to life and made me break with a standing policy about not using real people as models for my characters. Tom Clancy, a mentor and friend, who has always been willing to give his all when I need help, which is frequently. Brigadier General Robert Frix and his lovely wife, Mo, for their assistance in arranging my visit to Fort Campbell, their review and comments on the first draft of *Bright Star,* and, most important, their friendship. Lieutenant Colonel Tom Garret, for a GREAT helicopter ride, his efforts, and the efforts of the staff of 1st of the 101st Attack Helicopter Battalion in planning the raid on Al Fasher, and his review and comments on the draft of *Bright Star*. Dr. George Gawrych and Dr. Bob Baumann of the Combat Studies Institute for their assistance and the review and comments on *Bright Star*.

Michael Korda of Simon and Schuster for his advice and assistance in making *Bright Star* a reality.

A special thanks to the soldiers of Task Force 1-32 Armor (The Bandits), for their help and cooperation while I learned the trade and craft of a soldier. Though you all have played a role in getting me to where I am, a special thanks to the following: Lieutenant Colonel John F. Swann, for selecting me as his operations officer and letting me learn the trade, regardless of how much pain I caused him. Major Jeff Givens, the Task Force XO and my partner in crime. Captain John Swart, my trusty right-hand man who handled all the nasty little jobs that make operations such a joy. To the company commanders, who made it all worthwhile—in particular, Clancy Mueller, Rick Murphy, Lief Hasskarl, Dave Lemelin, and last but not least, Glen Holloway. To my sergeants, the people who really make the Army work and kept me sane, safe, and aimed in the right direction. In particular, MSGT Gee, SFC Jenkins (a true man for all seasons), SFC Freestone, SSG Davis, SSG Selover, SSG Robinson, SSG Eversole and SSG Bicksler. To the crew of HQ 50, the M-1 I called mine but left to them to clean, maintain, refuel, rearm, and to be at the right place at the right time so that I could have my fun. Special thanks to Sgt. Williamson, my gunner, Spec. Young, loader and stand-in gunner, Pvt. Perdu, the loader, and Pvt. Andres, a driver with a large foot and an understanding that sometimes my left was not the same as his. Last, but not least, special thanks to Spec. Gardner, the driver of HQ 3, my Hummvee. Abused and misused, Gardner was always there.

I cannot fail to acknowledge the patience of my children, Sean, Kurt, and Sarah. And finally, to my loving wife, Pat: Without her support, cooperation, and assistance, this book wouldn't have been possible.

BIBLIOGRAPHY

The following are the primary sources used in the background research for *Bright Star*.

Ady, P. H. *Oxford Regional Economic Atlas: Africa*. Oxford: Clarendon Press, 1965.

Carver, Michael. *Dilemmas of the Desert War*. Bloomington: Indiana University Press, 1987.

Colucci, Frank. *The McDonnell Douglas Apache*. Blue Ridge Summit, PA: TAB Books, 1988.

Gabriel, Richard A. *Antagonists in the Middle East*. Westport, CT: Greenwood Press, 1983.

Gunston, Bill. *AH-64 Apache*. London: Osprey Publishing, Ltd., 1986.

Gunston, Bill, and Spick, Mike. *Modern Air Combat*. New York: Crescent Books, 1983.

Harkavy, Robert E., and Neuman, Stephanie G. *The Lessons of Recent Wars in the Third World*. Volume I. Lexington, MA: Lexington Books, 1985.

Heldman, Dan C. *The U.S.S.R. and Africa*. New York: Praeger Publishers, 1981.

Isby, David C. *Weapons and Tactics of the Soviet Army*. London: Jane's, 1988.

Lucas, James. *War in the Desert*. New York: Beauford Books, Inc., 1982.

Menon, Rajan. *Soviet Power and the Third World*. New Haven, CT: Yale University Press, 1986.

Nordeen, Lon O. *Air Warfare in the Missile Age*. Washington, D.C.: Smithsonian Institute Press, 1985.

Nyrop, Richard F. *Egypt: A Country Study*. Washington, D.C., GPO. 1983.

O'Ballance, Edgar. *Tracks of the Bear*. Novato, CA: Presidio Press, 1982.

Pitt, Barrie. *The Crucible of War: Western Desert, 1941*. London: Jonathan Cape, Ltd., 1980.

Porter, Bruce D. *The U.S.S.R. in Third World Conflicts*. New York: Cambridge University Press, 1984.

Richardson, Doug. *Modern Fighting Aircraft: AH-64*. New York: Prentice Hall, 1987.

Shaw, Robert L. *Fighter Combat*. Annapolis, MD: Naval Institute Press, 1985.

Spick, Mike. *The Ace Factor*. Annapolis, MD: Naval Institute Press, 1988.

Sumrall, Robert F. *Iowa Class Battleships*. Annapolis, MD: Naval Institute Press, 1988.

Sweetman, Bill. *The Great Book of Modern Warplanes*. New York: Crown Publishers, 1987.

Unger, Sanford J. *Africa: The People and Politics of an Emerging Continent*. New York: Touchstone, 1986.